EVERY HEARTACHE BEFORE, LED TO EVERY MOMENT AFTER

M.S. GORZA

OWL BOOKED UP PUBLISHING

Contents

To my fellow maladaptive daydreamers: The story that's been stuck in your head, the one that inadvertently causes you to ugly cry in your car and lay awake night after night paralyzed with fear: write it down! You know every detail. You've planned for every possibility. You've stressed over this story long enough. I promise it will be worth the time and energy required to get it out of your head. And you never know, you just might find your name on a book one day ;)

Content Warning

This book is intended for mature audiences and contains subject matter that may not be suitable for every reader. It contains detailed, explicit, on-page romance. It also deals with heavy topics including, suicide, death, child loss, domestic violence, and other types of abuse.

Please be mindful when you read.

Prologue

Can you imagine a girl whose mother doesn't love her? And it's not just that her mother doesn't love her. Her mother belittles and despises her, eroding her daughter's self-esteem, a generally fragile thing for a young girl to begin with, until she becomes a shell of herself, believing she does not deserve to be loved.

As a result of her mother's abuse, the girl loses all sense of self. She lacks confidence and never learns how to trust herself. Her eyes are hollow, anchored by dark bruises, and sad, so heartbreakingly sad. She rarely laughs, and when she does, it is a struggle as the muscles in her face never learned how to smile.

By the time she approaches womanhood and freedom, she is so beaten down, her reality so warped by the unpredictable monster parading as her mother that she doesn't know what it means to love or be loved. She doesn't know she deserves to be treated with kindness and respect.

So, she settles for a man who also never learned how to love or be loved. The man had been her friend in the last years of their childhood. As a boy, he had been a close friend, a point of joy in her life, a respite, a safe place. When the boy became a man, he became a monster, preying on her insecurities. When she mustered up enough courage to leave, he almost killed her.

So, you see, when she grabbed her freedom with both hands and built a wonderful life for herself, what a colossal achievement it was. She finally learned how to smile. She found joy, safety, and contentment within herself. But most importantly, she learned how to love another and receive love in return. And love hard, fiercely, and passionately she did.

She dug herself out of the pit of learned inadequacy and unworthiness, inch by torturous inch. She replaced her mother's degrading, bitter voice with one full of love and acceptance. Her heart overflowed with love and gratitude, and she celebrated with ferocious passion every happy milestone reached and every challenge overcome.

So, you also see how hard she must have fallen when this new wonderful life, one that she worked so hard to create for herself, was viciously ripped away in a single, horrific, irrevocable moment in time.

Can you now imagine a woman, defeated and broken anew, suddenly and maliciously thrown back into the pit, left to tumble down into the unending depths of despair, with nothing to anchor her or stop her descent?

Will she rise again and overcome adversity? Or does she succumb to the despair and surrender to the darkness?

Like She's Making Love

"**H**ello, darling. You look fabulous, as usual," Romeo, the bartender and my only new friend in five years, exclaims as I beeline to the stool tucked into a semi-secluded corner of the bar. A drink station divides it from the rest of the barstools, making it the perfect spot to avoid the other patrons. One corner of my mouth tilts up, a brief glimpse of kindness flashing out from my perpetual resting bitch face.

In a strapless, iridescent purple dress, I shimmer like the reflection of the twilight sky on a clear pond. The dress hugs my curves, rippling down my body to where it sits at mid-thigh. A sweetheart neckline accentuates my toned arms. My auburn-streaked, dark brown hair is pulled back into a sleek bun, and pearls adorn my ears and neck.

A man sipping a glass of red wine occupies the nearest stool on the opposite side of the drink station. I groan internally and roll my eyes. I should come in at three on Tuesday afternoons when it is likely far less busy. I yank the stool out from under the lip of the bar top, making it screech. As I move to sit, the wine-drinking stranger slips gracefully off his stool and places his hands on the back of mine. Sometimes, or more accurately, all the time, I wish chivalry was dead.

Or at least didn't come with a huge dose of expectation.

"Can I help you," I challenge, emphasizing the last two words of the sentence.

"My apologies," he concedes in a thick British accent, nodding slightly and returning to his stool.

As I ungraciously plop onto my stool, I catch his reflection in the mirror behind the bar, surprised to see nothing but genuine kindness on his handsome face.

Since when do you notice that kind of shit, V?

I have no interest in men, or women for that matter. Not in relationships of any kind, romantic or platonic, not anymore, not *after*. I've come to think of my life that way, simply *before the* worst day of my life and *after* the worst day of my life. It's the only way I can manage without having a complete mental breakdown. It's been five years, and I still can't get over it. If I'm honest with myself, I have not, until recently, even considered allowing myself to get over it. Now, I come here every Friday night intending to socialize and interact with other humans, but I just can't make myself do it any more than is absolutely necessary.

Romeo saunters over and places a wine glass in front of me. It contains sparkling water mixed with cranberry juice because I very rarely consume alcohol—not since *the event* that divided my life into *before* and *after*. Romeo is kind enough to help me hide that fact from the other patrons, who generally refuse to let a woman drink her non-alcoholic beverage in peace.

"Don't worry," he says to the stranger, jerking his chin at me. "Her bark is worse than her bite."

"My bite is sufficiently vicious when necessary," I deadpan. Like last week when some rich, entitled prick wouldn't take a fucking hint and leave me the hell alone.

"Ronnie," Romeo warns, but I've tuned out and don't register him speaking to me. "Veronica," he demands. I still can't believe he carded me, an 80s baby, that first night, nor that he remembered the name on my I.D. When I was a server, I never looked at anything except their birth date. I should quit being stubborn and get a legal name change.

"How many times do I gotta tell you, *Romero*? Don't. Fucking . . . call me that." He narrows his eyes at me but chuckles, unperturbed. He knows *exactly* how I feel about my given name. Yeah, it gets my attention quickly, but I hate it. My mother used to lace it with such venom that just hearing it sends a shudder down my spine. I glare at him over the rim of my glass. Still unperturbed, he jokes, "Reign it in, Ronda," eyes wide and lips pursed.

"You look like a constipated lemur. Anyway, I have no idea what you're talking about," I reply primly, lifting my chin. I can feel the stranger watching our exchange, and I take a deep, steadying breath. Romeo notices and warns,

"The bar has a two-strike policy, Ron, and I can't do anything to stop them from banning you."

"Fine. You have my word. Scouts honor," I reply, raising my right hand with the pointer and middle finger up in a salute. "However, if I remember correctly, which I do, *management* was happy to see him go. They banned him instead of me, remember?"

"We were all happy to see him go. He was a pompous ass." I nod and raise my eyebrows, giving him a 'you're welcome' look.

"Do I dare ask?" ventures the stranger, his deep, honey-smooth voice grating on my nerves. I would not be able to describe any other stranger's voice that I've heard in the past five years, but for some reason, I can't begin to fathom; this random British man's voice draws my attention. I place the back of my hand against my forehead, furrowing my eyebrows.

You're not sick, V, but something is definitely wrong with you.

That's the understatement of the century. Nothing in my life has been right since *the event* shattered my world five years ago. I flick Mr. British a sideways glare, warning him to mind his own business, then send Romeo a warning glare of his own. He smirks, ignoring me, and launches into the story with unveiled glee. I wouldn't be surprised if Romeo's middle name is 'The Suriel.'

"The pompous ass was a long-time regular, and we all hated dealing with him. Last week, he kept hitting on Ron here," he says gesturing toward me with a flick of the bar rag in his hand, "even after she had shut him down multiple times. As she walked past him in her tight little dress on her way out, he grabbed her arm and told her, 'If you dress like a slut, don't be surprised when you get treated like a slut'."

"Bloody prick and his fucking audacity," the man exclaims, shooting me an incredulous stare, green eyes intense on mine.

My thoughts exactly. God, that guy was such an entitled douche canoe.

"And the size of his balls," Romeo agrees, eyes gleaming. "Well, our delicate, timid little rose petal here," he continues, jerking his chin at me while he polishes a beer mug. I snort loudly.

"Let me guess," Mr. British interjects, "she kindly explained to him that a woman can dress however she so chooses and still expect to be treated with decency and respect?" I roll my eyes and huff out a breath even though I do appreciate the sentiment.

Romeo guffaws. "Oh no. She took a much more subtle approach. She smiled, which was the first warning the buffoon ignored, wrapped his tie around one fist, and snatched his glass of red wine off the bar—the second warning he stupidly ignored. She threw it in his face and all over his white suit. God, the look of horror on his face." Romeo chuckles, flashing me a knowing glance.

"A lovely sight, to be sure," the British hunk muses.

"For some, that would have been enough. But not for our dear Ron Ron," Romeo continues. I stifle a shit-eating grin and glare at him from under my lashes. "She ripped him off the stool by his tie and threw him to the floor. It was fabulous." Romeo finishes, singsong-ing 'fabulous,' eyes glazed like he's reliving the memory.

"Would've stomped his ass too if I had been wearing panties," I murmur under my breath. Out loud, I ask Romeo if he's ordered my food yet. He winks, then works his way down the bar, calmly and efficiently waiting on the other patrons.

I take a sip of my drink, then fish a pen and a worn book of sudoku puzzles out of my purse.

"Sudoku, huh," the determined stranger inquires. I nod without looking up. "I thought you could only find sudoku in the newspaper or on an app," he continues. I inhale deeply through my nose and rub my fingers between my eyes.

"I prefer the print copy because it's a better deterrent," I reply, waving the book at him.

"Deterrent for what?"

"Unwanted conversation," I reply, tone snarky. I know I'm supposed to try, but forcing myself to engage in meaningless small talk with strangers makes me want to vomit. I want to have a normal life again, but people are unpredictable. Most mean well, but simple questions and common phrases randomly trigger a flood of painful memories that I don't want to deal with.

"Hint taken," he replies.

See other men; it's not that hard. When she says no, you respect it and move on. Easy peasy.

I return my attention to the half-completed puzzle. I don't particularly enjoy Sudoku, but I can't read or mindlessly scroll social media anymore. Seeing people gush about their families or worse, complain about them, makes me want to throw hands. If only they knew how lucky they are to have a family to complain about.

I can feel the stranger watching me in the reflection of the mirror behind the bar. I try to concentrate on the numbers in front of me, but the weight of his eyes on me makes my heart race and my legs bounce. Exasperated with myself, I sigh and flick my eyes up. They're met with a piercing jade stare. I study him for a minute, taken aback by the intensity of his gaze.

That's enough of that.

I roll my eyes, tilt my head, and pin him with a wide, hard gaze, nostrils flared in silent warning. He drops his eyes from mine and attempts to hide a smirk by rubbing his close-cropped beard. My hand balls into a fist and the urge to reach over and wipe that smirk right off his handsome face washes over me. I stretch my fingers, forcing them to relax and return my focus to the numbers in their neat little boxes. After a few blessed minutes of peace, Romeo clears his throat before setting a delicious-smelling cheeseburger and mouth-watering fries on the bar before me.

"Ah," I say, "the Polynesian tonight. Exactly what I needed." Every time I'm here, Romeo orders one of three items for me: a regular cheeseburger, The Black n' Blue, which is a burger topped with blue cheese, bacon, and hot sauce, or The Polynesian, also a cheeseburger, this one wrapped in lettuce and topped with grilled pineapple, cream cheese, and teriyaki. It's the perfect system because I'm frequently too indecisive to make my own choice, and he hasn't chosen wrong yet.

"This looks amazing. Thank you."

I drizzle mustard and ketchup over my fries and take a huge bite of the burger, moaning a little when the flavors explode on my tongue. Good food. It is one of the few luxuries in life I can still enjoy in peace. There are too many voices in my head constantly vying for attention. Tiny Mildred loves to remind me that I'll never be good enough. Angry and bitter, past me loves to rile up guilt, despair, and grief, stirring the pot randomly so I live with a painful ball of emotions constantly roiling in my gut.

I shove a handful of fries in my mouth.

Fuck, I love this place.

If only I could have the whole restaurant to myself every Friday night. I know I'm *supposed* to interact and converse and all that bullshit, but I'm terrified of what I'll have to face if I let down my guard. I did promise I'd try, though, and constantly breaking that promise to myself is also starting to wear on me. Maybe I can try tonight. See how it goes. I hear Mr. British ask Romeo a question and decide he's safe enough. He's been kind and respectful; if things go terribly wrong, I'll never see him again. It's settled, then. I will attempt to converse with the British stranger if the opportunity arises.

You can do this, V.

"Ronnie," Romeo's voice cuts through my mental ruminations.

"What," I snap a little too harshly. He has always been kind and patient with me. "I'm sorry," I say and smile apologetically.

He smirks, that goddamned smirk, then drawls, "you know." Mr. Green Eyes finds my gaze in the mirror, eyebrows raised, head tilted.

"It's really nothing. He's just being facetious," I answer his unspoken question, then shoot a warning glare at Romeo.

See, that wasn't so hard.

"Oh, come on, darling," Romeo drawls. The 'Suriel' in him is a stronger temptation than my scowl is a deterrent. Plus, he's right, at least where he's concerned: My bark is worse than my bite. "She eats like she's making love," Romeo says, leaning a forearm on the bar. The only time you will ever see her real smile is when she is staring at that cheeseburger."

"I don't think Evan, you know, your boyfriend. Remember?" He smirks. "I don't think he'd like to know that you think he looks like a woman when you two sword fight."

"Really? That's the best you can come up with?"

"Oh, I can come up with better," I reply, leaning in conspiratorially, "but delicate ears are listening," I confide in a mock whisper, inclining my head toward the stranger who places his hands over his ears and whistles.

"Anyway." Romeo continues. "It's always, 'Oh my god, this looks amazing,' followed by her moaning after every bite."

Well fuck, V. He's got you pegged.

However, I'm pretty sure I've never uttered the words 'This looks amazing' while having a hot beef injection. I mean, could you imagine? The man gets naked, and your reaction is, 'Oh my god, this looks amazing.' I chuckle to myself and take another bite.

"See what I mean," Romeo says to Mr. Jade Intensity. I sigh. It's time to end this.

With grease still dripping down my chin, I mock, "Romeo, Romeo. Wherefore art thou Romeo?" He grins, and I drop the annoyed smile from my face, pinning him with a 'shut the fuck up' look. Romeo's grin stays plastered across his face as he saunters away to pour a drink.

I vaguely hear the stranger ask someone to recommend what to order. The young woman on his other side replies in a nasally, overly flirtatious voice, recommending the Ahi tuna salad. I make a pretend puking noise under my breath and roll my eyes. She's young and trying way too hard to attract attention to herself. I want to assure her that it's okay to eat whatever she truly enjoys because, let's be real, salad is rarely any woman's favorite food. And the guys that she's probably trying to impress don't care. But I bite my tongue and focus on my own meal.

The man thanks her, then says, "You don't agree?" It takes a few seconds to realize who he's talking to.

"What," I ask. "How do you figure?"

"It's written all over your face." I glance at my reflection.

Fucking traitor.

My first instinct is to deny his observation, but that opens up the door for further conversation, so I simply reply, "No, I don't. Agree."

"Then, what is your recommendation?"

"Do you like spicy Roquefort," I inquire, voice dripping with sarcasm, and shove a handful of fries into my mouth. He wets his lips with just the tip of his tongue and runs a hand through his dark, wavy hair.

"She means blue cheese and hot sauce," Romeo chimes in from down the bar.

"Ah. I am still not sure that I follow," Mr. British says, looking back and forth between us. I've officially reached my limit for small talk. My head pounds with each beat of my heart.

I rub my temples and bark out a demand. "Just order him the damn 'Black n' Blue, Rome."

Mr. Jade Intensity fires a question at Romeo, who assures him my choice is infinitely better than the Ahi, and I finish off the last of my burger. I am about to signal Romeo for the check when I catch him mouthing to the handsome British man, 'Here she goes,' and give him an exaggerated wink.

You are so predictable, V.

I am. It's true. It is the only way I can function anymore. I get up every morning at the exact same time. Go to bed at the exact same time and follow the exact same routine every day. When I stray from this consistency, I quickly spiral back downward. I wish Romeo a good night and turn toward the door. I feel the handsome, British stranger's intense green gaze follow me as I maneuver through the tables, but I don't look back, and when I exit the building, all thoughts of him flee my mind completely.

Not My Home

The air outside is still warm, almost too warm for this time of night, but the walk back to my apartment is pleasant, and by the time I get there, I am thankful for the warmth of the long California evenings. Back in Idaho, where I grew up and lived until five years ago, the sun would have long since dropped behind the mountains, making it too cool to be outside in this dress. Fuck, I miss those mountains.

Not too long ago, I stood on the edge of a cliff in my beloved mountains, my tumultuous thoughts a raging storm inside my skull. A part of me was determined to die, to throw myself off the precipice and let the mercy of the Rockies decide my fate.

It wasn't the first time I had fought that battle, either. I have stared at a handful of pills, down the barrel of a loaded gun, and at the lights of an approaching train, begging myself to be strong enough to do it. The pain I've endured since that unseasonably hot and humid May afternoon five years ago is so unbearable; I'm not sure how I've endured it this long. It's been five years since my perfectly wonderful life was shattered. Five years since I was thrown head-first into a downward spiral. I've only recently managed to slow my descent.

The part of me that somehow always finds a way to keep going and keep living won on that mountainside. Although it wasn't the first time I raged inside, wishing, yearning to die. It was the first time I decided to live, to truly live. I decided I could not continue to exist in this state of in-between, wanting to die but unable to end it. If I could not take that step, and clearly, I couldn't, then I would find a way to heal, let go, and move on. A few weeks later, I ate the best cheeseburger ever, and my Friday night tradition with Romeo began.

My biggest struggle right now is social interaction. Other people are too unpredictable, saying or doing things that unknowingly trigger feelings of guilt, despair, shame, rage, and anguish or cause a flood of memories so painful it cuts me down at the knees and makes it impossible to breathe. Living near my family and close friends, who know the cause of my emotional turmoil, is even more triggering.

So, a few months after my world imploded, I sold everything except a suitcase of clothes and a box of keepsakes and set out. I've been a modern-day gypsy ever since, wandering around the country from here to there on a whim, staying in one place for only a few days, and in another a few months, doing my damndest to leave my ghosts behind. Whenever I can muster up the courage, I swing through Idaho to visit my friends and family, who mostly support my new lifestyle. Everyone that is, except my younger sister, Victoria.

Podcasts and self-help audiobooks scored the soundtrack on the long drive to California after that fateful day in the mountains eight months ago, helping me develop a plan. Multiple options and scenarios twirled in and out of my brain like seeds in the wind. In order to thrive, I decided I must figure out how to manage my reactions when interacting with others. This meant I had to actually start socializing and stop door-dashing meals and staying at Airbnbs.

I forced myself to stay at a hotel and have an actual conversation with the front desk clerk. It was frustrating but safe, a short, simple interaction that didn't require a lot of thought or provide much of an opportunity to dive too deep. After a few, mostly successful rounds of this, I added dining out to my self-inflicted 'get better' plan. It was still safe but with longer, more in-depth interactions.

I started sitting at the bar when I felt pretty confident in my ability to interact with the staff, figuring it was time to branch out and open up the opportunity to have more peer-to-peer interactions. A solid plan in theory, but it just led to either getting hit on or getting asked super personal questions (thank you, alcohol for loose tongues and no filter) and pulling back further and further into my shell. In hindsight, I probably should have gone to the library or the park instead of the bar, but those places are triggering even without the social aspect.

Maybe it's time, V. Take a leap of faith.

I've been contemplating taking my wanderings overseas. Maybe interacting with foreigners will be less triggering.

As I turn the corner onto my block, I dodge a group of loud, tipsy young women. The sight of my sister, Victoria, standing on the bottom step of my building makes me stop short, and joy pulses through me, followed quickly by a jolt of trepidation.

"Hey, Ron," she says, bounding onto the sidewalk to hug me quickly. When she pulls back, I see trepidation lurking in the corners of her eyes, and a shiver of apprehension slithers down my spine.

Better not be another fucking intervention, Vic.

Before I can form a reply, she confirms my suspicion.

"I'm here to take you home, where you belong," she declares. No prelude. No, 'How are you,' or 'It's good to see you,' or 'Let's get dinner and catch up.' Just a straight sucker punch to the gut. We've been down this road before. She knows damn well that I'm not going back there. My stomach churns, and my heart pounds in my chest just at the thought of living in Idaho again.

"Victoria," I chide. "It's *not my* home anymore. Did you seriously come all this way just so we can have the same argument?" I ask, nostrils flaring. "Would it be so difficult," I continue, without giving her the chance to answer, "to come simply to spend time together? Is it really such an issue for you to accept that this is my life now," I ask, raising my hands, then dropping them to my sides with a forceful sigh.

"This is not your home, sis. Just like all the other cities you've called home these past few years were not your home. Your home is in Idaho with your friends and family."

Moving closer to the building, I take a wide step around her, arms up, fingers splayed in warning. "Vic, you do not get to decide that for me. It will never be my home again," I say, enunciating the words sharply as if I can drive acceptance into her thick skull.

"Why," she challenges, hands on her hips, tone just as sharp as mine.

"You really have to ask me that. You know why," I exclaim, throwing my hands in the air. "Since you can't get it through your thick fucking skull, I'll go ahead and reach into my chest and rip my fucking heart out, piece by piece–again–until you finally understand how hard it is. Without *him*—" I choke back a sob. "No, actually. No, I won't try to explain it to you anymore. I have asked you multiple times to stop pulling this shit and deliberately ignoring my boundaries. I am not going to tell you where I am anymore–"

"—Ron,"

"—No," I raise a shaking hand, palm in her face, "Stop. This stops now. I love you, Vic, but I can't live there, and you know why. You need to leave." I turn all the way around and stop dead in my tracks, and for one heartbeat, I forget how to breathe. My painstakingly and carefully mended heart shatters. After a long beat, I find my breath and, with it, my voice.

"What the fuck," I seethe, spinning on Victoria, jabbing a finger into her chest. "If you ever pull this shit again. Bring him to my *home*. You will *never* see me, ever again," I finish, voice low and hard, chest heaving. I spin on my heels and try to sprint past the man sitting on the stairs, driven by the need to get away, but the despair I see in his eyes mirrors my own, and it pins me on the top step.

Victoria continues berating me while I stare into those sad blue eyes that tear apart, bit by bit, the few pieces of myself I've barely managed to piece back together.

"You have to come home, Ronnie. So long as you're on American soil, I will find you and do whatever I can to bring you home," my sister promises.

"Ronnie—" the man starts, but I don't want to hear it.

"I'm sorry," I say, tearing my eyes out of his cobalt gaze and sprinting to the door. My voice breaks as the tears I've been holding back finally spill over.

"Let her go," he tells Vic. His deep tenor voice, thick with emotion, is barely audible over my heart pounding and the staccato click of my heels as I flee from the memories.

Several days later, I dig myself out of a mound of blankets, crawling on hands and knees out of the corner of the closet where I've been buried since I ran from Victoria and . . . and him.

A loud buzzing rings out behind me. I crawl toward my nightstand and slump against the bed, yanking my phone off the charger. Two faces light up the screen, and I almost decline the Facetime call but change my mind on the last ring.

"Do you two know what my darling little sister did," I blurt, throat raw from crying out my despair and screaming out my torment. Catherine and Sophie, my two best friends, sigh and quirk their lips into annoyed but sympathetic smiles.

"She didn't," Catherine says, pursing her thin, delicately shaped lips.

"Not again," Sophie agrees, shaking her head, platinum blonde bangs bobbing, hazel eyes narrowed with annoyance. I nod.

"How long?" Catherine asks, brushing her curly black hair out of her face. She doesn't have to elaborate; they've been through this with me enough times before that I know exactly what she means. I calculate the time based on the day and date on my phone.

"Only a week." A week since my sister pushed me overboard into a tumultuous sea of grief, guilt, and despair. A week lost, drifting through painful memories, weathering the tumultuous storm in a heap of blankets on my closet floor until it spit me back onto shore, battered and broken once again.

"Oh, sweetie," Catherine says.

"We'll keep trying to convince her to stop," Sophie continues.

"To help her understand and accept that you're doing what you have to do to heal," Catherine finishes.

I sigh, shoulders dropping wearily. "Thank you."

"So, where to next?" Sophie asks, bouncing in her seat, completely accepting of my gypsy lifestyle.

"More than likely Europe," I reply, voicing the thought that's been growing inside my brain for a while now.

"That sounds fabulous," Catherine says in a voice tinged with longing and envy. She has three amazing kids whom she loves dearly, but they make traveling a bit challenging.

"Which part of Europe? Turner and I thoroughly enjoyed Ireland and Scotland," Sophie says. She and her husband have traveled extensively–one of the many reasons they chose to remain childless.

"Probably all of it, eventually. If I do go."

"Will you come see us before you leave?" Catherine asks, voice carefully neutral. I know they wouldn't hesitate to come to me, but Cat has the kids, and Sophie's super busy working on getting a promotion at work. Not to mention, I've already secretly promised Turner I'd make a dining set and some other items for the home he and Sophie are currently in the process of building. I have only made a few pieces since I sold the woodworking and epoxy business I co-owned with *him* five years ago. I just couldn't keep doing it without *him*.

"If–if–I go. Either way, I'll visit soon. Please don't say anything to my sister, though, I don't want to see her right now."

"You'll go," Catherine says with a playful wink. I offer her a wry smile.

We talk for a while about other, less depressing topics, like Catherine's kids and Sophie's job, and when they hang up, I stand in the middle of the living room in the tiny, rented apartment, contemplating my next move. Europe has been in the back of my mind for a while now. Maybe a different country, on a different continent, will provide the space and distance I'm desperately seeking. Maybe it'll finally be enough to help me move on. Maybe.

Déjà vu

Charlie

"Pardon me?" I interrupt Theo's rambling about all the pints he will drink and the women he hopes to seduce this weekend. I cradle the mobile between my ear and shoulder and toss some chicken and veggies into a frying pan. "Did you say art studio? You and the boys want to go to an art studio?"

"Yeah, mate. Not just the boys, the ladies too. It was their idea," Theo replies. During the few months that I have known him, he has never shown much interest in anything besides work, throwing iron, a cold pint, or women.

"Then you have my answer."

"Jess isn't going, so it better be yes."

"I have heard that before," I say, jaw clenching. Clicking on the speaker, I set my mobile on the counter.

"Come on, boyo. Rumor on the street is that the artist is a gorgeous, single, American woman." I start, dropping the spatula onto the floor, and focus on the conversation. Could it be her, my Veronica? What I would not give to see her again. I brace my hands on the counter and drop my head between my shoulders.

"An American woman?"

"Apparently, she specializes in mixed media art, whatever that means. So, are you in or not, mate?"

"Yeah, yeah. I will be there. Text me the details."

Single, attractive, American woman? It is highly unlikely that this artist is the witty, frank, brown-haired, long-legged beauty from San Francisco, but a man can dream. A year later, any mention of America, cheeseburgers, or knickers still brings her to mind. I doubt she meant anyone to hear that enticing little tidbit, but I sure did. My cock twitches behind my slacks, remembering the image of her in that painted-on, iridescent purple dress and wondering, if I had slid my hand up her supple thigh, would it have met any resistance, or would my fingers have found bare skin.

I groan and turn to the skink to splash cold water on my face. Considering how curt, borderline rude, and uninterested she was, I should not be this infatuated with her. Fuck, she spent the night glaring daggers at me. Even though her rich, harsh brown eyes screamed at me the whole time to fuck off, they still haunt my dreams.

She hid it well, but my guess is that her abrasive attitude is a cover for a deep soul wound. I saw the sadness and despair she desperately tried to hide lurking behind the severity. And despite her best efforts to deter me, her quick wit and those few flashes of hidden turmoil drew me in. What has she experienced to make her don such a tough exterior? I doubt I will ever get the chance to find out, but I still wonder and think about her every day.

It is a trifle insane, considering how brief our single interaction was, but no woman since Veronica has sparked my interest. None of them compare to her, which is not surprising. None of them give a shit about me. Not that she did, either. That is part of the appeal, though. I get the feeling she would not give a fuck about a man's wealth or social status. She would strip him down to his soul to bare his true self. I have given up hope of ever finding such a woman. I suppose it is good that I have no interest in marriage and am content with myself.

The odor of burning poultry and veggies pulls me out of my thoughts. Bloody hell. My lunch has gone and burnt completely while I daydreamed about Veronica.

Veronica

The autumn sun shines brightly over the London skyline, illuminating vibrant yellow, orange, and red patches on the changing trees. The large windows lining the front walls of my studio are thrown open, letting the warm, fragrant air flow into the space. Autumn scents mingle with the smells of my trade: paint, resin, sawdust, canvas, paper, pencil shavings. The combination creates a lovely, inviting, peaceful ambiance in the gallery.

My agents and temporary studio managers, Kali and Kellan, who are identical twins, suggest, prod, and demand until they finally convince me to go upstairs to get ready for tonight's Grand Opening. For the past few hours, I have nervously wandered through the gallery, adjusting already straight paintings, wiping already clean tables, and generally getting underfoot.

After my younger sister Victoria staged her last intervention in San Francisco just over a year ago, I did exactly what Catherine and Sophie said I'd do–I left. Within two weeks of Victoria and I's heated fight, I packed my few belongings, made arrangements to travel for an extended time in Europe, and drove up to Idaho. I spent time with my dear friends and fulfilled my obligation to Turner, Sophie's husband, to craft furniture for their new home. Then, I spent a few months meandering my way from Greece up to Norway and back down through Scotland and Ireland to England. London has been my home ever since.

As soon as I got settled in London, I started therapy and hired a life coach, so I feel mostly confident that I can make it through this evening without a mental breakdown. But no matter how much therapy, meditation, life-coaching, or thought work I do–and I do *a lot*–the memories are still there, lurking and painful, and I still struggle with guilt, shame, despair, rage, self-loathing, and occasional bouts of debilitating depression. I am learning effective ways to deal with everything, though.

I strip off my sweaty, paint-smeared work clothes and step into the shower, letting the hot water wash away my fears and trepidations. *He* would be proud of you, a small voice whispers in the back of my mind. A louder, crueler voice screams a frustrated retort: "But *he's not* here!" I inhale deeply, silencing both voices, locking all thoughts of *him* and *before* firmly back inside their vault. I will do my best to be fully present tonight without letting the past haunt me.

When I finally get out and dry off, my skin is as red as a lobster. I twist my waist-long, auburn-streaked, dark brown hair into a towel and meticulously apply a thick layer of makeup. While I paint on this shield of sorts–a shield to hide my brokenness–I chant affirmations to myself in the mirror.

I am strong. I am capable. I am enough.

The black satin cocktail dress I'm wearing this evening settles over my body like a sheath, hugging my curves and accentuating my toned arms and legs. At 43, I am in the best shape of my life. Exercise is one of the anchors that tethers me to life when harsh currents and unexpected storms threaten to drag me off course, crashing toward self-destruction.

With trembling fingers, I fumble on a pair of my signature handmade earrings, pairing them with a matching handmade necklace. All three pieces are simple yet elegant: dried, purple pansies set in crystal-clear resin, beautifully framed in oval-shaped silver bezels. As I brush and dry my hair, I contemplate leaving it down even though I know I won't. *He* loved my long hair, so I always wear it up in public. Plus, I like the way the top of my only tattoo, delicately designed wings, peeks up over the top of the back of my dress.

To finish my look, I step into six-inch sparkly silver stilettos. As soon as they're buckled, I begin to pace, waiting for one of the brilliant twins to text me to join the party. Kali insisted that I arrive fashionably late. Kellan agreed, and they would not budge when I insisted on being early. After much deliberation, I deferred, seeing as they are the experts in this industry. A decision I now regret as my heart rate steadily rises and Tiny Mildred's muffled voice struggles to break free of its gag. In lieu of sprinting downstairs right now, I employ every tactic I've learned to remain calm. My nerves are just a little frazzled, and my feet are just starting to ache when the 'come hither' text finally buzzes through my watch.

When I first started working with Kali and Kellan, and they convinced me to open *Studio V*, I thought of them as the 'sour twins.' They are very stoic and taciturn until they get to know you and decide whether they like you. It only took a few weeks for me to recognize and appreciate their brilliance and for them to make their decision about me. They each have a wicked sense of humor and love to joke and tease. They also push me to the edge of my comfort zone with loving support. If everything goes well tonight, which I have no doubt it will, I plan to ask them to extend their contracts indefinitely.

Kali and Kellan are also both tall, lean, and fucking gorgeous. Their skin is a radiant, deep umber, and their eyes are a piercing sky-blue surrounded by a thick ring of charcoal. The only difference in their appearance is Kali's long, coal-black goddess braids to Kellan's perfectly round, shaved head. They are genuinely amazing friends and fucking brilliant businesspeople. I could not be more grateful for them.

Palms sweaty, I flick off the lights and snap the door shut behind me, pausing on the mezzanine overlooking the gallery. I focus on my breath, breathing deeply and evenly to center myself while I survey the gallery below. Kali and Kellan move fluidly through an already large crowd, smiling, shaking hands, and interacting with everyone they pass. Servers decked out in black and white attire weave through the crowd with trays full of hors d' oeuvres and champagne.

I square my shoulders and descend, chanting affirmations the whole way down.

I am strong . . . I am capable . . . I am enough.

Kellan intercepts me at the bottom, offering his arm before we seamlessly blend into the crowd. I agreed to be fashionably late but refused to allow them to make a big scene of my entrance. We meander our way through the crowd, and I manage fairly well by sticking close to one of my brilliant agents and managing not to panic if we occasionally become separated. The tactics I've learned in therapy and life coaching sessions, daily meditations, and workouts, combined with consistent thought work, are helping me regulate my thoughts and feelings.

Eyes downcast, I stride purposefully through the throng of people towards the small gift shop situated by the entrance. There's a handful of racks displaying small items that I make in between larger projects, like keychains, bookmarks, and other assorted trinkets, along with my best-selling item, jewelry, like the set I'm wearing tonight. As I needlessly reorganize the racks, giving myself a reprieve from the crowd, I catch the end of a conversation between two patrons as they head toward the exit.

Their voices are unmistakably American and instantly pique my curiosity. I turn to speak with them, but their words sink in and hit me like a sucker punch to the gut. My chest constricts, and my vision blurs as phrases like Buster, Potato Bowl, Vandals, and Bleed Blue assault my fragile heart. A crystal-clear image of *him* standing in front of a TV decked out in white and green, cheering as his team hoists a trophy, burns itself onto the back of my eyelids. I stumble away from the door, clutching my chest and struggling to suck air past the lump in my throat. Kali catches my elbow and hauls me into the dark, quiet workroom.

"It's okay, Ronnie. Breath. Match my breath. I got you," she says, exaggerating her inhales and exhales.

Fuck, fuck, fuck.

After a few minutes, my heart rate returns to normal, and I am finally able to breathe easily. I squeeze my eyes shut and shake my head to dispel the image. When I can breathe easily again, I straighten and nod to Kali.

"What happened?" she asks.

"I overheard two guys talking as they left." She raises her eyebrows at me.

"They were Americans . . . from the same state where I used to live."

"Ahhh," she replies, knowing that's all the explanation she'll get.

"Can you manage the last hour? If not, Kel and I will take care of it."

"Thank you, but I can manage."

"Then let's get back out there."

I Don't Care

K ali deposited me at the bottom of the stairs with strict instructions to hurry, or she'd come up and drag me back down to finish the night. She said it playfully, but I don't doubt for a second that she'd do it.

My shaking hands steady as I dab away the runny mascara under my eyes and reapply a fresh coat. I stare at my reflection for a long beat. The woman staring back makes me proud. She's a confident, successful creator and business owner who's been through hell and back again.

It's so fucking hard, though. Doing this without him.

Determined not to let two stray Idahoans derail an otherwise successful evening, I square my shoulders and march back out there, my stilettos striking a staccato rhythm on the mezzanine. I pause again at the top of the stairs to watch another small group of men and women file into the gallery. Eyes scanning the crowd as I descend, I easily spot Kali and Kellan. They stand out, their tall frames striking in matching sky-blue attire; Kellan looks smashing in a Richard James suit, and Kali is absolutely stunning in a silk, floor-length Sachin & Babi dress. Once again, I chant affirmations as I descend the stairs.

I am strong. I am capable. I am enough.

Halfway down, a pair of piercing green eyes pins me on the stairs, riveting me in place. Also transfixed, the man's eyes bore into mine with a palpable intensity. Shock and elation briefly cross his face before his sensual, full lips curve into the barest hint of a smile. He wets his lips with just the tip of his tongue and runs a hand through his dark, wavy hair. The gesture seems familiar, but it wasn't one of *his,* so I shrug it off.

"Ronnie. Ronnie . . . *Veronica!*" Kellan calls, breaking the trance, and I whip my head in his direction. My eyes are narrowed, and my nostrils flare.

"Just Ronnie, Kellan," I warn.

"Come, come, my dear. These lovely guests would like to make your acquaintance," Kellan purrs as I finish my descent. "If you would respond to Ronnie the way you respond to," I glare at him, and he makes a 'you know' gesture, "then I wouldn't have to resort to using it," he replies out of the corner of his mouth, all the while flashing his charming smile at our guests. I let it go for now, placing my arm in his, and retort with a sarcastic, "Yes, dear."

My palms are clammy, and my fingers tap nervously against my thigh. My gaze often darts back to Mr. Green Eyes, and each time, I find him staring at me. What is it about those eyes? A memory niggles in the back of my mind, but I throw another bolt across their vault. I will *not* have another panic attack tonight.

I continue sneaking glances at him while Kellan introduces me to the rest of his companions, although my gaze never lingers long on his. Butterflies flutter in my stomach, and a tinge of crimson crawls up my neck, settling high on my cheekbones at his scrutiny. Kellan introduces me to the last of the man's companions, a beautiful, blonde woman named Jessica. She reluctantly, but roughly, returns my handshake and I flinch, ripping my hand out of her crushing grip. Her cold blue eyes bore into mine, hard with warning and poorly concealed hatred.

What the fuck?

I glance at Kali out of the corner of my eye, raising my eyebrows. Unperturbed, she rolls her eyes and shakes her head, so I let it go. Jessica looks pointedly at Mr. Green Intensity, who hasn't taken his eyes off me since the stairs, then back at me before stalking off with the rest of their party.

Alright, Regina, he's yours. Trust me, I'm not interested.

He glares at her as she steps away and exhales forcefully through his nose, nostrils flaring, then sets his shoulders and captures my gaze once again, dismissing her completely.

Interesting . . . Not that I care.

Kellan introduces me for what feels like the millionth time tonight, and I extend my hand automatically, transfixed by the handsome stranger's jade depths. His grip is firm. His hands are large and calloused, which is rather at odds with his polished appearance.

"Hello Veronica," he purrs, caressing my name with the same sensuality as his thumb caressing circles on my wrist.

"Hello," I breathe, tilting my head.

"Charlie," he croons.

"Hello, Charlie." That memory niggles in the far corner of my mind, failing to break free from its vault. I'm lost on a sea of smoldering emerald, drifting through the intensity, lured by the sensual caress of his thumb and the predatory gleam in his eyes.

"Ronnie." Kellan's sharp tone snaps me out of Charlie's enchanting aura. I hop back, yanking my hand out his as if he shocked me, and shake my head, blinking rapidly to break his captivating stare.

"I need to borrow her for just a moment, mate," Kellan says to Charlie as he deftly tucks my hand into the crook of his elbow and steers me away.

Ho—ly fuck.

I have never experienced anything like that before. I hope Kellan can't feel my sweaty palms through his suit or hear my heaving breathing over the cacophony of voices. Without looking, I can feel Charlie's eyes stalking me. Goosebumps pebble across my skin as the unsettling feeling of déjà vu slithers up and down my spine.

What is it about those eyes and why does his stare feel expectant?

What do you want from me, handsome stranger?

"Oh, my dear," Kellan exclaims in a hushed tone. "You just had a moment with that scrumptious, sculpted, Adonis-in-the-flesh."

"I did no such thing," I scoff, a hot wave of scarlet crawling up my throat.

"Oh, honey. You are so cute when you're in denial. I know you don't like people, but for the love of all things beautiful and desirable—which yon specimen is the God of," he jerks his chin over my shoulder, "at least sample the wares. Find out if he's more well-endowed than his stone counterparts."

"Kellan," I scold, hiding my grin and deepening blush behind my palm, and glance over my shoulder. Charlie leans against one of the massive, exposed wooden support beams running down the gallery's center. He does look as if he's sculpted from clay with his corded arms crossed over his lean chest and long, powerful legs crossed at the ankle in front of him. His eyes tracking me is the only movement detectable on his still form. The barest hint of a self-satisfied smirk tips up one corner of his full lips when he catches my eye.

"You know, Miss Ronnie, there are a lot of activities you can do with a man that do not involve talking." Kellan's low voice pulls me back to our mildly inappropriate conversation.

"Yes," I agree, shoulder rising in a dismissive shrug. "However, the effort of getting to those *activities* is rarely worth the meager reward."

"Darling. A man like that will, undoubtedly, lavish you with rewards."

"Oh really, *darling.* And you know this how?"

"The power of observation. He's been undressing and devouring you with his eyes ever since he stepped through your door."

"And that's all the undressing or devouring he'll be doing. Unless you need me for something important, I'm off to bed." The sophisticated smart-ass wiggles his eyebrows at me. "Alone," I insist, shooting him a look before releasing his arm.

"Regardless," he says, smiling and waving farewell to someone on their way out, "I would be willing to bet 'Big Bertha' over there that our exquisite statue is a bloody voracious lover." I roll my eyes and head straight for the stairs.

"Let go, Ronnie. Live a little."

Kellan's words hit me with the force of a gale, and I clutch the banister.

Oh, Kel. I'm trying so fucking hard.

He sees my daily struggle but doesn't understand my sorrow; he doesn't understand why it's so fucking hard to find a reason to keep living. Self-loathing, guilt, and grief pummel my chest, threatening to break the battered tethers keeping me afloat, and pull me into the unforgiving current of despair.

Not again, fuckers.

I focus on calming my breath and do my best to embody the confident, successful, creative businesswoman I saw reflected in the mirror upstairs. The pain and memories may have caught me unaware earlier, but I have come too far to let them consume me. I straighten up to my full height, pride bolstering me against the gale. Gratitude for this life I've been fighting so hard to create for myself blooms in my chest as I sweep my gaze around the room one final time.

As I place my foot on the bottom step, Charlie detaches himself from the beam and strides purposefully toward me. I grab the banister to propel myself up the stairs but hesitate and take a deep breath instead. He closes the distance between us with effortless strides, stopping beside me to rest his tall, lean, well-dressed frame against the banister. He fairly exudes casual confidence and quiet sexuality.

Still and quiet as a statue, his eyes lazily scan the room from an outwardly calm face, but a penetrating energy radiates off him, charging the space between us and betraying his calm exterior. I study him surreptitiously from under my lashes and bite the corner of my lip. There's no denying that he's fucking gorgeous. Kellan hit the nail right on the head, naming him Adonis.

His dark hair is styled in perfectly disheveled short waves, and a few days' worth of stubble dusts his strong jaw. His attire is simple yet sophisticated: a cream Irish Aran sweater paired with dark jeans and polished Brandy Leather boots.

Leg shaking and fingers drumming a nervous rhythm on the banister, I wait for him to speak. Should I say something? Or I could give in to the urge to run, walk right up the stairs, and retreat to the solitude of my flat. Somehow, I doubt he'd let me go without making a scene, and I have to admit I am intrigued. My fingers tap, tap, tap as the silence between us stretches on.

Get a grip, V. Just say something, anything.

But my voice gets caught in my dry throat, and I let out a strangled sigh. I can't even remember how to initiate a conversation anymore. A smug smile pulls up the corner of his full lips. Then, *finally,* he moves, gesturing at the abstract landscape painting titled Cliche of Fusion, displayed on a large easel in front of us. I once read an article describing the city that inspired this piece as such, and it stuck with me.

"It reminds me of San Francisco," he observes. His rich baritone voice sounds like honey drizzled into hot tea—viscous and smooth.

"SF was, in fact, my inspiration for this one. Thus far, you're the only one who's made the connection. I take it you've been?" Strong emotions flash in his eyes; expectation, disappointment, doubt, and determination morph so quickly back to their previous intense cast that I question whether I imagined them.

"Yes, I have," he replies, raising an eyebrow and dipping his chin.

Why does he keep looking at you like he expects something, V?

Fuck if I know. "What do you think? Did I capture the feel of the city?"

"Yes," he answers without hesitation. "You are a bloody talented artist, Veronica." I clear my throat, look away, and fidget with the rings on my fingers.

"Thank you." I try to infuse my voice with the sincerity that I feel, but it sounds forced. I cringe internally and press my lips into a thin line, hoping he didn't notice.

"Interesting," he purrs.

"What?"

"You do not like compliments." I scoff, brushing him off, but he's right, I fucking hate them.

"How do you figure?"

"It is written all over your beautiful face."

"Ugh," I groan, dropping my face into my hands. "More like traitorous." Even as a child, when hiding my thoughts and feelings was essential for survival, I couldn't do it no matter how hard I tried. He chuckles but mercifully doesn't push it.

"Cliche of Fusion, I get, but Big Bertha," he ponders as we move towards the piece in question, our bodies naturally falling in step.

The massive piece is made of two giant canvases covered in a riot of colors and textures, a mash-up of mediums with no apparent thought or theme. But it's there, a pattern within the chaos. Stark white and harsh black lines offset the vibrant colors, mirroring the dichotomy of human feelings, a consistent thread woven through life's tapestry of triumph and failure, success and ruin.

He delicately traces a finger over one of the black lines and I shudder. I wonder how his fingers would feel on my skin.

Don't be ridiculous, V. You don't care about that shit anymore.

"The black-and-white lines are deliberate, yeah?" I nod, the movement almost imperceptible, but he notices.

"Obviously, each stroke is deliberate, but these feel . . . " He trails off, considering the piece with his fingers, tracing a line of white resin from the point where it starts, through a patch of swirling purple and neon green paint, over its harsh white slash, and across a patch of pink and yellow fabric to pick up the distinct white trail a final time before it ends at the edge of the canvas.

"They are constant. Representing the extreme dichotomy of good and evil, maybe. And the colors represent the chaos of everything in between."

Tremors slither up and down my spine, and I feel as if I've bared my soul to this intense stranger. I do my best to school my features and try to figure out a reply that won't give away any more of myself, but my mind is reeling. This is the piece that I poured the most of myself into, and he sees it for what it is.

I look at him, fully intending to confirm his observations, but the words get stuck in my dry throat, and it is his turn to squirm under my scrutiny. He runs a hand through his hair and wets his full lips with just the tip of his tongue. His eyes dart back and forth between me and the canvas, and I decide right then and there that I like flustered Charlie. Not that it matters because I *really* don't care.

You'll probably never see him again anyway, V. Which is for the best.

"That's a very astute observation, Charlie," I reply dryly. A fucking brilliant smile spreads across his face.

"She seems deceptively simple, but I see a new detail every time I look. She would look bloody smashing in the right setting." He moves to look from a different angle, and his arm brushes briefly against mine, spending a jolt of his vibrating energy straight into my soul. I jump, placing a hand on my heaving chest, and struggle to settle the riot of butterflies in my stomach.

"Right here, for example," he says, voice pitched so low that I have to lean in close to hear him, so close my chest grazes his arm when I inhale. A smug smile tugs up the corners of his mouth, and mischief dances in his eyes. I chide myself for falling so easily into his trap, clear my throat, and take a pointed step back.

"This circle of red. If you look closely, you realize that it is two shades of red, not one, merging and diverging in an intricate dance. I think they represent two sides of the same coin, two strong emotions often considered opposites, which are actually more similar than most care to admit."

How the fuck is he inside my head.

"Which emotions," I ask on an unsteady exhale.

He turns fully toward me, and I unconsciously mimic his movement. The little space left between us is charged with intoxicating tension. I wait, breath held, greedily absorbing his vibrating energy.

Don't you remember, V? This is what it feels like to be alive!

"Love and hate," he says, grazing his fingers up my arm from wrist to elbow. Or maybe it represents emotions more closely related. Love and lust, for instance," he finishes, mirroring his tormenting movements on my other arm. I swear sparks ignite the hyper-charged air between us.

"Charlie. Let's go." Jessica's shrill voice slices the tension between us, severing the charge. I dig my nails into my palms to suppress the urge to glare at the bimbo and release a shaky breath, relieved to be free of this too-charming stranger's enchantment.

Charlie's eyes remain locked on mine, but his hands fall from my elbows, setting me adrift on a sea of swirling emotions. Multiple pairs of eyes settle on us, their judgmental weight making my shoulders hunch. I know it's ridiculous, but tendrils of guilt and betrayal twine up my legs, and I shift from foot to foot, trying to break their hold.

He's gone, V. You can't betray someone who's not in your life anymore.

"Umm, you're being summoned," I say, and when he makes no move to acknowledge Jessica, I reluctantly prod, "your friends are . . ." His eyes narrow to slits, and I trail off.

"Let's make one thing clear, Veronica. No one summons me, especially *her*," he sneers.

Touchy, touchy, but he's cute all riled up. No, V. You don't care, *remember.*

"Ronnie, my dear," Kali calls from across the room, manicured hands planted on curved hips, eyes wide and demanding.

"I better get over there," I whisper, sad to see him go while reminding myself that it is probably for the best. His face falls, and he runs a thumb delicately across my cheek.

"I will see you around. Goodnight, Veronica."

He looks at me one more time as his party leaves, and I grudgingly admit to myself that I hope I do.

Maybe Just Maybe

*H*o-l-y *shit! What a night.* You survived all the socializing–and–whatever that was with Charlie without having a complete mental breakdown. You deserve a fat reward, V.

For this exact reason, there's a slice of tiramisu cheesecake in the fridge, delivered this morning from my favorite bakery. An hour after Charlie left, I finally convinced the brilliant twins to call it a night. They were phenomenal, mingling with our guests with poise and grace and kindly yet firmly keeping me focused and on my feet. The constant pain that radiates from my shattered heart is dull for once, muffled by contentment and satisfaction.

Moaning in pleasure, I step out of my damn stilettos, stretching my toes, a huge yawn contorting my sleepy face. As I drop my dress to the floor, leaving it in the living room right where I'm standing, I wonder what Charlie's doing with the rest of his night. I find that it's easy to picture him at the pub, sharing a pint with his friends, coolly yet courteously halting Jessica's advances. She may have tried to lay her claim on him tonight, but he didn't seem to want anything to do with her. At least, I hope I read that right.

Still, my imagination runs wild, picturing her pressing her frustratingly ample bosom against his arm and batting her fake eyelashes at him; him leaning in to press his luscious, full lips to hers. I inhale sharply through my nose, startled at the ferocity of the jealousy snaking through me at the thought of him with someone else.

For fucks sake, V. YOU. DON'T. CARE.

It really doesn't matter anyway. If the past six years have taught me anything, it is my inability to let go of him. Releasing an exasperated sigh, I flop down onto the small cream-colored sofa, naked, and throw an arm over my face. I focus on breathing evenly to calm my racing heart, fully intending to get up, eat the cheesecake, and do my nighttime routine. But I fall asleep after a few rounds of deep breathing . . . and regret it in the morning.

A woman stood on the small front porch of a cute little cottage nestled in the pine trees on the edge of town. A man, tall and lean with kind blue eyes, stood on the step below, gazing longingly into her chocolate eyes. The woman tilted her head up, lips parted in invitation. The man lowered his lips tentatively to hers and kissed her softly.

The man leaned back to search the woman's eyes. Finding permission and yearning in their dark depths, he leaned back down and kissed her more fervently. The woman's heart sang with joy at the promise in his kiss. He broke their embrace before they got swept into the throws of passion. His face shone with contentment and desire. The woman saw her future written in his eyes.

A gallery of still-life images flashed through the woman's mind, a series of their life's milestones playing out in sequence. The images passed by faster and faster until they were a blur, too fast to decipher the individual images. An entire lifetime passed before her eyes, and she wept with joy at what their future held. The man left, placing a loving kiss on her forehead, and the images stopped so abruptly that the woman staggered. The final image, stuck on pause, clouding her vision, turned her joy into dread. Nausea roiled within her.

No, she screamed. No. She begged. No, she pleaded, despair toppling the woman to her knees.

No, she screams. No, she begs. No, she pleads to whoever might be listening. No, no, no, no. Not again, please, not again. The image doesn't budge, but the nausea breaks free and moves up her esophagus. No, God, no. No, no, no, no . . . I scream myself awake.

Another nightmare. Thank fuck I have them less often than I used to. They are so vivid, so real that they leave me raw and exposed, chest flayed open, freshly mended heart shattered once again.

Why? Why did you leave me?

Sometimes, I miss *him* so much that my legs buckle, and I struggle to draw breath. Like now: legs drawn to my chest, skin cold from falling asleep naked on the sofa, face tear-stained and contorted from the effort to stop hyperventilating.

Inhale, V... Now exhale. And again.

After a few minutes, I am able to get up and brew myself a cuppa, cup of tea, as the Brits say. Too afraid to go back to sleep and risk falling back into the nightmare, I write in my journal, meditate, and do some mobility work instead–all things I should have done last night before falling asleep. The aftershock of the nightmare won't wear off for a while, but at least I feel more grounded now, if not still raw and drained.

When the first rays of sunlight peak over the London skyline, painting the sky in beautiful shades of orange and pink, I walk to Fitness First, letting the peaceful morning soothe my battered soul. I punch out my rage on a heavy bag, cursing the universe for dealing me such a shitty hand.

I pump, twist, and push away my despair, wishing that I could go back and change the past with every fiber of muscle being stretched and rebuilt. But I can't, so I run. I run until my breaths come in ragged, heaving gasps, and my legs shake with the effort to keep going. I run from the guilt and the grief, replacing the never-ending pain of the soul with the temporary and fleeting pain of the body. Reluctant acceptance and transient absolution rest heavily in my limbs, and a few pieces of my heart have been carefully fitted back into place when I'm done. At the very least, I'll be able to focus at work today.

I run smack dab into something made of granite. Of their own volition, my hands pat and poke the specimen until my brain catches up and realizes that it is, in fact, a man and not a statue standing in front of me.

A honey-smooth voice drawls, "Good morning, Veronica." Mouth hanging open, I stand there staring like an idiot, palms resting on his abdomen. Fuck, he's ripped. The strong urge to run my hands over his sculpted torso startles me, and I quickly pull back as if he scalded my fingertips. I drop them to my sides and curl my hands into fists before I make a fool of myself. Brilliant green eyes regard me with warmth and humor, and the most beautiful smile blooms on his full lips. Which I'm staring at.

Holy crap, V, pull yourself together!

I blush, an amusing shade of red based on the look on his face, step back, and stammer out, "H-hello, Charlie."

He chuckles. "Hello, Veronica. Do you come here often?"

"Yeah, pretty regularly. You?" I manage to get out an entire sentence. He is so handsome, with that easy confidence and radiating intensity, turning my insides into fluttering mush.

"Occasionally. Which gym I use depends on what I want to accomplish," he says cryptically. "Do you box or do any MMA?"

"I haven't recently." Hitting a punching bag doesn't count.

"There's a kickboxing class starting in a few minutes. Do you want to join me?" His smooth, warm voice sounds hopeful.

"Maybe another time. I have to get back to the studio soon. Even though technically we're equal partners, Kali and Kellan run a tight ship."

Charlie makes a pirate joke, but I miss the punchline, my attention drawn to a man walking towards where we stand in the doorway. I step closer to Charlie to let the man pass, but he rams me into Charlie's sculpted chest, accidentally grabbing my ass, and mumbles, "Stupid American," just loud enough for us to hear. I yelp, and Charlie's hand, fast as a viper, strikes out and grabs the man's arm, flipping him around and pinning him against the wall with a forearm in his throat.

"Next time," he purrs in the man's ear, that honey butter voice low and menacing, "keep your fucking hands to yourself and watch your fucking mouth." My eyes go round, and my heart starts racing.

"Piss off," the man rasps as he tries unsuccessfully to dislodge Charlie's arm from his throat. Charlie shakes his head and waves a finger in the man's face.

"Nuh, uh, uh, uh. You owe her an apology."

I fight back the urge to ogle and fan my heated face.

Careful, V. Swoon too hard, and you'll faceplant.

The man swivels his head as far in my direction as possible and manages to blurt, "I'm sorry." Charlie's arm remains locked across his throat. He looks at Charlie and repeats his lame apology. When the corded forearm still doesn't budge, the man forces out, "Christ, mate. I said I was sorry." Charlie looks at me, eyebrows raised. I nod, and he releases the man, who stares Charlie down for one tense moment before stalking away.

That. Was. Hot.

Charlie reaches out tentatively and runs his fingertips down my arm, goosebumps pebble across my skin in their wake. I shiver visibly, and he smirks. "I will see you around, Veronica." And again, I hope I do.

But I shouldn't, right?

I take the long way home, contemplating our two brief interactions. That unwarranted feeling of betrayal swells in my chest again, and tears prick my eyes. I splay my palm hard against my chest, reminding myself that my therapist said these feelings of betrayal aren't serving me. I chose to live. Having friends, maybe even someone who is more than a friend is a natural, normal part of the human experience.

Being attracted to someone is not a betrayal to *him*.

Am I attracted to Charlie? What does attraction even feel like?

Let's see. Erratic breathing, check. Butterflies in my belly, check. Unable to form coherent thoughts and sentences when around him, yup, that's a problem. Notice his every physical detail when I haven't cared about that for years, yup. Am I secretly hoping to see him again, definitely. If I were thirty years younger, I'd say I have a crush, but I'm not a young girl anymore, so I'll call it what it is: an infatuation.

The social hurdle has been steadily lowering, bit by bit, as I do the work on myself, becoming easier and easier to jump. Kali and Kellan are smoothly morphing from taciturn, intimidating agents to shrewd, empowering business partners to kind, fun, supportive close friends. Together, we work hard and play hard, loving and supporting each other through life's ups and downs.

The question I really need to answer for myself is whether I'm open to having a romantic relationship. Am I ready to jump that hurdle? Am I willing to even try? Maybe pursuing this thing–whatever it is–with Charlie isn't such a bad idea after all.

But I'm scared.

Making and maintaining friendships is one thing; being in a romantic relationship is a whole different ball game. Throughout the long, grueling workday, my thoughts bounce back and forth between no-fucking-way and maybe-just-maybe. I continue to contemplate my predicament while I eat a quiet sushi dinner and perform my nightly routine without forming any conclusions. Mind and body exhausted, I fall into a mercifully dreamless sleep, having decided to find out if he's even interested in me before I worry too much more about any potential thing between us.

Cows Aren't Easy

The melodies of my favorite classical composers chime out of the speakers, providing creative inspiration, while I add some final touches to a few pieces at the end of a productive workday. *Studio V* is divided into two parts, the gallery in front and the workroom in the back, separated by a half wall topped with windows to let in as much natural light as possible.

The brilliant twins and I are working out a contract to become long-term business partners, and once it's finalized, they'll run the business aspect full-time. Until then, they manage the gallery, gracefully sharing their vast knowledge with me whenever we have a spare moment, while I spend my time in the workroom, creating and hiding. When I co-owned a similar business years ago in the States, *he* also managed the business while I mostly created, and *he* utilized every available opportunity to educate me, much the same way Kali and Kellan do.

God, I miss him *so much.*

I splay my hand over my chest in a futile attempt to relieve the ever-present pain that radiates from my shattered heart.

He's gone, V. Accept it. Move on.

It shouldn't be this hard to get over someone. But man it is.

Despite my mental turmoil, I am vaguely aware of the steady stream of customers trickling in and out of the gallery. Some watch me through the glass, but I ignore them, my attention divided between work, him, and *him*. The lower half of my face is hidden behind a respirator (a necessity when working with resin), so I can't even offer them a smile regardless.

Twenty more minutes, V. You can do this.

Debussy's *Clair de Lune* plays in the background, and I pause, moving my hands in the air before me, miming the chords as if caressing real ivories. Mid-chord, my breath quickens, my palms get clammy, and butterflies fill my belly.

My eyes flick to the glass, and piercing green eyes lock onto mine. Transfixed, I stand there, hands raised and body half turned. Hopefully, this damn respirator hides the blush blooming on my cheeks. The hair on my arms stands on end and a shiver courses through me at the intensity he radiates even through the barrier that separates us. I shake free of the trance and give him a small wave. A beaming smile spreads across his handsome face.

Eyebrows raised, he points at the stylish *Arnold & Son* watch on his wrist. I noticed it the other night, noted the brand, and looked it up. The intricate inner gears and wheels are displayed on a blue PVD flange (whatever that means) and are visible through a glass face set in a stainless-steel case. The value of the watch could cover my rent for a few months. I would love to have one of their timepieces, each more gorgeous than the last, but I would never spend that kind of money on myself.

Financial Advisor or entertainment industry executive, maybe?

Unless he inherited his apparent wealth, but he doesn't possess that arrogant entitlement I've noticed in most other trust fund babies.

I hold up all ten fingers in response.

Why are you here, Mr. Green Eyes?

I doubt it's solely to see me. He's probably here for some other, purely professional reason. And this infatuation will pass soon. Yeah, he's gorgeous and charming, intelligent, insightful, and intense. Not to mention that stunt with the asshole at the gym. That was panty-melting hot. The only other time I've felt this strong of a connection was with *him*, and that was real. So, fucking real, I live in a constant state of pain and inner turmoil.

Nope. Don't go there, V.

I return my attention to the abstract blue and gold-covered canvas, enjoying the soothing process of popping stubborn air bubbles in the resin. As I move a torch back and forth across the swirling colors, I focus on using my breath to clear my mind. Inhale, exhale. In, out. I don't look back as I finish. I know Charlie's there, waiting. Like a passionate caress, I feel his eyes on me as I work. It is oddly exhilarating. Goosebumps pebble my flushed skin, and his eyes linger on me as I walk to the private loo connecting the gallery office and the workroom.

I stare down in resignation at my paint-splattered jeans and t-shirt. There's probably paint in my hair as well, but I can do nothing about it now. The tiny, glittery avocado stud earrings in my earlobes, made by yours truly, twinkle as I freshen up and examine myself in the mirror for a moment. I decide Charlie's going to have to take me as I am on such short notice, then take a deep breath, let it out, and step into the office.

"Adonis is here to see you," Kali says in a sing-song voice as I try to slip past her unnoticed.

"You have senses like a jungle cat, Kal," I quip at her back. She continues rapidly tapping on the keyboard.

"Oh, I'm not actually working. I've been sitting here pretending to work since he walked in."

"What? Why?" I look more closely at her monitor and see my reflection displayed clearly on the black screen.

"To watch you stammer and blush while the delicious hunk flirts with you."

I scoff. "Remind me, again, why I pay you," I jest as I move toward the door.

"Because I'm brilliant."

"Don't forget humble," I throw over my shoulder as I walk into the gallery, slamming the door in her face.

"Hello, Veronica," Charlie says before the bang of the slammed door finishes echoing through the gallery. Two simple words— spoken in that voice, as smooth and rich as honey—and my insides instantly melt.

Wait, what?

His greeting finally registers in my brain. He calls me Veronica, and I don't hate it. I kind of . . . like it. And who wouldn't, coming from him, a sensuous caress rolling off those full lips?

"Hello, Charlie. What brings you in today," I ask, a bit breathless.

"Two reasons." He holds up a hand, pointer finger raised. "One. To oversee the packing and loading of my newly purchased artwork. And two," he raises a second finger, "to see you, of course." He shrugs casually as if reason two was obvious.

Does that answer your question, V?

I'm not ready to find out yet, so I respond to the safer option, knowing what his answer will be. "Oh, really? Which piece is that?" I smile knowingly.

"Yes, Big Bertha. I promise you she will love her new home. I bet you would, too. You should visit her after she is installed," he says, shrugging and quirking one side of his mouth.

You sly devil.

"Maybe someday," I reply neutrally, then add, "Cool watch," and gesture towards his wrist with my chin.

His face momentarily tightens before he answers with a curt nod of his head.

Touchy, touchy.

Riled-up Charlie is adorable. "No, really, it is an interesting watch. I've never seen one with the gears displayed like that. And that color. A mix of Prussian and Midnight blues, like the deep twilight sky of a moonless night at the moment right before the sky fades to black. It's a fucking hard color to replicate with paint," I clarify.

His eyes flash sideways at me, and his shoulders drop away from his ears. "Oh, yes. I'm told they use a very distinct method of assembly for their timepieces, as well."

"It's hard for me to imagine. Working on such a small scale with such delicate materials."

"I can see that," he says wryly, gesturing at my artwork, each piece massive in scale. Crimson slowly parades up my neck, and I fight the urge to glare at Kali, who has emerged from the office and conspicuously adjusts a large resin geode directly behind Charlie, which is already perfectly displayed.

"Which is perfect for us collectors who have large spaces to fill."

I have a space you can fill.

Well, that escalated quickly. I expel a huff and consciously draw my shoulders away from my ears. "I am relieved it's being received so well thus far. It took quite a bit of convincing to get Kal and Kel on board," I say, nodding at Kellan, who matches his twin in sophisticated white and black casual business attire. They've converged on our side now, heads tilted together as they direct the packaging and loading of sold pieces. I know for a fact they are paying more attention to Charlie and I's conversation than their work. So, I nonchalantly wind around a few of the wooden support beams to create some distance between us and them.

When I stop, Charlie raises his eyebrows and jerks his chin at them. "My condolences," he jokes.

I snort. "Have you ever tried to coax a herd of cows to cross a bridge?"

"I have, believe it or not."

"Not," I blurt, clapping my hand over my mouth. There's no way he's serious. Without pause, I babble, "It's easier. The cows. They're easy. Not easy. Cows aren't easy. Getting cows to cross a bridge is easier than trying to change Kal and Kel's minds."

Oh my god, V! Just shut up.

My leg jiggles, and I press my lips into a thin line.

"You don't believe me," he prods. I keep my lips pressed firmly together. "Why not?"

"Because you don't look like a country boy." And he doesn't in his perfectly tailored black slacks, still crisply starched white shirt devoid of wrinkles or stains after what I'm guessing was a long workday. Top that with a charcoal vest and matching tie, and he looks like the cover model for a romance book about a sexy billionaire CEO who loathes his arranged marriage but doesn't like to share 'his wife.' Feelings that have been long submerged bubble up, and I don't know what to do with them, so I cross one ankle over the other, squeeze my thighs together, and clasp my hands in front of me.

Charlie scrutinizes me, but I refuse to meet his gaze for fear of him seeing straight through the glass to the truth of my feelings. He reaches forward, a smug smile plastered on his face, and runs the rough fingers of one large, calloused hand down my arm. I shiver.

Shit. That feels good.

I forgot about his hands. How did I forget about his hands? Well, I didn't. I haven't stopped thinking about his touch and the way it feels on my skin. I just assumed the calluses were from the gym. I risk a quick glance at his hand as it lingers on my arm.

Big hands, V. And rough. Your favorite kind.

He also had large, rough hands. Fuck me.

"Let's make one thing clear, Veronica." His voice, whispered directly into my ear, pulls me out of my spiraling thoughts and sends more shivers down my spine.

"I am *not* a boy."

"Obviously," I hiss, whipping my head toward him. His face is so close to mine that our noses almost touch, and I can smell the mint on his breath. Flustered, I step back, crossing my arms over my chest, eyebrows raised.

"I grew up on a farm with cows. I still go there often to help my parents: throw hay bales, fix fence, and plow the fields."

You can plow—stop!

Charlie may be striking as the rakish, well-dressed businessman, but the thought of him dressed in jeans and a T-shirt, sweating and sun-drenched while working on the farm has me drenched.

Woah, Nellie.

A loud bang draws our attention to the twins and the movers. We watch in charged silence as they carefully package the two halves of the enormous piece. I am hyper-aware of Charlie standing next to me, the small space between us vibrating with delicious tension. I sneak a sideways peek at him. He's younger than me by about a decade, I'd guess, but he possesses the easy confidence of someone closer to my age. Someone who is perfectly at ease in their body, who intrinsically knows he has every right to take up space in this world. Someone who never had to make himself small and invisible and defer their right to exist.

He leans casually against a wooden beam, arms folded across his muscular chest, ankles crossed casually while he watches the proceedings intently.

He catches me looking at him, but I don't look away this time. I stare at him boldly. The vibration between us intensifies, enhancing those feelings I thought I had lost forever with *him*.

God, I miss him.

So much it hurts. Most of the time, the pain is a consistent dull ache. During moments like this, though, when it sneaks up on me, it's like a knife stabbing clean through my sternum and straight into my heart, repeatedly.

My eyes cloud over, and I struggle to draw breath. I grip the back of the nearest sofa hard enough to turn my knuckles white. I struggle to pull air into my lungs, and a memory breaks free from its vault. *He's* cutting wood shirtless. I watch his muscles ripple as *he* swings the axe. *He* catches my gaze and looks at me with naked desire. My lips part, and I inhale the smell of the forest so forcefully that it burns down the back of my throat.

Someone gently taps my shoulder and calls my name—my given name. I flinch, and reality crashes into me. Charlie's hand on my shoulder steadies me, and I take a few measured breaths before meeting his eyes.

"Are you okay, Veronica?" His voice is so tender that I almost step into him and fall apart right there in the middle of the gallery. Instead, I straighten my spine.

"Yes and no," I answer. He steps in front of me and lifts my chin with his knuckle.

"Is there anything I can do to help?" he asks, genuine concern making his voice soft and intimate. I shake my head, but he doesn't let go of my chin.

"I'm fine, really." He presses his lips into a thin line but refrains from calling me out. He simply waits, holding space for me. "This happens sometimes. Panic attacks," I clarify, rolling my hand between us. "This one was pretty mild, though, thanks to you." I give him a small smile. His expression relaxes, and he drops his hand.

We both turn back to observe the movers who carefully feed 'Big Bertha' through the garage door. I had the doors installed on the studio's front wall specifically for this reason.

I like to make big pieces. Kali also opens them in the afternoons. The early fall weather here in London has been absolutely beautiful, creating an earthy, calm atmosphere in the gallery.

"I have to meet them at my place, but I ah, I have been meaning to ask you something," he says tentatively, and I detect a note of nervousness in his voice. "Um, I would love to take you on a date. Would you go out to dinner with me tomorrow?" He stands with his shoulders slightly hunched and his hands in his pockets, peaking at me out of the corner of his eye.

Nervous Charlie is almost as cute as riled-up Charlie.

"I can't tomorrow. Kali and Kellan need me here all day. I can Sunday, though." I twist the rings on my fingers, surprised that he is still interested after seeing the panic attack.

Maybe crazy and unstable is his thing, V. Don't overthink it.

"Sunday sounds lovely. I will pick you up at 7," he states, not exactly a demand but not a request either. He's a man who is used to getting what he wants.

"Perfect. I'll see you then." That brilliant smile of his blooms across his face. He leans down, places the lightest of kisses on my cheek, and saunters out the door, nerves vanishing the moment he gets what he wants. I stand there absently caressing my cheek, staring after him long after he's gone.

"Ronnie, Ronnie. Earth to Veronica!" Kali calls. A wonderful shade of crimson crawls up my throat. I jump into action, rearranging the racks in the gift shop as if that's what I'd been doing instead of gawking after Charlie.

"Oh, Kal. Let her have her moment," Kellan scolds, shooting me a sly smile.

"I did *not* have a moment, Kel."

"As much as I love to argue with my arrogant brother," Kali says, struggling to keep the amusement off her face, "I must agree with him on this one. You definitely had a moment with that tall, fine hunk of meat. Mmmm."

"Kali," I chide playfully

"What? He's gorgeous. Right, Kel?"

"Oh, I already know Kel's opinion on the matter. He gave me an uncomfortable earful of it the last time Charlie was here."

"Ah yes," Kali replies, "your other 'non-moment' with Mr. Adonis-in-the-flesh."

"Okay, yes," I concede, "the man is gorgeous. Happy," I ask, flinging my hands up. A pair of Cheshire grins stare back at me, and Kellan's eyes dance with mischief.

"Oh no. Not this again. I don't do relationships. I don't even do people in general. You guys know this."

"But you could . . . do him," Kali jests with a devilish wink.

"I walked right into that one, didn't I?"

"Come on, Ron," Kali goads.

"You are gorgeous, yourself, love," Kellan states.

"And, in your prime," Kali agrees. My palms are sweaty, and my heart races just listening to these two. The thought of getting naked and tangling with a man that attractive and self-possessed, not to mention so much younger than me both intrigues and terrifies me. I may be in the best shape of my life, but I've got scars and saggy bits and stretch marks from another life. Tiny Mildred pipes up, reminding me that I'm also too tall, too muscular, and not feminine enough to garner a man's attention.

"Like I said before," Kellan continues, "there's plenty of activities you can do with a man like him that require very little talking."

"Hardly," I counterattack before Kali has a chance to fire off her agreement. "If I was interested, which I'm not, I highly doubt we could get to those activities with very little talking."

"Oh honey," Kali fires. "All you'd have to do is crook your finger at him, and he'd come without a single word."

"Really, Kal? Eww," I say at the same time as Kellan says, "Nice sis. That was a good one."

"You two are way too open about sex for brother and sister," I say, scrunching my nose.

"Oh, come now, darling. We're all adults here," Kellan points out.

"And we're just innocently encouraging you to go have a little fun," Kali continues their tandem barrage. These two just might wear me down eventually. They're the cheerleaders I need but don't always want.

"Innocently," I ask, crossing my arms over my chest and pinning her with a wide-eyed stare. Kellan guffaws.

"Yes. Innocently in the sense that after you play 'park the car in the garage' with sinful Adonis, you share all the juicy details so we," she gestures between herself and her identical twin brother, "can live vicariously through you."

"You're perfectly welcome to play hide the sausage with him yourself if you're that interested," I shoot back, surprised at the feral surge of possession the thought of him with someone else sparks within me.

"Oh no, darling. Our sculpted Greek God has eyes only for you," Kellan clarifies.

"Then you two nymphos will just have to keep dreaming. Like I said. I don't do relationships."

"And like I said," Kali declares, finger pointed at the ceiling, "you can do—"

"Oh my God. Stop already," I say, chuckling despite myself. "Isn't it about time to close up," I attempt to change the subject.

"I pulled the sign and locked up when Adonis himself left," Kellan says, raising one eyebrow. I point a finger at each of them.

"Don't. . . say anything. I'm going to bed. Alone," I emphasize.

"Such a pity," they reply in unison as I flip them the bird and stalk upstairs while their unorthodox encouragements ring in my ears. They don't need to know about our date until I see how it goes and decide whether there will be more.

You could take their advice and skip the talking.

But casual sex isn't my thing, and I get the feeling that Charlie and I could never be casual. I'll just see how this date goes and go from there.

That's a First

"Good morning." I greet Sophie over Facetime.

"Good night," she chuckles. "It's so good to see you, Ron."

"What's up with you two?"

"T's on leave for a couple of weeks." The man himself leans over his wife's shoulder and flashes an easy smile.

"Any cool flights lately," I ask the Air Force pilot.

"That's top-secret info, Ron," he replies, shaking his head.

"I know. But one of these days, I'm going to get lucky, and you'll slip up and tell me that you flew over an active volcano, saw a megalodon from the sky, or solved the mystery of the Bermuda Triangle."

"I wish. Did Soph tell you we're getting a new puppy in a few weeks?"

"I haven't had the chance yet," she says, shooting her husband a playful glare. Longing slices through my chest, but I cut it off swiftly so neither of them see it on my face.

"That is exciting. What kind?"

"A husky," Turner answers. His wife pushes him in the chest.

"Hey now," she whines. "Don't forget Ron is *my* friend. Off with you for a minute." He disappears, good-naturedly counting, one . . . two . . . three . . . as he disappears. Sophie and I giggle, and I consciously push back another wave of longing for the past and do my best to stay focused on the present.

"How's the promotion going," I ask.

"I haven't got it yet."

"You will. They'd be stupid not to give you the position."

"The waiting is wearing on me. I feel like I'm under a microscope with the office jockeys scrutinizing everything I do."

"That sounds exhausting. Is that prick Harry still running the ER?"

"No! He got fired last week," she says, eyes wide.

"What?" I gasp. I worked as a labor and delivery nurse at the same hospital that Sophie still works at forever ago, and Harry strutted around, acting like he was king of the ER.

"He got caught having an affair with a young intern."

"No way. Serves him right, though. He always gave me the creeps."

"Me too," she agrees. "Is the studio still busy?"

"Yes, thanks to Kal and Kel. They are brilliant."

"I'm so proud of you, Ron. This is a huge step forward for you, and I'm sure it's been challenging. But, you're doing it, and that takes a lot of damn strength."

"Thanks, Soph. It is, but it's also been really rewarding." The conversation lulls, and my mind drifts to Charlie and our disturbingly intense attraction. I have been half tempted to cancel on him tonight. I debate whether to ask Sophie for advice but hesitate, knowing she'll encourage me to go.

She ends my mental debate when she says, "I see the wheels turning. Spit it out, lady."

I roll my eyes and sigh dramatically. "I was trying really hard to keep that off my face," I pout.

"I hate to break it to you, sweetheart, but I don't think you'll ever master your face. Plus, I'm your best friend. You'll never be able to hide much from me."

"Fine, then," I gulp, forcing out my next words. "I need some advice," I admit, grudgingly.

Her eyebrows rise almost to her hairline. "That's a first," she says.

"I. . . met a guy, and we're supposed to go on a date tonight, and I'm—." The rest of my sentence is drowned out by Soph and Turner (who's no doubt been sitting just off camera this whole time) shouting, "Yes, girl," and "Do it!"

"Would you two chill out already!" I say, laughing despite my trepidations. "I am barely holding it together here. I might not go. Now that I've had time to think about it, I'm not sure it's such a good idea."

"Go, Ron," Sophie encourages kindly.

"Yeah. If it doesn't go well, then you never have to see him again," Turner agrees. Somehow, I don't think Charlie would let me walk away that easily. But I can't stop thinking about him, so I guess I may as well figure out what this is between us.

"I don't know what I'm doing. I haven't been on a date since," I make a 'you know' gesture. "I don't know what to do. I don't know what to say. I don't know what to *wear*!" I flip the phone screen. It looks like the closet threw up on the bed.

"Okay, okay. First things first. What are you doing on this date?" Sophie asks, surprised. I have sworn to her since *the event* that I would never date again.

"To dinner," I say.

"That's a start. Where? Is it fine dining, casual?" Turner asks pragmatically.

"I don't know," I whine. "I didn't think to ask. I don't know what's wrong with me. I feel like I can't think straight around him. It could be either, really. He's been to the studio a couple of times. Bought my most expensive piece, actually. He showed up to oversee them loading it, decked out in luxury business attire. But then again, he also told me he was raised on a farm." Twin expressions of curiosity stare at me from my phone screen.

"Don't ask."

"Take a deep breath. It will be okay. You will do just fine." Sophie's simple words do wonders to calm my racing heart.

"Zoom us in closer. Let's see what we are working with here," Turner chimes in. These two are some of my favorite humans. I would have never made it through everything without their support. It's rare to catch them both at home since Turner is an active-duty Air Force pilot, and Sophie works crazy hours at the hospital.

"You could go with the little black dress. That's always a safe choice," Turner rationalizes.

"Shit," I smack my forehead a little too hard. "He's already seen me in that dress." Turner harrumphs but nods in agreement.

"Hold up the one on the top left. No, no, my left. Is that a jumper?" Sophie asks.

"Yes, yes. That is a great look for her," Turner agrees.

I hold it up to my body. White and brass-colored flowers are splattered across the olive-green bodice, which accentuates my narrow waist. The back dips low, displaying my one tattoo: a pair of large wings, starting at the nape of my neck and flowing in delicate black swirls down the outer edge of my back to my sacrum. Words and numbers are hidden in the pattern, a tribute to another life.

"You two are lifesavers. Literally. Wish me luck!"

"We want a full report tomorrow," Turner demands.

"Don't you two have anything better to do," I joke. "My dating life isn't exactly existent, let alone exciting."

"It's existent now, and we're invested," Sophie says.

I chuckle. "You two are ridiculous. Go see a movie or something."

"Nah. We've just been married forever, and you know John and Cat are even bigger homebodies than us, which makes for very little entertainment," Turner says.

"Fine, but don't set your expectations too high."

"That's the spirit," he says.

"Talk to you soon. Love you." Sophie blows a kiss, and I return the gesture.

"Love you guys, too."

I chuck the phone on the bed and stare at myself in the mirror, stomping down the urge to cancel on Charlie. Curiosity gets the best of me, and I decide to follow through and determine the nature of this attraction between us.

Well, shit, V. You're really doing this.

I Hope I Do

Several hours later, I wander down to the gallery and sift through the racks in the gift shop. The other day, I made a batch of earrings that would go perfectly with my jumper: large gold triangle bezels with a single, small fern cast in resin. Sometimes, I feel like such a fraud, living here in London and being an *artist* of all things. Developing my new personal style (aka not sweats and hoodies), always wearing heels (unless I'm in the workroom), and jewelry that I've made helps me believe that I truly am this new version of myself. Imposter Syndrome Ivy is a bitch I battle daily.

The last rays of sunlight filter through the single large window on the gallery's west-facing side. It's bright and warm, and I bask in its glow like a cat as I sketch out an idea for a new piece. Minutes or hours later, I'm not sure which, as engrossed in sketching as I am, a shadow falls over me. Without looking up to confirm who is standing there, my breathing immediately quickens, and butterflies fill my belly. I take a deep breath, then raise my gaze to meet piercing green eyes. I hold his eyes for a moment, momentarily emboldened, then slowly put away my sketchbook, hoping it will give me time to center myself. However, the weight of his gaze following my every move makes it impossible to calm my nerves.

You can't back out now, V. Get your ass out there and get on with it.

When I've stalled as long as I possibly can without being rude, I set my shoulders and walk out to greet the handsome enigma.

"Hello, Veronica," he purrs. Those simple words that are quickly becoming my favorite two-word phrase. I haven't allowed anyone to call me that since I was little, not even *him*. My mother said it in the most manipulative, shaming, and demeaning ways. She could infuse such contempt and malice into those four syllables that I'd end up buried in my closet, shaken and balling.

"You look gorgeous," he drawls, dipping his chin.

"Thank you," I reply, a light shade of red blooming on my cheeks. "As do you." He wears snug, dark jeans that sit low on his hips and a white Sunspel T-shirt under a black suede trucker jacket. His hair is gelled back into a pompadour, and he's sporting a five o'clock shadow, which sinfully accentuates his full lips.

Quit staring at his mouth, V.

A smug smile slides across his face when he notices my eyes on his mouth. His eyes track the blush that creeps up my throat, observant as a cat who's cornered a mouse.

"We're dining at the pub a few blocks down. Do you mind walking? Or I could ring my driver around," he asks.

Driver? So, entertainment industry then.

"Let's walk," I answer. He seems decent enough, but I don't want to find out the hard way that he's not. He offers his arm, watching me closely. Hopefully, he can't read my face as well as Sophie or feel my clammy palms through his jacket.

Charlie and I speak little on the walk to the pub, which suits me just fine. The sun hangs just above the horizon, shining its last brilliant rays over the London skyline, and a gentle breeze rustles the leaves on the dazzling, dusk-illuminated trees. The last of the day's warmth lingers in the air, creating a peaceful atmosphere that helps to calm my nerves.

The young hostess greets Charlie and me both by name when we enter, and he returns her greeting warmly, then requests a specific table, surprising me. I'm not sure why, but I assumed we'd sit at the bar. As we pass, he exchanges jokes with the bartenders, and they nod at me. I haven't created a bond with them in all the times I've been here, unlike I did with Romeo. I wonder if Charlie's seeming familiarity stems from us having previously crossed paths here. I was just here two days ago, as this is my new Friday night haunt. We arrive at our table, and my pondering ceases.

I am not disappointed in Charlie's choice. The table is set off the main dining room on a small, raised platform nestled in a nook between three floor-to-ceiling windows. The view of the city is breathtaking. The pub stands on the corner of the block, and this table looks down a street lined with ancient trees and old, beautifully restored buildings. It opens up at the end, perfectly framing the Tower Bridge looming over the Thames in the distance.

"Veronica?" Charlie waits patiently while I reluctantly pull my gaze away from the windows.

"The view is breathtaking," I say.

"Yes, it is," he replies, eyes roaming over my face.

I unsuccessfully attempt to stop the blush from blazing up my throat. I'm focusing so much on keeping my nerves in check that it takes a moment to register the server taking our drink order from Charlie, who orders for me: sparkling water mixed with cranberry juice in a wine glass.

What the fuck?

I sit back, cross my arms over my chest, raise my eyebrows, and pin him with a wide, demanding stare. He examines me for a few seconds before answering, unconsciously licking his lips with just the tip of his tongue and raking a hand through his hair. "You truly do not remember me, do you?"

"Remember you?"

"We met. Well, maybe we did not exactly *meet*," he contemplates, changing tactics. "I was in San Francisco about a year ago. Ate a delicious cheeseburger topped with spicy Roquefort. It was a rather . . . interesting evening. You were—"

"Rude, more than likely," I interject, and the memory of that night breaks free from its vault.

You forgot about this gorgeous hunk? Really, V?

He chuckles. "I would say blunt or straightforward. Also witty and standoffish. But, without sounding like a completely arrogant twat, it was refreshing."

"What? To not get hit on. To not have women throwing themselves at you, knowing the whole time that they don't really give a damn about you?"

"Yes, exactly."

"Does that happen often?"

"Often enough to make me wary."

"Why? Are you some famous actor or something?"

He chuckles again. "No. I co-own a large financial firm with my father and brother. We've made a good name for ourselves and are on course to generate over one hundred million in revenue by the end of the year." I raise my eyebrows.

Ah-ha, finance then.

"As you can probably imagine, it attracts the fakes and gold-diggers." Disgust briefly crosses his face. There's a story there.

Do I ask about it on the first date, though? Fuck it.

"Did one of them play her part a little too well?"

"Yes, my ex, I guess."

"Ex, you guess?"

"We had only been casually dating for a few months when she started talking about marriage. I thought maybe we could have had something real, but that made me suspicious. She lost her mind when I reminded her that I had no intention of getting married, which I had made clear from the beginning."

"Sounds like you dodged a bullet with that one."

He nods. "She had never ended things with the guy I thought was her ex. She fully intended to marry me, then quickly get divorced and take as much money as possible with her on her way out. For her and Fabio, of course," He takes a long sip of his beer.

Not the marrying type, eh?

That's actually perfect. I contemplate him for a minute, then change the subject.

"It all makes so much sense now," I say. His answering smile is amused, but he goes along with it.

"What does," he inquires.

"The déjà vu. Did you feel it, too?"

"No," he replies without hesitation.

"Oh?"

"I recognized you immediately," he says, voice thick with an emotion that I can't quite place.

"You did? It's been over a year," I say cautiously, afraid to decipher the emotion on his face.

"Yes, it has. But, between your banter with Romeo and the burger, which was amazing, by the way, thank you." I stick up my nose and 'hmph' primly. "And the account of the assault—"

"Assault on me, I hope you mean."

"Of course," he replies. "And something about a lack of knickers,"

My mouth drops open. "You heard that?"

"Yes," he replies. "Do you often frolic about in such a state of undress?" I press my lips into a thin line, and his eyes track the blush crawling up my throat, setting my cheeks ablaze.

The server stops to take our order, saving me from further embarrassment. We both order cheeseburgers. I raise my eyebrows at Charlie. He shrugs.

"Cheeseburgers are *amazing*, don't you agree?" I shake my head and try not to smile. A pang of guilt pops up, and I take a long sip of my drink in an attempt to drown it. Even though *he's* gone, I still feel like this date with Charlie–flirting with Charlie and being attracted to Charlie–is a betrayal to *him*.

It's been six years, V. You've paid your penance.

Charlie stares at me intently, no doubt sensing my inner turmoil and rising panic. Before he says anything and inadvertently opens the floodgates, I change the subject again.

"So, Charlie. What's up with you and Jessica? Was I sensing some tension between you two the other night?" His face hardens, mood souring immediately. "I'm sorry. I didn't mean to intrude. It's none of my business, really." I apologize.

"No, no. It's fine. Her refusal to accept that there is nothing between us is frustrating," he replies.

"Hmmm. She did try to lay claim on you."

"Fuck."

"Yeah. I could tell that you were annoyed, though, so I dismissed it."

"I was annoyed. Extremely. I have told her so many fucking times that I do not return her feelings, but she will not accept it. I told my mates not to even call me anymore if she is involved." I sigh internally, relieved to know I won't have some British chick show up randomly, angry that I went to dinner with her man.

"Can I ask why you don't reciprocate her feelings? I mean, she's pretty."

"I think you mean petty. She may be pretty on the outside, but she certainly is not on the inside. And I would bet my left bullock that she does not fancy me so much as my image."

"Ahh, she's after a sugar daddy, eh?" He nods, nostrils flaring. "So why come to the studio then?"

He pauses, a fry halfway to his mouth. "I originally agreed to go partly because she was not. Unfortunately, she decided to join us at the last minute. I was already committed to attending; I was looking forward to seeing you again," he declares.

Oh shit, oh shit, oh shit.

I know my mission tonight is to determine the nature of this attraction between us, but I am terrified of the answer he's giving me. My leg bounces under the table while he waits for me to say something, but I don't know what to say, so we just sit staring at one another.

"Why London?" he asks, finally breaking the awkward silence.

"I love the feel of the city."

"That was enough to prompt you to put down roots in a foreign country?"

"Not just that, no."

He tilts his head, eyebrows raised.

"The rich culture. The long history. The castles, museums, art. The ballet. The fact that I can live in a foreign country and not have to learn another language." And there are no ghosts here, I add silently. At least not any of mine.

"No language barrier—that is always a plus. Have you always been an artist?"

"No."

He tilts his head. "But you are now."

"Sure." He looks at me expectantly again.

"I don't feel like an artist."

"You don't?"

"No."

"Is it always this challenging to get information out of you?"

"Yes, it is," I reply without apologizing.

There are lots of secrets to keep safe.

"Okay," he says, acceptance plain on his handsome face. "Would you be willing to explain to me how you came to be the owner and creative mind behind *Studio V*?"

"I started drawing in college. When I searched for a place to rent here, the lettings negotiator showed me the flat above the studio. I immediately fell in love with the whole place. The old tenant had left behind loads of art supplies. I argued with myself for a few weeks before I finally said, fuck it. Signed the lease the next day." I argued with myself the whole time, worried I'd regret the commitment. There are still days when I get the itch to pack up and leave, but I am mostly content here in London or as content as I can be.

"And...?" he prompts.

"Right. I meant to get rid of the art supplies, but I started painting and got sucked into an insane creative spell. I started posting my pieces for sale online because they started piling up, and I figured, why not." I was perfectly content with that method, too. I could justify the expense of the space and make some money with very little human interaction. It was perfect. And then Kali and Kellan happened.

"That is very serendipitous. How did that turn into *Studio V*?"

"Smartass," I quip, and he gives me a shit-eating grin. "Kali and Kellan found my work online, then convinced me to meet with them and eventually open the studio. Like I said, they are as stubborn as mules once they've made up their collective mind about something." I am grateful to them for pushing me to do this. My own methods weren't getting the results I'd hoped for. And now they are my dear friends, and I am on a date, of all things.

"I am glad they found you," Charlie says, drumming his fingers on the table with deliberate precision while he takes a long, slow drink of his beer. I stare at his fingers, remembering the feel of them on my skin. My heart beats an erratic rhythm in my chest. The drumming stops, yet I continue to stare, mesmerized by his long, graceful fingers. He runs one of them through the condensation on his pint, and I suck in a breath through my teeth when he starts drawing lazy, wet circles on the glass tabletop. I feel each circle burrowing into me deeper and deeper with each rotation, spiraling straight to my core.

The server brings our food, and I sigh, relieved. To steady myself and hopefully erase any trace of desire from my face, I take a slow sip of my drink. When I finally work up the courage to look up, he's slouched back in his chair, arm draped casually over the back, watching me, a self-satisfied expression on his face. He winks, then takes an enormous bite of his cheeseburger. I relax my shoulders and pop a fry into my mouth.

The burgers were fabulous, as usual, and our conversation was light-hearted and fun for the remainder of the meal. Charlie is easy to talk to when he reigns in the charm.

Even though conversation flows easily between us and I start to relax, I am still hyper-aware of him. The way his eyes twinkle with mischief when he tells a joke. The way he drapes himself over the chair, oozing casual confidence and quiet sexuality. It makes me want to climb over the table and straddle him. I notice how his bicep ripples when he signals for the cheque and the hard look Charlie gives the male server whose eyes linger on me a little too long when he drops it off.

And I wonder. I wonder if the intensity that so often radiates off him stems partly from a quiet, simmering violence. The kind that a man cultivates and keeps primed and ready to use when the need arises, like the other day at the gym. I am not surprised to realize that I like the way it made me feel when he slammed that man against the wall to defend me. *He* never hesitated to protect and defend nor shied away from using violence when *he* felt it was necessary.

The quietly simmering part of me that yearns to live and thrive flares hot in my chest, straining towards Charlie's ferocious internal riptide. Exhilaration thrums through my veins at the remembrance of Charlie's overt display of domination and masculinity on my behalf. My long dormant feminine desire to be cherished and protected surges back to life, yearning for more. And it fucking terrifies me.

Ever the gentleman, Charlie offers to walk me home, and I gladly accept. It may only be a few blocks back to the studio, but I'd rather not walk alone after dark. We stroll in companionable silence, arms linked until he stops. I stare at him with raised eyebrows, fighting back the urge to run my hand up his arm to cup his cheek.

"This is you, yeah," he gestures towards the studio. I blush and step away, digging my keys out of my bag.

"Right, yes, it is. Um, I had a great time tonight, thank you," I stammer.

"I did, too," he replies, leaning down to place a quick kiss on my cheek. "Good night, Veronica. I will see you around."

And again, I hope I do.

Bouquet Like That

Charlie

Sweat dripping into my eyes, I glance at the French doors leading to the hallway for the hundredth time this morning. Obviously, she is not going to walk through them, but I cannot stop myself from hoping. I have deliberately stayed away from Fitness First these past three days to give her space. Were it not for my regularly practiced self-discipline and my father's voice in my head, I would have demanded a second date right there on the pavement in front of her studio Sunday night. But, in this case, my father would advise patience and space. It's good advice, too. She is not a woman to put up with being pressured.

Veronica fascinates me. She is witty and reserved, intelligent and straightforward. And fuck, if it was not hot when she challenged me about her drink at the pub. She was ready to hit or split, or both. I could see it plain on her face. I would not say her beautiful face is overly expressive, but everything she thinks and feels is plain to see if you simply pay attention.

And Christ, every time that delectable blush crawls up her neck, my cock twitches. I badly want to kiss the bloom on her cheek and trail my lips down its path to nuzzle in her neck and wallow in her intoxicating, citrusy scent. My cock swells in my joggers just thinking about it, and I abandon the gym for a cold shower.

Thoughts of Veronica follow me to work, where I spend the morning wondering what caused her carefully hidden sorrow in between business meetings and client calls. Something weighs heavily on her. I want to gain her trust and figure out what it is so I can ease her pain. But I must be patient. First, I have to court her and show her what we could have together, then hope she will give me a chance.

Tired of fretting and waiting for her to make the next move, I pull up a list of florists and dial the one closest to *Studio V*. I gladly pay the extra fee for them to have the bouquet ready in an hour so I can hand deliver it myself.

Veronica

Bright afternoon sunlight blazes through the gallery into the workroom, illuminating the rich sunset hues on the piece I'm currently painting. I finish the last few strokes of the base layer, plop my brush into a murky glass of water, and then make my way to the loo where I hang my paint-splattered apron on the hook next to the door. I quickly wash up, then step into the office to see if lunch has arrived yet. Delectable aromas of curry and marsala greet me, and I hum, grateful for the twins and their love of good food.

Kali and Kellan are perched on the high stools of our favorite table, tucked into the corner of the gallery under the row of large windows. We eat most of our meals here, soaking up the sun when it deigns to shine, and people-watch while eating takeout and sipping mineral water. Kellan loves to make up elaborate stories for the passersby while Kali and I add details, each one more ridiculous than the last.

Today, we watch a tall, well-dressed man cross the street toward us, face and torso obscured by an enormous bouquet of peonies, the blooms as large as my hand. Kellan speculates that he's a cheating, soon-to-be ex-husband on his way to apologize to his disgruntled wife. She'll throw the vase at his head after he delivers an utterly pathetic apology, we postulate.

"Soon-to-be ex-husband can only mean one thing," Kali posits.

"His cheating wasn't enough," I question, making a face.

"Marriages last after cheating all the time, Ron," she answers. "He either cheated with her sister or her best friend."

"It was her dad and his best friend at the same time," I deadpan. Kellan guffaws and Kali snorts. That's the only explanation for ruining such a stunning bouquet," I clarify, popping a large bite of chicken and noodles into my mouth with a shrug.

"I would keep the bouquet to let him think that I forgave him. Then I'd divorce the cheat and take everything."

"We would expect nothing less from you, dear sister," Kellan teases around a large mouthful of chicken and mushrooms.

The man turns, and just as he passes our window, he shifts the flowers to the opposite arm, revealing his handsome face. I start, and Kali hoots while Kellan sprints to the door to hold it open. Kali hops off her stool, nimble and graceful as a gazelle in her pointy-toed, white stilettos. She grabs me by the hand and hauls me across the gallery, stumbling behind her with all the grace of a newborn giraffe.

Eyes crinkled with amusement and a private, knowing smile on his face, Charlie saunters through the door. Not wanting Kali to pick up on my nerves, I pull my clammy hand out of hers and hold back a step, waiting on the fringes while Kellan and his sister fawn over Charlie and the stunning bouquet. He gracefully accepts their praise, giving them his full attention, and engages in their joking with a witty remark that prompts both the twins to bark out laughter.

This could be your life, V, if you allow yourself to have it.

Surprisingly, I can easily see this future, where Charlie drops by occasionally to have lunch with us, clapping Kel on the back and dropping a kiss on my forehead before heading back to the office. A dwindling voice in the back of my mind, one that falls weaker day by day, strains to remind me that I don't deserve this, not after everything I've done and all the mistakes I've made. But I want it. I want it so fucking bad.

Attired in an all-black suit, Charlie radiates casual confidence and quiet sexuality. I suppress the urge to haul him upstairs by his tie.

With my heart pounding inside my chest and butterflies swirling in my belly, I motion for him to follow me. I wipe my clammy hands on my jeans and shoot a warning glare at Kali as we head toward the workroom.

I've spent the last three days replaying our date over and over in my head, debating whether to pursue a relationship with him. I gave Sophie and Turner a very abbreviated version, and, of course, they think I should go for it. And despite everything that happened six years ago, my general brokenness, and numerous misgivings, I'm inclined to agree with them. But now that the decision is staring me right in the face, I'm flooded with fear and trepidation.

I am so caught up in the storm of what-ifs raging inside my skull that it takes a few tries before I punch in the right code to unlock the door. What if I'm too broken? What if he turns out to be an abusive narcissist? What if he's great but doesn't work out—or worse, it ends badly? What if, what if, what if.

Charlie clears his throat, pulling me out of my thoughts. Heart beating an erratic rhythm in my chest, I turn toward him and start at the riot of large pink, white, and yellow blossoms he's still holding.

"Oh, shit. Here," I gesture, moving items off a table under a back window. He sets down the bouquet, and I run my fingers over the fragrant petals. He reaches out, cupping one of the pink blossoms in his large hand, and caresses its delicate edge with his thumb. I suck in a breath and a shiver runs up my spine. A chuckle rumbles in his chest.

Christ. He knows exactly what he's doing to you. Pull it together, V.

I take a deep, steadying breath and turn toward him. "They're beautiful, thank you." One corner of his mouth tugs up, and his eyes twinkle. He leans against the wall, crossing his ankles and sliding a hand into a pocket. Eyes avidly scanning the workroom, he runs a hand through his hair, causing the unbuttoned top of his crisp white shirt to pull apart, baring a hint of his sculpted chest. My eyes devour the sliver of exposed skin, and my fingers drum against my thigh, itching to touch him. His Adam's apple bobs, the movement reminding me that there's a man under that tantalizing skin. With great effort, I raise my eyes to his.

"My pleasure," he purrs, and my thighs involuntarily squeeze together. "So, this is where the magic happens, huh?" he asks, and it takes a moment to realize he's not talking about *that kind* of magic. Kali and Kellan's constant teasing and joking are rubbing off on me (pun intended).

Pulling my mind out of the gutter, I answer with a simple "I guess." We both gravitate toward the large workbench that occupies the center of the room,

"You guess?"

"Yeah."

"Veronica." He waits until I raise my eyes to his. "You are a bloody talented artist, even if the term makes you uncomfortable. What you create out of a blank canvas and seemingly random materials is incredible." My leg jiggles and my fingers drum a nervous rhythm on my thigh at his praise. He waits, giving me the space to share more on my own, which makes me feel comfortable unmasking for him.

"I feel like a fraud most of the time. Imposter Syndrome Ivy is a good friend of mine. So," I shrug and move to stand beside him. I can feel him looking at me, but I keep my eyes glued to the half-finished painting on the table.

"What is this one?"

"I don't know yet. Lately, the sunsets have been so vibrant and beautiful that I just had to capture them. But it doesn't feel like a landscape, so we'll see." What I want is to add a lake surrounded by mountains with a broken woman staring out of the lake's reflection, but I'll never share her with anyone.

"I cannot wait to see it finished. But, unfortunately, I must get back to the office. Are you free tonight?"

"No. Kali and Kellan have us booked solid." Disappointment quickly flashes in his eyes. "But I do have some free time tomorrow morning after my workout. We could go for coffee."

"I will join you, and we can go for breakfast afterward."

"Okay. Meet you there?"

"I will come here and walk with you. London streets early in the morning are not safe for a woman to be alone."

"Uh hu, okay. Enjoy the rest of your day, Charlie."

"See you tomorrow, Veronica," he replies and softly kisses my cheek before waltzing out the door, leaving a curious duo of onlookers in his wake. I knew they were watching, and I'm sure he did, too. My first instinct is to seek solitude and overthink this whole scenario, but I fight the urge and head into the gallery instead. I could use some brilliant twin unorthodox cheerleading right now.

"What . . . Was that," Kali exclaims as soon as I open the door.

"Shhh," I hiss, glancing at the handful of customers roaming the gallery, one of whom approaches tentatively. She's petite and flighty. Her eyes dart away often while we speak, and she fusses with her rings throughout the entire conversation. We spent several minutes discussing the different mediums I work with. She's a student at The Royal College of Art and researching for a big project she's preparing for next term. I send her off with my business card and an open invitation to contact me if she needs help with a project or just wants to discuss art. IS Ivy taunts misgivings in the back of my mind, but I do my best to block out her criticisms. I roll my eyes and sigh when Kellan calls for me as I try to sneak away after the jittery art student leaves.

Just get it over with, V. They'll pester you until you spill the beans.

I kind of love them for it. I get stuck inside my head too often, and it's rarely a pretty place to be. To prevent the customers from hearing our conversation, I park my ass on a small sofa tucked into the opposite corner of the gallery.

"Please tell me he confessed his undying love for you, and you need us to plan a winter wedding," Kellan begs, palms pressed together in front of him. The innocent jest plunges a serrated knife into my heart. Pulling my core muscles tight to prevent my body from curling into a ball, I blink away the image of *him* in a tux. Instead, I point a finger at my mouth and pretend to gag. Kali chuckles and swats her brother playfully on the arm.

"Have you ever been told you have an overactive imagination, Kel," I ask.

"Regularly since he learned to talk. But don't change the subject, missy," Kali replies. Twin ice-blue gazes pin me in place. Like two curious owls, they stare me down until I relent.

"We're going for breakfast tomorrow. No big deal," I say. They both scoff.

"A bouquet like that for breakfast on a first date?" Kali asks her twin. I relax my face and stare blandly into the middle distance, but I don't fool either of them. Kellan pins me with a stern look, and I sigh, resigned.

"Ah, technically, it is our second date. We had dinner Sunday night." Neither astute twin looks satisfied, so I add, "It went well. He was the perfect gentleman."

"Good. He'd better be, or Kali will hunt him down, and I will thrash his arse," Kellan promises.

"Thanks, Mom and Dad," I quip, flaring my nostrils and pursing my lips.

"On the other hand," Kali postulates, looking at her brother like I'm not even sitting there. "She could use a healthy dose of ungentlemanly behavior."

"Can't we all," he replies wistfully. "Just imagine . . . playing the beast with two backs in the sheets with Mr. Adonis-in-the-flesh—"

"We have customers in here," I scold, clenching my legs together.

"Okay, okay. We're genuinely thrilled for you, Ron," Kali says.

"We know that you don't like people, and we're proud of you for putting yourself out there. We know how hard that can be," Kellan adds.

"Thanks, guys. Maintaining acquaintances and friendships has been challenging enough. A relationship just feels unattainable. And I had a bad experience that messed me up."

"It is completely normal to be apprehensive after a bad break-up, Ron. It's easy to dwell on all the things that could go wrong, but don't forget to consider all the ways it could go right, too," Kali offers.

"A relationship could be the thing that helps you, the thing that heals you and makes you happy. Give it a go, love. We'll be here for you however it plays out," Kellan says with a half-smile.

"And let us know the details. Where you two are going and when," Kali insists. "Not because we're nosy–we are–but for your safety, okay?" I nod, comforted by their concern and support. Kali and Kellan return their attention to work while I head back to the workroom to utilize the rest of the day's sunlight. The doubts and fears, the painful memories and incessant feelings of guilt, shame, and despair, threaten to consume me, but with some effort, I set them aside like my therapist taught me, to unpack with her at our next session and I manage to squeeze in several more hours of work.

Don't be Surprised

Charlie arrives early the following day, stepping into the studio like an angel materializing out of a cloud with thick tendrils of fog floating around him. He licks his lips with just the tip of his tongue and runs a hand through his damp, wavy hair. "Veronica," he calls to the stillness. From the shadows upstairs, I watch him. Fuck, Charlie is so like *him*, tall, lean, muscular. My heart breaks into pieces at the thought of what I've lost; the thought of what I might gain summons butterflies to flutter the pieces back into place.

As I descend the staircase, he stops in front of a vibrantly covered abstract on canvas painted with alcohol inks and topped with a clear coat of resin. He crosses his arms and props his chin on a fist. I chuckle at the sight of him studying high-end art in sneakers, gym shorts, and a black *Wright & Sons* hoodie.

His head cocks to the side, and the hint of a smile pulls up the corner of his mouth. He makes no further indication that he's aware of my presence, but I know he is. He stands still as the statue he is, and the second he tipped his head, I felt his intense energy reaching out to me. Keeping an even, measured pace, I cross the gallery and slide in between him and one of the wooden beams that run the room's length.

We stand in charged silence for long minutes, his eyes moving across the canvas, mine stealing sideways glances at him until I can handle the suspense no longer. I turn toward him, eyebrows raised, and he smirks. I roll my eyes and run my tongue across my teeth. He turns and steps toward me in one motion, crowding me back into the wooden beam behind me.

"Hello, Veronica," he purrs, dropping his head slightly.

I inhale deeply, filling my nostrils with his earthy, minty scent, and forget to exhale when my chest brushes against his upper abdomen. After an embarrassingly long pause, I find my voice. "Hello, Charlie." Sinking back into the beam as far as possible and taking shallow breaths, I ask, "What do you think?" indicating the painting with my chin. He braces his forearm on the beam above my head and leans down.

"Beautiful," he answers, eyes locked onto my face. "Fucking, gorgeous."

I know he doesn't mean the painting, but I stammer out a, "Thank you," because I don't know how to accept compliments gracefully, especially ones given by a reincarnated Greek god with such searing intensity. Heat blooms deep inside me, spreading like an inferno, blazing a path up my neck and across my face. His eyes drop to follow the blaze, and he leans against me. Delicately, he trails his fingertips from my collarbone up the column of my throat and wraps his fingers around the nape of my neck, weaving them into my hair while his thumb traces circles on the sensitive skin just below my earlobe. My lips part on a silent exhale, and my hips press into his of their own volition.

Fuck this feels good. I forgot how good it feels to be pressed tightly against a man's solid, warm body. His other hand drops to my waist and grips me hard. My eyelids flutter closed, and I revel in the sensation of his hands on me and how right it feels to be this close to him. Charlie moves his hips against me, a tiny, almost imperceptible movement, and even though it's been years, there's no mistaking his erection pinned against my stomach.

Holy fuck, V.

My eyes fly open, locking onto his luscious, full lips. For a brief moment, I wonder what it would feel like if he dropped his mouth to mine. Then his eyes drop to my lips, and he lowers his face closer to mine. I jolt, panic making my heart beat even faster than it already is, and I slip out from between him and the wooden beam.

"We should get going," I say, voice unsteady.

Charlie dips his chin and adjusts himself, then leads me outside with his hand on the small of my back, his touch sending hot desire coursing through me. It will be an enormous challenge to focus at the gym. We take a few steps down the pavement before he hooks my hand into the crook of his elbow, and we walk the handful of blocks in charged silence, stealing occasional glances at each other.

Charlie opens the door to Fitness First, ushering me inside with his hand on the small of my back. I can't help but imagine that hand touching me all over.

"Do you prefer to work out together or split up?"

"If we're going to have enough time to grab breakfast, we should probably split up. Meet back here in thirty?" He nods and saunters off to the boxing room. There's no way we'd get anything accomplished if we stayed together. It's going to be hard enough for me to stay focused after that moment in the gallery. The intensity of my desire to get him naked terrifies me. It's been so long since I've had those desires.

I find a quiet corner and perform my warm-up, a sun salutation, using it as a form of meditation to clear my mind. Surprisingly, I manage to get in a solid workout, cutting it off a few minutes early to tidy up before meeting Charlie to head to breakfast. He raises his eyebrows as I walk toward him.

"What," I say, feigning ignorance.

"You changed," he states.

"Do you know what it's like to wear a sweaty bra any longer than necessary? I got an extra minute of cardio in, just trying to get the damn thing off," I joke.

"Probably about as comfortable as a sweaty jockstrap," he quips. I snort and shake my head. As we approach the door, I can't help but remember how fucking hot his overt display of masculinity was last time we were here. A white-hot flame of desire bursts through me when he tucks my hand into the crook of his elbow.

Fuck, V. Get it together. It's six o'clock in the morning, and you both have to work.

We walk to a popular cafe, or *caff*, as the Brits call it, and grab a booth by the window.

"What's good here," I muse, flipping through the menu.

"I have no idea, but it all looks smashing," he says, eyeing a tray of food carried past by a hustling server.

You look smashing. Ten out of ten would smash you.

I need to reign in these thoughts. The brilliant twins will not be impressed if I'm late getting back to the studio. "Let's get a few different meals and share," I suggest, batting my eyelashes at him.

"Superb idea. We need a big helping of bacon and eggs. Good source of protein."

"Definitely. The drop scones with fresh fruit also look delicious."

He nods absentmindedly and turns a page on the menu. "Shall we order those and the sausage rolls?" he asks.

One Charlie sausage roll for me, please. For fucks sake, V.

We place our order, complete with tea, milk, and honey for him and just honey for me. The food is delicious, as expected. We devour our meals while discussing our favorite foods from around the world.

Charlie catches my subtle attempt to check my watch, then asks, "Is our time up already?" I nod, frowning. Guilt and shame flame hot in my chest.

It's okay, V. You are no longer obligated to maintain your loyalty to him.

But what happened—it's all my fault. I don't deserve to be happy.

No, it's not, and yes, you do. It's time to forgive yourself and move on.

I don't know how. I don't understand what Charlie even sees in me. I'm broken. I have random panic attacks and severe depressive episodes. I push everyone away and run every time life gets hard. Charlie deserves someone better than me. Someone young and full of life and more emotionally available than I am.

What kind of person he wants as his partner is his choice, V. Besides, you don't have to decide anything right now anyway.

With less effort than expected, I put these thoughts into my brain's 'analyze later' compartment. All those therapy and life coaching sessions are paying off.

I sense his eyes on me and look up. "Fascinating," he breathes.

"What?"

"I would love to get inside your head and hear the conversations you have with yourself."

Stupid traitorous face.

The one time in my life I meet a man who is even remotely observant is the one time I'd prefer him to be oblivious. At least he hasn't been pushy or demanding thus far.

I flush red. "It's not a very nice place to be. I need to go," I answer and rush out the door.

He throws some pounds on the table and follows, long legs quickly catching me up. He gently grabs my elbow, stopping my flight. "I'm sorry, Veronica. It wasn't my intention to upset you," he says sincerely.

I take a deep breath and exhale, deciding. "It's okay, really. I get frustrated with my inability to hide my thoughts and feelings. And it is a little disconcerting how observant you are. Most men aren't." I shrug.

"I see," he says, contemplating. "I may be the one who generally does most of the talking, and I get the feeling you prefer it that way," he pauses, and I nod. "But I can also be a good listener," he offers simply without expectation. I look at him thoughtfully and take a step down the sidewalk. He falls into step beside me, offering me his arm.

"I have been overwhelmed with feelings lately," I start tentatively. He turns his head slightly towards me and nods. "For the past few years, I've lived numb to the world, shutting out everything and everyone, chiefly because I didn't want to feel anything anymore. And now I struggle to socialize and process my emotions."

I breathe deeply, deciding whether to say more. Charlie waits patiently, slowing our pace as we near the studio. "If I'm not mindful, I'll expend too much time over-analyzing every thought and feeling. It still takes a lot of energy to stop and compartmentalize. Save the heavy stuff for therapy." We stop, my hand still on his arm, and I look up at him, wanting him to understand but hoping he won't push for more.

Half of his mouth tilts up in a small smile, understanding evident in his green eyes. He simply looks at me, and, after it's clear I have no more to share, he says, "I understand. What do you need from me?" I tilt my head, eyebrows scrunched together. "I mean, would you like advice or someone to simply listen," he clarifies, thoughtful as ever.

"Umm, wow. Most people either immediately word-vomit unsolicited advice or hijack the conversation. Just listen, thank you."

"My pleasure," he says.

I remove my hand from his arm to fish my keys out of my bag. "I really gotta get to work. If I'm not ready when the twins get here, they'll make me walk the plank," I joke as I step toward the door.

"Wait," he grabs my elbow, "When can I see you again?"

"I'm pretty booked right now. Kali and Kellan are selling pieces almost faster than I can make them, and they have a family event to go to next weekend, so we're going to be open every day through next Friday. So yeah, we could plan something for next weekend if that works for you."

"I do not want to wait that long to see you again, but I will make do." My palms grow clammy, and butterflies riot in my belly at his admission. "What would you like to do? Is there anything you have wanted to experience since you moved here but have not gotten to yet?"

"Yes. Do you like hiking? There are some trails I've been wanting to check out before winter sets in." A lazy, confident smile flashes across his face.

"That sounds like a smashing idea. I will pick you up at nine o'clock next Saturday morning." His eyes flash, and his nostrils flare with the words. "And Veronica," he waits for me to look at him before he continues, "don't be surprised if you see me before then."

"I hope I do."

He places another brief kiss on my cheek and waits until I am inside before leaving. I take a quick shower and have already started on a project when Kali and Kellan arrive.

The following several days mercifully fly by in a blur of sweat, sore muscles, PPE, paint, epoxy, canvas, and the brilliant twins' business lessons. Twice during that time, the hustle and bustle stalled, the blur dissipated as one point crystallized into sharp, brilliant focus: Charlie.

Once, when I ran into him at the gym.

Did I even do one full set that day?

I remember nothing besides watching his sculpted muscles contract and ripple as he moved through his workout.

And twice when he stopped by the studio to 'see my new work.' He wore dark jeans and a black T-shirt, fairly exuding casual confidence. I knew he was there before I even saw him. I was painting the base layer on a new piece, lost in thought when my breathing became erratic, my palms became clammy, and the butterflies swirled to a frenzy in my belly. I looked up and was met with such intensity from his fathomless green eyes that I almost fell off my stool. I practically ran to him but regained some composure as I unlocked the door between the workroom and the gallery.

So much for this 'little' infatuation dying, eh V?

The weather has been shit these past two days, mirroring my mood, as the potential for torrential rainfall threatens to derail our plans for Saturday. I look forward to seeing Charlie again, which surprises and terrifies me. The reality of my life, losing *him,* coupled with this potential relationship with Charlie, hit me hard, and I've been grappling with myself during the rare quiet moments I've had during the crazy, busy past several days.

A battle has been raging in my mind between the me who wants to move on and the me who can't let go of the past. I miss *him and them* so God-damned much that sometimes my knees give out, and I crumble under the weight of their loss. How can I move on? How can I not? How do I reconcile two great loves (if Charlie is to become one) in one lifetime when I was only supposed to have one?

I vowed to love *him* for all the days of *my* life. *My* life, not his life. Can I honor that vow and still move on with someone else without betraying *him*? Is it fair to Charlie to be with him but never be able to give him all of myself? To only be able to give him a small part of my heart because the rest belongs to someone else? These opposing thoughts swirl in my brain, the hot, swift current of my possible future colliding with the cold, vast, deeply sunken island of my past, creating a maelstrom of guilt and acceptance, resentment and contentment, loneliness, and longing.

This isn't the only battle I've been fighting, either. I guess you could say I'm at full-blown war with myself. I've been trying to deny certain growing feelings I have for Charlie. Namely, my brain commanding that I remain celibate indefinitely, and my body defiantly yelling back, "fuck that!"

My body's baser urges initially vanished after *the event*. Then, one night a few years later, they returned rather abruptly. I was soaking in the tub of some hotel in Miami, chugging vodka straight from the bottle in a useless attempt to drown the pain. I had been wandering the country for a while at that point, fleeing from the ghosts that lurked in every corner of my previous beautiful, wonderful life.

I don't remember how I ended up in Florida, but there was dancing at the hotel where I was staying. I sat at the bar drinking whiskey and watching couple after couple dance the salsa or the tango. The way the men and women moved together was sensual and sexy. I watched the entire set, transfixed by the details; hands on hips, faces buried in necks, pelvises writhing in unison.

I thought about the dancers while I soaked and was surprised to feel an insistent throbbing grow between my legs. Absent-mindedly cupping my breasts, I rolled my nipples between my fingers, imagining it was *him* touching me as I slid one hand down my belly to the warmth between my legs.

After *the event*, I was sure I'd never have a physical relationship with anyone ever again. I did have a few one-night stands since that night in Miami, on the rare occasion when the need for human connection became overwhelming. But this is different. As much as I don't want to admit it, I want Charlie. I sit with this reluctant admission, sifting it through my mind, dissecting it as openly and objectively as I can. I decide to go with the flow and trust myself to make the best decision.

Penny for Your Thoughts

Friday night rolls around, and I am exhausted from the insane hours the twins and I spent in the studio. We close the gallery early so they can head to France for the weekend. I also go through my nighttime routine early, donning a pair of baggy black sweatpants, an oversized white hoodie, and my favorite skull studs, preparing for another kind of date. What would Charlie think if he knew I was going on a 'date' with someone else? Would he unleash that primal masculine violence and claim me as his own? The thought floods hot desire through my veins. But I don't have to worry about it tonight, as I'm not actually going anywhere with anyone.

My phone vibrates on the coffee table, Sophie's face illuminating the screen. I press accept, and we Facetime for hours, sharing small talk, pleasantries, and gossip about back home. I want to ask her for advice, but I don't. I worry too much that my friends are sick of hearing about my problems. She's a great human being, though, and she knows me well.

"What's eating at ya, Ron? Spit it out. I don't mind being the one to listen once in a while," she says pragmatically after a lengthy discussion about Turner departing for his fifth tour in Iraq and Sophie's promotion (she finally got it) to Chief Nursing Officer.

"I think I want to try having a relationship with Charlie, but I am struggling to let go of the past. How do I honor *him* and the life we had but also move forward," I say, shrugging my shoulders and holding back tears.

"Oh, hun. He's gone, and that's not going to change," she says softly, sensitive to my wounded heart. "You are allowed to live and love however you choose. You don't owe anyone any explanations, and *he* would understand. No one blames you, Ron. I know it doesn't feel like it because you're still healing, but there is room in your heart for both of them. Just keep picking up the pieces and putting them back together, and you'll see. It's not going to be easy, but I'm going to guess it'll be worth it."

"Thanks, Soph, you're the best. I don't know what I'd do without you," I say, a pained smile on my face. I miss her so much, but I don't visit often. I can't handle the ghosts.

"I miss you too. Maybe we'll remedy that? You're still coming home in a few weeks, right?"

My face falls. "No. I won't be able to make it until the holidays. Everything got switched around when Kali, Kellan, and I negotiated our new contract. You still have the same plans for Christmas, right?"

"Yes. Turner will even be home, and John, Catherine, and the kids will be here too."

"Okay, good. I'll probably come for a few weeks," I question, eyebrows raised.

She smiles lovingly, "You are always welcome here as long as you want, Ron. Charlie, too."

"Umm, we'll see how things go between now and then. But I promise not to back out this time. I'll even book a non-refundable, non-transferable plane ticket," I raise my right hand, the first two fingers raised, "scouts honor."

"I'll hold you to that, missy," she teases. "What about Victoria and her annual New Year's Eve party?"

"We've been texting a little. I understand why this is so hard on her. I'm the only family she's got left, and she doesn't have friends like you and Cat. I've forgiven her; I just need to tell her that." She nods, but her answer is drowned out by pitiful howling in the background.

"Okay, okay. I'm coming, you needy little shit," she says, laughing. "Next time we get a puppy, Turner is retiring so he can get up at all hours of the night to potty train."

"Little Cooper still isn't sleeping through the night?" Another howl sounds, and Sophie rolls her eyes.

"Mostly, yes. I just forgot how much work they are, but I love the little furball."

"I can't wait to meet him at Christmas."

She smiles. "And he can't wait to meet his auntie. Probably eat your socks, too. But until then, my dear friend, take a deep breath, let go, keep rebuilding, and move forward. We love you."

"I love you too, Soph. Give Turner my love next time you talk to him."

She's been such a great friend. I always feel more grounded after talking to her.

Glorious, bright sunlight streams through the window on Saturday morning, caressing me awake and instantly erasing my bad mood. As I go through my morning routine, nervous excitement and a thread of trepidation course through me. I focus on calming my nerves and opening my heart to the possibilities that lie ahead with Charlie.

I fill a small hiking pack with water, snacks, a raincoat just in case, and other necessities, then head downstairs to prepare the gallery for Monday even though I'm taking the day off. Kali and Kellan were ecstatic when I told them I was taking a three-day weekend. My ears need a deep cleaning from the sheer number and absurdity of all the sexual innuendos I've heard since they found out.

Remembering Kali's farewell, 'If you can walk when we get back, I'll be *sorely* disappointed in you,' has me shaking my head when the butterflies start fluttering in my belly. I fly to the door before my palms or breathing have time to catch up. I briefly wonder if it's obvious to Charlie how much he affects me or how much I adore him. Then, I wonder why it matters. He keeps coming back, and I'm not into playing games. As they say (whoever *they* are), honesty is the best policy. Unless it's about *before*, that subject is completely off-limits.

I open the door and hear my favorite two-word phrase, "Hello Veronica," roll off those full, inviting lips. I stare at them until one corner pulls into a smug smile.

"Hello, Charlie," is all I can manage as a reply. A brilliant smile blooms across his handsome face, crinkling the corners of his jade eyes with warmth. He sports a few days' worth of stubble and wears simple gray joggers and a green shirt that complements his eyes so well they're even more intense than usual.

"You look beautiful as always," he says as he points to a sleek, black sports car–some model of Audi–parked right in front of us. "This is our ride."

I open the passenger door, or what would be the passenger door if we were in America, and then stare at the steering wheel for a minute before my brain processes the situation. Charlie chuckles, preventing a wave of embarrassment from taking over. I press my lips together and roll my eyes exaggeratedly, muttering, "It makes more sense for the driver to be on the other side," as he leads me around the car with his hand on the small of my back. His touch sets my skin on fire, quick and all-consuming like a wildfire in a hay field. Ever the gentleman, he opens the door for me. I almost burst into tears as I slide into the car. The gesture is so reminiscent of *him*. I take a few deep breaths to center myself before Charlie gets in and remind myself of Sophie's advice: let go and move on.

We drive in companionable silence for a bit. At first, I enjoyed the beautiful English countryside, but my attention kept returning to Charlie. Eventually, I give in to the urge and turn toward him, tucking my feet under me. I'm staring and do not try to hide it, honesty, right? He is fucking gorgeous in profile. I want to reach out and touch him, to memorize his face with my hands the way I'm memorizing it with my eyes.

What if one day I wake up and he's gone too?

I push that thought way back down. Not just down, out. Completely out of my mind. I refuse to let the fear that the past will repeat itself control my thoughts. Whatever happens, I can handle it. Whatever happens, I can handle it. If I repeat it over and over and over again, eventually, I'll believe it, according to my therapist, at least.

He looks pointedly from my bouncing leg to my restless fingers to the crimson crawling up my neck. Our eyes lock, and I am transfixed and riveted to my seat, unable to breathe. A lazy, arrogant smirk tugs up the corner of his mouth. The urge to kiss him returns, and I can all too easily imagine ravaging him as we drive through the foothills of whatever mountains these are. I knew their name before we left. Now I am consumed by Charlie, kissing him, touching his bare skin, feeling him inside me.

Reign it in, V! Go with the flow, remember?

It seems the flow is heading straight for Charlie's bed. Twin flames of guilt and betrayal flare in my chest, making it hard to breathe. I close my eyes and pull steady, even breaths through my nose.

"Penny for your thoughts."

I startle at the sound of his voice. Caught off guard, I reply, "Ahh. I was just thinking about how beautiful England is."

"How does it compare to America?"

"Apples and oranges."

"What?"

"You can't truly compare the two. Many parts of both countries are beautiful in their own way. Can you compare the ocean to the mountains? The tundra to the jungle? What did you think when you visited the States?" One question from him and my nerves are instantly calmed.

"I did not see enough of the country to form an opinion, but I learned that I much prefer the warm waters of the Pacific to the cold ones of the Atlantic." He's laid back, so at ease in himself. One hand guides the wheel, and the other rests palm up on the console between us. My hand twitches to grab his, but I keep it fisted firmly in my lap. He has big hands, working man's hands. My favorite kind of hands. For the millionth time, I wonder what they would feel like caressing my skin. And just like that, my mind's back in the gutter.

Focus, V.

"I agree. I hate being cold. Which is kind of weird, I guess, since I prefer the mountains."

"You are about to get your fill," he replies as he pulls into the parking lot at the trailhead. I hop out and quickly use the loo. I do not want to have to pee in the woods on my third date with Charlie. No fucking thank you.

Conversation flows freely on the trail, out in the open air, instead of confined in a small space so close to him. As we head towards the summit, we talk about everything and nothing, everything about him and nothing about me.

"Have you hiked this trail before?"

"Not this one, no. I have not yet had time to hike the trails in this area of Britain. I grew up near Manchester and only just moved this past winter to open a new company office here in London."

"Couldn't wait to get off the farm," I tease.

"I love the farm. My brother and I helped our parents build it and the company from the ground up. I enjoy the physical labor of farm work, but I excel with numbers," he explains.

"Ah. Numbers, eh?"

"Yes, numbers. They are constant, consistent, and always straightforward," he says as we begin to move down the trail. I scoff a bit. He eyes me skeptically. "You don't think so?" he asks, eyebrows raised.

"I don't like numbers. They're boring. One plus one is always two. Where's the mystery? Where's the spontaneity? When you have all these thoughts crowding your brain, feelings clogging your chest, and emotions tying your belly into knots, how do numbers help you alleviate the pain," I state, not expecting a response.

"Numbers are the best way to alleviate the pain. When everything else in your life is chaos, numbers are always constant. When your emotions are a jumble, and you don't know whether to laugh or cry, at least you *know* that one plus one always equals two and that it always will," he states simply, not arguing, just sharing his thoughts.

It's not fair that someone this attractive is also intelligent, kind, and intuitive.

The trail narrows, forcing us to walk single file.

Has a nice ass, too.

Before I fall too far down the rabbit hole of imagining what he looks like sans the gray joggers, the trail opens back up, and he waits for me to come up beside him. My phone buzzes in my pocket, vibrating both our legs. I quickly silence it through my leggings and look ahead. It immediately starts buzzing again. I huff and rip it out of my pocket.

You have the worst timing, sister.

I silence it again, and again, it buzzes immediately. Frustrated, I step away from Charlie and type out a quick reply, promising to call back later. Charlie's posture is rigid, and his eyes study me warily when I turn back toward him. I am momentarily confused, but then I remember our conversation at the pub.

"My sister," I say, waving my phone before slipping it back into my pocket. "She's a little high-strung and very impatient." His posture relaxes, and a sympathetic smile spreads across his face.

"I am impressed you got service up here."

"Eh, it happens a lot back home. There was this one place I used to frequent, way up, higher than this. It always had service."

"Interesting."

"Yeah. I mean, you did have to be frighteningly close to the edge of a huge drop-off. Kinda like that one." I point to the small opening in the trees and the cliff edge a few inclined meters in front of us. He raises his eyebrows, and I nod.

He leans down and whispers in my ear, "You go first, then." His breath is a warm caress on my skin. I fight back the urge to push him against a tree, moving forward instead to get a clear view of the scene before us.

Carefully, I step through the trees to the edge . . . and my fragile heart shatters to pieces.

Mountain View Doppelgangers

The view is breathtaking . . . and so achingly familiar that I struggle to breathe. I feel like I've been punched in the gut and barely keep myself from doubling over into the fetal position. If mountain views had doppelgangers, this would be the British version of my spot in America, where I stood just over two years ago contemplating life or death. A tremor of despair runs through me, and I inhale sharply. Charlie's head snaps toward me, eyes soft with concern, and he rubs light circles on my back.

Stupid glass face.

I look away quickly, focusing on my breath, in and out. Let the past be. Live. Move forward.

LIVE, V!

"Veronica, are you ok? Do you not want me touching you," he says. Seriously, a gentleman.

"No, no. Everything is fine. I don't mind you touching me. I quite like it, in fact," I answer more boldly than I feel, eyes still forward. He turns toward me, puts a finger under my chin, and tilts my head, holding it up until I look at him. He's so fucking handsome, face so open and concerned. So like-yet-unlike *him* that tears prick my eyes. I lean into Charlie, pressing my lips firmly together to prevent damning words from escaping.

I pull air deep into my lungs and suppress the urge to scream at the universe. Why? Why did you take *him away*, then give me Charlie? How can I leave the past alone and move forward with all these damn reminders? Fate, if that even is a thing, is a cruel mistress. Maybe more fittingly, life is a bitch. Charlie waits patiently, one hand still caressing my back, the other holding my chin, watching the internal struggle play across my face.

"I . . . Something happened a few years ago, something horrible. And now people, music, smells, places, and moments can randomly trigger strong emotions and painful reminders. I've been running ever since, keeping everyone at a distance along the way. Until now."

His look turns thoughtful. He lets go of my chin but doesn't let go of me. He slides his hand slowly down my neck and arm, then around my back, pulling me into a hug. I let out a long, shuddering sigh and melt into him.

My racing heart calms, syncing to the steady rhythm beating in his chest. I breathe in his earthy scent and dig my fingers into his taut back muscles. The protective wall inside myself that I've painstakingly built since I lost *him* shifts to make room for Charlie, and I step away.

We stand silently for a long beat before he asks, "Do you want to talk about it?" I fall a little harder for him, grateful that he offered to listen without expecting an explanation.

"No," I answer. "Charlie, I probably will never tell you what happened. It hurts too much. If you really want to do this," I gesture between us, "whatever this is, I need you to accept that. It's slowly improving, but sometimes, the reminders and memories overwhelm me, and I cannot function. Like, literally can't get out of bed, or eat, or sleep. You should know before you decide about us that it's not going to be easy or normal."

He places his hands on my shoulders, trailing them down my arms until he holds both of my small, soft hands in his large, rough ones. "I do not need to know what happened in your past—unless there is a jealous ex-lover that I have to worry about showing up at some inopportune moment?" he asks with raised eyebrows. I shake my head.

"No. No, there's no ex," I reply, my heart cracking at the admission.

"Good. Then, I am not asking for your past. I will not even ask for your future, not yet. All I want is the present. That is it. If you go to the past during our present, I will be here waiting for you to return to me, offering whatever support you need. I have been infatuated with you since the moment we met. I have adored you since I walked into your studio a month ago and saw you floating down the stairs like an angel."

I blush and look away. He waits till I meet his eyes again. "You should know that I would have come to your Grand Opening no matter what. Even if Jess had been part of the plans from the beginning. As soon as Theo said 'attractive, single, American woman,' I was hooked."

Ah, that's why his explanation at the bar seemed vague.

"Do you want to know why?" I nod, my heart beating erratically in my chest. I will my hands not to get clammy. "Because if there was even the tiniest chance that it was you, my Veronica, I had to find out."

"And when you realized it was me?" I hold my chin high while a brilliant smile blooms across his handsome face.

"I knew it was fate, and you were just as witty, intelligent, and stunning as I remembered." I make a face and shake my head. "What?"

"I don't know if I believe in fate. Was my life always destined to take this path? Was I always meant to suffer this much? Do I have no free will? Do I have no control over my own life? Sometimes, it makes it easier to deal with, to believe it was fate and completely out of my control. And sometimes, it is easier to scorn the idea of fate, holding tight to the what-ifs. What if I had made a different choice that day? Would the outcome have changed? Either way, fate is a cruel mistress, and life is a bitch. I was thinking about this just now, actually."

His mouth curves into a wry smile. Oh, that mouth. I'm staring at it. Very obviously staring. He closes the small distance between us and places my hands on his chest, wrapping a hand around the small of my back, splayed out and possessive, pinning me against him. His eyes never leave mine as his other hand tenderly cups my cheek. Locked in his gaze, molded against his body, I've forgotten how to breathe. My hands lay limp against his chest. I'd crumble under his intensity if he weren't holding me up. He is the sun, shining so bright and beautiful, and I am Mercury, the wall I've built around my heart melting away.

He lowers his head to mine, pausing right before impact, eyebrows raised, silently asking permission. I nod. The smallest of movements loudly shouting, yes, fuck yes, please kiss me already. His lips on mine are soft and tender, slow and promising at first. He pulls back slightly to look at me, and I whimper. He chuckles against my mouth.

Oh, you like that, Adonis, don't you?

When our lips meet the second time, there is no sweetness or tenderness. I am no longer melting; I am liquid fire ignited. Feelings and emotions buried deep, deep below my inner crust, bubble up and burst through the cracks like molten lava. My hands cling to his shirt, pulling him against me, desperate to mold our bodies even closer together. My hands snake around his neck, one going into those gorgeous brown waves of his. Small, contented moans escape me as he tastes my mouth with his tongue. His hands roam over my face, neck, shoulders, and back, eagerly exploring. I feel him start to harden against my belly, and the pulse between my legs intensifies into an excruciatingly delicious throb.

He grabs my hands, prying them out of his hair as he pulls back, breaking the magnetic force drawing us together. A small, frustrated sigh leaves his lips, followed by the most brilliant smile I've seen yet. "We should head back down before we get caught in the rain," he says, resting his forehead against mine while our breathing regulates.

We silently make our way down the mountain, smiling like teenagers after their first kiss. I am strung tight as a bow, an internal battle raging between the me who doesn't want to let go of the past and the me who does, trying to keep it from showing on my face. Guilt and betrayal bubble up, and the worry that I don't deserve to find happiness again simmers deep within.

Those feelings have no merit, V. They can all go fuck off, okay?

We arrive at the trailhead, and I walk to his car in a daze. He stands by the passenger door, still holding my hand, perfectly composed. The me who wants to move forward wins. I take a deep breath, square my shoulders, and look up at him.

He smiles warmly, looking at me with open, patient eyes. My wall almost completely crumbles and my crust cracks almost completely open. But there are too many things buried there that cannot be free.

"Like I said," he places a hand on my cheek, "I'll be here for you, waiting till you come back to the present. Are you back? What do you need from me?" What a loaded question. Deep crimson crawls up my neck, and he flashes me a brilliant, knowing smile. He pins me against the car and kisses me, a deep, passionate kiss. "That will have to do you for now. Shall we head to the caff?"

"You see too much, Charlie. Let's go."

A Game for Two

S till holding hands, we follow the hostess to a booth tucked into the back corner of the caff. I sigh in relief when Charlie slides onto the bench opposite me. I need a little space to think clearly. Conversation flows easily between us again, with him doing most of the talking and me drinking in the sight of him. He's draped over the back of the bench, laughter and mischief twinkling in his eyes, straight exuding casual confidence and quiet sexuality.

Kali and Kellan pop into my mind like twin devils, their teasing and unorthodox encouragements ringing in my ears. I can practically hear Kellan praising 'Mr. Adonis-in-the-flesh', and Kali chiming in with a "Come on, Ron. Let him clean the cobwebs with his womb broom." When I let slip how long it's been since I've been with someone, she was disgusted and appalled and doubled down her efforts to end my self-imposed celibacy.

Sometimes those two make me want to repeatedly bang my head against the wall with their incessant good-natured teasing, joking, and constant banter, but I still adore them. I didn't know how much I needed friends who treated me as a whole, competent, strong person and didn't unintentionally tiptoe around everything so they wouldn't upset me.

The food arrives, pulling me out of my thoughts. I tell Charlie how much I enjoy the meal and his choice of caff.

"Thanks, love," he drawls. "Do you want dessert?"

Okay, Adonis, two can play this game.

I am a grown-ass woman. I am beautiful and intelligent, and he is obviously into me. I am going to go for what I want. I have spent too long in limbo, living but not really living.

"Yes, but not the kind they serve here," I reply, slowly looking him up and down, somehow managing not to blush. He throws his head back and laughs, a deep, masculine, throaty laugh like butter being spread over toast, melting into all my cracks and crevices, settling there to patch me up and make me whole again. The pulse between my legs returns, throbbing so forcefully that I squirm and shift in my seat. He throws some pounds on the table, grabs my hand, and rushes us out of the restaurant. He pauses long enough to open the door for me, and then we're racing down the streets of London. My mind finally catches up with us, and I ask where we're going.

"To my flat. To visit 'Big Bertha,' of course," he adds as an afterthought.

"Can we stop at my place first? I need to check on the studio, shower, and change."

"Yes. No, and no. You can shower and change at my place, 'Big Bertha' *really* misses you," he replies with a wink.

"Bossy, bossy. What if I am not okay with that arrangement," I ask primly, more curious to hear his answer than because I'm not okay with it. I am more than okay with it. Hopefully, he'll join me in the shower.

"I would never force you to do anything you don't want to do," he replies, sincerity resting softly in his eyes. I assumed as much, but hearing it from him is still reassuring. We walk into my studio holding hands, but I let go at the bottom of the stairs.

I am not ready to share my space with him, so I tell him to wait in the gallery. He nods, and I fly upstairs and grab something to change into. There's no way I'm letting him peel me out of these tight, sweat-dried clothes. I quickly clean up, brush my teeth, and comb my hair before I pull on a flowy, yellow halter dress that sits at mid-thigh and nothing else.

On the way to Charlie's flat, the enormity of what we're about to do hits me in full force, and I begin to panic. We've already crossed the point of no return with one foot. If we have sex and, more importantly, decide to be together, there's no going back, not just between me and Charlie, but me and myself. If I choose this to be in a relationship, I am also choosing life for good. I can't change my mind when someone else is involved, and my actions will affect a partner as powerfully as they would affect Charlie. I may never share my past with him, and I may never look to the future. But I can do my best to give him my present, and that's all he asked for. I need to tell him not to ask for more, ever. It's not going to happen. I already gave my future to *him,* and it was all ripped away in the blink of an eye.

He reaches for my hand as he skillfully navigates the London traffic, weaving in and out of those famous red, double-decker buses like they're standing still. "We're almost there. See that building to your left. The tall black one that's mostly windows?" I nod, eyes wide. "The whole top floor is all mine," he says, pride momentarily overpowering the desire in his voice. I crane my neck to see the top, at least fifteen stories up. "You're going to love the jacuzzi tub," he states, mildly arrogant. But do I also detect a smidge of nervousness in his voice?

Oh shit, oh shit, oh shit!

He's going to see me naked. Fuck. Why didn't I pick something with a camisole underneath? Maybe he'll be too engrossed in the sex to notice the scars.

Wishful thinking, V.

He is the most observant man you've ever met, and you're about to get naked with him during the middle of the day in a flat that is all windows. At least I can tell him part of the truth about the scars without worrying that he'll push for details.

He navigates into the dark parking garage under the building and pulls into a spot labeled 'Mr. Wright.' I can't help but giggle, then burst into nervous laughter when he shoots me a sideways glare. In a mock sotto voice, I say, "Oh, Mr. Wright. Right there," he chuckles with me, humor and mirth glowing on his face, which is illuminated only by the dim lights lining the wall. "How many times have you heard that," I tease, rolling my eyes dramatically.

"The real question here," he says, voice low and full of promise, "is how many times am I going to hear it today after I take you upstairs? On second thought, I quite enjoy a challenge. How often do you think I can coax it from your lips right here in the car?"

"None," I breathe.

'Challenge accepted' flashes in his green eyes. He effortlessly plucks me out of the passenger seat and sets me on his lap, straddling him. He grabs my hips, grinding me down on his erection, and I briefly wonder if we're even going to make it upstairs. We kiss with carnal hunger and need, tasting, biting, sucking. Wait—sucking?

Fuck that.

"Do not give me hickeys. And, as much as I am enjoying this," I declare, rotating my pelvis against him, "I do not want our first time together to be a quickie in your car."

I try to move off him, but he locks his fingers around my waist, rubbing himself against the sensitive flesh between my legs. I whimper, biting my lip to prevent myself from saying what he wants to hear. Determination radiates from his beautiful, intense green eyes in response to the unspoken 'challenge accepted' he sees in mine.

"We can go upstairs when you say it." He runs one hand up my side. His thumb finds my nipple, taut and hard, and caresses it in light, teasing circles. It takes all my willpower to stifle a moan and sit perfectly still on his lap. No longer able to withstand the torture of the too-soft, too-gentle caressing, I grab both his wrists and bring his hands together between us. The absence of his touch leaves me light-headed and adrift on a raging current of desire.

I look at him with raised eyebrows, silently telling him, you won't win this one. He sighs and disentangles our bodies, setting me gently on the passenger seat, a smug smile on my face. "Wait here," he commands, grabbing my bag from the back seat before jumping out and slamming the door. He opens mine, offering his hand. I place my small hand in his large one, and he pulls me out of the car, slamming my door, too.

"You don't like to lose, do you, Mr. Wright," I tease, giving him my best mischievous grin. "Or maybe you're just not used to not getting what you want. You're not used to being told no." It's not a question.

His nostrils flare, and searing intensity pours from his green gaze. He places both hands on the car, one on either side of me, standing just close enough so that we're not quite touching.

"You may have won this round, Veronica, but I will not be so merciful once I have you naked in my bed," he says, rewarding me with a brilliant smile and a quick, chaste kiss. Any more than that, and I'd let him bend me over the hood of his car and fuck me right here in the parking garage. He grabs my hand and leads me to the row of lifts, pushing the button on the one furthest to the right. We stand facing forward, only our hands touching, breathing ragged, and each lost in our own thoughts.

A small ding sounds when the doors open. We ascend the first couple of floors in silence. "This is a private lift," he offers, looking at my reflection in the mirror on the opposite wall, face etched with desire.

I shrug a shoulder and lick my top lip. The mirrored door slides open, and I stand there staring, mouth open. His flat looks like it was cut right out of a luxury homes magazine. He was not exaggerating about the windows. He steps off, pulling me with him.

Immediately to the left on a raised dais sits a baby grand piano. It is gorgeous, black, and shined to perfection. He could bend me over that and, holy fuck, V! I am wound so tight, the throbbing between my legs so unrelenting, I can't fully appreciate the beauty of the space and the view of London until after. Right now, everywhere just looks like a good place to fuck: the sofas, coffee tables, kitchen counters, the floor. I'm not picky.

Intelligent and intuitive as ever, Charlie grabs me around the waist and lifts me into his arms, setting me on the half wall that divides the piano from the sitting areas. I rip off his shirt and run my hands through his dark, wavy hair. It is silky and thick, and he groans in satisfaction when I dig my fingers into his scalp. In turn, he rakes his nails up my sides, cupping my breasts and kneading my nipples through the thin fabric of my dress. My eyes roll back in my head, and I moan, bucking my hips forward. His strong grip drops around my hips and prevents me from falling off the wall.

Fingers digging into my hips, he rests his forehead against mine, our labored breathing sounding unnaturally loud in the silence around us. "I need to see you without that dress on. I can feel the lack of anything under it, and it is driving me fucking insane. I need to feel your skin against mine; I need to be inside you. Now."

"You first, Adonis," I say, slipping his grip to hop off the wall. I will not get fully naked while he's still half-dressed. Grabbing the tie of his joggers, I admit, "But, I do like it when you're commanding." I push them down, and he springs free. I lick my lips, and he yanks them off the rest of the way, chucking them forcefully across the room. He is so fucking hot, built like a fucking superhero, all sculpted muscles, planes, and angles. After letting me look him over hungrily, he unties my dress and slides it down my body with excruciating slowness. My chest heaves, and my leg jitters as he eases it over my hips, letting it fall to the ground; he steps back to rake his eyes over my body.

"Fucking beautiful," he breathes. He can't possibly see this body, marked with the evidence of so many struggles and torments, and think that.

They're just scars, V. Faint, faded scars. Look at the desire on his face. He doesn't think less of you because of them.

Still, after years and years of trying, I can't get my mom's cruelly critical voice out of my head. My body could be pristine, perfectly shaped, and lacking any blemish, and I'd still feel inadequate; ugly, unworthy of adoration, too big, too muscular, too curvy, not feminine enough, not enough. Never enough. Never enough for her and, therefore, never enough for myself or anyone else.

Objectively, I see the evidence of Charlie's desire, his hardness and shining green eyes devouring every inch of exposed skin, and I believe he speaks truthfully. But it is fucking hard to trust his words. A small voice in the back of my mind will always be skeptical that someone could truly think kind things about me.

Charlie groans my name, drawing me back to the present. Looking down while the crimson burn of shame crawls up my neck, I cross my arms over my stomach. He closes the distance between us with one determined stride and gently raises my chin, waiting patiently while I work up enough courage to meet his gaze. "Veronica," he rasps, prying my arms away from my stomach. He holds them out to the side and steps back, raking his eyes over me again.

"You are the most fucking beautiful woman I have ever seen," he says, his voice earnest and raspy with desire.

Although I believe he means what he says, the statement does little to alleviate my insecurities. But instead of dwelling on my body's imperfections and ruining my ability to enjoy this time with him, I run my hands from the tops of his thighs up his sculpted torso and twine them around his neck. He claims my mouth with his and lifts me off the floor with little effort. His powerful legs carry me to his room in just a few purposeful strides.

Not missing the thoughts that must have shown on my face, he whispers into my ear, "You *are* fucking gorgeous, Veronica. Anyone who has ever made you feel otherwise is not worthy of you." Choking back a sob and tired of feeling inadequate, I grind myself against his stomach and kiss him ardently. He kisses down my jaw and nuzzles into my neck, causing me to erupt into a fit of giggles. He throws me onto the bed and pounces, tickling me all over. I squeal and try to reach past his long arms to get at his ribs. When we're both laughing hard and breathing heavily, he sits back on his heels, a smug smile tilting up the corners of his mouth. I roll my eyes but smile back, thankful for him breaking the tension and getting me out of my head.

"Scoot up and spread your legs, Veronica," he commands, and I obey with alacrity, sweet anticipation coursing through me. Pupils dilated and eyes dark with hunger, he yanks open a drawer from the nightstand next to his bed. He fishes out a condom and rips open the foil packet with his teeth. I briefly consider telling him that it's not necessary but decide to wait till later. Confident and sure, he locks his gaze on mine and slowly, so excruciatingly slowly, rolls on the condom.

I buck my hips and whimper, urging him to hurry as he kneels between my legs. No longer able to stand the sweet torture of anticipation, I cup him with one hand and stroke him with the other. He moans, dropping his head back, and breathes out a strangled, "Fuck."

The need in his voice unravels the little restraint I have left, and I beg, "Charlie, please. I need you inside me."

He pushes me onto my back and trails his fingertips up and down my thighs. "Wider," he demands, and I shift my knees even further apart for him. He rubs my clit with the tip of his cock, and I buck harder.

"Fuck, Charlie. Please," I plead.

"Uh, uh, uh," he purrs, shaking his head. "Say it, Veronica."

The demand in his voice sends a jolt of pleasure through me, and I cup a breast in my hand, rolling a nipple between my fingers. "Fuck me."

He raises his eyebrows and leans back just enough to break contact. "No mercy, Veronica, remember? Say the words I want to hear." I shake my head and whimper, reaching for him with my free hand. He grips my wrist and shoves it above my head, positioning himself at my entrance. "Veronica, say it," he demands.

I press my lips together and shake my head again. He rocks forward, careful not to push inside me, and pulls a nipple into his mouth, sucking and flicking it with his tongue. I writhe and buck my hips. He chuckles and releases my nipple with a pop, looking at me expectantly. I keep my lips pressed firmly together so he ducks his head and sucks my other nipple into his mouth.

His hand trails up and down my body, touching me everywhere except where I'm wet and throbbing. The sensation is excruciatingly delicious. I try to continue holding out, reveling in this moment and memorizing this ecstasy, but he removes his hands and lips from my body and stares at me, head tilted and eyebrows raised. He's not going to give in this time.

Oh my God, V. Just say it already.

"Please, Mr. Wright. Fuck me," I beg. His smile boasts, 'I win' as he thrusts into me all the way to the hilt. We both gasp at the powerful intensity of our joining. The musky aroma of our mingled desire fills my nostrils while the silk sheets rub delicately against my skin, and fuck if he doesn't feel fucking fantastic pounding inside me.

"Fuck, Veronica. You feel so fucking good," he says as he rocks back onto his knees, gripping my hips to pull me with him. His eyes travel lazily down my body to watch where our bodies join. I try to focus on the sensation of him inside me and his hands on my body, but that shitty little voice in my brain takes over, reminding me that there are scars and stretch marks and jiggly skin, and Charlie is definitely disgusted and will never want to be with me again.

Stop! Look at him, V. He fucking loves this. He'll go for round two as soon as he can get it up again.

Whatever. It's easy to love it at the moment, but it's also easy to regret it after. Grimacing, I close my eyes and drop my head to the side. He's obviously enjoying this. It's also obvious that he's truly interested in me and wants to be with me. I look at his naked body and see only perfection. No criticisms come to mind—*because he is literally perfectly made. W*hy is it so impossible for me to trust that someone could look at me the same way?

Jesus, V. You're having sex with the hottest, sweetest, most thoughtful man you've ever met. Get out of your head and enjoy it already.

Bitch, I'm trying. Charlie withdraws from me and says my name questioningly, returning me to the moment. He searches my eyes for a second before asking, "Are you still okay with this?" Not trusting my voice to betray whatever thoughts he hasn't read on my face, I nod vigorously and cup his cheek. He studies me for another second before scooting down the bed and licking my clit with long, wet, lazy strokes. My eyes roll back, and the voices in my head shut right the hell up.

"Mmmm," he purrs, picking up the pace. "You like that, don't you, Veronica?" He plunges two fingers inside me, curling them to hit that sweet spot while his tongue rubs quick, firm circles over my clit, and I can't think enough to keep playing the game of wills.

"Yes, Mr. Wright. It feels so fucking good." Pressure builds as he strokes and licks, starting in my toes, and I arch my back, fingers digging into his hair, and then I'm panting and murmuring, whimpering and urging him to keep going, right there, until sweet, delicious, all-consuming pleasure explodes inside me.

I'm still panting, still floating on ecstasy when he drives back into me, pace fast and hard as he chases his own release. I grip his ass, reveling in the feel of his muscles contracting with each thrust, and kiss him, open-mouthed and needy. I fucking love tasting and smelling myself on him. I meet him thrust for thrust, bucking my hips to meet his, and he buries his face in my neck, his breaths coming in ragged pants.

"Your turn, Adonis," I whisper in his ear, and it is his undoing. He shudders and pumps into me twice more before his whole body goes rigid. He releases a long, shaky breath, then collapses on top of me, his head resting tenderly between my breasts. I run my fingers through his hair and trail them up and down his back while our breathing evens out. Tiny Mildred is thankfully quiet in my mind, so I mentally catalog every single detail of our tryst. I want to be able to remember this moment with as much detail as possible. Leaving out my mental struggles, I recount everything from our kiss on the mountain to our meal at the diner and our game in the car. Joy, awe, and contentment bloom in my chest as I fix the details of the past hour into my memory. Other memories threaten to bubble up and pull me down, but I fucking drown them before they even get the chance to taint this moment.

Not Soon Enough

The sun is starting its westward descent when Charlie wakes me with light kisses on my neck, trailing his fingers over my back in a delicate caress. His hand slides up my ribs, cupping my breast from behind. He pinches my nipple and nibbles on my earlobe, causing my back to arch, my ass pressing against his erection. He glides inside me easily and moves in a gentle rhythm. His hand leaves my breast, snaking down my belly to my pulsing center. He gently massages it as he moves inside me, building speed and pressure as we both near climax. We ride the wave together, cresting at the apex of release, then crashing in a sea of tangled limbs and contented sighs.

"Food or shower," I vaguely register the question. My brain says sleep, while my sore, languid limbs crave a hot soak. But, my belly rumbles, winning the battle. He chuckles, "Food it is, then." He disentangles his legs from mine, standing and stretching his arms overhead, entirely at ease in his nakedness. Suddenly shy, I cover myself with the sheet.

"Where's my dress?" He shrugs and winks, tossing me the shirt he was about to pull on. I quickly pull it over my head, feeling more comfortable under a layer of cloth. Carefully pulling my legs from under the black, fluffy down comforter, I scoot to the edge of the bed, my quads, glutes, and hip flexors groaning in protest. I stretch my arms overhead, then bend my elbows like chicken wings, and twist left and right to loosen my upper back muscles.

Charlie notices the warmth in my eyes and my content smile, flashing one in return as he leads me to the kitchen. "What do you fancy for dinner?" I purse my lips in thought and run my eyes down his body. "Food, Veronica. We both need real food. Then, a hot soak. Then, and only then, will I give you more of this," he says, gesturing at himself. I crinkle my nose and stick out my bottom lip. His deep, warm laugh fills the air as he saunters over to me. His lips meet mine, his tongue tasting my mouth until I am breathless. "That will have to do you for now," he says, chuckling.

I shake my head and follow him into the kitchen, plopping onto a stool at the island that separates the kitchen from the sitting room. Charlie winks and starts gathering supplies to make dinner, but my smile falters when he turns away from me. This all feels so foreign but so achingly familiar. I allow myself one long inhale to miss *him* and the beautiful, wonderful life we had together. Clutching my hollow, aching chest, I release a long, shaky breath, trying to let *him* go with it. I'll never be able to fully eradicate *him* from my heart, mind, or soul, and I don't want to, but I hope that I can learn to love *him* and miss *him* and look back on my past with fondness, while joyously anticipating my future with Charlie.

Charlie's gaze pulls me back to the present. When my eyes focus on him, a kind, tender smile spreads across his face, and he gently inquires, "Are you back with me?" Wanting to break the tension inside me and bring some levity to the moment, I give him a cheesy smile and two thumbs-up.

He snorts and throws some flour, baking powder, and salt into a large metal bowl. He stirs, brows furrowing together, then glances at me. He inhales as if preparing to speak but exhales without saying anything. Slowly adding a Boddington's to the bowl, he takes another deliberate inhale. I watch him in awe. Usually, he's self-possessed and hard to read, but right now, I can tell he's musing over something. Having stirred the batter to his desired consistency, he sets the bowl aside and rummages through a drawer for a peeler. He takes another preparatory inhale, vigorously peels potatoes, and sets his shoulders. Rushing out the words on a quick exhale, he asks, "Do you mind if I ask how long it has been since you have been with someone?"

'Mr. Calm and Collected' gets flustered talking about sex. How adorable.

"Been with someone how," I reply, eyebrows furrowed, head tilted.

He gives me a 'you know' look. I shrug my shoulders and press my lips into a thin line. He huffs in annoyance, "When was the last time you had sex?" He says it slowly, enunciating every syllable and giving me a pointed look.

"About two minutes ago. Remember? You were there." I *am* enjoying this.

He abandons the potato and peeler and leans on the counter, large hands splayed in front of him. He squints his eyes and purses his lips. I have no idea what he replies. I want dinner and a soak to end quickly so I can have dessert again because it has been a long time since I've enjoyed it this much. He snaps his fingers in front of my face, grins, and shakes his head. "You know very well what I'm asking, Veronica. How long since the last time you had sex before two minutes ago?"

"About two hours before that." His face darkens as I reply. He steps toward me, and I raise my hands, "Okay, okay. It's been a long time, okay? Well over a year. And since the . . . the *event* I mentioned yesterday," he nods, "It didn't happen often and when it did, it wasn't all that enjoyable. There. Are you satisfied now?"

"Love." My heart skips a beat. "I have been thoroughly satisfied since I pulled you off the lift earlier today." A brilliant smile shines on his face. "That answer, though, is a little vague. I am going to need some details." He slices the potatoes into thin chips, eyebrows raised.

I raise my eyebrows and quirk one corner of my mouth. "What details, specifically?"

"What was your sex life like before the *event*, why did it change or what changed about it after, and what caused a long span of celibacy?" A shiver runs up his spine, and he shakes his head as if trying to remove the thought from his brain.

"Wow, umm, okay," I reply, pausing to gather my thoughts. "Before, my sex life was amazing," I admit. "Why did it change? Because sex is so much better when it's with someone you have an emotional connection with. After the *event*, the few times I did have sex, it was a one-time thing. The last one was bad." He looks at me thoughtfully, and I answer his question before he can ask it. "He was an arrogant, selfish asshole who was so full of himself that I'm surprised he even allowed another person in bed with him."

I see all the questions he wants to ask dancing behind his eyes, so I tell him the story. *After* the *event*, I only gave in to the need for intimacy a handful of times. I was upfront with those partners about it being a casual, one-time occurrence. Except for the last one, they all respected my rules. He tried to prevent me from leaving after we'd finished.

"Charlie, you would not believe this guy! This is what he said to me: "No girl really means that shit. And every girl always comes back for more because I am the best they've ever had and the best they will ever have." Like, what!?!" Charlie splashes oil over the side of the fryer, trying to contain his laughter. "Oh, it gets better," I continue, "I told him that he was the worst I'd ever had, he was by far, and he better get the fuck out of my way. He was physically blocking the door. He refused, then grabbed my shoulders and tried to force me back to the bed."

"No, he didn't," Charlie growls, thunder rolling across his eyes.

I raise my hands in front of me, patting the air. "Don't worry, we were in Montana, where I just so happen to have a concealed weapons permit. I pulled a pistol out of my purse, pointed it at his tiny, pathetic penis, and told him again to get the fuck out of my way."

Deep, booming laughter fills the air again, followed by a string of expletives. Charlie, laughing hard, dropped the battered halibut into the fryer, splashing hot oil on his arm.

"Are you okay," I say, quickly rising off the stool.

"I'm fine, I'm fine," he holds up his unmarked arm for proof. "Just a small drop that startled me." I lower back onto the stool, belly rumbling. The food smells amazing.

"Every time I learn something new about you, I am amazed and impressed," he says, admiration evident in his voice. Warm crimson crawls up my neck as he serves me a plate of fish and chips.

Conversation flows easily as we eat. We talk about Britain and America, his career and family, and where he grew up. Everything and nothing; everything about him, nothing about me. He's taking on a new client starting Monday and will be working as many hours a week as I do.

After we're both stuffed, I insist on clearing up and washing dishes since he cooked. He tidies up the rest of the flat, retrieving our scattered clothing, and checks his company email while I dry the dishes and put them away.

He returns from his office as I finish, placing a sweet peck on my lips. "Are you going to give me the grand tour now," I ask.

He holds out his arm, elbow bent, bowing slightly. "Milady." We both giggle as I take his arm, his mock formality hilarious in our state of disheveled half-dress. "This way," he gestures toward the sitting room containing the lift. The entire right wall and the wall in front of us are floor-to-ceiling windows overlooking the London skyline. The baby grand piano sits on a dais in the corner, framed by two half walls. I ascend the three steps up to the platform and play a couple of lines of my favorite classical song, *Clair de Lune*, by Debussy. I could sit here all day drumming out melodies on these ivories, watching London from above.

I fold the fallboard back over the keys and turn to continue the tour. I stop, riveted in place by Charlie; intense longing, desire, and possessiveness radiate out of his eyes, which are boring into mine. My heart leaps in response, and my eyes reflect similar feelings back at him: longing, desire, and surrender.

He reaches for my hand and says, "Come, my dear, we have just begun."

The sitting room wraps around the lift. My old friend 'Big Bertha' hangs on the side wall of the lift, the focal point for this section of the room. White and black chaise lounge chairs, small sofas, and oversized armchairs sit in two separate groups around modern-style wood and iron coffee tables. The group behind us faces the windows and the amazing view of London. The group in front of us faces my artwork. He was right, this is the perfect setting for her. He stands next to me, hand on the small of my back, while I admire my work for a few moments.

"Charlie, your place is amazing," I say.

"Wait till you see the rest," he declares, raising his eyebrows. He takes my hand and leads me down a hallway, nodding at the first door on the left, "the master suite, which you are well acquainted with." I blush, and one of those brilliant smiles lights up his face. The second room on the left is his office, and the door across the hall is a spare bedroom. The other door on the right leads to an enormous, lavishly appointed bathroom. The large walk-in shower is lined in black and white marble tiles, with a bench running the entire length of the far wall. There are five total shower heads, one on each of the shorter side walls, two on the far wall, and a mister hanging from the middle of the ceiling.

"So, where's this famous jacuzzi tub," I inquire.

He chuckles, "Patience, V."

He opens the double French doors at the end of the hall to reveal a well-appointed home gym, complete with an infrared sauna. I look at him, surprised. "Why do you go to a public gym when you have this at home? If I could combine your flat with my studio, I would never leave."

His feet shuffle, and a slightly embarrassed look crosses his face. "I generally do not use public gyms. I spent most of the night at your open house checking you out, and I assumed you probably frequented the gym. So, I googled the one closest to your studio and went there, hoping to run into you." He looks at me and shrugs one shoulder, his easy confidence returning.

"Oh, you sly devil," I exclaim. He looks me up and down and bites his lip. I clear my throat and look around the room. The wall to the right is all windows and the one to the left is all mirrors. His gym is as well stocked as a commercial gym. My hands itch to get in there and get to work, but neither of us is exactly dressed appropriately.

"You are welcome to use this anytime you want. I will set up a passcode for the lift so you can come and go as you please."

"Really? We're at that point already?"

He turns toward me and pulls me into his arms. "Listen, Veronica. I want to be with you, here and now, in the present. And like I said before, I do not need your past, and I will not ask you to promise me your future. I do not date casually. You are the only woman in my life. I want you to be comfortable here and think of it as your second home. If you would rather come here than go to Fitness First, even if I am not here, that is fine with me," he says matter-of-factly.

"I would like that very much. Thank you, Charlie." He kisses me tenderly, and I pull back before it becomes more insistent. "Will you understand if I don't give you a key to my place right away?" He nods. "I want to be with you too. You're the only man in my life, and I'm not hiding anything. I just need a safe place for myself, where I can be alone when life gets overwhelming." I look at him, eyes pleading for him to understand.

"No sweat, love, I get it. I trust you," he replies.

"Now, about this hot soak," I say, pressing my hips into his. He leans down, kissing me, tongue hungry and insistent until we're both panting, his need pressed up against my belly, mine dripping down my thighs. He lifts me to straddle his waist, carrying me down the hall, and, kicking open the door to his room, he sets me on the floor. He leads me across the room to another set of French doors, flashing a brilliant smile as he opens them and steps back. The room is massive, twice as big as the other bathroom. The entire far wall has floor-to-ceiling windows, and the view is breathtaking. The last rays of the sun are just peaking over the London skyline, painting the sky in muted blues, purples, pinks, and oranges, illuminating the white and gold marble that covers every surface of the room.

The jacuzzi tub is framed in the middle of the wall of windows. It could easily fit six people. A toilet and urinal sit to the left, partitioned off from the room and each other by elaborately decorated black, white, and gold folding shoji screens. A long vanity, equipped with two huge sinks and topped by a large, ornate gold-rimmed mirror, spans half the length of the right wall, ending in a built-in, sit-at vanity. There are two showers, one in each far corner of the room, as big as the shower in the main bathroom and set up similarly. A large black and gold armoire sits between the left shower and toilets.

"Holy shit, Charlie. I would never leave. But you get naked in here every day," I ask, wrinkling my nose.

"The windows allow us to see out but prevent others from seeing in."

I step into the bathroom, running my fingers along the smooth marble vanity. He stalks up to me, green eyes boring into my reflection as he grasps the hem of his shirt and lifts it over my head. He runs his hands up my sides to cup my breasts, rolling my nipples between his thumbs and pointer fingers. I moan and arch my back, rubbing my ass against him. He drops his hands and takes a step away from me.

"I said hot soak first, Veronica," he admonishes, playfully reprimanding me.

I lift my hands in mock surrender. "Excuse me, Mr. Wright. If you can't finish, don't start."

Smirking and tilting his head at an arrogant angle, he drops his pants and fists his cock. "My dear, Veronica, I can finish well enough. I can also be very, very patient when I so choose."

He saunters to the tub, looking like a statue come to life in this marble palace, his sculpted body part of the adornments.

Adonis-in-the-flesh indeed.

The setting sun highlights the rich chocolate tones in his hair, and I long to run my fingers through it, but I settle on the bench opposite him. I shudder out a sigh of sweet relief as the jets massage tight muscles. Charlie clicks a few buttons on a remote, dimming the lights and playing some classical music in the background, then moves to sit near me, and we stare at the London skyline in companionable silence for a long time.

When I can stand the heat no longer, I exit the tub, staring at Charlie over my shoulder as I walk toward one of the ginormous showers, swishing my hips provocatively. Feeling bold, the usual criticism blessedly quiet in my head, I pause at the door, arch my back, and raise my eyebrows. Arm draped over the side of the tub, radiating that casual confidence and, right now, overt sexuality, he stares me down, naked desire in his intense emerald eyes. He rakes them over my body and moves a hand beneath the water, pumping himself before rising to follow me.

The glass door is cool and smooth beneath my fingers, and the lukewarm water feels delightful on my heated skin. After turning on each faucet, I stand in the middle of the shower, slowly rotating with arms outstretched, strengthening the barrier in my mind behind which I store the painful memories, troublesome emotions, and critical voices. Charlie twirls me into him with a hand on my arm, my back against his front. He runs his hands up my back and removes my ponytail, letting my hair fall down my back.

"I cannot believe how long your hair is, Veronica. It is so beautiful. Wear it down more for me?"

"For you, I will." A pang of guilt breaks past its barrier and stabs through me as he gathers my red-streaked, dark brown locks into his hands and massages shampoo into my scalp.

Let it go, V. He is never going to run his hands through your hair again. Don't ruin what's right here in front of you for something long gone.

With some force, I shove the guilt back behind its barrier and return my focus to the present. Wrapping his soapy hand around my throat, he tilts it back into one of the multiple streams of water, gently rinsing out my hair. We communicate silently, palpable intensity radiating from his eyes, which never leave mine. He scrubs my body methodically, lingering frustratingly too short on my sensitive parts.

You want another battle of wills, Mr. I-Can-Be-Patient. Well, so can I.

I never thought I'd have this chemistry with another man again. And now that I do, I am—despite the fucking slippery sea monster inside me that just cannot let go of the past—going to take my time and savor every precious minute I get with Charlie.

I lather up a loofa and begin scrubbing him down, moving slowly across and down his body, deliberately avoiding his erection. His desire is evident, but he is patient and true to his word, allowing delicious tension to build between us. After scrubbing almost every sensational inch of him, I slip my hands up his chest and around his neck, gently tugging him forward so I can wash his hair. As he rinses himself, I drop to my knees, lathering my hands with the remaining suds on the loofa, and begin to stroke him. His hands remain in his hair, fingers laced together, eyes boring into mine. I start slow and delicate, methodically increasing the pressure and pace until his eyes close and his head drops back into his hands.

He remains still as the statue he is, chest barely moving with each measured breath, his handsome face revealing nothing of what he's feeling. My confidence dissipates, and Tiny Mildred's mocking permeates my thoughts. *"You can't please him; look at your old, scared body,"* it taunts mercilessly.

My grip falters, and the strokes along his silky, hard length become shaky and unsure. His eyes pop open, locking immediately on mine, and he reads my face through his haze of lust. On the verge of tears, choked with embarrassment, and frustrated that it's so fucking difficult to just be, to just live in the moment, I cling for dear life to his knowing, sure gaze. He drops to his knees and cradles my face in his hands so tenderly it takes every ounce of will I have to hold the tears at bay.

"You have no idea what you do to me, do you," he states, green gaze searing straight into my soul. "One look, one touch, and I fucking come undone for you. My patience departed the moment you knelt before me, naked and determined and mine." He grips my neck and pulls my forehead to rest against his. "You are enough, Veronica, for no other reason than simply existing. There's no need for more, for me or us, or any other pressures someone else has thrust upon you. You are enough, and fuck anyone who has ever made you feel otherwise. For this, I do have patience. The patience to figure out who planted these thoughts in your mind, and destroy every last one of them."

My broken, bruised heart flutters at the thought of Charlie going toe to toe with my mother on my behalf, and another terrible, selfish wish that I've denied for the past six years bubbles up, and, for once, I let it. I let myself wish so fucking bad that the fucking douche who decimated my life was still alive so I could watch Charlie rip him apart.

Instead, not knowing how to respond and not wanting these thoughts of vengeance to consume me, I throw myself into Charlie's arms and crash my lips against his. There's nothing tender or patient about this kiss. It's fueled by need and desperation—the need to feel alive and the desperation to forget and allow myself to believe Charlie's words.

You are enough, V. You always have been.

Powerfully and gracefully as a jungle cat, Charlie rises with me in his arms and backs me against the slick, cool glass wall. Without breaking our hungry kiss, he shifts my hips and slams into me. I cry out, mumbling nonsense and urging him on.

"Oh, yes. Fuck, yes," I groan into his mouth as he pounds relentlessly into me. My shoulder blades bang against the glass with each thrust, and my nails dig into his back, his neck, and his scalp. My legs are draped over his toned forearms, and his large, rough hands firmly grip my ass as he drives us close to the edge, but I need more. I try to wiggle my hand between us to touch myself, but I whimper in frustration because there's not enough room to get the friction I so desperately need.

Pleasure rumbles deep in his chest and, in one swift motion, he drops me to my feet and pins me face-first into the glass and, holy fuck, do I love being manhandled by him. Without further direction, I arch my back and wiggle my ass, and he glides slowly into me. I can't believe I forgot how fucking good it feels to be with a man I adore, who adores me back.

My mind wholly focused on the sensations coursing through my body and the man creating them, I try to drive back and regain our frantic pace, but Charlie's iron grip on my hips prevents my efforts, and I plead urgently, the glass cool against my flushed face.

Sunk fully into me, his large, deliciously rough hand slithers up my spine into my hair and pulls, bringing my ear to his lips. "I have found my patience again, Veronica," he breathes into my ear, "You are now at my mercy." I hum in acknowledgment and shudder, my breath going ragged at the command in his voice.

He wraps my long, wet hair around his forearm and begins moving inside me, slow and measured. Whenever I try to drive back to meet him, he pulls my hair tighter around his fist.

"What's the rush, love?" he purrs, pinching my nipple and giving it a firm tug.

For a few long, torturous minutes, he moves lazily inside me, toying with my nipples. "Charlie," I beg, back arched and legs trembling.

"Who, Veronica?" he demands. He may have found his patience, but mine fled the minute he assuaged my insecurities. My general competitive and stubborn nature turns pliant when his hands are on me, and his cock is buried deep inside me. I want to defy him, but my instincts to obey him take over, and I give in easily.

"Mister," I breathe out on a long exhale, "Wright," I finish, whimpering as he drives into me. And then my eyes roll back, and all logical thought floats away because he positions the shower head between my legs, hitting my already swollen and sensitive clit with an excruciatingly intense stream of water. The dual sensations send wave after wave of pleasure crashing through me, each one bigger than the last, building and building, pushing me to the brink of orgasm while Charlie manages to maintain his steady, even pace.

The biggest wave yet starts rolling through me, and I breathe through my nose, readying to crest the climax when Charlie removes the shower head and stills inside me. I whimper and whine and beg him to continue, but he merely whispers in my ear, "Patience, my love." I exhale forcefully through my nose and sag against the glass. How many times we repeat this process, I don't know, but by the time he loses himself to the frenzy, increasing the speed and ferocity of his thrusts, I can think of nothing but the sensations, the cool glass against my face, my hair wrapped around his forearm, him pounding into me, the tormenting vibration of the water, and the need for release.

Just when it all becomes too much, and I feel as if I'm going to explode from the inside out, he demands, "Now, Veronica," and we both come undone, groaning and screaming our pleasure, him stiffening behind and in me, and me shuddering and clenching around him. If it wasn't for his steel grip around my stomach, I'd collapse. I am completely and utterly spent, body drained and mind blank. It is a relief to simply exist without the constant war in my head, without feeling uncomfortable in my own body.

Charlie gently scoops me into his arms, grabbing a towel and draping it over me on his way out the door. With tender, soft strokes, he dries me off then applies soothing lotion to my used, satiated body. He pulls back the comforter and helps me into bed, tucking me in and dropping a sweet, tender kiss on my forehead. The silk sheets feel luxurious against my skin as I fall instantly into a deep, dreamless sleep, for once at peace.

Charlie

Chest still rising and falling erratically, I return to the bathroom to clean up. That was the most amazing sex I have ever had. But, I fucking hope she did not bloody say what I thought she said as I tucked her in. If she did, could I let her go after the day we had? Yeah, the sex was phenomenal, and her body, fuck I am getting hard again already just thinking about her luscious curves. But it is more than that. She smiled today, easy and genuine, and laughed, eyes bright and carefree. I want to beg her to promise me the rest of her life just so I can coax that smile onto her face again and again and ease the pain she tries so hard to hide.

I adore her amazing body, but I also love her brilliant mind. The way it works and the way she sees the world are vastly different from mine. When she lets her guard down and opens up to me, I live for those moments. I could listen to her talk about her career for hours, not just because it is interesting on its own but because of the light it brings to her rich, chocolate eyes.

And after today, fuck, I want to know all her secrets. What do the words and numbers intricately woven into her wings tattoo represent? What happened to make her feel so broken, so unworthy? Shitty parents? Abusive ex? I could have sworn she mumbled another man's name just now as she snuggled into my bed, but I also cannot believe that she would play me like that. God knows, in the past, that would have been enough for me to call it off immediately and never speak to her again, but I am in way too fucking deep. Deep enough that I am willing to trust her and give her the time and the space to share her story on her own terms and in her own time.

She said that I am the only man in her life, and I will just have to trust that for now, but the world fucking help us both if it happens again.

Just Veronica

I chuckle as I drop a tea bag into a giant mug of steaming water. Charlie would be horrified, but I prefer my tea contained. I place the mug on a saucer to carry outside, stopping by my nightstand to grab my journal and sketchbook. An idea for a new piece has been brewing for a while, and I need to get it out on paper. The morning is blue and clear, the sun shining warmly on me as I sit on my small balcony overlooking a beautifully manicured city park.

Okay, V. It's time to go through the overflowing 'analyze later' compartment.

Most of the thoughts are easily processed, and the compartment is empty except for one lingering issue. I can't quite wrap my head around the idea that I can honor my past love *and* move forward with Charlie. But I decide to trust Sophie regardless and keep slowly rebuilding my heart, hoping that someday there will be room for both men when enough of it gets repaired.

I return my journal to its place on the nightstand and order takeout for lunch. While I wait for the delivery, I jog up and down the stairs, stretching my stiff legs. As I munch on the delicious Gyro, I sketch. The images swirling in my mind flow easily onto the paper. While engrossed in my work, the sun disappears around the building, taking its warmth with it. A powerful shiver courses through me, startling me out of my creative trance, and I realize that my toes are numb. I quickly tidy up the balcony and head inside. My tingling feet carry me to the workroom before my brain consciously decides to go down.

I blast some classical music and get lost in the process of creating, finishing the entire piece in one sitting. That'll make the brilliant twins happy when they come in tomorrow.

My back pops in protest as I rise from the stool and look out the windows to see the last rays of the setting sun painting the sky in warm oranges, golds, and reds. The natural light quickly dissipates, so I flip on the lights to tidy the workroom and fully return to reality. My stomach growls, and I contemplate ordering in again, but weariness takes over as I ascend the stairs. The past few weeks have finally caught up with me. I grab a banana off the counter to tide me over till morning and fall into bed, still fully clothed, with my nighttime routine forgotten. What a bad idea that was.

The woman stared in awe at her reflection in the mirror. Her hair and makeup were done to perfection. Her white, strapless lace dress hugged all her curves; the train trailed behind her like water over rocks as she walked toward her destiny. She had eyes only for the man, who was stunning in his black tux: tall, lean, and clear blue eyes beaming. Tears of pure joy rolled down both of their faces. They kissed, a long, passionate kiss on the happiest day of their lives.

Images swirl around too fast to decipher: white lace, friends and family dancing around them, rose petals on white sheets, the man and woman dancing, eyes fixed on each other, pavement covered in debris. No, no, not again! The reel stops and the woman stands alone in a cold, metal room on the worst day of her life. A hand hovers in the corner of her vision.

You're dreaming. Wake up! Wake up before the sheet gets pulled back.

An arm reaches out, "No, no, no, no, no!"

I scream myself awake.

Hyperventilating, I sit in dawn's cold, gray light, soaked in sweat and tears. Heart racing and mind reeling, I flail my arms, trying desperately to untangle my legs from the sheets. Once they are finally free, I swing them over the side of the bed and focus on calming my breath. One, two. In and out. I slip into my slippers and robe and pad to the bathroom to splash cold water on my face.

Ooof. You look like shit, V.

As I splash some more water on my face, a small flashing light in the mirror's reflection grabs my attention. I dry my face and quickly retrieve my phone from the nightstand. The screen displays two missed calls and four new texts from Charlie. The last of which reads:

I hope everything is okay. If you have gone to the past, I will be here waiting for you when you return. Please do not make me wait too long. –Mr. Wright

I hit the call button and almost immediately hit end. Two seconds later, his face flashes across my screen.

"Hey. Sorry if I woke you. I didn't realize how early it was."

A sleepy smile spreads lazily across his face as he rolls onto his side. He waves away my apology. "You can call me anytime, day or night. I have been worried about you. Are you alright?" he asks, concern evident in his eyes. There might be a hint of distrust lingering behind the concern, but it's too early for my brain to function properly, especially after the fitful night's sleep I had.

"Kind of. I'm sorry I didn't answer last night. I spent the day holed up in the studio. I was so tired when I finished that I fell asleep in my clothes." I angle the phone down so he can see me dressed in the same outfit I had on when he dropped me off yesterday morning.

"No worries," concern lines his brow. "You don't look like you slept very well," he says, not asking but giving me an opening to share if I want.

"I didn't eat before bed. I was just restless all night." I shrug it off.

"I will bring you some breakfast then," he states.

I breathe slowly, deciding. "That would be lovely."

A brilliant smile blooms on his face. "See you soon, Veronica."

I pull my damp hair back into a sleek bun as I descend the stairs wearing a simple black blouse and pencil skirt, having spent all my time layering what feels like pounds of makeup on my face. Large silver teardrop earrings sway as I move, the glitter and multiple tiny, colorful flowers in the clear resin reflecting the few rays of the early morning sun peeking through the clouds. With a huff of weariness, I plop onto a small sofa by the coffee table nearest the door, and not two seconds later, butterflies flutter to a frenzy in my belly.

A cool breeze ushers Charlie through the door, and I'm in his arms before he has a chance to put down the bags of food he has in his left hand. With his right arm still locked around me, he maneuvers us backward and places the food on the coffee table. He puts his other arm around my waist, loosening his hold just enough to lean back and look at me. He raises his eyebrows slightly and cocks his head to the side. I shake my head once.

I definitely don't want to talk about it.

We kiss for a long time, slow and chaste, until my rumbling stomach finally separates us. We eat in companionable silence for a few minutes, drop scones and sausage rolls, which are delicious.

Charlie lounges, an arm slung across the back of the chair, a foot propped on a knee. He's dressed for work in a perfectly tailored black suit over a crisp, white dress shirt, the top two buttons undone, showing just a hint of his sculpted chest. Casually draped over the chair like that, impeccably dressed, groomed, and confident in his place in this world, in his right to take up space, he exudes casual confidence and quiet sexuality. There's also a hint of that danger lurking in the corner of his eyes that silently offers a warning: fuck around and find out.

"How was your first day with the new client," I ask.

He scoffs. "It was tedious. The man is young, arrogant, and a fucking imbecile. He has no business sense whatsoever, having never worked a day in his life. His grandfather passed away, leaving the bloody dolt his entire fortune. He is going to lose it all if he gets his way." He waves it off, asking me, "Did you enjoy your day off?"

"Yes, I did. Very much. Come see." We clean up, and I lead him to the workroom. I punch in my code on the keypad, turning on all the lights as we enter. Rain clouds build in the sky, threatening a miserably wet and cold day ahead. He stands in front of the worktable, feet set firmly in a wide stance, an elbow propped on the arm crossed over his chest, his chin propped on a fist.

"This is incredible, Veronica. Truly incredible." He turns, adoration shining in his eyes. "My flat is going to become a private Veronica—" he pauses, eyebrows raised.

"Just Veronica," I answer.

"A private Veronica showroom if you keep creating pieces like this," he declares, waving a hand in front of him. "Consider it sold. I will negotiate the price with the twins later this week." My heart swells a little, both for his support of my career and because he doesn't push; he simply accepts what I'm willing to give. I decided not to change my name after *the event*. I don't want to lose that part of *him*, too. And 'Gorski' is uncommon enough to garner lots of questions. Questions that I do not want to answer.

Charlie holds out his hand, asking, "Are you back?" I place my hand in his and nod. "Well, my darling, I must be off. Thankfully, I do not have to deal with that pompous little prick in person today."

I turn, and he pulls me into his arms. "Try to have a good day," I say, shrugging my shoulders up. He dismisses his client with a sardonic smile.

"So, about last night," he says, changing the subject. I furrow my eyebrows at him. "We did not. . . use a condom," he offers, eyes darting around the room and body tense. It takes all my focus to keep my face serious, delighting in those rare moments when Charlie is unsettled.

"No, we didn't."

He narrows his eyes at me. "Well, I wanted to apologize and say we should always use one." I nod and pretend to consider his words. His fingers fidget on my waist, and I smirk at him.

"What," he demands.

"You are just so fucking adorable when you're flustered. I'm trying to draw it out as long as I can." He spins us around and traps me between him and the table.

"You little—" he accuses, trailing off and shaking his head.

"I accept your apology, although it isn't exactly necessary since we didn't discuss it beforehand. Also, we don't technically have to use them. I've had a hysterectomy. I would prefer, however, that we share doctor's notes that we're both clean. I have one from a few months ago."

"That is a lot to digest, but okay and okay. A few months ago," he asks, scrunching his nose, "I thought you said it had been over a year since your last partner?"

"Yeah, it has. But I was in for a yearly check-up anyway, so I had that checked too."

"Well, then. I will go in as soon as I can to get checked," he replies nonchalantly.

"Uh-huh."

"What," he replies innocently.

"When was the last time you were with someone else," I ask sweetly. He stares down at me, nostrils flaring.

"Do you truly want to know the answer to that?" he purrs.

I clear my throat and push against his chest. "Ah, nope. Got me there. I really don't."

"That's what I thought." He pulls away, a smug smile plastered on his face.

"Did I ever tell you about that time I hooked up with that—" His eyes narrow again, and he stops me with his lips on mine. When he finally breaks the kiss, I smile smugly. "And *that's* what I thought."

"I wish I did not have to get to work so I could remind you who is the only man ever allowed in your bed again, but fuck, I do," he growls, gripping my hips. I playfully swat his hands away and shoo him toward the door.

"Yeah, if you want to get to work on time, you need to quit that shit right now, or it's not gonna happen."

Unperturbed, he saunters a few steps, then turns abruptly.

"One more thing. A few of my friends are meeting for drinks Saturday night at the pub to watch the football game. Do you mind if we meet up with them after dinner? I would like them to meet you."

I purse my lips, contemplating. I want to keep us in our safe little bubble, but that's not feasible long-term. "Sure, why not?"

He drops a sweet kiss on my forehead, smiles, and moves his lips to my mouth, lingering until we're both a bit breathless. "I will see you soon, Veronica."

Slow clapping sounds from the door behind us, and we freeze, arms still loosely wrapped around each other. A slow burn crawls up my neck, and a lazy, arrogant smirk spreads across Charlie's face as we turn together toward the sound.

"It's about time," Kali mock whispers to her brother out of the side of her mouth.

Kellan nods, looking us up and down before he answers. "Look at her positively glowing, Kal."

Don't say it. Don't say it. Don't fucking say it.

"Mmm-hmm. You know what that means, Kel?" I shoot them both warning glares that are promptly ignored.

"She finally sampled the wares."

"Bloody smashing."

"Smashed him, more like."

Charlie vibrates with suppressed mirth, and I bury my face into him, hiding a smirk.

"And that's our cue. Yours to leave," I say, ushering Charlie toward the door. "And yours to kindly shut the fuck up," I singsong as we pass the twins. Kellan stops Charlie to shake his hand, and Kali gives me a sly pat on the ass, and I feel like my face is going to combust. Charlie manages to kiss me again before I kindly but insistently shove him out the door and turn on the twins.

Sour twins today because of that little stunt. Shitheads.

"You two are insufferable," I chide half-heartedly.

"Come now, darling. You have nothing to hide or be ashamed of," Kellan insists.

He's right, V. What happened isn't your fault. You are allowed to be happy with Charlie.

But, telling myself this and believing it are two very different things.

"So," Kali purrs, dropping gracefully onto the small sofa and patting the seat next to her, "how was it–taking the magic bus to Manchester–with Mr. Adonis himself?"

I open my mouth to dismiss their curiosity and scold their teasing but drop onto the sofa, resigned. Their good-natured teasing only bothers me so much because I feel guilty and ashamed and like I'm breaking a promise that, due to circumstances outside of my control, can no longer be kept anyway.

So, I take a deep breath, give them a sly smile, and, in my best imitation of Kellan (which is fucking awful), reply, "It was fabulous, darling. He is a bloody voracious lover." Before either of them has the chance to reign in their surprise, I jump off the sofa and saunter to the workroom, exaggerating the swing of my hips. Kellan's barking laugh and Kali's throaty giggle echo behind me as I slam the door and get to work.

You Are Mine

Saturday night, after a delicious meal at a local seafood place, we glide through a sea of red. Most are sporting red and white Arsenal jerseys, but there's a splash of Manchester United red and yellow sprinkled in as well. We meander around tables and groups of patrons to the back of the pub where Charlie's friends longue in a large corner booth.

As we approach, I wipe my clammy hands on my jeans and take a few calming breaths. Halfway there, Arsenal scores a goal. The bar erupts into a deafening roar. Stools get knocked over, and beer gets spilled as spectators celebrate. I step directly behind Charlie to avoid an especially rowdy group of guys. But, as I move to pass them, a hand clamps around my arm in a bruising grip. The man's eyes rove over me as he yells to his buddies, slurring drunkenly, "Look here, mates. I've caught a pretty little thing to keep us company for the night. Isn't that right, pet?"

"Not a fucking chance in hell," I sneer, attempting futilely to break his hold on my arm. Charlie's fist flies past my chest and slams squarely into the man's flabby gut. He grunts and doubles over, releasing me to clutch at his stomach. Charlie yanks the man's head up by his hair, then squats until he's only inches from the man's face.

In a low, menacing voice, he says, "She is not a pet, you sick fuck. And she is no one's *pretty little thing*. She is a woman, a fucking human being, who deserves to be treated with respect." He pauses, gesturing behind with his free hand to where I'm standing, then continues. "Your eyesight must be shite, mate, because she is clearly fucking gorgeous.

And here is the kicker, *pet:* she is mine. And nobody—nobody, touches her without her consent." Charlie stands, pulling the man up by his hair.

"Since you are not worth my time, I am going to go easy on you tonight, but if I ever catch you or any of your fellow *pets* over there treating another woman like that ever again . . . Well, let us just agree that it will not be enjoyable . . . for you. Me, on the other hand, I will thoroughly fucking enjoy teaching you a lesson."

Charlie stares into the man's face for one long second before releasing him. Then he straightened the last fraction to his full impressive height and adjusted his coat, making eye contact with each man before turning to me and offering me his arm. My heart thunders in my chest, the blood pumping through my veins thrilling, yearning toward that violent, protective energy I feel coursing through him. He plows forcefully through the throng of people. If he detects the way my body sings to him, he doesn't show it.

As we near the table, a woman's voice calls Charlie's name, and I feel him stiffen and mutter, "Fuck," under his breath. Delicate hands with fingernails painted blood red snake around his neck, pulling him into an embrace, and ice blue eyes meet mine over his shoulder. She purses her lips and glares at me as Charlie uses his free hand to disengage himself.

With a wink, he pulls out the chair at the end of the table for me and slides in next to a man named Theo, whom I vaguely remember meeting at the studio. Theo's handshake is firm, his brown eyes warm. As he summarizes the first few minutes of the game for Charlie, I scan the rest of the faces in their group. The two men sitting on my left and another woman sitting at the other end of the table next to Jessica all nod in greeting. I nod in return. Jessica glares daggers at me, and I stare blandly back at her.

A squat, older gentleman stops to take our drink order. The others order another round of pints, adding one for Charlie, and the waiter merely raises his eyebrows when I decline one myself, opting for sparkling water instead.

"Hey, Ronnie," Jessica calls out over the noise of the pub. She emphasizes my unconventional name, elongating the soft vowel in the first syllable and cutting off the second in a staccato sneer. I exhale quickly through my nose and look at her, eyebrows raised. "Have a pint with us," she taunts, barely concealing her malice.

I feel Charlie inhale to answer, but I stop him with a hand on his arm. "No. I'm good."

The man sitting across from her chimes in. "Come on, love. Have a pint." Charlie's arm goes rigid under my hand at the man's casual use of the endearment, and his face blanches at the dark look Charlie gives him.

I kindly, but firmly repeat myself. Jessica redirects the attention back to her, crossing her arms on the table and leaning into them to accentuate her ample cleavage. "Afraid you can't keep up with us Brits?" she asks, her contempt poorly disguised by a playful smile.

"I don't drink. Oh, look," I point to the TV, "Ronaldo just scored. Manchester tied it up!" It's a sufficient distraction for a table of Arsenal fans. Alcohol reminds me of shattered glass and scattered limbs. I shudder and take a deep breath to steady myself. Charlie leans in and murmurs in my ear.

"Are you okay? We can leave whenever you are ready."

You can handle one little vindictive hussy, V.

I assure him that I'm fine. He kisses me and replies, "Yes, you are," against my mouth.

With a private smile on my face, I look up and straight into Jessica's ice-blue glare. Without breaking eye contact, I pull Charlie's arm around my shoulders and snuggle into him, placing my hand on his sculpted chest, smirking at the little cunt. Understanding the gesture for what it is, Charlie chuckles and drops a kiss on my temple, a cocky grin on his handsome face.

Theo, Charlie, and I carry on a three-way conversation, the two men getting louder and more animated as the liquid in their pints disappears. I block out the game in the background as much as I can. I knew it would drum up painful memories, but I came prepared to deal with them. Theo is boisterous and laughs easily, an infectious laugh that has us all rolling more than once. Charlie is more relaxed around him and less controlled than normal. Theo's one of those people that just brings out the fun in everyone. Everyone except Jessica, who still has a stick up her ass.

Let her be jealous and petty, V. Charlie chose you.

When the whistle blows for half-time and commercials pop onto the screen, Charlie and Theo get up to use the loo. Jessica immediately jumps up to 'do the same,' eyeing me coyly as she hurries to catch up with them. She runs her hand up Charlie's arm and leans into him. He does a silly spin move around Theo, placing him between them and eliciting a loud guffaw from Theo. I make a face, a little sad for her. She should do herself a favor and move on. There is a natural lull in conversation then, and her behavior makes it awkward for all of us. I pull out my phone and check my email to prevent any more awkward interactions.

The other three people in Theo's group speak in low tones, trying to sneak surreptitious glances at me. Jessica's friend giggles at the end of the table, covering her face and looking over her shoulder. One of the men flashes me a contemptuous glance, and then they all promptly ignore me, talking quietly amongst themselves. I hear phrases like 'can't believe he'd—' and '—not his type,' and the woman forgets to be quiet when she says, "Bloody Yank isn't even pretty. I don't know what he sees in her over Jessica."

Caught off guard by their contempt, shame, hot and cruel, crawls up my face. I turn away, pretending to rummage through my bag. Tiny Mildred pipes up, eagerly reminding me that they're right. There are so many reasons why I am so wrong for Charlie, chief among them being that I am too old for him. Fuck, I'm not equipped to deal with this petty drama. I spend most of my time fighting my own demons; I can't handle the added weight of deflecting other people's shitty opinions. But, I haven't gone to countless hours of therapy and life coaching and done so much work on myself to let these strangers get inside my head.

So, I focus on my breath and methodically strengthen the barriers in my mind, forcefully shoving back the shame and pushing out the opinions of people who don't matter. I read a text from Sophie and block out their conversation as best as possible while waiting for Charlie to return.

I am chuckling to myself as I read an account from Sophie about their new puppy when he returns, plopping down in the chair next to me. I type a quick reply, drop my phone into my bag, and look up into frigid ice-blue shallows. I recoil slightly, expecting warm, intense green depths, and raise my eyebrows. Jessica turns a friendly smile on Theo, who has also returned, asking him to grab her pint. She sips on it companionably and pretends to watch the game.

Where the hell is Charlie?

I scan the room until I see the familiar sweep of his dark, wavy hair above the throng of people. He's standing by the bar, talking to a couple of middle-aged men in rumpled business suits.

"You're not welcome here," Jessica says quietly.

"Excuse me," I hiss.

"You heard me. You need to leave," she replies.

"No. I'm not leaving until Charlie is ready."

"That's not what I mean. You need to leave Charlie alone. Go back to America. You. Are. Not. Welcome. Here." She punctuates each word, savagely driving home her meaning.

"No, I'm good right where I am. I am not going anywhere." I emphasize the last word but stand to find Charlie, grabbing my bag as her hand clamps around my wrist. Theo notices and quietly hisses,

"Jess! Let go of her, or Charlie is going to wallop us both."

I may have told her I'm not going anywhere, but that itch to run slithers up my spine. All the horrible misgivings I have been silently fighting break free and crash through my mind, threatening to drown me. What the fuck am I doing here? I don't belong in London. I don't deserve a successful career without *him*. And I certainly don't deserve to be happy with Charlie. Pressure builds behind my eyes, and panic creeps up, threatening to take over.

I stare her down for a second, then yank my hand from her grasp. Charlie is no longer by the bar, but I don't care. I don't waste time trying to find him as I beeline for the door. Unlike when we entered the pub, I am the ship parting the waters, cutting a straight path through the sea of red. Maybe I can't handle one vindictive little hussy after all.

IS Ivy. I really fucking hate you and your penchant for popping up at the most inopportune moments.

The cool night air calms my flushed face as I walk to the corner of the street, breathing deeply while trying to find my bearings. The walk arrow flashes white, and I cross anonymously with a group of pedestrians. I slip into a coffee shop and sit at a small table next to the window, foot tapping a fast beat while I wait for an Uber. I should just call Charlie, but Jessica and the others laid bare all my insecurities.

Do I belong here in the UK?

Who am I to have a successful business in a foreign country?

Should I let Charlie go to live a normal life?

After a short drive, the Uber pulls up from my studio on the opposite side of the street. I tip the driver and get out, pausing in the middle of the street when I see Charlie's Audi parked in front of the studio, not sure of how he will react to my abrupt departure. He gets out of the car, walks around the front, and leans against it, arms folded across his chest. I hold my breath while he stares at me for a few seconds. He sighs and opens his arms. I walk into them and rest my head on his chest. We stand there embracing, neither sure of the other, for a long time before Charlie pulls back. He waits for me to look at him before he speaks, his green eyes soft and comforting.

"Will you come back to my flat with me, or do you need to be alone?" He's always so considerate. I don't answer. I reach for the door he's leaning against and open it. The lights of downtown London whiz by in a blur, the whir of the engine loud in the silence between us. Frustrating thoughts, annoyance, irritation, and fear swirl around in my brain—as if I don't live with enough fear already.

Why did you let that bitch get under your skin so easily, V?

Frustrated with the constant stream of 'you're not good enoughs' flowing through my head, I bang it back against the seat and sigh forcefully through my nose. Charlie eyes me warily, eyes darting between me and the road. I can tell he wants to say something but is holding back. Fuck, now he's probably mad at me too. Sweat dampens my armpits and my heart starts pounding. I focus on keeping my face blank to avoid setting him off.

Take a breath, V. He's not the type to get physical with you. Removing yourself from bad situations is okay. It's not running; it's self-preservation.

I shift in my seat and reach to place my hand on his arm but let it fall back in my lap instead. He grips the steering wheel so tightly that his white knuckles stand out stark against the black of the night. His set jaw and flared nostrils are illuminated by the dash lights. My thoughts are still running circles around each other, and I'm on the verge of a panic attack when we pull into the parking garage. He jumps out and quickly makes his way around the car to open my door, offering his hand. I let out a sigh of relief. He must not be that upset with me.

I find the floor's wood grain in the mirrored lift fascinating as it slowly ascends all fifteen floors. I briefly consider punching the 'close door' button and fleeing home after Charlie steps off, but that won't solve anything. He walks briskly to the kitchen and puts the kettle on for tea, then grabs a bottle of scotch off the shelf, pours a finger's width into a glass, stares at it for a moment, then pours it down the drain.

"Does it bother you when I drink?" he asks, back still towards me, shoulders hunched over his large hands which are splayed out on the counter.

"No," the silence hangs heavy between us as I wait for him to face me. He inhales deeply, shoulders rising to meet his ears, then exhales forcefully. He turns and leans against the counter, one foot crossed over the other, arms crossed over his chest; the casual confidence oozing off him is mixed with a hint of danger. His intensity is palpable. His control of himself is absolute. At this moment, I realized he would never unleash his anger toward me, but to protect me, he would destroy anything and everything in his path.

I hope he didn't freak out on Theo, but Jessica can go to hell.

"I don't mind. If you got shit-faced all the time or were a mean drunk, then I would care." I cross the kitchen and place my hand gently on his face. "Alcohol played a role in the destruction of my life," I add in response to the question he's too tactful to ask. His arms slide around my waist, and his forehead drops to mine.

He wets his lips with just the tip of his tongue. "I am so fucking furious with them. I told Theo no more Jess, but he fancies her friend, the brunette," he raises his eyebrows and shakes his head. I nod. "He fancies her, and they're good mates." He shrugs his shoulders. "What did she say to you?" he asks, the words laced with steel.

I pull back slightly, needing to see the warmth and surety in his green eyes. "She told me to leave you and go back to America."

"That fucking b—" He must see the effect of her words on my face, which he now cups delicately with both hands. "She is petty and jealous. You belong here, Veronica. Here in London. Here, enjoying massive success with your career. And here with me." A small sob bubbles out of me, and his lips crash against mine. We're clinging to each other, hands and mouths proclaiming possession and offering surrender, each touch shouting, 'I am yours; you are mine.'

I rip his shirt over his head as he flings my jacket aside. Our mouths meet again, greedy in our need for one another. He lifts me off the floor, and I wrap my legs around his waist. He carries me across the kitchen and sets me down on the island counter. He removes my shirt and bra in one motion, tossing them over his head to join the rest of our clothes on the kitchen floor. His mouth is hot and demanding on my breasts, sucking and biting my nipples so deliciously that my back arches off the counter. I want to scream his name and stake out my claim on him, but I remain silent; only small whimpers escape my tightly pressed lips. I am afraid of what I might say; whose name I might utter in these moments of surrender and wanton abandon.

Charlie slides his hands up my thighs, and I raise my hips off the counter, giving him just enough room to rip them off. He pushes me onto my back and buries his face between my legs. His rhythm starts slow and light, methodically building as I start to tremble, more uninhibited moans escaping my lips. He slides his left hand up my torso to grip a nipple while he slides his right hand down, inserting two fingers inside me, almost instantly pushing me over the edge. I cry out then, unable to hold back my release any longer.

"Charlie. . . Charlie. . . Charlie."

I'm still floating in the clouds, breath coming in gasps, when my feet hit the floor. I emit a small shriek and tense slightly when my breasts meet the cold countertop, but I relax and stretch my arms above my head, back arching as Charlie penetrates deep inside me. He is not afraid to stake his claim on me, entering me forcefully over and over again, pulling all the way out, and then slamming back into the hilt. My body surrenders to him completely—though a few scattered pieces of my heart refuse to budge—rocking my hips back to meet his every thrust. Urging him deeper, silently answering his demand. . . *You are mine. . . yes, I am yours.*

After he is spent and satisfied, he gathers me tenderly in his arms and carries me into the en suite. He sets me down gently on the ledge next to the jacuzzi tub and fires up the jets. My limbs, jelly only moments ago, are now stiff, muscles tight from despair, need, adrenaline, and exertion. I try to lower myself into the tub, but my body is completely drained. Already in the water, Charlie notices my struggle and plucks me off the ledge like I weigh no more than a feather. Concern, and maybe shame, cloud his eyes.

"Was I too rough, my love?" he asks gruffly, fierce desire and anxious tenderness warring inside him. I look at him, and he easily reads the feelings that are laid bare on my face. I place my hand on his heated cheek to reassure him.

"No, I needed that, wanted that. The reassurance and conviction that I belong here. In London. With you."

Not There Yet

Waterfalls . . . pressure . . . noisy rivers . . . pressure . . . floating down noisy rivers towards waterfalls . . . Rocks dropping on my stomach as I float past tall cliffs . . . warm water swirling around my legs . . .

My eyes fly open, and I sprint to the bathroom, thankful that I don't have to remove any clothes before I relieve myself. My shoulder pops, and a spot in my back catches as I twist to clean myself. Every muscle in my buttocks and legs protest as I rise from the toilet. I move slowly in the dark gray of pre-dawn and do a double take as my brain processes the number on the clock.

Five am already, eh V. The first two rounds last night weren't enough to satisfy you? You just had to have another.

When the sex is that good, yeah. Charlie and I are both generally early risers, but his breathing is still deep and even, so I climb back into the warm oasis and curl up behind him, resting my cheek against his back and wrapping an arm around his waist.

A few hours later, the soft light of the late fall morning gently caresses my face, and the smells and sounds of breakfast being prepared waft in from the kitchen, waking me. I stretch my arms, reaching for the ceiling, and yawn, a huge, groaning yawn. I seriously debate going back to sleep until loud rumbles gurgle from my belly. Goosebumps ripple across my flesh as I sit in the cool morning air. Maybe if I burrow back into the covers, Charlie will serve me breakfast in bed. My chest tightens at the thought of him. I'm not sure if we reconciled everything last night. He may still be upset with me for running.

He's not Kyle, V. Just go talk to him. Trust that he's the man he's shown you over the past few weeks.

I throw off the comforter and swing my legs over the side of the bed before the warm, cozy oasis lures me back in. The white oak hardwood floor is cold on my feet as I tiptoe around Charlie's room, looking for something warm to put on. I catch a glimpse of myself in the tall mirror that takes up a large portion of the wall opposite the bed. There are deep purple bruises on my hips and shoulder blades and a delicate love bite on my right upper trapezius. After thoroughly considering my reflection, I spot clothes nicely laid out over the armchair in the corner of the room next to the bed. How thoughtful of him.

I slip into the kitchen, easing onto a stool, then grab a steaming cup of peppermint tea with honey and survey the spread on the counter.

"Are we expecting company for breakfast?" He's made enough food to feed us for a week. He chuckles and places another heaping dish on the counter.

"No. I am meal prepping," he says primly.

I raise my eyebrows and smirk, one side of my mouth curling up. "Meal prepping?"

"Yes. You know. You cook a bunch of food at once and—"

I snicker and cut him off. "I know what meal prepping is. But this," I wave my arm, gesturing in front of me, "is going a little overboard, don't you think? It will take you forever to eat all of it." He looks at me pointedly while sipping his black coffee.

"I am not going to eat it all by myself. We are going to eat it together. This weekend."

I shake my head skeptically, and we fill our plates. There's a lull in conversation as we both enjoy the meal. Charlie is a very good cook; *he*, on the other hand, was not. I inhale, rolling the thought back and forth in my mind like you would roll a leaf between your fingers, then sigh, freeing the thought to gently float away like a leaf on a breeze. We finish our breakfast in companionable silence, content to simply sit with each other, neither ready to acknowledge the unresolved tension suspended between us.

I set down my fork and tuck a foot under my thigh. Wrapping my arms loosely around my leg, I inhale.

"Are you angry with me?" He looks at me sharply, confusion clouding his eyes. "For bolting last night," I clarify.

He takes a few measured breaths, wetting his lips with just the tip of his tongue, and runs a hand through his hair. "I wasn't angry, just confused, until I saw the smug expression on Jessica's face, and Theo started apologizing. Mostly, I was relieved to catch you at the studio. And then even more relieved when you got in the car and did not leave the moment I stepped off the lift."

Guilt quickly flashes in my eyes, and I grimace. "Yes, I saw the thought on your face, and I could have cursed myself for ever letting go of your hand."

"I'm sorry," I say, guilt floating heavy in my chest.

"I appreciate it, but you do not have to apologize. You did not necessarily do anything wrong. You merely removed yourself from a shite situation." He's right. I didn't ghost him, and I would have called to explain my behavior sooner than later. I have every right to protect myself.

"The boy I dated fresh out of high school . . . Let's just say it ended badly. I tried a few times to set boundaries or 'remove myself from shite situations,'" I say in an atrocious British accent garnering a chuckle from Charlie. "My 'running' made him furious." Charlie reaches across the table and grips my fingers.

"When you need space, when you feel that urge to run, tell me, and I will either open the door and cheer you on your way or run with you."

"I can't make any promises, but I'll do my best to give you a heads up," I say wryly. Charlie gives me a lopsided grin.

"This guy sounds like a real piece of work," he says, eyebrows raised, silently offering to listen if I want to talk about it. I don't. I slam down hard on the torrent of memories trying to surface, and surreptitiously wipe my clammy palms on my sweats.

Breathe, V. Kyle can't hurt you anymore.

Charlie's thumb, drawing rhythmic circles on the back of my hand, pulls me back to the present.

"Are you back," he inquires gently. I nod, and he considers me for a moment before saying, "I am sorry if I pushed you to meet my friends too soon or pressured you to come home with me last night."

"No, no, Charlie. One of the things I love most about you is that you never push. I always feel like I have the space and the respect I need from you." I assure him.

That brilliant smile I love so much crosses his face, a hint of smugness creasing his eyes. I cock my head to the side and narrow my eyes. "We should fight more often. That is the second time you have said that word within twelve hours."

I purse my lips, tapping a finger against them. "What word," I question, feigning ignorance.

He jumps up from the stool and breaks into song, doing his best impression of Frank Sinatra's *L-O-V-E*. He's surprisingly good, his singing voice just as deep and smooth as his speaking voice. I giggle and playfully push him away when he pulls me into his arms and spins me into the sitting room as he belts the lyrics.

Mostly to prevent further ruminations about 'love,' but also because I've been dying to try it out, I prance up the stairs and plop onto the piano bench. My skills aren't as rusty as they used to be. I found a keyboard at a charity shop after I decided to stay in London. It was in great condition, so I bought it along with a stack of music books, and I've been playing most days. I hadn't played since I was a kid, so it's a hobby I can enjoy without having to fight off a deluge of painful memories. I run through a few scales to get familiar with the piano, then start fingering the melody to accompany Charlie.

Ironically enough, a book of love songs was in the stack of music books. I meant to throw it away, but, bored of playing the same tunes on repeat, I tried a few of the least familiar songs and found that learning them was more therapeutic than painful. Since I started playing again, music hasn't been as big of a trigger as it used to be. My therapist approves, claiming music is a powerful healing tool.

After a few practice runs, I start the song again, and Charlie joins in, holding a fake microphone and leaning on the piano, tilting his imaginary trilby hat and winking at me every single time he sings 'love.' After he belts out the song's last line, he pulls me off the piano bench into a twirl and dip, then slowly guides me back up, chest to chest. We are both breathing hard and laughing. His eyes twinkle from merriment as he leans down to kiss me. When he pulls back, I raise my eyebrows. He merely smiles and winks.

"We are not there yet, my love. We never have to be there either." He shrugs one shoulder lazily. "That does not mean I do not enjoy hearing you slip up and say it occasionally though. Will you play me another tune?"

We spent the rest of the morning playing and singing, dancing and laughing, and munching on all the food he made for breakfast. After a long, hot, steamy, and glorious shower together, we decide to enjoy the unseasonably warm fall day and hit up Piccadilly Circus once more before the cold weather sets in for good.

"Shall we take an Uber, darling?" Charlie calls from the sitting room as I finish getting dressed. "Or are you ready to learn how to drive on the *correct* side of the road?"

"Hilarious," I deadpan. "Get an Uber. Why aren't you driving though?"

"Well, if you are up for it, I booked us a reservation at Cicchetti, then I have a little surprise planned for after dinner."

"That sounds wonderful. Does Cicchetti have a dress code?" He pops his head around the door into the bedroom, "You look beautiful just the way you are. We will grab appropriate attire for the evening at one of the shops down in the circus." He grabs my coat off the rack, helps me into it, and then offers his arm, "Milady."

Uber, My Ass

"Charlie, what could we possibly be doing after dinner to need such fancy attire?" I ask again, gesturing at my Castleton green, beaded, and sparkling evening dress, which beautifully complements the auburn tones in my hair. He just smiles and rakes his eyes up and down my body. He leans forward, speaking quietly, a mischievous look in his intense, deep green eyes.

"Well, it will most definitely require hiking that gorgeous dress up around your hips, and . . ." He raises his eyebrows, and I bite my bottom lip coyly in answer. I feel beautiful and fancy and ridiculously lavish all at once. The dress fits like a second skin, with a hip-bone high slit baring my leg when I walk and a deep plunging neckline that tastefully accentuates my average cleavage, which feels like it's pushed up into my chin thanks to the ultra-padded push-up bra the lady at the lingerie store sided with Charlie on me wearing.

I've never participated in spending so much money in one afternoon on completely unnecessary shit like I did today. And Charlie insisted on paying for all of it. At first, I was very uncomfortable. My mom never gave simply out of the goodness of her heart. There were always strings attached, always ulterior motives—the need for control—and always a score being kept, a game being played, and I never understood the rules. But once I accepted that he did it because he genuinely wanted to do something nice for me, I thoroughly enjoyed being pampered by him.

Charlie also insisted—he's not so much a stubborn man as a man who knows what he wants and settles for nothing less—on having my hair and makeup done professionally. While the cosmetologist, Emily, skillfully painted my face and piled my curled hair up in a beautiful coronet, and a masseuse rubbed my hands and feet with calming lavender and frankincense oils, Charlie disappeared. I was too relaxed by the afternoon's attentions to care where he went.

After Emily was satisfied with my hair and makeup, she helped me into my dress. She was a kind, funny, and warm older woman who had aged gracefully. After she helped me with the clasps on my sparkly, 4-inch gold pumps, she spun me around to look in the floor-length mirror.

'You look stunning, my dear,' she said, pride dancing in her eyes as she stood on her tiptoes, peering over my shoulder. The comment brought unexpected tears to my eyes. How many times had I longed for that kind of recognition and kindness from my own mother?

Hold it together, V. Don't you dare ruin Emily's hard work crying over Mildred.

As I dabbed gingerly at a stray tear, careful not to mess up Emily's handiwork, I heard the bell over the front door chime and a collective gasp from the women up front. I grabbed my coat and clutch, knowing without a doubt it was Charlie who had just entered. He stood by the front window, magnificent in a perfectly tailored black pinstripe suit. His hair was gelled in a sweep over his brow, and he sported just the beginnings of a 5 o'clock shadow.

The breath was knocked out of me when he turned and looked at me full in the face. The intensity radiating from his fathomless green eyes was thick enough to cut with a knife. He crossed the room in three powerful strides and pulled me into his arms. I had never felt as loved or beautiful as I did then. *He* had loved me too, very, very much. But it was a much different kind of love, calm and sure and safe. It was passionate, too, but not this fierce or intense.

The waiter, a shorter, thickly built, handsome young man dressed in a crisp white button-up shirt, pressed black slacks, and a long, clean black apron, runs Charlie's card right at the table with a portable card reader while wishing us a nice evening. Charlie stands, adjusting his gold cufflinks, drawing the attention of almost everyone in the room, especially the women. He is truly a sight to behold, all sculpted lines and strong angles. He holds open my coat and offers me his arm, a gleam of excitement in his eyes. I make bold, direct eye contact with as many women ogling Charlie as I can on our way out.

"Okay, Mr. Wright. Where are we going?"

"Patience, love," he replies as he opens the door of a black, chromed-out limousine. *Uber, my ass.*

The inside of the limo is simple yet elegant. There are two bench seats of polished black leather, one up against the closed divider between us and the driver and one along the far side. A mini-bar, complete with a variety of liquors in crystal decanters and an array of delicacies, lines the side by the door. Warm, yellow lights glow from under and behind every surface, creating a calming, inviting atmosphere.

"Nice Uber," I snort, rolling my eyes. He smirks, draping his arm on the bench behind me. I scoot closer to him and whisper in his ear, "Is this the part where you hike my dress up around my hips?"

His pupils dilate with a feral possessiveness. He places his free hand on my exposed leg and slowly runs it up to the hem of the slit. He places a quick, delicate kiss on my lips, murmuring, "No, not yet." I stick out my bottom lip and pretend to pout as the limo comes to a stop. He exits quickly, buttoning his suit coat, and offers his hand. I look up at the huge, neon-red marquis advertising *Moulin Rouge!,* situated over stone arches. My face lights up with aww, and a brilliant grin blooms on Charlie's face.

"You brought me to the theater?" I turn toward him, opening the curtain on my glass face. "This is wonderful, Charlie! Thank you."

"The pleasure is all mine, my love," he replies, emphasizing pleasure with sweet promise.

"Does that mean we're taking the fancy Uber home?"

He leans to whisper in my ear, warm breath sending shivers down my spine. "Yes, my dear. And we are taking the long way home, too."

The theater is grand, boasting three levels of seating, and magnificently decorated in reds and golds. A steward shows us to our seats, floor level about mid-way up, the perfect seats with the best view of the stage. I look around in awe as the seats fill, anticipation for both the play and our private encore making me fidgety. A few minutes before the curtain, I noticed that the seats directly in front of us for a few rows were empty, and I commented about it to Charlie.

"I bought those seats to make sure your view of the stage would not be obstructed."

"What? Charlie! That is so thoughtful, thank you. But you shouldn't have. There are eight people out there right now who wish they could be at this show tonight."

"Do not fret, darling." He pauses, a genuinely content smile on his face. He makes a circular gesture towards the empty seats and ours. "I also paid for these same seats for tomorrow night's show. I will post in the Piccadilly Theatre Facebook group tomorrow, and whoever claims them first gets to enjoy the show on me." Another tiny, scattered piece of my heart leaps back into place, and my chest swells with adoration for Charlie and his depthless generosity. Smiling broadly, I grasp his hand, holding back tears of joy.

From the moment the lights dim and the lush, red, and gold curtains open, I am captivated. I ooh and ah, clap and laugh enthusiastically, and I catch Charlie watching me instead of the play more often than not. Christian's despair when Satine dies punches me in the chest and rattles my heart, re-scattering a few of the newly repaired pieces. I clutch my chest, hyperventilating, and tears stream down my face.

Will his *loss ever stop hurting so fucking much?*

Charlie gently dries my face with a handkerchief and holds my hand. His steady reassurance helps calm me, and I am composed when the actors take their final bow and the lights come up.

"Are you back?" Charlie asks as we wait to exit our row. I cup his cheek tenderly in answer.

"Today was simply amazing, Charlie. Thank you."

He dips his head and guides me into the aisle in front of him, hand on my waist. We meander through the crowd, in no rush to leave, simply content to fully enjoy the experience. However, when we finally make our way outside and up the street to the limo, we barely make it inside before he claims me with his lips and hands.

With an outstretched hand, Charlie feels his way back to the cool leather seat with lips still locked on mine. I straddle him and quickly unbutton his shirt while he slides the straps of my dress down my arms to free my breasts. He catches a nipple between his teeth, nibbling firmly. I emit a breathy moan and arch my back, hips grinding against his erection. I tug his hair, wanting to capture his lips with mine again, but pause at the sight of my bright red lipstick smeared all over his face.

Let's smear the lipstick all over his . . .

He reaches up to pull me in for more, but I stop him with a hand on his chest and wide, demanding eyes. He looks at me quizzically but smirks, oozing arrogance, and sexuality, slinging an arm across the back of the seat, desire evident by his bulging pants. Dropping between his legs, I grab a napkin off the bar behind us, wipe both our faces, and fish my clutch out from under the seat. Without breaking eye contact, I slowly twist up and re-apply the bright red lipstick to my kiss-swollen lips.

With deliberate slowness, I flick open the button on his slacks and pull down the zipper. His erection strains against his white briefs. A hum rumbles in his chest as I grip him over the smooth fabric and begin stroking him. I stare at him boldly, reveling in the power I feel, knowing that I can make him lose himself completely. I rarely get stuck in my head anymore when we're intimate, and it's so fucking freeing.

Charlie moves a hand to his waistband, but I stop him, grabbing his wrist and flinging it to the side. I wave my finger at him and, flashing a devilish grin, I release him. His nostrils flare, and he sucks air through his teeth as I run my hands up and down his thighs. After teasing him a few more times, I curl my fingers into his briefs and free him. Gripping the base firmly, I lick up the underside of his cock and swirl my tongue around the head, then suck it into my mouth. A guttural growl emanates from his chest as I take him deep into the back of my throat. I set an excruciatingly slow pace at first, up and down, up and down, moving steadily faster until he can stand it no longer.

A thrill of heady empowerment courses through me when he shudders and demands, "Come here," lifting me onto his lap. Glistening with desire, I slide onto him slowly, pausing when I've taken every hard inch of him deep inside me, then begin rocking back and forth to rub my sensitive clit against him. He slides a hand between us and stimulates me with his thumb while I ride him fast and hard. His head drops back onto the seat, and I feel his body tense. Before either of us reach that sweet release we're chasing, the limo pulls right up to the bank of lifts, and I huff a sigh of frustration, leaning to move off him.

Charlie grips my hips firmly and continues slamming into me. "Don't fucking stop," he demands. "Rub yourself, Veronica, and get ready to cum with me." Unable to do anything but obey when he uses that commanding tone, I slide my hand between us. It doesn't take long, and we're both shaking and moaning, and he goes rigid inside me while I turn liquid around him, sweet release surging through us both.

Early the next morning, after Charlie drops me off at the studio, I find Kali seated at our favorite table, tucked into the corner of the gallery. She stares out the large window with a wistful expression, two steaming mugs of tea on the table before her. I plop onto the stool, tired and deliciously sore from a late night with Charlie. She doesn't seem to notice, which is completely out of character for her.

Waving my hand in front of her face, I sing her name. She still doesn't acknowledge me, but a private smile tugs up the corners of her mouth, and I study her. She's glowing. I carefully sip my tea, assuming the extra cup is for me, and wait, watching thoughts and emotions play across her usually unreadable face.

Someone had a good weekend.

Long, silent, but not unpleasant minutes pass before she finally notices me. She snaps her delicate, red-tipped fingers to her chest, squeaking out a surprised exclamation.

"Good morning," I tease, arching my brows and giving her an exaggerated wink. She blushes! I can barely detect it, but Kali, stoic, unmoved, unruffled, Kali blushes. I throw my head back and laugh, clapping my hands together loudly enough that the sound echoes through the otherwise empty gallery.

"Well," I drawl. She shakes her luscious goddess braids and looks down her nose at me, the portrait of prim and proper. I snort and continue. "Spill the beans already. Who is . . . she?" I prod. Kali ducks her chin, hiding her face. "Oh, he then? I assumed the gorgeous gallery manager from a few weeks ago, but okay. And I'm not even going to ask how it was because it's written all over your face. Is it serious or getting serious?"

"Jesus, Ronnie," she drawls sarcastically, and I purse my lips, rolling my eyes at her.

"Now you know how I feel every damn day, Kal," I throw back at her. She flicks her hand between us, acceding the point, but presses her lips together in a firm line.

"Oh, I see how it is. I won't quit pestering you until I wear you down and you give me all the details. I will channel my inner sour twin determination. I have a lot of work to do in the office today, so you better just tell me now," I prod shamelessly.

Ha! Give her a little of her own medicine.

"Fine," she relents. I flash her a triumphant smile, thoroughly enjoying being the interrogator for once.

"She, the gallery manager, and I haven't been able to coordinate a time that we're both free, but I'm hopeful."

"So, not serious then?"

She contemplates me for a moment before replying. "Possibly in the very distant future, but for now, no. I don't have the time or the interest in serious. I don't want to be tied down and all mushy and cute like you and Charlie."

"Oh, no, you don't," I admonish, waving my finger at her. "I see what you're trying to do. Don't change the subject. Why are you dancing around the subject of 'who'? Do I know him?"

She takes a long sip of her tea and finally says, "Theo."

I choke on my own steaming tea, sputtering and coughing hard enough that Kali jumps up to give me two hardy thumps on the back. "Theo," I manage to choke out. "As in Charlie's friend Theo. Hmm, for some reason, I didn't peg you as interested in white boys," she guffaws. "And he is, like, super white boy. I'm pretty sure there's room for nothing else in his pretty little head besides beer, women, and sports. Doesn't really seem like your cup of tea, if you will," I offer, gesturing at our mugs.

"He's handsome and fun. And, I don't need anything in his pretty little head. Just need it to function well. And, yes, before you ask, it did, thank you very much."

I offer her a genuine smile, "I'm happy for you, Kal. Even if it's not serious, you're glowing, so it must have been something you needed. I don't know Theo well, but Charlie speaks highly of him. Oh my God, Charlie. Can I mention this to him, or do you prefer to keep it between us?"

"Go ahead. He's probably going to hear about it regardless."

"Dang, girl, did you rock his world that good?"

"You know it," she replies over her shoulder as she waltzes into the office.

Estimated Time of Arrival

B uzz . . . Buzz . . . Buzz

What is that infernal noise?!

My phone, buried under sketches and other art paraphernalia, vibrates my whole desk, shattering the silence I share with the twins in the office. I ignore it, focused intently on the preliminary sketch I'm working on, but the phone starts another round of fucking irritating vibrating. Absentmindedly, I fish it out of its hiding place and swipe blindly. Glancing at the screen without registering whose face looks back, I answer with a terse, "Veronica."

"Veronica, huh?" My best friend's voice snaps me back to reality. "Europe," she drops her voice low, "and Charlie," she playfully emphasizes his name, "have corrupted you! Veronica, psssh." I shrug and make a shooing motion with my hand. In all the years she's known me, Cat has never heard me use my given name.

"Catherine," I chide playfully. "It's still 'Ron' to you, my dear friend. I miss you. How's everyone?"

"We're good, everyone's good. The kids are getting big. It's chaos. You know how it is."

"Yeah, I do," I reply, the sadness in my voice evident no matter how hard I try to hide it. Shoving down the painful memories threatening to bubble up, I ask, "Who's doing what this time of year."

"Jake is taking guitar lessons. Cora is doing gymnastics. Little Lanie just joined some dance classes, and they are all doing basketball."

"Oh, mama. You have got your hands full. How are you doing?"

"I'm good. As much as I grumble about it, you know I love it. I tend to thrive off the chaos. You know how that works for those of us who grew up in chaotic, dysfunctional homes. Oh, and we're also gearing up for Halloween."

"I do, and I do, and I don't envy you there. I thought I dodged the dress-up-and-drown-in-memories bullet being over here, but they do celebrate. It's a bit different, though. They call it 'Guy Fawkes Day,' and they shoot off fireworks at bonfires, burn effigies, and dress up, but only as a select few characters." I shrug one shoulder, furrowing my brows, and continue.

"Charlie wants me to go to a bonfire at his parents' house. But it's like a five-hour drive, and I'd have to take time off work. I don't know if I could handle staying with his family for two nights. I want to use work and the twins as an excuse, but they adore Charlie and he knows it. I need to just tell him no." I let out a huge sigh and scrunch up my nose.

"Ron . . . I see how hard you've been working on yourself. I am proud of you. Charlie seems like a great guy. I'm sure he'll understand. And, maybe, without giving too much away 'cause I know you're not ready to spill the beans just yet, give him a heads up." I raise my eyebrows and tilt my head to the side. Cat purses her lips and nods, the movement exaggerated.

"You're right, you're right. I can already feel the shit storm brewing. Remember two years ago?"

Her smile falls, and she nods. "It snuck up on you."

"And sucker punched me right in the gut. I am prepared this time, though. I have my therapist, life coach, and other things I've been doing. And Charlie's very patient with me, but he'll probably push a wee bit more than I want him to if I randomly disappear with no explanation." Her face is full of love and understanding. We both start to tear up, remembering.

"So, I talked to Soph the other day. Said you're coming home for Christmas? Are you gonna bring that British hunk of yours so we can meet him?" Sniffling, we both chuckle and quickly dry our eyes.

"I want to, but no. I don't want to ask y'all to lie for me."

"Lie for you?" she asks, eyebrows raised.

"Yeah. I don't want to tell him about . . . " I roll my hand in front of me in a 'you know' gesture.

"Oh, sweetie, that's not lying. It's your story to tell, not ours, and we really want to meet him, so we'll keep it under wraps. Promise."

"Thanks, Cat, I'll think about it."

"Will you go to Vic's New Year's party?"

"I don't know yet. We've been texting occasionally. She apologized, and, of course, I forgave her. I understand how hard this is for her. It's been just the two of us since Dad died, and she doesn't have close friends like you and Soph."

"Hence why she always invites us to the New Year's bash—"

"—but makes it clear she doesn't really want you to show up? Yeah, it's jealousy. She's still got a lot of shit to work through. I wish she would get therapy, but she's convinced herself she's above getting help."

"Soph and I will come this year. We'll wear matching shirts that say, 'I go to therapy to deal with people who need to go to therapy but won't.'"

I huff a soft laugh. "The joke would be wasted on her. But I do want to mend things between us, so I'll probably go."

"The kids are ecstatic that you're coming. The girls have already started their shopping lists, and Jake thinks his gag gift from Uncle Turner will be epic this year."

"I am excited to see you all too. Give the kids hugs and kisses from Auntie Ronnie. Kellan's giving me the side eye." I roll my eyes at him and make a saltshaker motion with my hand near my mouth, garnering a dramatic eye roll. "Better get back to work. It was great to hear from you. I love you, dear friend," I say sincerely. In these moments, I am grateful for my glass face.

Catherine was right. Despite his disappointment, he accepted my decision gracefully. The thought of meeting his family terrifies me. When he talks about them, they sound wonderful and . . . normal. *His* family was wonderful and normal, and it felt so good to be accepted by them after being raised by a covert narcissist and an emotionally unavailable pushover.

My dad was amazing and did his best to take care of me and my sisters, but sometimes, a girl just needs her mom. And then you find your place in another family, only to lose that acceptance and sense of belonging. I'm not strong enough to endure that again. I want to keep Charlie and me in this bubble where it's just the two of us, at least for as long as I can. Bringing him home to my friends is even more terrifying. What if they slip up? What if he finds out? What if I fall to pieces, and he gets tired of not knowing why?

What if, what if, what if. These what-ifs are going to eat you from the inside out if you let them, V.

Charlie

"Uncle Charlie!" My nephew yells for the bloody hundredth time. My brother gruffly tells him to leave me alone. I love my family, but right now, I need space. My nerves are on their last rope, and I am one flick away from snapping. I spent the weekend being patient and keeping up appearances for my family's sake. Pretending to be content and having a fun time. I do truly appreciate this time with my family, but I miss her. Every time my brother has the opportunity to snuggle his wife, to show my sister-in-law some affection, and he ignores her, I want to bloody throttle him. What I would not give to have Veronica here celebrating with us. If she were, I would not ignore her. I would lavish her with affection. What a bloody idiot.

"Charlie, darling, there you are," my mother says as she leans next to me against the fence that has been holding me up all night. I spent most of the day helping my dad haul hay for the horses while my brother and nephew built the bonfire for tonight's celebration. I would have insisted on overseeing the festivities in past years, but I could not have cared less today. I am itching to get back to London. Tomorrow, I tell myself. As soon as morning chores and breakfast are over, you can leave.

"So, tell me about this girl. She must be very special to you for you to be moping around like this on Guy Fawkes Day," she says without judgment.

"She is a woman, mum, and I am not moping." I cannot see her face clearly in the gloom this far away from the bonfire's light, but I know the expression it wears—patient understanding.

"Veronica is, well, Mum, she is beautiful for starters, inside and out. She is a brilliant artist who is extremely dedicated to her work. She is kind, intriguing, and reserved. She's not like the others," my mum nods, clearly remembering the fiasco that was my last almost-relationship with a girl who *only* cared about material things.

"Her thoughts and feelings are written on her face, and as much as she hates it, they are easy to read if you just pay attention. She is sad and," I pause, sighing, "broken. She is like a shell of herself, Mum, and every day, I see her work so hard to put herself back together. It breaks my heart a little, and I badly want to help her, to ease her suffering. To bring a little joy back into her life." My breathing is a bit erratic after my passionate speech, my chest heaving ever so slightly.

"So. . . you love her," my mother says pragmatically.

I have never felt this way about another woman before. When posed with the question, 'How do you know if you love someone,' people older and wiser and more experienced than I often say, 'When you know, you know.' I used to scoff at that ridiculous notion. Before Veronica, life was logical. It could be explained in numbers or equations. A squared plus B squared always equals C squared, so you love somebody because they fit perfectly into your equation.

But Veronica does not fit into any logical equation. She is a living, breathing conundrum, longing for her past, afraid of her future, wielding the present like a shield that will protect her from both. She is witty and talented, disciplined, and a bit challenging, but in the sense that she challenges me. She challenges my view of the world and my ideals. She challenges me to be more patient and less demanding. She challenges me to be a better man. I know that sounds like a cliche, but she makes me want to be worthy. Worthy of her time, her attention, her trust, and, yes, her love.

"Yes, Mum, I love her," I say, smiling ruefully.

Veronica

Deep breaths V. He gave you the key. Told you to come and go as you please.

I consider the many reflections staring back at me from the mirrored lift walls.

Just admit it, you missed him. A lot.

I did miss him way more than I care to admit. I keep telling myself that I'm finally using his gym because of that idiot who wouldn't leave me alone at Fitness First the other day.

Be real. He's only called you about five times in the past three hours to tell you that his ETA is two o'clock.

And I just so happen to be walking in his door at one thirty.

Maybe I should work out naked?

But half the fun is in getting naked.

I plan to mess around until he gets home, not get too focused or too sweaty, but after a few minutes, I blare some classical music and get lost in my workout. I'm halfway through my third set of squats when I notice his reflection in the mirror. He's leaning against the wall, watching me with possessive intensity, ankles crossed in front of him, one hand shoved into a pocket, the other holding a hoodie slung over a shoulder. He's wearing snug, dark jeans and a white T-shirt. One corner of his mouth quirks into a cocky grin, and his tongue darts out, wetting his lips in a long sweep as he watches me drop slowly into a squat.

He continues watching me like a predator locked onto its prey as I rack the weights and get a drink. I grab a towel and turn my back to him, wiping the sweat from my face and neck, watching him watch my reflection. When I am done, I drop the towel in the bin and stand there, arms dangling loose at my sides, head tilted to the side, waiting for Charlie to make the next move. He slings the hoodie off his shoulder, drops it to the floor, and takes three powerful strides across the room, closing the distance between us. We haven't seen each other in over a week, and the tension between us is palpable. Longing, yearning, need, desire, and a smidge of uncertainty create waves of tension between us.

He's so close behind me, without touching me, that I can feel the heat of his body and the barely suppressed emotions vibrating through him.

"Fuck, I missed you," he purrs, nuzzling into my neck, voice raspy with need. He grips my hips and pulls me against him, pressing his erection against my ass. I moan and arch my back, wiggling against him. I stare boldly at his reflection, straight into his intense green eyes.

Several weeks ago, when we first started dating, I would have balked at getting naked in this room of windows and mirrors—did balk at simply getting naked in front of Charlie at all. My insecurities and fears, the constant stream of criticisms that runs rampant through me, have ruled me and kept me stuck in my head for the better part of the past six years. Patient, kind, passionate, and a little demanding, Charlie has methodically helped me quiet the unrest in my mind in just a few short weeks. Now, I crave being intimate with him, crave the power I feel knowing I can lose myself in his arms and bring him to his knees with a single look.

"How much did you miss me?" I ask, voice breathless with anticipation. He grips the hem of my tank top and slowly drags it up my body over my head, discarding it on the floor. I didn't bother wearing a bra. Molten green eyes lock onto mine in the reflection, and as he stares me down, a small twinge of nerves slithers through me. Tiny Mildred tries to shout her criticisms from the back of my mind, but I've almost completely silenced her for good.

Charlie rips his eyes from mine and lazily moves them down my body. Pure male satisfaction shines from them as he cups my breasts in his large, rough hands, pinching and rolling my nipples between his fingers. I moan and arch my ass into him more insistently. One glorious hand roams down my belly and slides under the waist of my shorts. His eyes blaze with desire when his fingers brush bare skin. I didn't bother wearing panties, either.

"Take them off," he demands, voice rough with need.

I push my shorts down over my hips and let them fall to the floor. My head swims with the heady rush of power I get from standing completely naked in front of a fully dressed, aroused man surrounded by floor-to-ceiling mirrors and windows. I feel vulnerable and exposed but also confident and powerful. He moves his hand between my legs, massaging my clit with such excruciating slowness that I whimper and writhe against his hand, urging him to give me more. He pinches my nipple hard; pain and pleasure intertwine and course down my body, settling into an exquisite pulse between my legs.

"Charlie," I plead. The circles stop, and he releases my nipple. "Charlie, please," I whimper.

"Who," he breathes against my ear. I shake my head and bite my lip. He pinches my nipple again, tugging hard, and angles his body to bare my ass. He lands a solid smack on one cheek. I yelp in surprise and a new, more intense throb pulses between my legs. "Say it, Veronica," he says, demanding this time. I stare at him, biting my lip, hands balled into fists at my side. He tilts his head, and I receive another tandem pinch and smack. The pain and pleasure weave together beautifully, sending powerful tremors through my body.

Charlie's fingers still, resting lightly against me and waiting for me to give in, a determined, mischievous glint shining in his eyes. I don't. I've been waiting all fucking week to have his hands on me again, so I am in no rush. He stares me down, intensity radiating out of his eyes, which are so dark with need that the green is barely visible. This time, the pinch and smack come without warning. I gasp, trembling as the need for him drips down my thighs.

"Alright, darling, you want to play? Let's do it right then. You need a safe word."

"Hyacinthe," I answer without hesitation. I've never needed a safe word before, but I used to be an avid reader, and my favorite female character used this one.

"Say it, and everything stops, no questions asked." I raise my chin and set my shoulders.

Smirking at my stubbornness, he dips just the tip of one finger inside me, holding me in an iron grip around my stomach, preventing me from bucking forward to take it deeper. Finger slick with my wetness, he rubs my clit with delicate, too-soft, too-slow circles. I throw my head back against his shoulder, whimpering, body trembling from head to toe. He raises his eyebrows at me in the reflection. I raise mine right back at him and press my lips firmly together.

A deep, devilish laugh rumbles through him as he glides a hand up my spine to lock his fingers in my hair. Pressing harder against my back, he commands me to move forward. We stop at the cable machine, and Charlie gruffly instructs me to grab the rope and hold it tight. I eagerly obey.

"When you're ready to cum and get filled," he states, grinding his cock against my ass, musing nonchalantly as if we're conversing about the weather, "you know what to say." I lick my lips and wiggle my ass against him, and his nostrils flare, eyes narrowing to savage slits. He lands a solid smack on my ass, chest heaving slightly, and I hum in pleasure, fucking high on the empowerment I feel in obeying him, yet defying him at the same time, watching him fight not to lose control of himself.

Charlie sets his shoulders and masters his breath, circling me like a predator, deciding the best way to devour his prey. I follow him with my eyes as best I can, delicious anticipation crashing through me in waves that have me trembling again without him even touching me. I close my eyes briefly, and he strikes; the sound of his hand against my ass echoes through the room. I suck in a surprised breath and moan as he pushes two fingers inside me. He lets me ride them for a short time, sucking a nipple into his mouth and biting it roughly, then wiping away the pain with a pleasurable swipe of his tongue. I cry out at the loss when he pulls his fingers out of me, and then he's circling me again.

I don't know how long I hold out; time has ceased to exit. He pinches and smacks, licks and sucks, deftly weaving a delicious thread of pain through the pleasure. I'm sagging on trembling legs, barely able to grasp the rope, when I finally utter his two favorite words.

"Mr. Wright," I breathe, and he pauses, finger resting on my swollen clit. "Please, Mr. Wright," I groan, loud and clear enough for Charlie to hear this time. He wastes no time, fingers rubbing furiously at my clit, swiftly bringing me to a powerful climax. He holds me in a vise grip while I scream his name and hang on for dear life as I ride out the waves of the orgasm crashing through me.

When the last small wave retreats, Charlie helps me to sit on a bench, then squats down in front of me and asks, "Are you okay, my love? Are you done?"

"I haven't given you the safe word yet, have I?"

A positively feral, triumphant grin tugs up the corners of his mouth, and he stands, efficiently shedding his clothes. "Then get on your knees and brace yourself on the bench." I flash him a smug smirk and sink to the floor. Arching my back, I buck back to meet him as he slams into me. I fucking love it when he rides me this hard; when he pushes me to a place where there's no room to think about anything but him and the pleasure.

Charlie wraps my ponytail around his arm and pulls my head up. Leaning in to speak against my ear, he says, "Look me in the eye while I fuck you, Veronica." I find his eyes in the reflection and another wave of pleasure crashes through me. I never thought watching myself have sex would be such a fucking turn-on, but when it's with Mr. Adonis-in-the-flesh . . . fuck. With one hand wrapped in my hair and the other gripping my hip, he fucks me hard and deep and fast. I feel another orgasm building, and I can see that he's getting close, so I drop one hand down to rub my clit.

Letting go of all restraint and losing himself inside me, he drops both hands to my waist and pushes the pace even faster; the sound of our bodies slapping together rings out in the silence. Sweet, fucking pressure builds, starting in my toes, barreling up and connecting with my fingers, erupting into pleasure so intense that I'm shaking and moaning, clenching tightly around him as he continues to slam into me, chasing his own release. I ride him through my orgasm, urging him to follow me over the edge, greedily milking every drop of pleasure that he'll give me.

"Fuck, Veronica," he groans, pumping into me twice more before collapsing, chest heaving against my back. After our breathing regulates, Charlie gently eases out of me, scoops me into his arms, and takes me to the en suite where he administers gentle, loving aftercare. My mind remains blissfully quiet throughout and for a long time after.

Big Girl Panties

I will forever think of this week as the week of 'big girl panties.' I have thought, 'put on your big girl panties,' enough times this week that it's become an unexpected mantra.

First, I dealt with my youngest sister, Valerie. She disowned me and Victoria when we decided to go no-contact with our mother in our early twenties. Valerie is the baby of the family, and it was painfully obvious that she was our mother's favorite. Mildred treated her like the favored evil stepsister and the rest of us like Cinderella.

About once a year, Valerie contacts Vic and me, frantic about some fabricated issue or another. It is always a thinly veiled attempt to get us to reconcile with Mildred the Dreadful. Which is never going to happen. It's too much of a relief to not have to deal with her anymore.

However, I would love to reconcile with my sister and meet my nieces and nephews, but Valerie refuses unless I also reconcile with our mother. And that's not going to happen. She's been calling, texting, and emailing me multiple times a day for weeks.

Instead of my usual reply, "Valerie, I love you, little sister. But I cannot, for my own mental health and emotional well-being, have a relationship with Mildred. Please understand. I miss you, though, and would love to meet your kiddos." I told her to quit contacting me if it had anything to do with Mildred. Then, I provided her with a secondary email address and blocked her on everything else.

Second, I mended things over the phone with Victoria as best as possible. Forgiveness was given by both, but I fear she'll never be able to live and let live, and I'm fucking done putting up with her meddling.

And finally, I'm heading over to Charlie's for dinner tomorrow to give him 'the warning.'

I will never get tired of lurking in the shadows on the mezzanine and watching Charlie as he wanders the empty gallery. He is powerful yet graceful, so sure of himself and his place in this world. His muscular frame is well-defined, and his muscles ripple with a powerful grace under his navy Charles Tyrwhitt suit.

He leans casually against a beam, his ankles crossed and his arms loose at his sides. He is poised and sophisticated, making him seem older than I'm guessing he is. I take a deep breath and let it out, mentally preparing for our impending conversation as I descend the stairs. He watches my every step, radiating that intense energy toward me. Some primal part of me thrills at the possessiveness in his eyes. I love the feeling of belonging to someone, especially someone who is fully in your corner, willing to claim you and support you and protect you at all costs.

"Hello Veronica," he croons, voice deep and raspy. Joy brightens his eyes, making them a rich, sea-foam green. A lazy, confident smile spreads slowly across his face. Two simple words uttered from his sensual, full lips, and I'm thrumming with desire. "New earrings?" he asks, tapping the shimmering, black heart studs with one long, calloused finger. A shiver runs down my spine as he tucks a strand of hair behind my ear. It took some time and inner grappling, but I can finally wear my hair down without the anguish of missing *him*.

"Fuck, I have missed you, V. Only getting a few stolen moments with you during these long work weeks is killing me."

I suck air through clenched teeth. An image of shattered glass, warped metal, and scattered limbs flashes in my mind. Unseeing, glassy eyes morph from cobalt to emerald, and I squeeze my eyes shut, grasping Charlie's arm hard to make sure he's real. He places his hand over mine and asks, "What is wrong, my love?" I briefly consider brushing it off, but I've already put on my big girl panties, so I tell him an abbreviated version of the truth.

"Can you not say that 'killing me'. . . It, ah, doesn't sit well, you know?"

"Of course, of course. My apologies," he replies sincerely.

I step into his arms and run my hands up the hard planes of his back, inhaling his earthy scent deep into my lungs. The tightness in my chest eases. Tears well in my eyes, and I dig my fingers into his back, wishing with every fiber of my being that I could hold *him like* this one more time and hating myself for not being able to let go.

Charlie's hand rests warmly on my thigh as we navigate the busy London streets. The silence is thick between us, impregnated with words that need to be said. No doubt sensing my anxiety, he folds my hand into his, giving it a reassuring squeeze.

While Charlie cooks, we chat about my studio, his company, and his friends and family. He grumbles about Arsenal's disappointing season. To avoid the pain, I quickly redirect the conversation and ramble on about the upcoming Broadway shows I'm excited to see.

I wait until we are both almost done eating, take a deep breath, and begin.

"Charlie," I swallow audibly, breathing heavily. His head snaps up and he eyes me warily, concern and trepidation clouding his eyes. He places his knife and fork on his plate and folds his hands in his lap.

I take another deep breath and wipe my sweaty palms on my jeans. "I need to tell you something. Um. . . give you a warning of sorts, actually." I raise my eyes to his to gauge his reaction. He reaches across the counter with both hands, resting them in front of me, palms up, in invitation. His large hands engulf my small ones, the touch calming me. I take a few breaths and gather my thoughts.

"Do you remember I told you something terrible happened a few years ago?"

"Yes, the event," he replies neutrally.

"Next May will mark seven years since it happened. There's a pattern to my year now. The end of June through the beginning of October are the good months. During this part of the year, I function fairly well. Then, October ends, and holiday season rolls around, the memories bubble up to the surface more often, and despair starts setting in. I can still function most days, but my motivation to do so steadily plummets, and by February, full-on depression has taken over, and I struggle to get out of bed."

"There are large chunks of time that I can't remember because I completely check out. I won't answer the phone or the doorbell. I barely eat. I dissociate from life, from the pain." Charlie opens his mouth to speak, but I plow ahead to the conclusion. "I figured it would be a good idea to give you a heads-up." I rush out, shrugging a shoulder, and wait for his reply.

He licks his lip with just the tip of his tongue and runs a hand through his wavy, dark hair. "I appreciate it. I try to respect your time, give you space when you seem to need it and be patient when we do not talk or see each other as much as I would like."

"And you've done a great job of it," I interject quickly because he has. I fold my hands on the counter in front of me and nod for him to continue.

"But you and I both know I would come banging on your door if you disappeared without a warning." He looks at me thoughtfully for a long moment. "How can I best support you through this?"

What a gem.

He's not pushy or demanding. He's not arrogant, assuming he knows how to handle these situations best. Nor does he automatically spew unsolicited advice.

We analyze our options, negotiating and compromising until we have a plan in place. I give him the codes and keys to the studio and my flat, with the promise that he will not use them unless absolutely necessary. I promise to do my best to communicate with him at least once daily, and he grudgingly promises to wait a full week of silence before he comes to check on me, should I go silent.

November flies by in a blur of gray, rainy days. Charlie and I fall into an easy routine–long work weeks punctuated by briefly stolen moments together and weekends spent wrapped in each other's arms. Occasionally, we go out for dinner or down to the circus to catch a show. But, more often than not, we hole up in Charlie's flat, him cooking while I sit at the kitchen counter doodling, me plucking out tunes on the baby grand while he reads the paper.

And the sex. Oh my God, the sex. I thought *he* and I had had an amazing sex life, although, by the end, the intimacy was severely lacking, but it was nothing like what I now share with Charlie. Maybe it is maturity, the lack of kids, or the financial stability of our successful careers that have created space in our relationship for such unbridled passion. However, I suspect that for my part, at least, it is the wisdom I've gained from having loved and lost and knowing firsthand how quickly the ones you love can be ripped from your life that drives my need to give into every physical impulse and desire I feel for Charlie.

Consequently, while we dine at the pub on the first snowy night in December, I think I have no qualms when he runs his hand up my tights-clad thigh to rub his knuckle ever so softly over my clit. With a bland smile plastered on his face, Charlie sips his pint nonchalantly while continuing his infuriatingly feather-light ministrations beneath my dress. I drop a half-eaten Devils on Horseback on the plate in front of us and cough in a weak attempt to disguise the moan that threatens to slip between my lips.

A chorus of deep laughter draws my attention to the three male bartenders standing in a cluster at the opposite end of the bar. One of the men wiggles his eyebrows while another playfully elbows the third, and my face flushes red. They are not looking in our direction, nor do they give any other indication that we are the subject of their amusement, but I can't help but feel ashamed of being caught.

Charlie gently kisses my hot cheek and removes his hand, draping it across the back of my barstool. Caressing my back, he muses, "So, you are not an exhibitionist, then."

"No, no I am not." It was drilled into me from a young age to hide in the shadows and not bring any sort of attention to myself. Not to mention how the expectation to suppress all sexual desires outside of fulfilling a man's needs warped my view of acceptable behavior between partners.

"Do you want to get out of here," he purrs.

I open my mouth to say, 'fuck yes,' but decide there's no need to rush. "No, we can wait until after dinner," I say, giving him a sly look out of the corner of my eye and raising my glass. We clink glasses, and one corner of his mouth curls into a sinful promise.

"What about you? Do you like having an audience?"

"Never tried it and have no desire to."

"The thrill of getting caught never had much appeal for me, either. The hypervigilance could never let me relax enough to enjoy it."

"Was it your mom, dad, or both who instilled that hypervigilance into you?" I blink my eyes rapidly at his abrupt change of topic. I shouldn't be surprised by how intuitive he is, but he catches me off guard occasionally.

"Mom. I know that all these years later, it seems weird that she still has such a negative effect on me, especially with all the therapy and whatnot," I say, shaking my head.

"It is not weird, Veronica. It is perfectly normal. I am going to go ahead and assume that you endured years and years of narcissistic abuse," I curl my lip and arch a brow in response. "Narcissistic abuse causes the same issues as complex PTSD. That is not something that is easily fixed if it ever can be fixed. Do not feel bad. You are doing everything you possibly can to heal. That is all that matters."

Now, I blink rapidly to hold in the tears. "Jesus, Charlie. How is it that you always know what to say?"

He shrugs a shoulder. "I pay attention."

The bartender delivers our meals, and we eat quickly, then bundle into heavy coats. We sprint through large, lazy snowflakes to Charlie's Audi, parked halfway up the block. Before he opens the passenger door, he pushes me against the car and kisses me, plunging his tongue into my mouth. I kiss him back, fisting my hands into his coat and pulling him against me. When we part, our mingled breath steams, rising into the air in a little puff of white.

As Charlie expertly maneuvers the Audi over the snow-covered streets, I palm his cock through his jeans and stroke him. He lets out a surprised hiss, quickly becoming hard under my ministrations. He grips the wheel tightly with one hand and, biting his lip, slides his other hand under my dress.

I revel in the feel of Charlie's hand on me as we weave through downtown London. I revel in the way he feels under my hand. For a split second, I allow myself to remember the feel of *him*, my mind straining hard to grab onto the fleeting memories. The realization that I can barely remember the rhythm of *his* heartbeat or the way it felt to be touched by *him* makes me double down my efforts to memorize every precious moment I get to be with Charlie. When he pins me in the corner of the lift and grinds his erection between my legs, I don't hesitate to give in to the desire.

I use the mirrored walls to my advantage, memorizing every angle of our joining, searing the image of his ecstatic face into my brain. I never want to take advantage of time again, assuming that I'll always have tomorrow with him at my side. As our chests heave and our breaths mingle, I place my hand lovingly on his cheek, willing myself to never forget the look of pure ecstasy and adoration he gives me as he pulls me to him and holds me tenderly.

The next morning, during breakfast, I don't have any panties on, but we have another big girl conversation. I dodged the Halloween bullet by purposely holing up in the studio and throwing myself into work. I explicitly forbade the twins from opening the gallery at all on that dreary Thursday in October. And the Brits don't celebrate Thanksgiving, so I've been functioning pretty well, especially compared to prior years. I am not going to be so lucky at avoiding Christmas, though, and it's the toughest holiday of them all.

After I finish tidying up the breakfast mess—I always insist on being the one to do it since Charlie always cooks—Charlie drapes himself lazily on one of the sofas in the sitting room overlooking the London skyline. The sky is a dreary slate gray, the same color it's been for days upon days. I head toward the piano, but Charlie plucks me around the waist on my way past and snuggles me on the sofa next to him.

"Can we discuss Christmas, V? You mentioned heading back to the States sometime this month," he says, his hand drawing delicate patterns up and down my arm. I turn to face him, pulling my legs onto the sofa, crossing one under the other.

"I am heading to the States soon. I'm hoping Kal and Kel will say that's too long, so I have a good excuse to keep the visit short." I tilt my head to the side and half roll my eyes. Chuckling, he nods.

"That is wishful thinking, I fear."

I sigh, and, not wanting to feel ungrateful, I add, "Yeah, you're right. I haven't spent much time with Catherine and Sophie since I moved. I am genuinely excited to see them. It's just hard to be in Idaho for too long."

"That is completely understandable. But you do not need an excuse to leave when you need, love. Cat and Soph know your struggles. I'm sure they are grateful for whatever time you give them and do not begrudge your time apart."

"Thank you. I needed that reminder."

He fidgets with a loose thread on the hem of my shirt, his chest rising and falling a few times before he meets my gaze. "My family is celebrating early. My brother and sister-in-law invited us to join them at their house. Will you come with me?" he asks quietly. I can see the war in his eyes. He badly wants to demand, but he waits respectfully, allowing me to make an uninfluenced decision.

I am prepared for this question, having considered my options extensively since the last time he asked me to meet his family. When I stood on the precipice that beautiful June afternoon over a year ago, I chose to step away and *live*. On the drive to California a few days later, I made a plan to figure out how to not just live but *enjoy* life. A few months ago, I chose to be with Charlie. And I wake up day after day and continue to choose to be with him.

As much as I want to keep him to myself, to keep us in our safe little bubble, it's not realistic. Other people are important to him, too. I cannot keep expecting him to choose between spending time with them and me. It's not fair. And who knows, maybe his sister-in-law and I will become friends.

"Yes, I'd love to," I reply. One of his brilliant smiles beams across his face.

"Thank you," he says, voice husky. He clears his throat and continues in his normal timber, "Does Kel and Kal have you booked up next weekend?"

"They are going to rearrange the gallery, but they don't need me there. I usually just end up being their comedic relief anyway. Plus, they always encourage me to spend as much time with you as possible." He raises a sardonic brow. "They still love to live vicariously through me even though they get plenty of their own action. It's all your fault," I say, pointing an accusatory finger at him.

"Mine," he scoffs.

"Yes, 'cause you're so fucking hot. And you radiate sex appeal."

"Oh really," he muses. I look him up and down, biting my lip. "Well then. Let's bloody give them something to enjoy."

Afterward, we make plans for our weekend in Manchester with his family. He also reminds me of the important details about his family. How his parents have been happily married for fifty-two years. And although they had hoped for more, they only had Charlie and his older brother, James. James and his wife, Cynthia, started dating as teenagers and have been married for fifteen years. This is the tricky part; they have two kids: George Jr., who is eight and named for Charlie's father, and little Ella, who is six.

You can handle it, V. It's only three days.

Charlie assures me that his niece and nephew are quiet and well-behaved, though that's not the issue, and that I won't have to interact with them much. He assumes I don't like kids.

If only it were that simple.

Nervous and Nitpicky

"Charlie will be here in thirty minutes. Are you two all set for the weekend? Do you remember which ones are finished and ready to be sold?" I ask, aimlessly moving around the studio. The anticipation makes me nervous and nitpicky.

Kellan gently grabs both of my shoulders and looks at me thoughtfully until I quit fidgeting. He pulls me into a hug, embracing me long enough for my breathing to sync with his, calm and measured. I sigh and drop my shoulders, releasing all the tension I've been holding there.

"Thank you," I say as he steps back.

Kali pats me on the arm. "Everything is going to be okay. We have things under control here, and Charlie is not going to let you drown at his brother's house. He adores you." She emphasizes 'adores,' stretching out the 'or' sound.

"It will be good for you to see him in a different setting. See how he treats his family and whether he's good with kids. You don't want to wait and find out five years down the road that he's an ass to his mom," Kellan adds pragmatically.

"Exactly. Plus, traveling is always a good test for any new relationship," Kali agrees.

Kellan insists on carrying my luggage down while I grab my purse. When I join them a few minutes later, Charlie is chatting with the twins, his back to me. I wish I could see his face because it looks like the twins, despite their adoration for him, are giving him the 'you better not break her heart' speech that's normally reserved for overprotective fathers of teenage daughters. Charlie accepts their admonishing stoically, clapping Kellan on the shoulder and dipping his head to Kali.

I blink rapidly, holding back unshed tears. Kali and Kellan are the kind of friends I didn't know I needed, and I cherish them very much. I hug them each, and then Charlie and I get on the road.

During the long drive to Manchester, Charlie and I talk about everything and nothing. Only this time, it's everything about me and nothing about him. Thus far, he has been content with the mystery of not knowing. Maybe now that I am meeting his family, he doesn't want to be embarrassed by just how little he knows about me. I answer his questions as best I can. I am prepared for them as I figured they would come sooner or later.

"Veronica," he says. I tear my eyes away from the drab, misty British countryside to look at him. He looks back, contemplatively. "Do you mind if I ask some questions about your family? I know some parts of your past are off limits, but would you be willing to answer what you can?"

I love how considerate he is. "Sure," I answer. "What do you want to know?"

He takes a steadying breath, then exhales without speaking, his fingers drumming an anxious beat on the steering wheel. I grab his left hand and rest it in my lap, interlacing our fingers.

"How, um, I am by no means trying to be rude, but how old are you?" he asks in a rush. I press my lips together to hide a smile. He is usually so self-possessed and confident. These moments when he stumbles over himself are so endearing.

"I'd wager I'm about a decade older than you. What are you. . . thirty-three?"

He glances at me with wide eyes. The green is deeper than usual, mimicking the rain-drizzled forest we're driving through.

"I am thirty-five," he says, dignified.

"Yup. I was right. I'm forty-three."

"No," he exclaims. "That is not bloody true."

I laugh and shake my head. He quickly composes himself and moves on to the next question.

"Your parents. . ."

"My dad passed away unexpectedly eleven years ago. Heart attack. I miss him every day." I pause, thinking about how differently the past decade of my life might have been had he been alive. "His death was hard on me and my sisters. We each had a unique, special bond with him. He was our rock and the buffer between us, besides Val anyway, and our mom." I trail off, allowing myself a few moments to feel the grief of missing him.

"Is your mom still alive?"

"Mildred the Dreadful," I say, elongating the spaces between the words. He raises his eyebrows at this. "As you've surmised, she was a shit mother. We've been no-contact now for the past twenty years. It's a story for another day," I say, not wanting to dive in too deep. I need all my mental energy to make it through this weekend without having a breakdown. "She lives in an assisted care facility near my youngest sister."

"So, you have two sisters," he ventures.

"Three," I say, closing my eyes and bringing my oldest sister's face to mind. How does one person deal with so much loss? My heart stutters and my throat constricts, making it hard to breathe. I should have had this conversation with him last week. I am not strong enough to wade through these memories and fight off *the other* memories that being around Charlie's family is sure to dig up.

You can do this, V. You are strong. You are capable. You are enough.

"Vera was the oldest. Twelve years older than me. Out of the three of them, I was closest to her. She got the worst of Mildred's abuse, being so much older than the rest of us." I pause, eyes brightening with unshed tears, and swallow hard. "She committed suicide when I was 17."

"Oh, Veronica. I am so sorry." A corner of my mouth tilts up gratefully. I take a deep breath and tell him why. I tell him how our mom was cruel, how she beat us with her fists and lashed us with her sharp tongue. I explained how she was so unpredictable that any tiny, little thing would set her off and we never were able to figure out a pattern.

"My sister was kind and beautiful and generous and sweet, so sweet to everyone. She came home for an unexpected visit. She had fled to LA to be an actress as soon as she graduated high school. She was tall, taller than me even, and powerfully built. Mildred constantly criticized the two of us for our height and our muscles. No matter what size we were, to her, we were always too tall and too big, not feminine enough."

"Bollocks. What a blind old bat. I love me a tall, curvy woman."

I roll my eyes at him. "Well, as you can imagine, it became a major insecurity for both of us, but Vera took it especially hard. She went to audition after audition in between other jobs and got rejected often enough that she was ready to quit. But I encouraged her to do one last audition for this play she had been talking about non-stop for weeks. So, she mustered up all her courage and did the audition and . . . she got the part. I was so proud of her, so happy for her." I smile at Charlie, eyes bright with unshed tears.

"The other actresses were unbelievably cruel to Vera, picking and poking at the wounds our mother's constant criticism had left festering. A few days into her visit home, she somehow wound up home alone with Mildred. The three of us older girls stuck together to ensure that happened as little as possible." I take a sip of my water and look out the window, wishing I could go back to that day and–

"Your mother," Charlie says, voice venomous, "I am assuming, started in on her when what she needed was a loving, comforting shoulder to lean on."

"We don't know the specifics, but we do know that things got bad between them. Vera sent out a volley of texts and voicemails to my dad, Vicki, and me, begging us to get home. She couldn't just leave, it was the dead of winter, and she had no vehicle. My dad got home first, thankfully. He found her in the bathroom, an empty bottle of pills in her cold, stiff, blue hand."

Charlie rubs comforting circles on my thigh. "Veronica," he breathes, offering me more kindness and empathy in that one word than I had received from my own parents in the weeks and months following her death.

"She was my best friend. I missed her so much when she left for LA. We talked every day. I was her tiny shadow growing up, and she protected me as much as she could from our mother's cruelties. I wasn't allowed to be upset when she died; my mom couldn't handle any display of emotion that wasn't her own. And my dad was too lost in his own grief to console us girls. It fell on my shoulders to comfort my younger sisters."

"You should have never had to go through that alone. Your parents failed you."

"I was angry at my dad for a long time after Vera passed. I knew he tried to protect us, tried to be a buffer between us and Mom, but he was gone most of the time, working himself to exhaustion to support her drinking, smoking, shopping, and prescription drug addictions. When he was home, they fought constantly, leaving very little of himself to give us."

"You had every right to be angry with him, V," he says, thumb still rubbing soft circles up and down my leg. "You still have every right to feel how you feel. To have emotions. It does not make you a nuisance or a burden."

It is remarkable how he always perceives the unspoken hurts, the buried truths, and then always knows what to say to soothe them. "It took time and tons of therapy to accept that. I'm thankful that I had the opportunity to mend my relationship with my dad before he passed. He finally divorced Mildred when I was about twenty. We enjoyed thirteen amazing years with him, free of her control."

Charlie smiles, and we fall silent for a few minutes while we drive through the rain-soaked English countryside. Then Charlie gently prods, "What about your other sisters? Are they younger?"

"Yes. Victoria is eighteen months younger than me. We became close after Vera's suicide but grew distant after *the event*. She doesn't approve of how I deal with it, withdrawing and running away. I think she feels like I abandoned her when I sold everything and became a modern-day gypsy."

"Abandoned?"

"Yeah. For so many years, it was just her and me. Our oldest sister, the one we both adored and who was a better mother to us than our actual mother, was gone. Our dad, gone, and our baby sister and egg donor, estranged. And *after*, I just couldn't stay and deal with the constant bombardment of reminders. When the urge to get out and get far, far away settled into my gut, I went from a non-functioning zombie to all worldly possessions sold and flying across the country in a matter of weeks. We had become each other's constant, and, in her mind, I left her to fend for herself."

"I can see why she might feel that way," he replies neutrally. "I know you talk with her often. Do you visit her when you are in the States?"

"Yeah. It's rocky, but we try. She throws this huge New Year's Eve party every year. I try to make it as often as possible. It's always good to see her, but our relationship is strained. The ease and comfort we once shared is gone."

"You two have been through a lot." I give him a half smile and nod.

Oh, Charlie. You have no idea.

"And then there's Valerie, the baby, only a year younger than Vic. She was Mildred's golden child. She disowned Vicki and I when we disowned our mother. She has four kids. I wish I could get to know them. Be their auntie for real, ya know. She comes out of the woodwork once a year and tries to get us to reconcile with Mildredful." I roll my eyes and shake my head.

He accepts that as a good enough explanation for now. "So, Cat and Soph must be—?"

"My best friends. Sophie is a nurse, recently promoted to Chief Nursing Officer. She's married to Turner, an Air Force pilot who is deployed on his fifth tour in Iraq. They love dogs and children they can return." He looks at me side-eyed and tilts his head. "They like their friend's kids but do not want their own," I clarify. He nods, rubbing his chin, and the stubble against his rough fingers makes a soft scratching sound.

"And Cat, Catherine, works in insurance. She's married to John, an engineer. They have three kids who call me auntie." The rest of his questions are relatively harmless and provide a distraction from my growing anxiety.

When we arrive, Manchester glows eerily in the dusk, the drizzle quickly turning to pounding rain. Charlie's questions die out, and he removes his hand from my jittery leg to navigate the slick, freezing roads. James and Cynthia live ten minutes outside Manchester on the city's opposite side. George Sr. and Anne, Charlie and James's parents, are joining us there tomorrow, which is a relief.

I'm sure Charlie suspected that I would be overwhelmed meeting them all at once, so he orchestrated the staggered arrivals. As he skillfully weaves through the city, his focus firmly on the road, my anxiety builds. What-ifs play on a loop through my brain.

What if I have a breakdown and embarrass Charlie?

What if they don't approve of me?

What if I have a nightmare and scream myself awake?

Thank fuck that hasn't happened with Charlie yet.

Befriending the twins is one thing. In our safe little bubble, being in a relationship with Charlie is one thing. Spending three days in a house full of people I don't know is another thing entirely. I can already feel the memories straining against their vault door, fighting to break free. How am I going to manage to retain my composure?

Shit, this was a bad idea, V.

My heart beats erratically in my chest, and my mouth is so dry that it's hard to swallow. Last year, around this same time, I fell completely apart. I was at a gas station and had to go inside to pay because the damn card reader at the pump was broken. A beautiful little blonde-haired girl latched onto my leg, looked up at me, and said, "Mommy, can I pwease, pwetty pwease have some candy?" with the biggest, bluest eyes. It was like a knife piercing straight through my heart, twisting it to shreds.

I managed to extract myself, pay the cashier, and drive myself home before shattering to pieces. I didn't snap out of it until well into January when Vicki, Sophie, and Catherine realized I wasn't at one or the other's holiday celebrations as I had claimed. Sophie found me buried in my closet unkempt, ragged, and rail-thin, desperately clutching an old stuffed teddy bear.

Not now, V. Focus on the present.

With some difficulty, I redirect my thoughts and focus on subtly cycling through a few breathing exercises to reign in my anxiety. Inhale for four counts . . . *You are strong . . .* Exhale for six counts . . . *You are capable . . .* Repeat . . . *You are enough . . .*

By the time we pull into James and Cynthia's driveway, my heart rate has returned to normal, and the anxiety that threatened to consume me has abated. Charlie leans across the middle consul and kisses me tenderly.

"Shall we," he says, gesturing to the house. I take a deep breath and nod. "Wait a moment." He grabs an umbrella from the back seat, opens his door, and sticks the umbrella outside to open it. He quickly circles the car, opens my door, offers his hand, and leads me to the house, my small, cold hand firmly ensconced in his large, warm one.

He strides purposefully up the driveway with me tucked closely to his side. The door opens as we approach, spilling warmth and light into the dreary din of the evening. Over the pounding rain spatter, I hear small, high voices raised in exuberance, "Uncle Charlie, Uncle Charlie!"

A solid streak of blue launches itself out the door, crashing into Charlie's chest. Gangly arms and legs wrap around Charlie, clinging to him like a monkey as we step out of the rain and into the house. A second, slightly smaller form locks her arms around Charlie's waist. He sets the umbrella to the side and throws his head back, laughing.

I swallow hard, pushing back the wave of emotion that threatens to drown me. He is magnificent in this moment. I have seen him dressed to the nines, utterly naked, and everything in between. But I have never seen him so carefree and relaxed in his light jeans and black *Wright & Sons* hoodie, hair disheveled from the rain, his niece and nephew clinging to him with pure joy on their cherubic faces.

"Alright, alright, you two," Charlie says on the tail end of his laughter. "You better run! Here I come."

George Jr. jumps off Charlie and, grabbing Ella by the hand, runs, shrieking into the house. Charlie is quick on their heels. A female voice titters next to me. I turn toward the sound and offer a tentative smile before a petite, blonde woman pulls me into a quick hug. She pulls back to look at my face, leaving her hands on my arms.

"I'm Cynthia. It is so nice to finally meet you." Her smile is genuine, but I sense the exhaustion she's trying to conceal. I reach my hands up and squeeze her arms affectionately.

"You too." It is in moments like these that I most appreciate my glass face. James materializes from the inner part of the house, where we hear high shrieks and low, booming laughter. He holds out his hand.

"Veronica, my pleasure," he says in a voice just a tad deeper than Charlie's. I shake his hand but falter in my response. I inhale to correct him, but Charlie sweeps into the foyer and stands behind me, wrapping me in his arms. He fixes his older but shorter brother with a mock-serious stare.

"Only I am allowed to call her Veronica." He turns up his nose and looks down at James, a mischievous smile playing in the corners of his mouth, "You may call her Ronnie like all the other peasants." We all laugh, and I cuff Charlie on one arm at the same time as James punches him in the other, which causes us all to laugh even harder.

Still chuckling, Cynthia shoos away the men to go entertain the kids and links arms with me, "Come, my dear. I'll show you to your room."

The tightness in my chest eases, grateful for her thoughtfulness. I do need a minute to gather myself. I didn't realize how much I missed this feeling of belonging and being part of a family. I did not grow up experiencing this type of warmth and love, so when *his* family accepted me much the same way Charlie's has tonight, I clung to it greedily. And when it was all torn away, I mourned it just as much as I mourned the loss of *him*. *His* family didn't push me away *after*, but I couldn't stand to be a part of it without *him*.

The bedroom is large and tastefully decorated in navy blues and pale yellows. Fresh flowers are artfully arranged in a beautiful, handmade clay vase on the dresser. There's also an en suite with his and her sinks, a large walk-in, glass-walled shower, and a jacuzzi tub. These Wright sons spare no expense on the luxury of their homes.

I pat a little cold water on my flushed cheeks while giving myself a quick pep talk in the mirror.

You are strong, you are capable, you are enough.

I slip on the smaller of the two pairs of slippers left at the foot of the bed, no doubt by Cynthia, and, blinking back tears, head back downstairs.

If you're not careful, V, this family of thoughtful people is going to do their damnedest to dismantle the wall around your heart.

Which is not necessarily a bad thing, I consider as I descend to the main level. My breath catches in my chest at the sight awaiting me in the living room. James lounges on a massive sectional sofa, drinking a pint and watching TV. Charlie is draped across one of the corners of the sofa, his niece and nephew tucked in next to him, listening intently as he quietly reads them a book.

My eyes cloud over, and I grab blindly for the railing, pulling shallow breaths in through my nose. The vision in front of me blurs and sways, and when it comes back into focus, the man's hair has lightened, and he sits on a loveseat in a small cottage with small, blurry figures tucked in beside him. His affectionate azure gaze pierces through me, straight into my soul. His loving eyes morph into a vacant stare that burns a hole through my heart. I clutch my chest and slide down the wall, falling onto the stairs, blinking rapidly to clear the image from my mind.

Resting my elbows on my knees, I drop my head into my hands and suck in long, steady breaths. When my heart rate evens out, I take a deep breath, square my shoulders, and go to Charlie, dragging my fingers along the soft, smooth fabric on the back of the sofa.

Charlie drops his head back, grinning widely. I grab his face in my hands and plant a quick kiss on his full lips, pulling strength from his lips. The kids both giggle.

"Is Cynthia in the kitchen?" He nods, and we share a private smile. "I'm going to give her a hand." He raises his eyebrows skeptically but refrains from adding any commentary.

Sex Advice

Cynthia's kitchen—not *James and* Cynthia's because I get the distinct impression he rarely participates in the care of his home—looks like it popped straight off the pages of a magazine. An enormous island, complete with a small rinsing sink, a range-top with six gas burners, and a built-in chopping block, dominates the middle of the room.

A cute, quaint breakfast nook sits nestled in the crook of a bay window to my left. An intricately decorated vase on the wood tabletop displays a gorgeous arrangement of vibrant flowers, freshly picked from her greenhouse.

Walls in front and behind me boast crisp white beaded cabinets, cut cleanly down the middle by tidy, well-organized, and beautifully decorated black marble countertops that perfectly match the black marble floor. The backsplash is a checkerboard of mostly black and white tiles, with a random pop of color mixed into the pattern. The wall to my right is dominated by more cabinets surrounding two large, gleaming, black, double wall ovens.

Cynthia stands at the island, stirring something in one of the four pots cooking on the range top. It smells divine in here. She doesn't notice my entrance, so I take a second to consider her before I announce myself. She is obviously exhausted, and it's no wonder. I'm sure they have a cleaning lady and, more than likely, a nanny. Regardless, keeping up with all this house, a garden and greenhouse, a large yard, two kids, and a husband who is rarely home, is a lot. Especially if the mostly absent husband doesn't lift a finger when he is home.

We're gonna have a little chat with Charlie later, V.

"What can I help with," I say as brightly and genuinely as possible.

Cynthia's response is a knee-jerk, "Oh, don't worry about it. I've got this covered."

I walk around the kitchen island to stand beside Charlie's neglected sister-in-law. I place a hand on the arm that's stirring what must be her famous brown sugar and port cranberry sauce.

"Please, let me help," I say earnestly. She looks at me contemplatively for a second before a grateful but rueful smile spreads across her face. I purse my lips and shake my head.

"Did Charlie tell you that I can't cook?" I ask, mirth warming my tone. She nods her head while I shake mine.

That shithead!

"I am actually quite a good cook. He just never allows me to show him," I say, mildly exasperated.

She resumes stirring and gives me directions to check the prime rib that's resting in the bottom right oven. James calls from the living room as I walk back to help her with the potato leek soup.

"Cynthia, love, bring me and Chuck here another pint."

My nostrils flare, and my jaw clenches. It is moments like this that I curse my glass face. Cynthia quickly tries to downplay the situation, but I have no patience for the blatant disrespect. I fix my gaze on her, nostrils flaring.

"How much backlash will you receive if I intervene right now," I ask, raising my eyebrows.

"He won't hit me or anything if that's what you mean."

Well, then. Let's dance asshole.

"We're balls deep in making you boys a fancy, delicious early Christmas dinner in here. I think you can manage to grab your own pints, just this once. Don't you agree, Chuckie?" I give Cynthia a 'that's how it's done' look. Charlie bounds into the kitchen only a few seconds later, giving me a look of his own. I shoot one right back at him.

No, I will not mind my own business. Fucking men sometimes.

After returning home from celebrating Guy Fawkes Day with his family, Charlie mentioned how annoyed he had been with his brother's treatment of his wife. I tried to come here without any prior biases, but as soon as I saw Cynthia's poorly hidden exhaustion, I immediately became protective of her. Stay-at-home mothers deserve so much more respect, support, and praise than the judgment, isolation, and neglect they tend to receive.

While we eat a fabulous meal of prime rib, praline chestnuts and sprouts, Yorkshire Pudding, parsnip and carrot puree, English Trifle, and Cynthia's famous brown sugar and port cranberry sauce, an idea forms in my mind. My leg jitters under the table in anticipation of telling Charlie. He places his hand on my thigh, which has the opposite effect than I assume he intended. My leg does indeed steady, but I squirm in my seat to ease the throb that has now settled between my legs and accept my third glass of champagne.

Since *the event,* I have rarely imbibed, but I wanted something to help take the edge off tonight. If we weren't staying put at James and Cynthia's, there's no way you'd catch me drinking or getting in a car with anyone who had been. Plus, using alcohol as a crutch to numb the pain and silence my mind is too strong of a temptation. It's one that I gave into during those initial months after everything changed, and if I hadn't left Idaho, I would have drank myself into an early grave.

By the time Charlie and I take our turn tucking the kids into bed and retreat upstairs after I helped Cynthia clean up the kitchen, I've completely forgotten about the writhing knot of pain that lives in my chest. I planned to tell Charlie what I was scheming during dinner as soon as we were alone. There's no way he missed it, but as soon as he closes the door behind us, he spins me around and pushes me up against the wall face first. He pins my hands above my head with one hand and roughly palms a breast with the other.

Sober me would feel uncomfortable and disrespectful towards Charlie's family and decline his advances. Tipsy me doesn't give a fuck. Tipsy me craves the oblivion that comes with being with Charlie, and I crave the quiet mind and sense of peace I feel after. Tipsy me is also infinitely more defiant and stubborn than sober me, and she has no intentions of submitting to any of Charlie's demands tonight. In vain, I fight against his iron grip on my wrists and hiss quietly in frustration when it doesn't budge even an inch. He snickers and drops his hand from my breast to my hip, pinning my pelvis against the wall and grinding his erection against my ass. Wet, hot desire dampens my black lace thong, but I still try to shift away from him.

You're gonna have to work for it tonight, Mr. Wright.

In a clumsy attempt to surprise him enough to loosen his grip, I throw my head back against his shoulder and buck my hips. He doesn't so much as budge. Amusement rumbles in his chest, and he places a line of biting kisses up my neck.

"Hmm," he purrs, and huffing an exasperated breath out of my nose, I try to jerk my hands out of his. "You are not going to break my hold on you, feisty. If you want me to let go, you have two options," he continues, licking the edge of my ear, "say 'who' or 'flower'; otherwise, you are at my mercy." I'm glad he can't see the proof on my face of how much I fucking love goading him on, of how much I want him to push me. The more we play, the longer we draw it out, the quieter my mind becomes for longer.

So, while my body thrums with anticipation and heady desire, my mouth blurts, "Fuck. You." Sometimes, I really miss tipsy me and her shenanigans.

Charlie's teeth clamp down on my earlobe, and he grinds my hips into the wall hard enough to bruise. My breath hitches at the jolt of pain that courses through me. He shoves a knee between my legs, and try as I might, I can't stop him from spreading them wide apart. His fingers slip under my dress to find my thong drenched with need for him, and he hums, whispering in my ear. "It would seem, feisty, that you *want* me to fuck you."

I tremble with the need to have him inside me, filling me, and from forcing my body to remain still when all I want to do is to wiggle my ass against his cock and urge him to just fuck me already. He rubs my swollen, throbbing clit over the thin material, and I bite down on my lip to keep from crying out. I hold my hips perfectly still, refusing to give in. With a swift, rough swipe, Charlie moves my thong to the side and plunges two fingers deep inside me. My hips buck of their own volition, and I feel him smile against my neck.

Asshole. Bloody, fucking, cocky asshole.

After teasing me with his fingers for what feels like forever, he withdraws them and frees himself from his dress slacks. With a swift, rough yank, Charlie rips my thong right off me and buries his cock deep inside me. I breathe hard through pressed lips and can do nothing but ride the wave as he slams into me over and over and over again. He uses an angle that feels good but doesn't quite hit the spot, and he tilts my hips so I can't rub against the wall to find that friction I so badly need. But I don't beg, I don't whimper, I don't say his name or my safe word. I know that, in this, I can outlast him.

"Fuck, feisty," he growls into my ear, chest heaving against my back. He pulls out of me, releasing my hands, and before he can take command of the situation, I spin and push him onto the bed. He lands sitting on the edge, lips tilted up in a smirk.

"You're gonna lay there and do as you're told, Mr. Wright," I hiss at him. He arches a brow at me, and a purely male, satisfied grin spreads across his face.

Fuck you and your handsome, arrogant face. Veronica's in charge tonight.

Maybe I'm not just tipsy but full-on drunk. How many glasses of champagne did I even drink earlier? It doesn't matter because I am high on the power of being in control. With more confidence than I've ever felt, I turn my back to him and slowly pull off my dress. I reach back and unhook my bra, staring at him over my shoulder as I hold it out and let it drop to the floor. I step in between his legs and pull his head to my chest. Charlie obliges me, sucking a nipple into his mouth, flicking it with his tongue, and teasing it with his teeth. Pulling roughly on his thick hair, he lets go with a loud pop, and I guide his mouth to the other breast.

I rake my nails up and down his back while he suckles my nipples until I've had enough and push his shoulders. "Be a good Adonis and lay down," I demand. As he obeys, I prowl onto the bed and up his body, positioning my knees on either side of his head. I lower onto his face, and he sucks my clit into his mouth, giving it the same attention he did my nipples. I writhe on top of him, stifling my groans in the upholstered headboard. The navy blue fabric is cool and soft against my face. I ride his face until I come in his mouth, and then I ride his cock until he comes inside of me.

Sitting astride him, both our breaths labored, I begin to laugh maniacally, bouncing on his cock that is still buried inside me. He grips my hips and thrusts, arching a quizzical brow at him. I collapse onto his chest and pinch his nipple hard.

He yelps and says, "Jesus, feisty, what has gotten into you?"

"You," I reply, laughing even harder. He snorts and rubs my back, shifting his hips to withdraw from me. The loss of him sobers me enough to call our meeting to order.

"Okay," I declare, pushing onto an elbow. "Now that we've got that out of our system, let's get down to business."

"What? No, Veronica," he says, flinging an arm over his face. "We just got down to business. Now it is time to sleep."

"Not yet, Adonis. You must know that I've been scheming."

"I do. And I am very afraid."

I playfully flick his nipple again. He yelps and flings his arm off his face, giving me an exasperated look.

"We are initiating operation Make James Appreciate His Wife."

He raises his eyebrows and shakes his head. "This does not sound good."

"Come on, Charlie. Cynthia tries to hide it, but she's exhausted. James neglects his wife. You said so yourself after the last time you were home. So, this is what we're gonna do." I plow ahead without giving him a chance to disagree. "Tomorrow, after lunch with your parents, we're going to take the kids to all the fun kid places in Manchester. Then the four of us are going to spend the night at a hotel so James and Cynthia can have some alone time."

He holds up a hand. "What about my parents?"

I stare at him blankly for a minute, then smack my forehead. "I totally forgot. Your mom called Cynthia while we were in the kitchen. She's not feeling well enough to spend the night. They are going to drive in for lunch, then head back home."

"How convenient," he says, voice dry with sarcasm.

"Exactly. Here's the plan. I am going to tell Cynthia and help her get the kids lined out. You," I jab a finger into his chest for emphasis, "are going to reserve a hotel, preferably a suite with two rooms. And, this is the important part, okay. You are going to give your big brother some advice. Tell him to draw his wife a bath as soon as we leave. Light some candles and put a glass of wine and her book on the bathtub tray. He can do kitchen clean-up duty while she relaxes." Charlie flings his arm back over his face and groans.

"No, no, no," he mutters.

"Yes, yes, yes," I reply. "You're also going to make them a reservation at their favorite restaurant. Which just so happens to be *Comptoir Libanais*. I did some digging; you're welcome."

Another head shake and groan. "That's not even how you pronounce it, V."

"Whatever," I say in my best Clueless impression. "Anyway. Tell James to take his wife out to eat. Then take her home and eat her out like she's the most—"

"Oh my god, Veronica. Stop, just stop," he pleads, but I will not be deterred.

"No. Listen here, Chuck," I emphasize the nickname his brother uses. "They need this. She probably hasn't gotten off in months. I can guarantee you she feels like it's just another chore on her already long list. And do you wanna know why?" I say, not really asking.

"No, no, I do not, but I suppose you are going to tell me anyway," he says, rolling his eyes dramatically.

"Because," I continue as if he hadn't spoken, "I bet he never goes down on her. Never puts in the effort to make sure it's good for her. And they probably only do it on their bed. Tell James to make the most of their time alone. Tell him to do his wife in every room and on every surface of this house outside their room."

"Seriously, Charlie. Impart this wisdom on your brother. It will only benefit him. This is what you tell him. Help out around the house a little bit more consistently, recognize and appreciate the work Cynthia does around here because it ain't easy, and make sure she gets off first every single time. It's not rocket science," I continue, on a roll. "He needs to get rid of this entitled attitude he has because he's the only one who 'works' because it's bullshit. She literally *never* gets a break. Never. I watched Cat go through this, and it almost destroyed her marriage. Guess what saved it?" I say, not asking again.

"A little bit of help, a little bit more appreciation, and lots and lots of oral," he says, mirth playing across his face.

"Yes. See? You get it. Charlie, we don't even live together, but you do those things for me naturally. If you didn't, I would get rid of you." At this, he flips on top of me, tickling my ribs.

"Stop, stop. Okay. Charlie. Stop!"

"Okay, commander," he says ruefully, "I guess I am on board, but you owe me. Giving my older brother sex advice, bloody fucking hell."

I giggle and squirm under him, grinding my hips into his. "I think you are *very* qualified to give sex advice."

We don't fall asleep till late into the night.

Staging an Intervention

I fumble with the buttons on my phone, trying to silence the alarm without waking Charlie.

Ugh. It's too early.

Especially after drinking and staying up so late last night. I roll off the bed, landing quietly on all fours, and drag myself to the bathroom. I shower quickly, throw my hair up in a messy bun, then pull on sweats and head downstairs to help Cynthia prepare an early Christmas lunch. I stumble down the first set of stairs to the landing, still half awake, even after the shower.

Fucking Charlie.

That was precisely the problem! We stayed up way too late last night.

Cynthia sits at the table in the breakfast nook, sipping a steaming cup of coffee. I decline her offer to have a cup and opt for hot tea instead. She pushes a box of pastries my way when I plop ungracefully into the opposite chair. She smiles conspiratorially at me over the rim of her mug as she takes a delicate sip.

Shit, were we that *loud last night?*

"So, how did you sleep last night, deary," she says.

"I slept like the dead, just not long enough," I reply. "Anyway," I say, changing the subject and calling our meeting to order. "Since George and Anne are not staying the night, Charlie and I are going to take the kids after they leave and disappear till tomorrow. Hopefully, *you* can have a night where *you* sleep like the dead for not long enough.”

“What?” she asks, setting her mug on the table.

I look at her pointedly. “I’m staging an intervention, and everyone better listen! If you think Charlie expects to get what he wants, you ain’t seen nothing, honey. After lunch, *you will* go upstairs and enjoy a nice hot bath that your husband will have ready for you. *Your husband* will take care of kitchen cleanup duty. Charlie and I will take the kids and disappear until tomorrow. And if Charlie holds up his end of this plan, then you may just have the best night you’ve had in a long time. And you’re going to enjoy it. Okay,” I demand.

She smiles at me gratefully as she slides her hand tentatively across the table to grasp mine.

“Thank you,” she says.

“You are so welcome.”

“I’m sorry, love, but I have a new best friend.”

Charlie pauses mid-buttoning the cuffs on his crisp, white button-up shirt, hands raised, crossed in front of his chest. He raises his eyebrows at me in the mirror. “Oh?”

“Yes. I *love* Cynthia,” I say. He finishes buttoning as he walks over to where I’m perched on the arm of the chair. He pulls me to my feet and wraps his arms around me.

“I am glad you two are hitting it off so well. Are you holding up okay, love?” he asks.

“It was a little rough at first, but I’m dealing,” I reply.

“Are you ready to meet my parents? Is there anything I can do to help make it easier for you?”

Seriously, the most thoughtful man I’ve ever met.

“Nothing beyond just being by my side. Can I have a moment to myself, though, to finish getting ready? Come get me in about ten minutes,” I ask.

“Of course, my love,” he replies, settling his vintage, green suede suit jacket over his shoulders as he walks out the door.

I finish putting on my green suede pumps and sit in the middle of the bed with my burgundy, 50s-inspired circle dress spread out around me. I made myself the cutest mistletoe earrings and a sparkly green bow necklace to match. I also made a set for Cynthia with a red bow instead as a Christmas gift. I drop into a quick meditation that my therapist taught me to ground myself. I focus on breathing and strengthening the barriers in my mind to keep the painful memories and turbulent emotions contained. I just have to hold my shit together for one more day.

You can do this, V.

When Charlie pokes his head in the door a few minutes later, I feel reasonably confident in my ability to make it through the next twenty-four-ish hours without a major breakdown. He helps me off the bed, pulls me into his arms, and kisses me tenderly.

"They are going to love you, my dear. Just as much as I do," he says.

Well, shit.

My heart stutters a beat, and I struggle to bring it back to a calm pace. I carefully store Charlie's roundabout declaration in the 'analyze later' compartment and return my focus to the matter at hand. Charlie offers his arm, and we head down to greet his parents.

Cynthia and James both look lovely, in their matching vintage-inspired outfits, which was Cynthia's idea. The kids are adorable mini versions of their parents. We hear footsteps outside, heads turning collectively as James steps forward to open the door. Anne crosses the threshold first, resplendent in a blue sheath dress adorned with tiny sparkling snowflakes. She is tall and slender; her mannerisms and demeanor are elegant and sophisticated.

She greets each person with a hug and a sincere smile. I can barely detect the lines around her eyes and mouth, the pain and fatigue she masks exceptionally well. I wouldn't notice them if I didn't know she wasn't feeling well. She delicately grips Charlie's biceps and looks at him affectionately, and my insides become a knot of longing. My mother never once in my life looked at me like that. Her cold eyes were filled with contempt and hatred.

Charlie's voice pulls me out of my thoughts. "Mum, this is Veronica. . . Call her Ronnie."

She turns her affectionate gaze on me, and my eyes immediately well with tears.

"Hullo, my dear. It is so nice to meet you," Anne says, embracing me. It takes every ounce of willpower I possess to hold onto my composure.

"You too, Mrs. Wright," I reply.

A strong, deep voice sounds beside me. "It's Anne and George, dear. We don't stand on ceremony in this family," Charlie's father says, voice booming.

"Okay, Anne. George," I say, nodding my head. He pulls me into a bear hug, and one single tear escapes the dam that's barely holding back the deluge. George gently wipes it away with his thumb, eyes questioning. I take a deep breath, centering myself.

"I lost my dad some years ago. He gave hugs just like you."

"Ahh. Whenever you need one. . ." he offers.

Cynthia claps her hands, herding everyone towards the dining room. The table is set with a beautiful china set that's been in the Wright family for generations, along with multiple arrangements of fresh flowers picked straight from Cynthia's greenhouse. This morning, after we finished preparing the meal, she patiently taught me how to cut and arrange the flowers.

Cynthia pours wine. I decline, still feeling the effects of last night's indulgence, while I pass around hors d'oeuvres. Charlie's father makes a toast to the importance of family, and we clink our glasses together. We all sit for a while, enjoying our drinks and appetizers, enraptured by George and Anne telling stories about their long, full lives. I drink in this moment, the neglected inner child inside savoring every last drop of love, affection, and acceptance offered, hoarding it greedily.

Before Cynthia and I serve the main course, she sends Georgie Jr. and little Ella upstairs with a more kid-friendly meal and stern directions to watch a movie and rest before tonight's outing. Conversation dies out as we dig into the meal, and I am grateful for Charlie's large, warm hand resting on my leg under the table, anchoring me. The memories are straining to break free and consume me, but with his steadfast presence at my side, I refuse to let them. I am learning that my ghosts have their place–in the past. I don't have to forget them; I never will. But I no longer have to let them dictate my present or future either. I can too easily picture spending every holiday like this, safe and welcomed in the bosom of Charlie's family.

After lunch, George and his sons disappear to a covered patio outside to smoke cigars and do whatever it is British men do after Christmas dinner, which certainly isn't yelling at the TV when their favorite football team loses. Cynthia and I join Anne in a quaint sitting room that overlooks her garden. I stand looking out the picture windows, admiring their well-manicured backyard.

"Wow. I bet this view is gorgeous during the summer when your garden is in bloom," I say.

"It is, trust me," Anne says.

"Don't worry," Cynthia adds, "you'll see it soon enough."

I nod, my back turned to the other two women, not trusting my voice.

"You will be back, right?" Cynthia asks.

"Of course," I reply, turning to face them. "Of course I will. You're my new best friend," I say, choking down the well of emotions trying to bubble to the surface. Anne gestures at the seat on the small sofa next to her.

"Come, my dear, sit here with me," she says. I scoot in next to her, closer than is necessary, but I am drawn to her effortless maternal nurturing. She turns slightly toward me, taking my hands in hers. "Charlie adores you. I have never seen my son care for someone the way he cares for you. And after his troubled dating history, I am surprised to see it." Cynthia nods in agreement. "He told us not to pry, so we won't. Just know this. We all already think the world of you and consider you part of the family. We're here to support you, whether you need a safe place to share your burdens or deal with them alone. We are here in whatever capacity you need us."

Cynthia and Anne look at me with twin expressions of sympathy and affection while I process Anne's words.

"Thank you both, really, so much. It's been a long time since I've felt like I belong somewhere and am supported and accepted unconditionally." The Wrights remind me so much of *his* family. I didn't realize until now how much I truly missed this feeling of being welcome and supported, of belonging. The well of despair I've worked so hard to drain and bury threatens to rush up and flood through me.

What if I lose him and them, too?

When someone has experienced as much loss as I have, it's hard not to go down the 'what-if' rabbit hole. Each loss is brutal in its own way, and you learn to deal with it, but recovering after each one becomes more and more challenging. Worry slowly creeps in, and everyone you care about becomes a 'what if'; what if I lose them too begins to play on repeat in your mind. Each time it becomes a certainty, an 'I did lose them,' you add another row to the wall around your heart, and the well of despair expands to consume a little bit more of the meager hope you have left.

While Anne and Cynthia discuss lighter topics, I focus on breathing calmly and evenly, using Anne's motherly grasp on my hand to ground me, tethering me to the present. Within a few minutes, I am again able to engage in the conversation. We spend a pleasant hour together before George Sr. waltzes into the room to collect his wife. The fatigue is more prominent on her face than it was when they arrived, and George treats her with genuine warmth and concern. My heart gives a little squeeze of hope, watching them together.

Cynthia brings the kids down to tell their grandparents goodbye, and we promise to get together again soon. Charlie and I retreat upstairs to prepare for our evening out with his niece and nephew.

"How are you holding up, my love?" Charlie asks.

"Okay . . . better than I expected, actually," I reply. "I think I'm finally figuring out how to manage the anxiety and minimize the panic attacks."

"You are doing wonderfully, Veronica. I will haul this down to the car and get the kids situated. Take all the time you need, love," he says.

"Yes, thank you, Charlie."

Next time I see Anne, I will thank her for raising such a kind, thoughtful, and percep-tive son.

Our night out with Charlie's niece and nephew flies by without any significant hiccups. Georgie Jr. and Ella stayed glued to their uncle's side while we toured the Science and Industry Museum. I hung back, following along like a watchful shadow, allowing them as much one-on-one time with Charlie as possible. And allowing myself space to process any emotions being stirred up by being around them. We did end up warming up to each other at the Play Factore, especially Georgie Jr and I. We partnered up, bonding over our shared competitiveness, and destroyed (good-naturedly) Charlie and Ella in every game we played.

The kids are both tucked into bed in the second room of the hotel suite, utterly worn out after finishing our evening festivities with pizza and hot chocolate. Charlie's warmth enfolds me as his arms wrap around my torso, resting across my abdomen. I lean back, relishing his quiet strength.

"What a beautiful view," I say. "Every place I visit on this continent is beautiful."

He chuckles, head resting against mine as we watch the rain gently bathe Manchester in ethereal beauty.

"Come, my love, let us retire for the evening. I am just as knackered as those two munchkins," he says, tilting his head toward their bedroom. Surprisingly, I fall into a deep, peaceful, and dreamless sleep, wrapped safely in the cocoon of Charlie's arms.

I rise early, slipping from bed to meet a courier in the hotel lobby. I haul my supplies back to the suite and begin preparations for breakfast. By the time the smell of bacon frying lures Charlie and the kids out of bed, I've filled multiple pancake pens with pancake batter, each dyed a different color. Charlie waltzes into the kitchen, rolling up his sleeves to take over, but I playfully shoo him to the other side of the counter. He sneaks a quick peck on my lips as he passes, retreating with a skeptical look on his face. I grin back at him with equal parts sweetness and arrogance. It's been a while since I've made any pancake art, but I'm confident that muscle memory, paired with all the creating I've been doing lately, will pull through for me.

I pull the bacon out of the oven, remove it from the pan, and place it on a plate lined with a paper towel. I set the plate on the counter in front of my audience of three, along with a carafe of orange juice, then take a quick mental inventory, ensuring I have everything I need to begin. Inhaling deeply, I clap my hands, drawing my audience's attention.

"I am about to blow your mind," I say with dramatic flair.

Layers of russet and tan, black and white, green and yellow, and gray and white sizzle on the griddle as the shapes of the animals from Georgie Jr. and Ella's favorite cartoon, *The Animals of Farthing Wood*, come to life. A collective gasp sounds from my rapt audience when I flick my wrist, flipping the first pancake with a little flourish to reveal a perfectly detailed fox. I hand Ella a plate, instructing her to hold it slightly off the counter out in front of her. I pause for dramatic effect, making eye contact with each of them before quickly flipping the second pancake to reveal a skunk; then, fast as lightning, I flip the fox high into the air, landing it face up on Ella's outstretched plate.

The three of them erupt in squeals of delight and applause. I bow, then repeat my performance with the frog for Georgie and the skunk for Charlie, earning even more giggles from the kids. The cute little bunny gets set aside for me. I carefully wipe down the hot griddle while Charlie and the kids slather their pancakes with butter and syrup, but don't turn it off yet, guessing they'll demand round two. My intuition is proved correct after only a couple of bites.

"Veronica, you've been holding out on me. These pancakes are delicious," Charlie says.

"Yeah, Auntie Ronnie! Make some more, please," little Ella exclaims, causing my heart to squeeze in my chest with equal parts joy and pain. I meet Charlie's eyes briefly, the love I find in them anchoring me to the present.

"Can you make the snake, the otter, and the mole, too?" Georgie asks, voice rising with excitement.

"And Superman, too," Ella shouts. I make pancake animals and superheroes until the batter is completely gone.

Stuffed and content, the four of us pack up and head back to their house, Ella reverently carrying two wrapped plates full of leftover pancakes. Charlie skillfully moderates an argument between his niece and nephew over who gets to present the pancakes to their parents while expertly navigating the wet Manchester streets.

The door opens as we ascend the four stairs up the small front deck, James and Cynthia expecting us. I sent them a heads-up text on our way back, just in case. James must have implemented Charlie's advice. For the first time all weekend, Cynthia looks relaxed, content, and like a woman who feels seen. She meets my eye, a slight blush staining her cheeks when I give her a mischievous wink.

"Mommy, mommy. Daddy, Daddy," the kids exclaim over each other.

"Look what Auntie Ronnie made for us," Georgie says, causing another crack in the wall protecting my heart. I reach out blindly, groping for Charlie's hand, grasping on desperately when his fingers lace with mine.

"These look amazing," James says.

"They're yummy, too," Ella replies.

The kids drag their parents to the kitchen, insistent that they eat the yummy pancakes immediately. I move to follow, but Charlie pulls me in the opposite direction.

"Come, my love. It has been a long weekend, and we have a long drive home." He pulls me up the stairs behind him to pack and head home to London.

Complete Emotional Wreck

The evening breeze rolled off the ocean, chasing away the day's heat. Laughter from many voices floated over the sand to where the woman sprawled on a lounge chair, a content smile on her sun-kissed face. She whistled at a tall, muscular figure as he chased three tiny silhouettes. His head snapped up, and he gave her a private, knowing smile. The man murmured to the three tiny figures, and they ran screeching to the others.

He sprinted up the beach and situated himself in the chair behind the woman, tucking her protectively against him. She rolled onto her side, laying her head on his chest. His heart beat a strong, steady rhythm against her cheek. Content to listen to the beat, she smiled, chest swelling with love for the heart, his heart, that belonged to her. The man tilted her chin up with a knuckle, then gently, reverently, kissed her. Tears of happiness trickled down her face at the tenderness and promise in that kiss. He wiped them away with his thumb and brushed his lips against her forehead.

He murmured silent words into her hair, absently caressing her back. The woman jerked her head up to search his eyes, unwilling to accept what he said. He repeated himself, assuring her that he loved her and that he just wanted her to be happy. He promised to meet her again in a place where there is room for every love. Encouraging her with his eyes and imploring her with his words, he told her to let go, to live and love without restraint.

Tears poured down her face, and her breaths came in great, heaving sobs. She shook her head, denying his words, and begged him not to leave her.

The man placed another kiss on the woman's brow and extricated himself. Without looking back, he sprinted down the beach. She shot to her feet and ran after him, but no matter how fast she pumped her legs, she couldn't catch him. He paused only long enough to gather the three tiny figures, then led them farther and farther away from the heartbroken woman until their silhouettes were mere dots on the horizon. She fell to her knees, heaving sobs wracked her body, and snot ran from her nose. She screamed and screamed, begging them to come back, to not leave her again.

The woman's silhouette fades into a dark smudge, and the warm, tan beach starts spinning faster and faster until it morphs into a cold, grey street. The woman's knees scrape roughly against the pavement as she fights against the arms restraining her. Kind but sorrowful voices try to comfort her, try to drag her away from the grizzly scene before her, but she's hysterical, fighting for dear life.

"No," she screams. "Please, no," she begs, her heart shattering into a million tiny pieces.

"No, no, no, no," I scream myself awake.

Strong arms wrap around me, pinning my thrashing, trembling body to the solid, warm presence behind me. I still momentarily, holding out hope that somehow, I caught the figure in the nightmare, yet knowing it can't be true no matter how hard I wish for it. A sob of despair wells up from the pit of my stomach and surges out of me. I roll in Charlie's grasp, burying my head in his chest, sobbing even harder. He holds me steadily, stroking my hair and murmuring words of comfort in my ear.

When my body stills and my breathing evens out, he pulls away.

"Would you like to sit up?" I nod. "Tissue?" I nod again. He also grabs a handkerchief out of his nightstand and tenderly wipes my face. I settle a little more, his kind gesture and solid presence anchoring me back to the present. I take the hankie from him, wiping the evidence of my distress off his chest. Efficiently extricating himself from the sheets, he stands, then deftly scoops me into his arms with minimal effort. He deposits me on the sofa facing the London skyline and brews us both a cuppa. We sip tea in silence for a few minutes before he slings his arm over my shoulders.

"I am here if you want to talk about it, and I am here if you do not. Whatever you need, my love."

"Let's just say being around your family brought up a lot of feelings, emotions, and memories that have been buried for a long time. I'll deal."

"I am sorry, Veronica, I should not have pushed you to come. I–"

"No, no, Charlie. I enjoyed it. I really did, and I'm glad I went with you. I think 'operation intervention' went off with a bang."

"Pun intended?"

"Of course. Did you see the difference in Cynthia?" I feel him nod against my head. "We should go up there every few months and take the kids out for the night. Go back to the Play Factore. Georgie Jr. and I dominated you and Ella."

"Bullocks. If we did not have to go to work, I would dominate you right now," he says, voice husky, pinning me to the bed. I buck my hips, grinding against him, and all thoughts of work fly out the wall of windows.

Knock, knock, knock . . . knock, knock, knock . . .

My hands, stained with all the earthy shades of the enormous landscape scene I'm painting, move across the canvas with precision, never faltering at the incessant pounding trying to break through my concentration.

Ronnie . . . Ronnie . . .

A tap on my shoulder jolts me back to reality. I jump and accidentally brush a stroke of black where I didn't intend to.

It's a happy little tree now.

I take a deep breath before facing Kali. She is a sight to behold and a force to be reckoned with. She stands, hands on her hips, tall and elegant in her crisp white pants suit and six-inch black stiletto heels. She towers over me, her expression slightly amused, slightly annoyed, slightly reprimanding.

"Your phone has been ringing incessantly for the past thirty minutes. I had to use the emergency code to get in here and get your attention."

"Sorry, I've been a little distracted or easily distracted. Or maybe, easily lost in a project to distract myself?"

"Exactly. Ever since you got back from Manchester. Are you sure everything went well while you were there? Is Charlie treating you well?"

"Yes, and yes. It's just . . . I have a lot going on, okay?

"Okay. You know Ronnie, Kellan, and I adore you. We can be good listeners if you need someone to talk to." I raise my eyebrows, and a sly smile spreads across her face. "Granted, you might have to muzzle us to get us to quit talking long enough, but," she shrugs her slender shoulders and laughs, dropping gracefully onto the extra stool at the workbench. I surreptitiously move paint, glitter, and other messy supplies away from her immaculate white-clad elbow, which moves animatedly while she talks. "I think Kel is seeing someone, but he won't tell me."

"Oh," I say, not surprised by the sudden topic shift. Kali is notorious for jumping from subject to subject with little warning. "Why won't he tell you?

"Because," she drawls, "I think it's a man."

"Do you . . . not approve?"

"I could care less. I've known since we were little, although he's never confirmed his tastes."

"He prefers men," I speculate.

"Not specifically. He doesn't have a hard and fast preference. He's dated plenty of women openly and always seemed genuinely attracted to them and invested in those relationships."

"I'm having a hard time believing your no-bullshit, confident, assertive brother would hide a lover, male or female. Why hasn't he 'come out' yet?"

"Well, we may have strong French roots, but our parents are rather closed-minded. Even though we don't see them often anymore, one cannot easily overcome that type of programming." I nod my head, understanding exactly what she means.

If only everyone was blessed with parents like George and Anne.

"I can understand that, trust me. I have been no-contact with my mother for many years. But he won't even confide in you? Surely you would support him, regardless of his sexual preferences."

She gives me a pointed look, and I stammer, "Obviously. It's obvious you would. No doubt. I'm sure he knows that, too."

"Oh, he does," she agrees. I don't doubt that she's made her feelings extremely clear to him. "He'll come around eventually."

"What about you, Kal? Is there a special man out there? Or woman. Have you seen Theo lately or the other gallery manager lady?" I bounce my eyebrows at her. She throws her head back and laughs, a rich, caramel-y sound that seeps into your pores, making it impossible not to join her.

"Put those bloody eyebrows away, Ron," she says, swiping a finger delicately under an eye. "I'm in the prime of my life. I will be shackled to no one, man or woman. You know that I prefer casual dalliances."

"I do, but that can change. That gallery manager is gorgeous. I bet she's a voracious lover," I tease in an atrocious Kellan impression. She snorts.

"Oh, stop. Enough about me. What about you and your fine hunk of meat?"

"Kali," I say, playfully swatting her arm.

"What? Inquiring minds want to know. Does the proportion of his massive hands translate to other areas?" Try as I might, I can't stop the heat that stains my high cheekbones a damning red. She grins at me like the lithe jungle cat she is. "Hmm," she purrs. "Well then. Does that brooding intensity also translate into the bedroom?" My blush deepens.

Fucking glass face.

Although I have to admit, it feels good to share this camaraderie with someone who knows nothing of my past. There are no shadows in her eyes, no worry lining her face, no pity.

"He's a very skilled lover," I confide. She elbows me in the side.

"Even for being such a young pup?"

I roll my eyes and shake my head. "You can just ask, you know. I'm eight years older than him."

"Cougar. Rawr." I giggle and elbow her again.

"He's sweet, though. He has infinite amounts of patience, with me at least. He's possessive but gives me space when I need it. Oftentimes, I don't even have to ask; he just seems to know what I need before I do."

"So why have you been avoiding him?" There's the blunt, assertive Kali I love.

"I don't really have a good reason, Kali. My past broke me. I've been running from it for so long, refusing to let anyone in."

"Until Charlie," she gently prods when I don't continue.

"Until Charlie. And everything is perfect between us so long as we stay in our safe little bubble. Meeting his family made me question whether our relationship can be successful *outside* of the bubble. I'm struggling to figure out how to reconcile everything I've endured with everything I stand to gain if Charlie and I can make this work."

She pats my shoulder affectionately. "Well, he adores you—worships you. There's no doubt about that. And I've seen you work through problems and find solutions these past months. I have faith that you can do the same with this situation. A few weeks off to go home will be good for you. Check your phone," she throws over her shoulder as she walks briskly back into the gallery, leaving the door open for me to follow.

If only it were that simple. Our time with Charlie's family shattered the vault door to the last, most painful repressed memories, allowing them to flow freely, threatening to consume me whole. Dealing with memories of *him* gets easier with practice. But, where the memories of *him* are like a match burning down too close to your skin, memories of the others are like a white-hot inferno, searing third-degree burns through every layer of self until only a charred skeleton remains. They leave no place inside untouched, no place safe, so I have been hiding outside, in my work and with Charlie.

Multiple notifications from both Catherine and Sophie fill my phone's screen. My heart starts racing, and I struggle to pull enough air into my lungs. No, please, no. I can't handle another emergency, another phone call that brings only loss and despair. I stumble upstairs, focusing on breathing to calm myself instead of the steps in front of me. As I walk through the door, my phone buzzes in my hand, startling me, and I fling it across the room. I slam the door and quickly retrieve it, and part relief and part dread settle in my stomach when I see both Catherine's and Sophie's faces on the screen.

I take another deep breath and swipe the green button. "Hey, guys."

"Ronnie. Are you okay," Sophie exclaims.

"Yeah, is everything alright," Catherine adds.

"What are you two talking about," I ask.

"We haven't heard from you all week," Catherine says.

"So, that's not unusual."

"Except that you promised to call us this week to lock in details for your trip home in THREE DAYS," Sophie exclaims.

"And it's that time of year," Catherine adds.

"You're right. I'm sorry. I've been working extra to ensure everything is kosher for Kal and Kel while I'm gone," I accede.

"You still only have one ticket booked," Sophie points out.

"You're not going to bring Charlie home to meet us?" Catherine asks.

"I haven't decided," I reply sheepishly. "We're going to talk about it tonight, I promise."

"Okay. Send us the info tomorrow," Catherine says.

"Promise," Sophie demands.

"I promise. I gotta get back to work. I have some projects I need to finish before I call it quits for the year. See you guys soon!"

Fuck. Fuck. Fuck.

I toss my phone on the sofa and hurry back to the sanctuary of the workroom, trying to leave all my worries behind, but they don't stay put. I'm barely holding on by a thread. I should have waited to meet Charlie's family until after my trip home. I was getting pretty good at dealing with thoughts of *him*. But he's only one piece of the puzzle. I thought I was ready to face the whole of what I lost. Fuck, was I wrong. None of the strict daily routines that I've been doing, even at Charlie's, daily affirmations, breathing exercises, playing piano, working out, on top of therapy and life coaching sessions, can prepare me to face those ghosts. Losing myself in projects, working a crazy number of hours since we got home from Manchester, and living in the distraction of work combined have just barely allowed me to maintain my sanity.

Can you handle a trip home with Charlie, V?

Can I handle it without him?

I know he's worried about me. We have hardly seen each other since early Christmas with his family. Every time he looks at me with such love and such obvious concern in his eyes, I almost unravel entirely. I've even considered telling him about *before*.

NO! It's too painful. He can never know. What will he think of me?

So much guilt. It's the one emotion that poses the biggest threat. Everyone who knows has repeatedly told me that what happened wasn't my fault. But, how can I believe them when I was so selfish that day? If I hadn't been, things would have turned out so differently.

STOP! V, stop. You don't want to lose another month of your life wallowing in self-pity. Knock, knock, knock, knock, knock.

I know it's Charlie without even looking. He always knocks like that, five quick, staccato raps on the glass. I take a few deep breaths, inhaling through my nose and exhaling forcefully through my mouth, trying to release the tension I've created arguing with myself. I go deep inside, bricks and mortar in hand, to quickly repair as much of the wall around my heart as I can.

"Veronica," he says quietly. "Veronica, sweetheart . . ."

I step into him, resting my face against his chest, finding a calming strength in his embrace.

Voice muffled against his shirt, I say, "I've decided. I can't promise I won't be a complete emotional wreck the entire time, but I'd like you to come to the States with me for Christmas."

Welcome to the Family

"This is where you grew up? It is beautiful from up here." I lean across him to look out the airplane window. The mountainous terrain is beautiful, covered in a blanket of fresh white snow, passing by quickly as we descend for landing.

As we walk to baggage claim I say, "I hope Cat and Soph don't go too overboard. I'm pretty sure they are more excited for me to have a boyfriend than I am."

"Well, that is unacceptable." He stops in the middle of the sea of departing passengers, pulling me to him and kissing me until my head spins. A devilish grin splits across his face when he releases me.

"Spoiled, English brat," I say to his back as he pulls me along behind him.

We just barely exited the luggage bay, two large rolling suitcases in tow, when I was accosted by shrieks and arms pulling me into a tight embrace.

"Hi, Soph," I say before Cat cuts in, pulling me into her arms.

"Hi, Cat," I say. I reach back, twining my fingers with Charlie's, pulling him forward to stand beside me. "Sophie, Catherine," I nod to each in turn. "This is Charlie."

They shake his hand and fawn over him for a few minutes before we go to the parking lot and load up to head to Sophie and Turner's house.

"I'm surprised you two made it out of the house by yourselves," I say from the back seat.

"It wasn't without a fight, that's for sure," Catherine replies from the driver's seat on the *right side* of the car!

"We finally bribed the guys into staying home with the kids with beer and grill duty," Sophie adds.

"We both got lucky with men who can cook. It sounds like Ron lucked out in that department, too," Catherine says.

"Yes, I am fairly skilled in the kitchen," Charlie replies, smirking at me out of the corner of his eye. "Did you know that, until recently, I was not aware that Veronica even knew how to cook, let alone was good at it?"

"What," my two best friends exclaim in unison.

"She's always the one who cooks when we're together. She's a fabulous chef," Soph says. Charlie tells them about our weekend in Manchester, the intervention, and his being pleasantly surprised at my culinary skills. The three of us women burst into a fit of giggles when he described the look I gave him when his niece and nephew declared me the better cook.

"Ron and her looks," Sophie says, shaking her head playfully.

The knot of anxiety that has been sitting heavy in my stomach since we left the studio to go to Heathrow loosens, and I breathe easy for the first time in two days. My goal is to simply enjoy this visit home without the guilt, shame, and despair that usually assaults me twice as hard as usual as soon as I cross the Idaho border. Sophie and Turner recently moved into a new house a few miles outside the city. It's free of painful memories, which should help me hold my shit together while we're here.

"Sophie," I breathe. "I don't remember much from the last time I was here, but this is beautiful. It came together exactly how you two imagined," I say as she pulls onto a long driveway lined with perfectly spaced young pine trees. The house is a vast, modern-day log cabin with an enormous wraparound deck and large picture windows facing the mountains.

"Wait till you see the inside," Catherine claims. "Jake and Cora have been raving about it since we helped them move in."

"And let me guess, little Lainey hasn't left Uncle Turner's side long enough to notice," I say.

"Nope, and he's been loving every minute of it," Sophie says, "especially the minute when he can give her back at the end of the day, sugared-up and exhausted."

"Wired and tired," I chime in.

"Thanks," Catherine deadpans.

Charlie looks confused, so I quickly clarify who's who before we head inside.

"Soph and Turner are happily married; you'll remember they love dogs and other people's kids. Cat and John are also happily married and have three kids: Jake, Cora, and Lainey. None of us are actually related, but we're family regardless."

We haul our luggage onto the wraparound deck and make our way to the back of the house, which boasts a cozy, covered porch with a built-in grill and firepit. The smell of food and the sounds of laughter precedes us as we round the corner. The sight of my best friends and their kids sitting around a firepit, BBQing, and laughing is so familiar that, for a split second, I swear I hear *his* voice in the cacophony and see *them* sprinkled in with the rest. I inhale, a quick, sharp hiss, and my step falters.

Charlie grips me around the waist with his free hand and murmurs in my ear, "I got you." His firm grip and calm demeanor anchor me to the present. At this moment, I am so thankful he's here, so unbelievably grateful for him that my heart swells with love, and a few more pieces are put back in place.

"Auntie Ronnie, Auntie Ronnie," Catherine's kids squeal as they bombard me with hugs. I hug them each fiercely with one arm, the other clinging tightly to Charlie.

"We missed you," Jake declares. His sisters nod in agreement.

"I missed y'all too," I reply. Then, I am pulled into one of Tuner's famous back-breaking bear hugs. Before letting me go, he wraps a playful arm around my neck, giving me a freaking noogie. He's the oldest of our group and acts like everyone's big ol' teddy bear of a big brother. Some of the tension I've been holding onto melts away, and I take a deep breath, giving him a grateful smile.

"Turner, Sophie's husband," I say to Charlie. And to Turner, "This is Charlie."

They shake, and I giggle when Charlie lets out a little yelp of surprise when Turner pulls him into a one-armed man-hug, slapping him on the back and saying, "Welcome to the family."

Charlie inclines his head, licking his lips and running a hand through his dark, wavy hair. I haven't seen him do that in a while.

Aww, Mr. Self-possessed is nervous. Fucking adorable.

"Ron," another familiar tenor voice says, and John pulls me in for a quick hug. "It's good to see you," he murmurs.

"You too," I reply, stepping back to introduce Charlie again. John skips the handshake altogether, pulling Charlie in for a quick hug instead.

"You want a beer?" John asks Charlie, who catches my eye, eyebrows raised. I nod.

"Yeah, mate. It has been a long couple of days," Charlie replies. John inclines his head over his right shoulder.

"They're in the fridge. Here, Ron. Let me take your suitcase. Charlie and I will take it in. San Pellegrino?"

I nod, and then the guys are off to the house. Turner follows with a plate of finished cheeseburgers that smell divine, especially after the less-than-stellar meal we had a few hours ago mid-flight.

I settle on a navy cushioned, white wicker patio loveseat and listen with half an ear as Catherine, Sophie, and the kids chatter about work and school. I feel the push in my mind of memories demanding acknowledgment. Instead of immediately fighting against them, I steady my breath and focus on my surroundings: Sophie's laugh, Catherine's gentle words for her kids, the dogs barking in the trees, the feel of the fire on my face, and the weave of the wicker under my fingers.

This is the present, V. Let the past be.

I objectively acknowledge the memories: *I see you; I know you're there.*

Then I tell them firmly but kindly: *Fuck off.*

After this little chat with myself, it is easier to be present in the moment. I engage with my chosen family more earnestly and even laugh easily when Sophie tells a funny story about her first week as Chief Nursing Officer. The guys return, rueful smiles plastered on all three of their faces, and pass out drinks.

"Here you go, my love," Charlie says, offering me a cold, slender can as he sits, casually draping himself around me on the loveseat. Even after all these months with him, I still marvel at his ease in himself, at the effortless confidence he exudes everywhere he goes. I can't remember a time ever when I felt truly at ease with myself.

"Chow's ready," Turner declares, and we all filter inside. Mouth open, I take in the finished interior of their beautiful home. The main level is one massive room with high ceilings filled with warm, cozy light emitted by multiple sparkling chandeliers. A large fireplace, bracketed by a wall of windows, dominates the center of the living room. A sitting area is arranged in front of the fireplace with oversized leather couches and armchairs. Maple burl end tables and a matching coffee table, made by yours truly, are tucked between the furniture. Behind the sitting area, a small entryway equipped with a bench and coat rack is tucked under a set of stairs leading to a loft over the kitchen.

The kitchen is another chef's dream. It's set up very similar to Cynthia's kitchen, with two double wall ovens and an island with a rinsing sink, gas stove, and built-in chopping block. The most significant difference is the open wood shelving that lines most of the entire back wall of the house. The kitchen is open on both ends, and there is a straight shot from the entryway through the kitchen to the dining area that is dominated by a large, live-edge maple dining table. The table itself is a work of art, and it's the last piece I made before I left the States over a year ago now.

Ever since I knew them, Turner and Sophie have aimed to buy property in this area outside of town and build their dream home. When I informed them I was going abroad, they were about ninety percent done with the construction of the house. When they first purchased the property, it was largely untamed. It contained a few of these beautiful bigtooth maple trees that they just couldn't avoid cutting down to make room for the house. Turner had them milled into slabs and burls and begged me to make a live edge, epoxy river dining table, and the other smaller tables spread throughout the house. He surprised Sophie with them when they moved in.

I was very reluctant at first, afraid of what I would feel, fearful of the memories of doing this project, a project I would have done with *him* at my side *before,* might free from the vault. But I eventually said yes, wanting to give back a little to these two who sacrificed so much to keep me going when I didn't have the will to do so on my own. So, I snuck out to Idaho to the site of the almost-finished house and spent a few weeks building these tables. The smaller tables are simple, each a small maple burl, sealed in clear epoxy resin and set on hairpin iron table legs.

The dining table is not simple. I built a custom mold for the behemoth. I chose to build it on-site because it is cumbersome and would have been a pain in the ass to move. *He* and I never trusted anyone else to transport our pieces after a fiasco early in our career with a shipping company that ruined a smaller but similar table, cost us thousands of dollars, and almost sunk our business.

The table boasts a river of matte black epoxy snaking between two slabs of maple, with another strip of the epoxy creating one smooth, long edge. The long side facing the inside of the room is live-edge wood. There's a matching live-edge maple slab bench running along the back side of the table, connected to the sturdy iron table base. Charlie and I slide onto the bench with Catherine's kids.

The joyous revelry we share during the meal is a temporary balm to my battered soul. Stories are told, laughs shared, clever quips exchanged. Charlie's steadfast presence at my side keeps me firmly anchored in the present. He fits in just as easily here, dressed down in jeans and a white tee, eating BBQ with upper-middle-class Americans, as he does dressed to the nines, sipping Macallan doubles at ultra fine dining in London. He's sort of a chameleon, shifting and molding to his surroundings while easily maintaining the core of who he is.

After dinner, I help Catherine tuck her girls into one of the spare rooms in the loft while Jake, who's fifteen, drags Charlie to the basement, which is mostly one big gaming room equipped with a pool table, foosball, pinball, shuffleboard, darts, pop-a-shot basketball, and a massive TV hooked up to multiple gaming consoles. After a quick round of pool, where Charlie easily beat Jake, I grab the other adults another round of beers.

We congregate outside at the fire pit, reminiscing about the recent past and sharing ideas, goals, and dreams for the future until it's too cold, even with the fire roaring. None of us are ready to call it a night, so we sprawl out in the living room, each couple claiming a sofa, drinking and talking and laughing till the wee hours of the morning. I fall asleep, head propped on Charlie's thigh, his fingers tracing shapes through my hair, the love and safety of my family surrounding me, easing my heavy burdens and allowing me to fall into a deep, content rest.

And to All A Good Night

Charlie and I wake early Christmas Eve morning to tickles and giggles, with Cora and Lainey jumping on the bed, which turns into an all-out pillow fight. As the only three, now four, early risers of the group, we do our best to be quiet. Charlie lands a particularly good hit on little Lainey, who flies off the bed, eyes as round as saucers. She's not hurt, but before we get out of hand, I send the girls to the kitchen to raid the pantry for snacks while Charlie and I get dressed.

While the girls clean up their impromptu breakfast, I snag a set of keys off the rack, click the remote start button, and hit the garage door opener. Quietly, we don our heavy winter coats and brave the cold to go to the store to stock up for the next few days. There's a nasty snowstorm moving in. Nobody will be going anywhere for a while. Charlie, who insists on driving (showoff), has barely begun backing out of the garage when the door swings open to reveal Jake. Throwing on his coat, he bounds down the stairs two at a time and jumps in the back with his sisters, rubbing his bare hands together between his legs to generate some warmth.

"Good morning, Jake," I say as Charlie heads down the driveway.

"Morning," he says, voice still groggy. "I heard you guys up and didn't want to miss another one of Auntie Ronnie's famous shopping trips."

"Auntie Ronnie's famous shopping trips," Charlie parrots, arching an eyebrow.

"I have no idea what they're talking about," I say primly.

"Whatever Auntie. Thing One and Thing Two over here didn't shut up about the last one for, like, ever," Jake disagrees. I hide a smile, turning my head towards the window. I'm surprised he wants to come, being at that age where he's too cool for his family, especially his little sisters.

"Enlighten me. What is so special about these . . . shopping trips," Charlie presses.

"We buy lots of stuff! Like ten carts full of stuff," little Lainey, who is seven, exclaims. We still refer to her as 'little' because she is just a tiny little thing, short and scrawny.

"It was only two carts, Lain. How would three people even push ten carts," Cora says with all the self-importance of a mock-sophisticated ten-year-old. Lainey sticks her tongue out at her sister.

"Whatever, Cora. And Uncle Charlie, she pushes us really fast. She rides the carts like a—scooter. And she lets us do it, too. Right, Cora?" I clutch a fist to my chest to keep the pieces of my heart from scattering on the winds of my emotions. Love and loss, courage and despair, contentment and resentment swirl in my chest, creating a maelstrom of conflicting emotions. I grab blindly for Charlie's hand, resting our intertwined fingers on my lap, and sync my breathing to his. After only a few breaths, I am able to return my focus to the conversation.

"She buys us lots of stuff, too," Cora is explaining. "Toys, clothes, pretty much whatever we want. And food, Uncle Charlie. Lots of food."

"My love language is food," I say, shrugging my shoulders as Charlie maneuvers Sophie's suburban into the shopping center parking lot. "Where to first?" I ask, turning to look at the kids in the back seat.

"Target," the girls shriek in unison. Jake rolls his eyes and sighs loudly.

"Look," Charlie points out his window. "There's a GameStop. Shall we divide and conquer?" I don't necessarily want to give up time with my nephew, but I nod. If we're going to beat this storm home, we can't take all day, and it will be good for the boys to have some bonding time. "We will come find you ladies in a little bit. Have fun!" He leans across the center console, quickly pecking my lips. The girls muffle giggles into their mittens, and I'm pretty sure I *hear* Jake's eyes roll. Their parents are not affectionate in public.

The girls and I spend the rest of the morning racing shopping carts, giggling, and hiding from the boys. Cora thought it would be hilarious if we could outmaneuver them as long as possible. After silencing a handful of calls, I discreetly texted Charlie, 'Come find us,' with a winky face to prevent him from worrying.

They finally find us in the food court two hours later, grabbing donuts and juice.

"Where do you plan to put all the food?" Charlie asks as we fill the suburban's back end with the morning's many purchases.

"I'll call Cat when we're checking out at the grocery store to meet us," I reply. "Everybody jump in. Let's go get all the goodies!"

As we drive the few blocks to the grocery store, Jake quickly fills us girls in about his and Charlie's morning adventures. Charlie isn't much of a gamer, and Jake has teased him ruthlessly all morning for how out of place he was in Game Stop. And from the sounds of it, Charlie took Jake on a wild goose chase, trying to find me and the girls, dragging it out as long as he could to give us plenty of girl time. I squeeze his hand and look at him gratefully. It's obvious the kids are having a great time, and I am, too, in large part due to his being here.

We easily fill three carts full of food, indulging the kids' every whim. Their parents allow me this one indulgence every time I visit–to spoil the shit out of their kids (and them). It helps assuage my guilt for everything I wish I had done differently. Catherine meets us in the parking lot, and we load the groceries quickly, eager to get out of the cold. Little Lainey falls asleep on the drive back, head gently cradled in her brother's lap. John, Turner, and Sophie meet us in the driveway to help unload our considerable haul. John carefully extracts Lainey from the back seat, so worn out she doesn't wake up even when the cold wind blasts her face.

We eat lunch on the go while we unpack and put away and start preparing all the food for the next few days. I command the kitchen, doling out orders to kids and adults alike. I love big kitchens for this very reason. It is the heart of a house, and when it's full of people and food, my heart is full, too. I get lost in the rhythm of the afternoon, mind and soul blessedly content and at peace, surrounded by all the people who mean the most to me, some in body, some in spirit.

When the late afternoon sun slants warmly through the windows, and all the food is prepped, everyone heads in separate directions to have a little downtime and quiet before the evening's festivities. I take a quick shower, letting the hot water wash away a few days' worth of grime and tumultuous emotions. Towel wrapped securely around my chest, I sneak down the hall to the spare bedroom Charlie and I share. I ease inside, locking the door. Charlie lies on the bed wearing only a pair of shorts, torso propped on pillows against the headboard, fingers laced behind his head. He's one of the few people I know in our modern culture who is content to just be without the need to always have his nose buried in a screen.

I drink in the sight of him displayed on the bed like a statue of a modern Greek god, all sculpted planes and angles. We have spent very little time together in the past few weeks because I shut him out and pushed him away. Yet here he is, on another continent, in a different country, spending multiple days with a bunch of people he doesn't know, constantly consoling me, his partner who spends too much of her time pining after her long-lost love.

Wow, V. What a fuckup you are.

A pang of guilt blooms in my chest, then pulses down my torso, morphing into an unbearable pulse of desire. I need to be with him, to feel his skin against mine. I need the peace and quiet that comes from being intimate with him. I need to show him how sorry I am and how much I adore him. I loosen my grip on the towel, letting it fall and pool at my feet. Charlie's eyes snap open, the green so dark with desire that they're almost black, fathomless depths that devour me from head to toe. He slides to the edge of the bed so I can step between his legs. His large, warm hands rest on my hips, fingers digging into my flesh possessively.

He peppers my chest and stomach with kisses as he drags his hands back to cup my ass. My eyes roll back in my head, and my back arches when he takes a nipple into his mouth, sucking and teasing it with his tongue before he moves to the other one. My fingers tangle into his wavy, dark hair as he slips a hand between my legs, thumb circling my clit, fingers sliding inside me. Quietly, conscious of our surroundings, I groan, "More, Charlie, more."

He flings me onto the bed and drops his shorts at his feet. Hunter-green eyes bore into mine as he settles between my legs, tongue working me towards climax until stars explode behind my eyes and my legs clench around his head. I'm still floating back to earth when he rolls me onto my side and settles behind me. Happy and content, I arch my back, tilting my hips. He slides into me slowly, inch by exhilarating inch. Then he withdraws just as slowly, repeating the two motions over and over again.

A deep moan rumbles through his chest, and his grip relaxes, pace quickening as his self-control disappears with the onset of his orgasm. He thrusts into me one final, deep, possessive thrust, chasing his pleasure until he is spent. Chest heaving against my back, he pants, "I have missed you," in my ear. We lay for a time after, limbs tangled together, bodies cooling, heart rates returning to normal.

"I missed you too. Charlie, I am sorry for being so distant lately."

"No sweat, my love."

"Thank you for always being so patient and understanding with me. For giving me a safe space to figure out my shit without being pushy."

"It is my pleasure, Veronica. I got you." I kiss him fervently, pouring everything I feel for him into the kiss. He rests his forehead against mine for a long moment.

"Well, love, we best get dressed for dinner," Charlie says into my hair. A groan escapes my lips as I roll over, stretching my arms above my head. I chuckle to myself, watching Charlie pull a pair of black Luca Faloni slacks and a crisp white button-up shirt out of the closet. I briefly consider throwing him to the wolves because it would be hilarious, but I opt for mercy.

"Really, hun? You just couldn't help yourself, could you?" I say, shoulders bouncing.

"What? Surely you did not mean 'casual dress only' for tonight and tomorrow."

I shake my head and pull on a pair of jeans and a cozy, red cable knit sweater. "Suit yourself, love. Don't get me wrong, you look fucking hot. Those kids out there, though, aren't going to give a shit if they ruin your fancy pants."

"Oh, bloody hell, Veronica," he huffs, throwing up his hands in mock exasperation. He carefully hangs the offending clothes back in the closet, then dons only slightly less fancy dark jeans and a plain, but still fancy, white t-shirt topped by a heather gray, soft cashmere shawl collar cardigan. We walk downstairs hand-in-hand, and Charlie sighs side-eyes me as he registers the similar attire everyone else wears. "Remind me to never doubt you again," he murmurs out of the side of his mouth. I playfully bump my shoulder into his. A shriek of glee followed by a blur of color assaults us as we descend the last step. Charlie deftly snags Lainey around the waist as she hurdles herself at him.

"Come play with us, Uncle Charlie," she says, energy fully restored.

"Please, please, please?" Cora adds.

"You promised me another chance to beat your ass at pool," Jake chimes in, completing the three-way attack on any resistance Charlie might have.

John playfully smacks Jake upside the head, "Mind your manners, son. Don't start talking shit and scare away the Brit. I don't think your auntie would be very happy with you."

"No, I wouldn't," I say, digging my fingers into his ribs. He emits an adorable (to everyone else, but mortifying to him) squeal, then snatches me around the thighs, throwing me over his shoulder like a sack of potatoes. I emit a loud shriek and pound him on the back, laughing and begging him to put me down. Cora and Lainey run the opposite way, meeting us behind the couch and assaulting their brother with small fists and laughter.

"Put her down," they cry. I land on the sofa with an 'oof,' high shrieks and deep laughter recede into the basement. I stand up, smoothing down my sweater, a few tears of laughter trailing down my face. Charlie stands there, hands in his pockets, looking a little stunned. His niece and nephew don't play quite as rough as mine, and even though Jake is only fifteen, I'm pretty sure Charlie's instinct is to track down and beat anyone who manhandles his woman. Turner pats Charlie on one shoulder and John on the other.

"Come on, man. Let's go wear those kids out, so they behave at dinner," John says, chuckling. I wink at Charlie and head into the kitchen with Sophie and Catherine to finish preparing Christmas Eve dinner.

As soon as the guys are out of earshot, Sophie gushes, "Ronnie! We *love* him!"

"Yeah, he's so good with the kids. And he seems so down to earth," Catherine adds.

A smile of genuine happiness crosses my face, but a shadow of guilt also flashes in my eyes quickly, but not quickly enough to escape my best friend's notice.

"Oh, Ron. We have no idea how hard this is for you. We won't pretend that we do. But we are here for you," Catherine says.

"In whatever way you need us," Sophie adds.

"You two really are the best friends a girl could ask for. If you see the pain cross my face, a nod, wink, smile, or simple pat on the shoulder is what I need most right now. Just the space to miss *him* and be with Charlie and feel all the feelings that come with both."

Catherine offers me a loving smile from across the kitchen island, and Sophie's hand settles on my shoulder for the briefest moment before she claps her hands together, exclaiming, "Let's finish dinner. I'm starving."

Christmas Eve dinner is ready relatively quickly, considering it consists of hors d'oeuvres, charcuterie boards, and All. The. Goodies. The girls have been Christmas baking for days and we did a bunch more this afternoon. I breathe in deeply, savoring the aroma of the numerous platters, which are artfully decorated with meats and cheeses, fruits and veggies, chips and dip, nuts, pickles, olives, candy, cookies, and all manner of 'mini' delicacies, meatballs, croissants, tacos, bell peppers, cheesecakes, and pies. Crockpots steam and bubble, wafting out the aromas of spinach artichoke dip, little smokies, cheesy cheeseburger dip, and buffalo chicken dip.

Sophie strikes a match to light the candles in the two beautiful centerpieces on the table: fresh pine boughs decorated with holly and red ribbon wrapped around an assortment of candles. The rest of her house is similarly decorated, with fresh pine boughs, red and green, and gold and silver, holly and mistletoe covering every surface. Santa and snowman figurines, gnomes, and elves watch serenely as the guys and kids filter upstairs. I follow the horde around the table, filling gold-rimmed glasses with wine and sparkling juice.

When everyone is seated, Turner rises from his place at the head of the table, wine glass held high. In his best Irish lilt, the candlelight highlighting the red tones in his beard, he blesses us:

"The light of the Christmas star for you.

The warmth of the home and hearth to you.

The cheer and goodwill of friends to you.

The hope of a childlike heart to you.

The joy of a thousand angels to you.

The love of the Son and God's peace to you."

"Saliente!" We cry in unison, clinking glasses. His words settle around me, enveloping me in a blanket of peace and joy. Charlie's presence at my side is a shield, anchoring me to the present and keeping the memories at bay. *They* are still here with me, but for the first time since I lost *them*, they stay in the background, buoying my joy instead of dragging me down to the depths of despair.

Dinner is a rowdy and joyous affair. Food is passed, wine is poured, stories are told, and laughs are shared. At one point, a game of tag breaks out between Jake and his sisters after the girls tattle on him. According to them, he does, in fact, have a crush, and they know who it is. John judiciously wins the game, snagging the girls around their waists, one tucked under each arm, and firmly, but kindly, deposits them back in their seats.

Charlie good-naturedly receives quite a bit of teasing from Turner, as he has a strong love for his Irish roots. By the end of dinner, they affectionately refer to each other as 'the Brit' and 'Mr. Paddy' respectively, exchanging jokes and quips as often as the opportunity arises. And as for us women, we gush over the kids and fawn over our men, skillfully delivering a handful of perfectly timed clever asides to keep them humble and on their toes.

"Man, I am stuffed," Turner says, rising from his chair, leisurely dismissing the rest of us from the table. We work as a team to clean up, and the whole operation only takes about twenty minutes with everyone helping. Sophie tops off everyone's glasses as we filter into the living room and settle in around the cozy fireplace.

Turner pulls a well-loved copy of 'The Nightmare Before Christmas' off the mantle and settles on a loveseat next to his wife, sharing a look of such tender affection with her that my heart clenches, the memories threatening to slip free until Charlie squeezes my leg and I turn to see a similar expression on his face, just for me. I immediately relax back into the peace of the evening, fiercely hoarding this forgotten feeling of joy. Turner clears his throat and opens the book, settling back into the cushion and propping an ankle over a knee.

"Twas the night before Christmas, and all through the house, not a creature was stirring, not even a mouse; the stockings were hung by the chimney with care, in hopes that St. Nicolas soon would be there."

His deep, animated voice weaves the story around us, skillfully commanding our un-divided attention. Little Lainey sneaks onto our sofa during a brief page turn, snuggling between us. As Turner nears the end of the poem, she starts to nod off. I whisper in her ear to stay awake—because presents—and she shoots straight up, rubbing her eyes.

"He sprang to his sleigh, to his team gave a whistle, and away they all flew like the down of a thistle. But I heard him exclaim, ere he drove out of sight, *Happy Christmas to all, and to all a good night*!"

We whoop and applaud as Turner stands, giving us a small bow. He extracts three presents from under the tree, a ten-foot-tall pine they cut off their property earlier this month. Its boughs are full, fragrant, and extravagantly decorated. He gives each of the kids a gift, and they wait patiently until he returns to his seat next to Sophie. He takes his time contemplating each of the kids, who return his scrutiny with warm, adoring smiles.

"Jake, you go first this year, bud," he declares. Jake wastes no time shredding the wrapping paper to reveal a plain brown box. His dad produces a pocketknife, and Jake carefully cuts down both sides and the center of the box. First, he extracts something pink and fluffy. Since Jake was five, this has been our tradition for the kids to open one present on Christmas Eve, courtesy of Turner and Sophie. And every year, Jake receives a gag gift along with something from his list. It looks like this year, his gag gift is a man-sized pink, fluffy bunny onesie.

"Well, put it on then, Ralphie," Turner says, falling into a fit of hysterics with John as Jake shimmies into the pajamas.

"What else ya get? A Leg Lamp, perhaps," Catherine teases. Jake shoots her a playfully annoyed look, then holds up one Xbox gift card and one GameStop gift card.

"Even better," he says, aiming a grateful smile toward his aunt and uncle.

"Okay, little Lainey. You're next, girlie," Turner says. The girls do not receive gag gifts since it severely backfired the one year Turner tried to give them one. Neither one has quite as broad a sense of humor as their brother. She squeals with delight as she pulls out a large, pink case labeled, 'Nail Art Studio.' Catherine quickly jumps in to assure her daughter she can do everyone's nails–tomorrow–before she has a chance to open it.

"Even yours, Uncle Charlie?" Lainey asks. He agrees with zero hesitation.

"Cora," Turner says to a very wired and tired pre-teen. "Last but not least." She carefully removes the wrapping paper, gently folds it, and hands it to her aunt Sophie before flipping over the small, square box to reveal her gift: a smartwatch.

"Oh my God. I am so excited. I've been wanting one of these, like, so bad, since my parents," at this, she looks at them, rolling her eyes. Charlie and I hide our mirth behind fists as John and Catherine roll their eyes right back at their extremely strong-willed middle child. "Won't let me have a cell phone," she finishes, rolling her eyes. They then patiently help their daughter set up her new watch while Jake discusses what to purchase with his gift cards with Turner.

"Hey, Charlie," Jake calls from his spot on the floor, "do you remember that gaming headset we almost bought at GameStop this morning?" Charlie extracts himself from the sofa, moving to the floor to sit between Turner and Jake. Lainey pulls me by the hand to sit with Sophie and the three of us discuss how she will do each person's nails in the morning. Before long, everyone starts gravitating toward their rooms, yawning and sharing a pat or hug as we pass each other on our way to bed.

Only a few seconds after Charlie closes our door, little Lainey knocks and pokes her head in. I rub a phantom itch on my nose to hide a conspiratorial smile. She holds out a silver and blue patterned rectangle gift box.

"A present for you, Uncle Charlie."

"For me?" She nods. "Well, thank you. I thought only the kids got to open a gift tonight."

"I won't tell anyone if you don't," Lainey replies in a whisper that's louder than her normal speaking voice.

"Okay," Charlie loudly whispers back as he delicately opens the box. He sets it on the edge of the bed and holds a red flannel shirt up to his chest, raising his eyebrows at Lainey. "What do you think?"

"It's perfect," she exclaims, clapping her hands. "Will you wear it tomorrow? Pretty, pretty, please?"

He looks at me dubiously over her head, then replies, "Sure. I would love to."

"Yay!"

"Okay, munchkin, off to bed with you," he says, closing and locking the door behind her. I school my features to neutral as he turns around, still holding the flannel to his chest, eyebrows raised.

"It's the same thing you wear at your parent's farm," I offer.

"Yeah, at the *farm*, Veronica. Not for Christmas supper!"

I laugh and shake my head. "It's gonna be okay. I promise. I mean, do you want to be the one responsible for breaking poor little Lainey's heart?"

"Oh, bloody hell, V. You're just playing dirty now."

"Don't worry, my dear. At least I talked her into matching your nails to your shirt instead of using the brightest, most glittery pink, in her case, like she wanted to." He inhales, long and slow, nostrils flaring. I pat him on the cheek and grab the offending garment from his hands. "You're welcome," I say, as I hang the Walmart flannel in the closet next to his John Smedley trousers.

Safe Space

"Good morning, sunshine," Sophie says cheerily, placing a steaming cup of tea in my hand as I enter the kitchen early Christmas morning. I raise my eyebrows at Catherine, who sits at the island, sipping on coffee.

"You're uncharacteristically cheery this morning, Soph," I reply, rubbing the sleep from my eyes.

"She was the first one awake, too," Catherine adds.

"Wow," I say, drawing out the *o* in an Owen Wilson style.

"And... she's already put out all the gifts and started breakfast." I'm pretty sure my eyebrows have merged with my hairline by this point.

"Did an elf crawl up your ass and set up shop or something," I tease.

"Yeah. Why did we even get up this early if you were going to do everything by yourself anyway," Catherine adds, gesturing between us.

"Ha, ha. Very funny, you two. I won't stand for this abuse, in my own home, on the *one* day of the year I happily crawl out of bed at the ass crack of dawn," she replies, raising her nose and looking down at us.

"How do you manage on the mornings when you work the early shift?" I muse as Sophie and I join Catherine at the island.

"I very unhappily crawl out of bed at the ass crack of dawn. And I wanted a bit of quiet girl time before the rest of the days' chaos." She shrugs.

We spend the next few hours sipping tea and munching on a light breakfast while catching up with everything that's been going on in each other's lives. John and Catherine have been doing a lot of work on their marriage, and she feels that it's finally paying off. She and John and, consequently, their kids are thriving. Sophie is not looking forward to Turner returning to Iraq a few days after the new year to finish his tour. She *is*, however, very much looking forward to him being home permanently when it's over. He finally decided to retire.

At nine o'clock on the nose, exactly as instructed by us women, the men and kids filter into the kitchen. The three grown men immediately seek out their partner, greeting her with a kiss and a "Merry Christmas sweetheart" (or 'love' in Charlie's case). The kids get Christmas hugs as they move through the kitchen to fill their plates. Catherine, Sophie, and I share surreptitious glances, struggling more and more to hide our amusement as no one notices.

Finally, after about five minutes of morning pleasantries, Jake stops in the middle of the kitchen with his hands on his hips, lips pursed in concentration. He looks at his dad, then his uncle Turner. His eyes meet mine briefly as they sweep over Charlie before he looks down at his chest. We ladies hold a collective breath as we watch him throw his head back and laugh. Conversation stalls as the men look back and forth from Jake to each other to us.

Jake's laugh dies down to a chuckle, and he simply points to each of the men in the room. They look down and back up in unison, and we all break into a fit of hysterics when they finally realize that the four of them are wearing the same shirt, courtesy of Catherine. I look up at Charlie, a huge shit-eating grin on my face, and say, "See, hun, I told you, you'd fit in just fine in that shirt." He smiles grudgingly as we herd everyone into the living room to take pictures in front of the tree.

The rest of the day flies by mercifully fast as we zoom from one activity to the next: opening gifts, decorating sugar cookies, and playing multiple heated (us all being competitive) rounds of the many games in the game room–anything to occupy our attention while we're cooped up inside as the winter storm rages outside. And, of course, everyone gets their fingernails painted by little Lainey.

I weather the raging internal storm well—better than in years past. Charlie stays close most of the day, acutely in tune with my struggles, easily settling me with a hand on my leg or a whispered, "I'm here, my love." My chosen family also helps, regularly offering me supportive smiles and warm touches. I return their kindness and support with silent gratitude and a silent promise to regulate my emotions as much as I can without relying solely on their support.

Even though I am upright and participating this year, a massive accomplishment for me, the ache is still there. The well of grief is still deep, so deep. And now, the dam that has held back the raging river of guilt is cracked, allowing it to flow more and more fiercely to mix with the grief, threatening ever more to pull me under and drown me. If it wasn't for the hours and hours of work I've done finally learning to cope and for Charlie's steadfast presence at my side, I'd have succumbed to the pull already. But I keep fighting; fighting to acknowledge the past, leave it where it belongs, and welcome the future with grace and love.

By the time Christmas dinner ends and we've all said goodnight, I am wholly and utterly exhausted. My heart hurts from constantly being pulled in opposite directions, and my head hurts from the effort it takes to hold my shit together. I clumsily strip off my clothes, throw on one of Charlie's shirts, and plop down on the bed, yawning wide enough to cause a stray tear to roll down my cheek. As I snuggle into the blankets, Charlie produces a small red gift box tied with a gold ribbon from his suitcase. I raise my eyebrows at him, my brain too tired to comprehend his actions.

He sits on the edge of the bed beside me, gesturing for me to take the gift. "Merry Christmas, my love."

The box is heavier than I expected. I set it gently in my lap to remove the ribbon. When I pull off the lid, I gasp, and my wide eyes shoot up to meet Charlie's. In the box, nestled on a tiny white silk pillow, is a stunning mini twin of Charlie's *Arnold & Son* watch. I remove it from the box reverently, marveling at the workmanship.

"Charlie, it's beautiful. I love it. They managed to make it both practically identical to yours but also more delicate and feminine. It's a brilliant work of art." I offer him a genuine smile. "Thank you, truly. For everything. This is the first Christmas I will remember fondly in quite a few years." He leans forward, gently cupping my face in his hands, and kisses me tenderly.

"You are most welcome, but it is *my* pleasure. To bring you as much joy as I can. To help ease your burdens. To see your face light up in delight. I will always be your safe space, my love."

A frigid wind, carrying the stench of burnt rubber and the coppery tang of blood, blew through a stand of trees, rustling the dry leaves. Four oaks, one, an ancient behemoth towering over three smaller saplings, stood century in a semi-circle in the center, set apart from the rest by a moat of barren earth. On each of the four trees, a set of dates is carved in deep, jagged strokes. A woman, eyes rimmed red and glistening, studies each tree, caressing each carving reverently and despairing more and more as the difference between the two numbers decreases to a painfully small number as she moves from the largest to the smallest.

Clutching her chest, snot now running down from her nose to mix with her tears, she stumbled back to the ancient, watchful oak and knelt at its base. The ground was hard, cold, and unforgiving under her aching knees and numb feet. No sound escaped as she sobbed, her throat so raw it felt like swallowing sandpaper. She beat and clawed at the rough bark, staining it red from her torn-up fingers.

The woman's lips formed words through her sobs: why, please, no. Devastation, rage, guilt, and despair bubbled up out of the place deep inside, where she kept them locked away and sunk their claws deep into her chest, piercing her heart and shredding it anew. She railed against the truth, the evidence right in front of her that her life was shattered, the pieces scattered on the wind six years ago.

Maybe six more years have passed by while she knelt in the oaks, keeping a tormented vigil until a hand rested tenderly on her shoulder. The touch was achingly familiar yet heartbreakingly foreign. So long had it been since she had felt it. No, no, please, no. Don't leave me again, she thought, afraid to look up.

"Ronnie," a familiar, loving voice murmured. "Ronnie," it said again, more insistent. "Look at me." The woman didn't want to, but she had knelt there for so long, her knees felt like they'd never straighten out again, and her eyes were almost swollen shut, and her fingers, she looked down at them, were a raw, bloody mess. With a knuckle under her chin, he gently raised her face. Seeing his handsome, beloved face broke the dam inside her, and a raging river of guilt crashed into a deep well of grief with such force that it shattered, sending searing splinters of pain through her, pulling her under so forcefully that she doubled over onto the ground, legs pulled tightly to her chest.

No, no, please don't. Don't say it, don't tell me to let go, the woman pleaded through her swollen eyes, but all she said aloud was, "I'm not ready."

"It's time, Ron," he said, kindly but firmly. He helped her sit up, placed a phantom kiss on her dry, cracked lips, then turned and strode into the trees. She tried to stand and follow, but her legs couldn't support her. She thrashed on the ground, writhing in agony of body and spirit, fighting to come up for breath.

Just as he disappeared into the fog, she found her voice and tried to scream, "Come back." The words came out as a tiny, gravelly squeak. "Please, please, don't go. Don't leave me." She mustered one last breath and put all her might behind it as he faded away completely:

"Daniel!" I scream myself awake.

Strong arms wrap around me, pinning my arms to my sides. Warm breath sighs across my face as calming words are murmured near my ear. I know at once that this is not the embrace I yearned for in the nightmare, but it's familiar and safe, and I am grateful for it, nonetheless. Charlie releases his tight grip around my chest and fits me into the hollow of his shoulder, caressing my hair and murmuring comforting words until my breathing regulates. Then, he delicately extracts himself from my embrace and reaches across to turn on the lamp.

His face is open and kind, but his eyes are troubled, and his posture is tense. *Shit.* He scoots to the opposite edge of the bed, contemplating me. After a few tense moments, he asks, "Are you going to be okay?" When I nod, he demands, "Who is Daniel?"

The wariness and hurt in his eyes cause a ball of trepidation to settle roughly in my gut. His only concern with my refusal to discuss my past is the possibility of a troublesome ex. And his only concern with the present is that I would be unfaithful to him.

It's okay, V. Tell him as much of the truth as you can. He'll believe you.

I clear my throat and muster up the courage to say *his* name. "Daniel," my voice wobbles, and my heart breaks, but I press on, "is someone who was once important to me. He still is important to me, but—" I emphasize the word when Charlie's eyes narrow. "But… he is no longer in my life. He's… he's gone, and you don't have to worry about him causing issues. And I am not—would not—cheat on you. Charlie, I adore you. You're my person. My best friend and my partner. Our relationship means everything to me. I would never compromise that." I am rambling by this point; anxiety over Charlie's evident anger and hurt triggers the beginnings of a panic attack.

He takes a deep breath—and then another—and then reaches out to tentatively stroke my cheek. I wait, breath held. He confidently grips my hands before saying, "Okay, my love. I believe you. I have a ton of questions, and I can't promise that I will be able to hold them in forever, but I will do my best to stifle my curiosity and be content with the information freely given."

I sigh, shoulders sagging in relief. He clicks off the light and climbs back under the covers, holding them open for me to snuggle in with him. "Now, come here and let me hold you."

Don't Give Up

"You look lovely, darling," Charlie says, looking over my shoulder at my reflection in the mirror. I've tried on every dress I brought, but I just can't decide what to wear to my sister's New Year's Eve party. I huff and strip off the current dress, a black velvet number, tossing it on the bed next to all the others. I finally settle on a floor-length glimmering silver dress with long sleeves and a plunging neckline and hang it carefully in the garment bag with Charlie's classic black slacks and white dress shirt. Frustration seeps out of me as I try for the third time to clasp my watch with sweaty, trembling hands.

"Here, V. Let me do it." Charlie's hands, nimble despite their size, settle the watch on my wrist, then hold my small, cold hands tenderly. "You're nervous about seeing your sister?" I nod. "Because of the nature of your recent relationship?"

"Yes. I don't know what else to do to mend the rift between us. Short of moving back, I don't think there is anything I can do. But the truth is, I don't want to. Even if my mental block was removed, I wouldn't go back there. My life is in London now, with you."

A smug smirk tugs up the corners of his mouth, and his intense green eyes radiate happiness. "Have you told her how you feel?"

"I have. And so, with every positive step I take forward for myself, I leave her behind feeling abandoned and disappointed."

"I do not agree with it, but I can understand why she might feel that way."

"Yes, I can too. I don't blame her. I did once, though, even though it wasn't her fault. I blamed her for what happened that day. She says she understands why and forgives my harsh words and actions, but it's never been the same between us. We've never been able to regain the ease we used to share."

"You blamed her," he parrots, giving me the space to explain if I want.

"I was out with her that day, shopping, eating, drinking," I huff. "I . . . I should've been, well, not there. But she convinced me to stay longer than I planned, and I was so angry, so devastated that I lashed out at her. It took a long time, perhaps too long, to crawl out of my despair and apologize."

"I can see how that could drive a wedge between two people." I nod, rubbing the bridge of my nose. "But, you keep trying to mend your relationship with her?"

"I do. She's my sister and I love her. As you know, I call or text her regularly. I was there when she delivered her babies and when her father-in-law was so sick he almost died. I do my best to show her that I can be in her life, that I can support her without living down the street."

"I'd hoped she'd start to understand more over time, but if anything, time has made her more frustrated. And that makes me even more nervous about her meeting you. I'm not entirely sure that she approves of our relationship or my decision to finally "settle down," I say, rolling my eyes and adding air quotes for emphasis, "on the opposite side of the globe." He nods and smiles ruefully.

"I hope she at least respects my decisions enough to be civil and keep her unsolicited opinions to herself. I don't want you to find out from anyone else." I lock eyes with him, imploring him to understand.

"If she says anything, I will remove myself from the conversation. I do not want to hear the story from anyone else either." He smiles reassuringly, and I relax, my shoulders dropping a small fraction from my ears.

"Well then," he says, turning to grab our coats from the closet, "now that that is settled. Shall we," he says, holding out my coat.

"We shall," I reply, offering him a grateful smile. "I promised we'd be there early to help set up."

Victoria's house is beautifully decorated, every surface covered in gold, silver, and glimmering black streamers, balloons, confetti, tablecloths, vases, and tableware. Multiple tiny disco balls hang from the ceiling, catching the dimmed lighting just enough to make the space feel like you're floating through stars in the night sky. Vicki and I eventually end up in the kitchen, alone for the first time all evening. I glance surreptitiously at her from the corner of my eye, trying to gauge her mood. She has been a kind, gracious host thus far, but I feel an anxious energy emanating from her.

What is she planning?

"Hey, Vic," I venture tentatively, "Is everything okay? You seem . . . anxious."

"Oh, no, no, Ron. Don't worry. Everything is just fine," she says, elongating the last two words of her sentence, which does little to ease my worry. She's either plotting something or trying very hard to keep her opinions to herself.

"I know things have been rocky between us these past few years, but if something is bothering you, please tell me."

She sets down a platter of food, studies me for a quick second, and then places a kind hand on my arm. "Really, Ronnie, everything is fine. I didn't start planning for tonight as far ahead as I usually do. That's all."

"And you've been helping your mother-in-law recover from knee surgery, too. How's she doing?"

"Yes, that too. She's healing well. And. . ." she gestures in a circle with her hand, looking at me meaningfully, "it is a lot to take in. You with someone else." I try to keep my face neutral, but despite the distance between us, she still knows me well. "I mean, he seems like a great guy, and it's obvious that he adores you. It's just. . . you know." I nod in agreement.

Yeah. It's all so fucking messed up.

"I understand. It's still a lot for me to take in sometimes. But we're good, Vic. Right now, at least. As good as we can be," I ask, desperate for my sister's approval.

An odd glint flashes in her eyes that makes me a little uneasy. There and gone so quickly that I'm not entirely sure that I actually saw it. But she smiles at me warmly and replies. "Yeah, Ron. We're as good as can be." Then grabs up the platter of food and takes it to the other room.

Guests start arriving soon after, a slow trickle of people, mostly old acquaintances with a few fresh faces sprinkled in. I do my best to greet them all warmly, surprising those who knew me *before* when I introduce Charlie. As they mingle with other guests, I see them whispering and throwing incredulous glances in our direction, not even trying to be subtle about it. Embarrassment crawls up my throat, and flames on my face. Charlie notices and leans in, speaking low in my ear.

"I do not especially care, and neither should you, but why is everyone here so obsessed with us?" The tightness in my chest eases, and I release a humorous laugh.

"They are confused because I'm acting normal, and they're waiting for me to snap and give them a good show. They're probably also surprised to see you," I answer, forcefully pushing the memories back into their vault.

"Oh, because I am tall, broody, and British?" I elbow him in the ribs.

"Obviously. Or, it could be because I had been very adamant that I would never date again."

"Well, I am honored to be the man who changed your mind," he whispers seductively into my ear. "Was it my devilishly good looks, excellent taste in art, or my prowess in the bedroom?" he finishes, raising his eyebrows. I shake my head and elbow him playfully.

"Definitely your 'excellent taste in art,'" I joke in a terrible British accent. He chuckles, then turns his head as Vicki greets another group of guests as they step through the door and shrug off heavy coats.

Fuck, Vic. How many people did you invite this year?

The door opens again, and my newly reconstructed and very fragile world shatters.

Tall and lean—like *him*. Gorgeous blue eyes—like *his*. And then a honey, smooth voice unintentionally caresses my name.

"Ronnie," he breathes, surprised. "It's been a long time."

I stifle a sob with a fist and clutch Charlie's hand so firmly that my knuckles ache.

"Daniel," I breathe unconsciously but loud enough for Charlie to hear. He stiffens next to me and whips his head toward me, green eyes shooting twin daggers of betrayal and anger at me. He rips his hand out of mine and turns to stalk away. Over Charlie's shoulder, *Darren*—Daniel's identical twin brother—looks confused.

"Wait," I hiss, catching Charlie's arm. "Charlie, please." My plea halts him in his tracks. "This is Darren," I say, finding my sister standing on Darren's right. I shoot twin daggers of betrayal and anger of my own at her. "Daniel's," my voice catches painfully on his name, "twin brother."

At this, Darren steps forward, offering his hand to Charlie. "The infamous Charlie," Darren says, awe and respect clear in his voice, "The man who finally convinced my ex—"

"Don't," I interject, raising my free hand. "Darren, please don't."

Charlie stiffens again, and he turns slowly. By this point, the entire party is hushed, all of them leeches, eager to witness the drama that poor, broken Ronnie always creates. Her pathetic life provides such great entertainment. Entertainment for them. But they never stop to think about what it is for me: my entire world falling apart, my heart being ripped out of my chest, and me being broken over and over and over again.

They are a bunch of fucking nosy, rude, disrespectful assholes.

"Your ex? Are you bloody serious, Veronica?" he grits out through clenched teeth, voice as cold and hard as I've ever heard it.

"He's not my ex, Charlie," I spit back.

"Then what, Veronica? What is he to you?"

"Nothing, Charlie. Just an old acquaintance." I wince internally at the look of hurt that crosses Darren's face.

"It seems that he," Charlie gestures toward Darren with his chin, "would disagree. No more lies, Veronica. I need the truth. Now, or I'm going back to London."

"I have only ever told you the truth, Charlie," I say, squaring my shoulder and taking a step closer to him. He waits, the tension so thick between us you could cut it with a knife.

"That's it. That's all you have to say?" he demands, disbelief morphing back into anger in the blink of an eye. I remove my hand from his arm and ball my hands into fists at my sides, holding my shit together by sheer force of will. I will not give these idiots the satisfaction of seeing me break again.

"I have suffered incomprehensible loss," I say, quavering voice low and heavy with anguish. "I have since contemplated taking my own life so many times because the pain has been too unbearable to live through one more day. Remember? I almost did not long before we met in California. You don't have any fucking idea how hard it is to keep going, to keep striving to have a life worth living when the freedom and oblivion that death has to offer is only one decision away. Before you came along, I fought that urge every single day. With you, it is a tiny bit easier to ignore, a tiny bit easier to allow myself to hope for the future." I hold out my hand between us, my pointer finger and thumb held mere millimeters apart.

"I have been honest with you every step of the way. I said my past was off-limits and that it always would be. You accepted that. I told you not to expect a future. That all I could offer was my broken but slowly mending self in the present. You accepted that, too. So, if you want to run at the first sign of challenge, Charlie, go. I have no intention of ripping my heart out of my chest and laying myself bare in front of all these nosy, disrespectful leeches just to protect your big-ass, fucking fragile ego." The onlookers snap into action, moving about and murmuring amongst themselves in a poor attempt to pretend like they hadn't been enjoying the show.

Chest heaving and tears held back by sheer stubbornness, I stare him down. He stares right back, his intense energy radiating out to me. I hurl it back at him. It churns between us in a charged circle for what feels like a lifetime. I see the moment he makes his decision, squaring his shoulders and clenching his jaw.

"I'm sorry, but I need some space." He steps toward me and caresses my cheek for a brief moment. "I'll see you back home, okay?" he says, voice tender and hurt yet hopeful as he places the keys to our rental car in my hand. I don't answer. I am incapable of answering. I stare mutely at his back as he walks away, leaving me there to face my demons alone when he promised so many times that he would always be there when I needed him. The sound of the door closing snaps me out of my trance, and I turn a violent glare on my sister.

"How could you?" I spit at her. "I *knew* it! I knew something was up. Why, Vicki? What was your goal in inviting Darren tonight and not telling me? It's the same shit you pulled in Cali but with much higher stakes this time. Were you deliberately trying to shatter the tiny bit of happiness I've managed to find? What, just because I haven't done things the way *you* think I should. It's my fucking life, Vic. *My life* that was ripped away. *My* life that I've been working so hard to rebuild. *Mine,* not yours! And you just fucking ruined it. *Again!*" I spit, seething with so many raw emotions I don't know whether to cry or scream or hit my arrogant, meddling sister right in her stupid fucking face.

"Again? What the fuck, *Veronica.*" My name flies off her lips in the exact way our mom used to say it, slapping me across the face so forcefully I take a step back. "I maybe, *maybe,* crossed the line tonight, but I had absolutely nothing to do with what happened to them, and you know it."

"Nothing to do with it?" I scoff. "You just wouldn't take no for an answer, would you? You kept pushing and pushing until I went out with you that night. I may not have told Charlie everything, but at least what I did share with him was honest. Can you say the same?" I ask, looking at her husband pointedly.

Her shoulders slump, and a look of remorse settles on her face. "Ron, I'm. . . I, I don't know. I thought if he showed up, you would, I don't know. Fuck! I thought it would remind you of all the people still alive that you left behind and bring you back to us."

"Really?" I exclaim, voice incredulous. "You thought that *his* identical twin would remind me of the people still alive and *not* the people who aren't? Or, was it really that you just can't stand the fact that I've rebuilt my life for myself, and it's not all about you? Tell me, Vic. Look me in the eyes and tell me that you could stay in this house—in this town—if the same thing happened to you. Tell me you could wake up every day and face the constant reminders. Tell me you could maintain a relationship with a man who looks *exactly* like your husband but isn't. Who has the same beautiful blue eyes as—"

I finally break, tears streaming down my face, shoulders shaking from the force of my sobs. Darren steps forward, arms outstretched, but I gesture for him to stop. It would be far too easy to fall into his embrace and never leave. To pretend that at least one part of my heart was still whole and on this earth with me. But that would be no kind of life for either of us.

"Ronnie. . ." Vicki says, but I don't want to hear it. I take the stairs two at a time, my four-inch pumps not hindering my speed. I slam the door to the spare room, undo the buckles, and chuck my shoes at the wall. Fucking furious with my sister, I strip out of my sweat-soaked dress, throw myself onto the bed, and scream into the pillow. I scream and scream, cursing fate for only allowing me rare, brief moments of respite between frequent, long stretches of hardship. I curse my sister for helping fate tear away my newfound happiness. I curse Charlie for running out on me when I need him most. And I curse myself for letting him go. After all, what would it change if I just told him? Why do I guard this secret so closely?

Because if you say the words out loud, it becomes real and you'll have to face it. That would probably be a good thing, V.

After crying myself into a weak, vacant shell, I roll off the bed and stuff my leaden limbs into warm clothes. I swiftly descend the stairs and beeline through the still-festive party, heading straight for the door. No one intercepts me, and I sigh, my shoulders drooping as the tension fades. The feeling evaporates when Darren steps outside and follows me to the rental car.

"Ronnie," he implores as I open the driver's door and move to get in. "Ron, please." I hesitate, back still turned toward him, shaking from all the feelings raging inside me and from the cold January night. "We miss you. My parents miss you. I miss you. You are part of our family. It hurts that we had to lose you, too."

"Stop, Darren. Just stop. I can't. I can't be a part of your family without *him.*"

"You mean you can't stand to look at me," he assumes, voice heavy with frustration and sadness. My heart aches for him. How hard must it be for him to not only lose his twin but to be a constant, painful reminder of that loss to everyone else?

"You have no idea how hard it is, Ronnie, to look in the mirror every fucking day and see my brother's face. To see the pain behind everyone's eyes every. Single. Time. They look at you," Darren says, voicing my thoughts aloud.

"I'm so sorry, Darren. I'll never be able to look at you without that pain," I say, back still turned. "I miss y'all, too." I muster up the tiny shred of courage I have left and turn to face him. "I'm so proud of you, Darren, for moving forward and making a wonderful life for yourself. Your wife and kids—" my voice breaks, and a fresh wave of tears freezes on my face.

He looks toward the house where they are safe, celebrating another year of life. "You're right, I do have a wonderful life. So you see, Ron? It is possible. Possible to move on and live even though they're gone. You could do it, too."

"I was, Darren. Can't you see that? I was building a wonderful life with Charlie. You and my sister and everyone else might just have to accept that you aren't going to be a part of it. You," I point an accusing finger at him, "managed to move on without *me* in your life. So you see, Darren? It is possible," I spit, tossing his words back at him. "Possible to move on while leaving the past in the past." We stare at each other for a heated moment. Pain etches weary lines across his handsome face, and his shoulders droop under the weight of his sorrow. I let out a long breath and, with it, the misplaced bout of anger. "Please, Darren," I relent. "Please, just let it go. Our time as a family has come and gone. Know that I love you all and wish you all well. I'm so happy for you, Darren, truly."

He smiles sadly. "I'm sorry about tonight, Ronnie. I thought, well, it doesn't matter. I hope you work things out with Charlie and find happiness or at least some peace. Take care of yourself."

"Goodbye, Darren," I reply, sliding into the driver's seat. I throw the car into gear and peel out of the driveway, hoping to catch a redeye to London. As the highway flies by and the darkness of the night embraces me, faces swim in front of me, blurring my vision. Charlie's hard with betrayal and disappointment. Darren's heavy with pain and sadness. *His* soft with love and understanding—the same look Darren gave me as I fled into the snowy night. Seeing his face—*his face*—tore open all my carefully healed wounds and shattered the vault door keeping my most painful memories locked up.

They stream out, a deluge of emotions bashing ruthlessly against my endlessly battered soul: pain, anguish, despair, anger, longing, desperation, hopelessness, and the desire for it all to end, violently stripping away my protective barriers, brick by excruciating brick.

A fresh onslaught of tears pours down my face, obscuring my vision, and dry heaves wrack my aching body. I manage to pull over without incident and it's only when I park that I realize I'm not at the airport at all. I stumble out of the car, catching my shoulder on the corner of the door as I slam it shut. I trudge slowly down the snow-packed trail, fighting the urge to curl up in a ball in the underbrush, go to sleep, and never wake up.

Four oak trees, one old giant, and three smaller saplings sit off the trail in a small clearing. Each tree is marked with a set of dates. I walk between them, running my fingers along the smooth carvings, a fresh wave of despair bringing me to my knees in front of the biggest.

God, Daniel. I miss you so much. Why! Why? Why . . . ?

Heavy, wet snow soaks my pants, turning my legs into icicles as I kneel in the clearing, alternating between sobbing and screaming until my voice scrapes like gravel in my throat. The snow beneath my hands is dotted red, stained from the blood slowly dripping from my ripped-up fingers. Maybe if I claw at the trees a little harder, the souls they represent will be released back into the world to live out the remainder of their lives—lives that were cut devastatingly short.

"I'm sorry, Daniel. So, so sorry. It's all my fault. I should've been more careful of who I allowed in my life. I should've worked harder to quit being a people pleaser. I should've told my sister no. If I had, none of this would have happened. I am sorry. So, so, sorry."

I fall on my side and curl into a ball. Time ceases to mean anything as I lay there, succumbing to the guilt and desperation, letting the maelstrom of emotions raging inside pull me down. Down, down, down. Down to the cold, black depths of despair. I float towards the cold embrace of oblivion, crashing from rock to rock along the bottom, for what could be minutes or hours or days.

"Ronnie. . .. Ronnie. . .. Ronnie. Wake up." The ghostly whisper of a comforting voice draws me back into my body. "Get up. You need to get up. Move! You're gonna freeze."

"I don't care," I whisper back.

"But, I do. So, get up."

"No, I want to be with you again."

"You can, but not yet."

"Why not? Why do I have to wait?"

"Because you made a promise to yourself and Charlie."

"Past me was stupid to make those promises."

"No, Ron, she wasn't. Now get up. Go get your happiness back."

"I can't be happy. Not without you."

"Yes, you can. Don't give up trying now. Get up, Ron."

"I don't want to. It's too hard."

"You can do hard things. Isn't that what you used to say every morning to our—"

"Stop!" I command, still, after everything, not ready to face those *memories.*

"Come on, Ron. Get up. Get up. Get up!"

"Fine!" I roll onto all fours and sway, vision blurry. Everything hurts.

"That's it, Ron, almost there. Come on, keep going."

"Give me a second. Fuck, it hurts." I manage to stand, my numb legs wobbling. I give my eyes a minute to adjust to the full dark of night, then look back at the four oaks one last time. "Goodbye for now. I love you," I say, then walk away into the night.

Already Forgiven

A thousand tiny needles prick sore, stinging legs.
Stiff fingers burn around the wheel.
A long, dreamless sleep over the ocean.
Forced pleasantries at the gallery.
Large white canvases covered in black, white, and grey; my art reflecting my emptiness.
Eat very little. Sleep riddled with nightmares. Work in the studio. Repeat.
Force a smile. Send a text. Ignore the calls.
Dodge questions. Avoid everyone. Spiral down, down, down . . .

A game of deflection:
"Yeah, yeah, Soph. Charlie and I are having a great time touring the States."
"I'll be okay, Vic. I'm not happy about what you did, but I still love you."
"I'm staying in the States for a bit longer, Charlie. Yeah, I'll call you when I get home."
"Kal, Kel? Tomorrow after we close, I'm going with Charlie for the weekend."

Phone off. Blinds pulled. Doors locked.
Lay on the floor. Stare blankly at the ceiling.
Lay on the bed. Stare blankly at the wall.
Lay on the sofa. Stare blankly at the door.

Burrow into the closet.
Clutch an old teddy bear.
Spiral down, down, down . . .

A moment of clarity:
Turn on the phone. Text everyone so they leave me the hell alone.
Close off. Turn off.
Lay and stare and clutch the teddy bear.

Work. Text.
Gone. They are all gone.
Alone. I am so, so alone.
Turn off. Close off.
Lay and stare and clutch the teddy bear.
Repeat and repeat, and most importantly, don't think.

Blue eyes and soft skin.
Love and laughter. Happiness and belonging.
Gone. It's all gone.
Cold metal against pale skin.
One deep cut through the sluggish blue vein could end all this pain.

Charlie

"Bloody fucking hell, Veronica," I mumble under my breath after looking over our last volley of texts, which consist of me begging her to pick up her phone and call me so we can talk, maybe fix this rift between us. She is right; I do have a fragile ego. She lets her past come between us by trying to omit it completely, and I let *my past* come between us by not trusting her. The truth is, I am jealous of *Daniel*, whoever the wanker is, and I do not know anything about him.

And her only answers are single-word responses unless she says, "I'm gonna stay stateside a bit longer." No doubt she is holed up in her studio, avoiding me. The need to find her is overwhelming, but I promised her a week. Fuck, I miss her. I am such an idiot for running out on her like that. She was agitated and on the brink of collapse—and I left. I did not even give her the chance to explain. I put her on the spot in front of a bunch of strangers and expected her to share something she had made clear from the beginning that she never would.

It has been weeks since I have seen her. I have driven past her studio so many times but did not have the nerve to stop. I want to see her, want to go find her, but I do not want to break my promise. Slamming my hands on my desk, I push back my chair and start to pace. With a silent plea to the universe, I type a quick text to John, hitting send instead of delete like I have multiple times since I last saw her.

I am terrified of ruining any chance there is to mend my relationship with Veronica, but I have to put her well-being above my fear. John's reply buzzes through and I eagerly tap into the text.

Please, please let her be safe in Idaho with her family.

John: Having fun in the sun in the Sunshine State?

Charlie: No idea what you are getting on about, mate?

John: We just got an update a few days ago from Ronnie about your tour of the States. Said you were in Florida enjoying the warmth.

Charlie: I am in London. Have been since New Year's Day.

"Hullo, John," I say, suspicion churning my guts inside out.

"Hey, Brit," he replies. "So, you're not in Florida?"

"No, I am not. She sent me home. Well, technically, I left. I guess you could say it was a joint effort, but I left on New Year's Eve."

"I'm guessing there's more to that story?" I harumph in reply. "So, where did she say she's at?"

"Bouncing back and forth between your place and Sophie's. She texts me every few days that she is, 'going to stay just a few more days.'"

"Huh," he replies. Then, voice muffled, "What, Catherine?" After a pause, he says, "Umm, Charlie. You're going to want to hear this," and hands the phone to his wife.

"Hey, Char."

"Hullo, Catherine."

"I just ran into Vicki," she says, voice tinged with accusation.

"Oh, and I suppose she told you about the incident at the party?" I answer resignedly.

"She did. She said that Ron had told her that she was staying with us. But she told us that she's touring the States with you."

"And she told me that she is staying in the States just a few more days," I answer, voice hard with frustration.

"So," John pipes in, "where is she then?"

And that is the fucking million-dollar question, isn't it? "I have a sneaking suspicion that she is holed up in her studio, giving us all the runaround." Worry roils in my chest, making it hard to breathe.

"Well, Charlie, what are you gonna do about it then?" Catherine answers expectantly.

"I promised her I would give her a full week of silence before I check in, and it has only been four days."

"That's very noble of you but trust me. You need to get over there ASAP. It's been weeks since any of us have seen her or actually spoke with her. Someone needs to get to her before she spirals any deeper into one of her episodes," Cat implores urgently.

"Okay, okay. I will go now," I say, my worry mirroring hers.

"Keep us updated?"

"Of course." I slam the phone on the desk, muttering fuck, fuck, fuck. I rip off my suit jacket and toss it over the chair, then loosen the tie that is suddenly suffocating me and run my hands through my hair. I swipe my keys and phone off the desk and slam the door, glaring down anyone who dares try to stop me on my way out of the building. Fingers drumming an anxious rhythm on the steering wheel, I maneuver quickly through the light traffic of mid-afternoon, grateful for this one small break.

The Audi's tires screech as I speed up to the curb in front of *Studio V,* my heart pounding erratically in my chest. *Please,* I beg the universe. *Please be here, and please be okay.* I cross the pavement in a few long strides and yank the door open, searching for her in all her usual spots. A few customers are in the small gift shop area, and another is in the back corner studying a large black-and-white abstract. Kellan and Kali hurry toward me, eyes wide with alarm.

"Where is she," I demand.

"She's not with you," Kali asks, eyebrows furrowed.

I give her a hard look and take the steps three at a time.

"We'll be here if you need anything." Kellan's words float up the stairs in my wake, but I hardly register them. I jam the key into the lock and shove my way inside. Please let her be here, I plead with whoever might be listening. Please let her be alive.

"Veronica," I inquire into the empty living room, closing the door quietly behind me. The remaining rays from the setting sun provide enough light for me to see blankets and pillows tossed haphazardly, a few dishes strewn across the counter, and random pieces of clothing scattered throughout the small space. The air is stale and permeated with an unnerving, desolate hopelessness. Fear squeezes my heart, and my breaths come in shallow, worried pants. She admitted that she still considers suicide an option, and I left her to deal with that by herself. Fuck. Fuck. Fuck. My chest tightens, and my stomach pulls into knots.

"Veronica?" I plead; voice laced with worry. She is not in the living room, kitchen, or small bathroom. I open the door to her bedroom, pausing to give my eyes a moment to adjust to the darkness. "Veronica. God, please, where are you?" The room is in total disarray. Blankets and pillows are scattered everywhere, and the sheets are pulled off the top corners of the bed and bunched in a pile towards the bottom. Dresser drawers hang open, clothes spilling out, and her journal lays face down against the far wall as if she threw it. Bloody hell, where is she? Please, please be alive.

"Veronica?" I beg, voice and hands shaking. A tiny, muffled whimper sounds from behind me. I whip my head around and listen, still as a hare caught in a wolf's stare. There it is again.

Heart in my throat, I cross the room in two strides and carefully open the folding closet doors. "Veronica. ... Veronica?" I fumble along the wall blindly for a light switch, then rip my phone from my pocket and click on the flashlight when I do not find one fast enough. Frantically moving clothes aside and searching the deep corners of the closet, I see boxes in one and a pile of blankets in the other.

Please, please, let her be alive.

"Veronica," I say calmly, gently nudging the heap of blankets, which elicits another soft whimper. "Veronica," I say earnestly, barely preventing myself from ripping the blankets apart to find her. Instead, I gently pull the blankets off one by one to finally reveal a small, ragged pile of bones barely held together by skin, curled tightly around an old teddy bear.

My stomach leaps into my throat, vying for space with my heart. I am surprised to hear a sob escape through the blockage. She is alive!

"Oh, love. Come here. I am sorry. I got you."

I scoop her into my arms, carry her to the sofa in the living room, and sit, cradling her carefully in my lap. She is frail. Her face is ghostly white, and her dull hair hangs limply down her back. Her breathing is so shallow that I can barely feel her chest move. "Sweetheart, look at me. I am here." Her cracked lips move, and her throat bobbles soundlessly. She tries again, but still, no sound comes out.

I snatch a glass of water off the side table and hold it to her lips. She takes a few sips, then lays back against my shoulder, exhausted.

"Oh, no, you don't. Come on, love, wake up. You need to wake up." Her eyes flutter open, and she stares into the space between us, unfocused and vacant. "That's right, sweetheart. Time to come back to me." Her hand, so small to begin with, feels like a tiny, fragile skeleton against my cheek.

"Daniel," the green head of envy rears its head inside my chest, but I push it away with some force of will. "Are you real?"

The longing in her voice is so raw that I want to say yes, to give her this one small respite, but I do not. It would not last anyway, and I know she would be more angry than thankful when she returned to reality.

"No, love, I am not Daniel. I do not know where he is or anything about him, I am sorry." She looks up at me, eyes going in and out of focus. "It is me, Charlie."

"Oh, Charlie," she says, a small measure of relief evident in her tone. Then she bursts into tears, silent, heaving sobs wracking her frail body. I grasp her firmly to my chest, holding her together so she can safely let go and fall apart. After a time, her body stills to an occasional hiccupping sigh. I murmur comforting words in her ear and stroke her hair while she takes the time she needs to come back to me.

"Charlie," she murmurs tentatively.

"Yes, my love?"

"I . . . I am sorry."

"Shh. Shh now. You have nothing to be sorry about. I am the one who is sorry. I walked out on you when you needed me most and have regretted it every minute since. I am sorry it took so long to pull my head out of my ass and come find you."

"I told you to go."

"You did not mean it?"

"No, I didn't."

"I knew that. Just like I knew Darren was not an ex-boyfriend. Just like I knew you did not betray me. I am sorry."

"It's okay, Charlie. Trusting someone who shares so little and asks you to blindly accept everything they don't say, can't be easy. And I knew it was a trigger for you, but I was too stubborn to even give you a little bit of reassurance."

"That is okay too. You were right, I do have a fragile ego. I could have set it aside and been there for you like I have promised so many times. Can you forgive me? In time, maybe?"

"I've already forgiven you. I forgave you before you even walked out that door. I was on my way to the airport just after you left, but I got sidetracked." She pauses for a second, gathering her thoughts. She shifts in my lap, lifts her shirt to her nose, and sniffs, nose scrunching in a cute little ball. "I'll tell you the rest, I promise. I need a shower first."

"And food," I add. "Let us get you in the shower. I will take care of the rest." Easily rising with her cradled safely against my chest, I carry her to the bathroom, gently set her on the vanity, then turn on the faucet, letting the water run over my fingers until it gets hot. I help her undress, wincing internally when I see just how emaciated and frail she has become. I place a gentle kiss on her forehead and help her in.

While she showers, I order takeout and quickly but thoroughly clean her flat. I also send John an update and poke my head out to reassure the twins that she is okay. By the time she is done, every surface is tidy and polished, the dishwasher is loaded and ready to run, and a load of clothes is in the wash. As soon as I hear the water shut off, I rush a folded pair of comfy sweats and her favorite baggy hoodie to the bathroom and knock softly.

"Come in."

"Here," I say, holding out the folded clothes.

"Thank you," she says shyly, clutching the towel tightly around her pale, thin body.

"I will wait out here."

While she changes, a soft, rap, rap, rap sounds from the door. I open it to find Kali holding our takeout, shoulders thrown back and chin held high.

"I'm coming in. I just want to see her for myself, and then I'll leave."

In a room full of stubborn people, of which we all are, her brother included, Kali is the most unmovable when her mind is set. I do not want to upset Veronica any more than I already have, but Kali is a good friend so I think she will understand.

"Let her in, Char."

Kali and I consider each other for another long moment before I step aside. She drops the food onto the coffee table and pulls Veronica into a fierce embrace. They speak quietly, and I force myself to calm the writhing possessive, over-protective prick inside me and go to the laundry room to give them some privacy. I am beyond relieved that she is alive, but so fucking mad at myself for all the mistakes I have made over the past month. The urge to protect her, to find everyone who ever contributed to pushing her to this place where she spirals into this deep of a depressive episode and make them atone for the pain they have caused her, burns inside me. As I fold clothes, my hands shake with the need to lash out at whoever hurt her. Kali hollers a "Toodle-oo," and I'm in the living room before the door closes.

My heart swells in my chest at the sight of her. Even in this fragile state, she is stunning, and a determined strength shines in her eyes. I love her so much, and my hands are trembling again, this time with the need to touch her—to make sure she is real and as okay as possible. At this moment, I vow to mend things between us and never leave her side again. I gesture at the food on the coffee table–not the kitchen table. I need to feel her sitting beside me.

She drops onto the sofa and carefully tucks herself into my side. Then she raises her eyes to mine, takes a deep breath, and says, "I'm going to tell you what happened. Why I'm so fucked up and broken."

Bring Back the Rainbow

Warm soup in my stomach does wonders to settle my nerves and calm my erratically beating heart. Charlie's solid leg resting against mine anchors me to the present as I prepare to delve deep into my past. I'm still a conflicted mess, desperately wishing it were possible to both cling to the past and *him* and build a future with Charlie. These past few days, or weeks maybe, but hopefully not months this time, have proven it's not. Speaking with Darren broke the poorly constructed damn holding me together, allowing the past to rush forward and drown me. But it also unearthed a small channel of cleansing water that has trickled in slowly since that night, filling my well with hope and possibility.

Charlie sits next to me still as a statue, casually draped across the sofa, one arm slung behind me, an ankle crossed over a knee. Any casual onlooker would assume that he's patiently waiting, but I can feel the intense vibration radiating from him. I can also tell he's trying hard to hold it back, to give me the space I need to say what I need to say.

"In the closet on the top shelf way back in the corner is a box. Will you grab it for me?" Lithe and graceful as a mountain lion, Charlie rises from the sofa and retrieves the box. He drops down beside me smoothly, offering it to me. I shake my head. Once it's found a spot in the back of my closet, I never touch it again until it's time to pack up and move once more. "Open it and set it on the coffee table," I instruct him. A single tear glides down my diverted face as he does so. "There should be a photo album on top." He carefully removes it from the box and sets it gently in his lap. I take a deep, steadying breath, pull my legs under me, and turn to face Charlie.

He raises a questioning brow at me, and I nod. On the first page is a single, grainy photo taken with a disposable camera more than two decades ago. We probably went through hundreds of those cameras during those few years that we were inseparable, my teenage friends and I. Charlie delicately traces his fingers across the five people in the photo as recognition dawns on his face. His finger lingers over the one in the middle. "This is you," he states. I nod as his finger moves to one of the two identical boys whose arm is casually draped over my shoulder, head thrown back in laughter. "And . . . Darren?" I nod.

His finger pauses over the other two boys pictured, then skims back across to the other girl. She leans into Darren, sharing his laughter. "Ah," he says after a moment, "Vicki?" I smile and brace myself as he traces back to the two yet unidentified boys. He points at a short, stocky boy with a shock of blonde curly hair whose hand is conspicuously behind the other twin and the apparent cause of the shocked look on the twin's face and the rest of our laughter.

"That was Kyle," I explain. He raises a sardonic brow at me. "Yes," I reply with an exasperated roll of my eyes, "he was your typical Kyle; a Monster drinking, heavy metal rocking, reckless driving, mean-drunk redneck. And for some reason, all the girls loved him, me included." I trail off, remembering with bittersweet fondness the easy friendship between the five of us. My chosen nephew Jake had explained to Charlie the slang definitions for the names Americans use to represent different stereotypes while we sat in the mall food court eating donuts and people-watching while in Idaho for Christmas.

"So, this," he says, bringing me back to the present, "I'm guessing, is Daniel?" I swallow hard and clench my teeth. From the moment I decided to tell Charlie, I've been holding back the tsunami building inside me, but when Charlie says Daniel's name with such careful neutrality, I let it break over me. For the second time since he pulled me from my blanket refuge in the closet, Charlie gathers me in his lap, holding me firmly but gently against his shoulder, and I let it all go. When the sobs die out, and my breathing returns to normal, Charlie gently sets me on the sofa and retrieves a glass of water, a box of tissue, and some ibuprofen. I accept all three gratefully.

"This is the story of how I died," I say ruefully. Charlie gathers the strands of my long, auburn-streaked brown hair, soft and still damp from the shower, and runs it through his fingers.

"I certainly hope not, my dark Rapunzel," he replies gravely.

"We were inseparable, the five of us, for most of high school. In the States, you go to high school from age fourteen to eighteen, give or take. We spent summers mowing lawns, swimming in the frigid mountain lakes of Idaho, and sneaking alcohol from our parents, getting drunk and stupid in the back of Kyle's jacked-up truck, hidden in the forest behind the twins' house. Vicki and I avoided being home as much as possible, even during the school year. Kyle did, too. And, often when he did go home, the next day he showed up with a black eye or bruised ribs, and once a broken arm, courtesy of his alcoholic father."

"I think Daniel and Darren were drawn to the three of us because they were 'fixers,'" I pause, considering, "and because we were reckless. Where they grew up with both loving, doting parents at home, Vic, Kyle, and I didn't. D & D, as we called them to their utter annoyance, grew up wearing perfectly starched shirts to church on Sunday mornings and enjoying nightly family meals. The rest of us grew up hiding under beds, covering up bruises, and avoiding our parents, well, Vic and I's mom anyway. Our dad was wonderful but could only protect us from so much. And he worked all the time while Mildred sat on her ass drinking, smoking, and shopping away all his hard-earned money. There were times when we only ate at school or a friend's house."

"Tim and Tam, the twin's parents, were surprisingly accepting of us. They knew what was happening at home, so they took us in. And, even though we got into a fair bit of trouble, they never blamed the three of us or shunned us. When the weather was shit, which is often in Idaho," we both chuckle, remembering the storm that ravaged us over Christmas, "we camped out in their living room, watching TV and playing video games."

Charlie's eyes narrow, and his lips turn down into a slight frown. He will try his hardest to remain silent during this long story, mainly because he is a good listener, but also because he's afraid he'll distract me and I won't finish. "You can ask questions and make comments, love. I promise I will tell you the whole story."

He lets out a sigh of relief. "Thank you."

"One time, all three of the boys got into a fistfight over a game of *Mortal Kombat*. Tim, who we all respected and adored, was able to quickly break them up with a firm word and had them all laughing and patting each other on the back within minutes."

"James and I got into more than one fight that our father had to break up."

"I can imagine." We both chuckle.

"There was never anything romantic between any of us until very late into our senior year—the last year of high school. We were all seniors except Vic; she was a year behind us. Things got bad at home for Kyle when his dad found out that he received a scholarship to play football at a local community college. That's like university, except it is cheaper, and you can only get a two-year degree there. Anyway, the night his dad found out, he went berserk. It was the only night Kyle ever fought back, too. If he hadn't, I think his dad would have put him in the hospital. Kyle worked whenever he could in between school and sports, and his dad took every penny he earned. And he had big plans for Kyle and the income he would bring in from working full time after graduation."

I pause and take a sip of water, remembering Kyle's bruises and how scared I was that night. I study Charlie's handsome profile, so fucking grateful for George and Anne.

"Are you doing okay, my love? Do you need to take a break?" he asks when I don't continue.

"I'm okay," I reply, touching his cheek. "So that night. D and D were out of town, and Vicki was off with this new boy she was fooling around with. Kyle called me frantic. He thought he killed his old man. It was natural to console him. I was always the one who was there for my sisters when Mildred was especially dreadful. We ended up kissing that night. I think we both had started having feelings for each other before, but we were ignoring them for fear of ruining our friendships." That night, I felt so safe in his arms and thought I was the luckiest girl in the world to be with him.

"I mean, we did eventually. At first, everyone was supportive of our relationship. Daniel, less so than the others. He told me later that he worried Kyle would end up like his dad. Unfortunately, he was right. But Kyle and I had a good year. He went and played football a few towns away from where I chose to go to get a nursing degree." Charlie raises his eyebrows, looking at me sidelong. "I know, right? I didn't even know back then about my artistic side. My only goal was to do something that would pay a lot so I could get out of there. Neither Kyle nor I wanted to go home for the summer after our first year in college, so we rented an apartment near his school." I was relieved to have somewhere to go where I didn't have to deal with Mildred's abuse.

"I was perfectly tailored growing up the way I did to overlook his red flags and shady behavior. It's like a switch flipped when we moved in together. He started drinking excessively and became extremely possessive to the point where he punched a hole in the wall right next to my head because I met up with Darren for a quick lunch one day while Kyle was at work. When I went home to celebrate Vic's eighteenth birthday, he threatened to commit suicide because I didn't call him at exactly eleven pm as I *promised*. I called him two minutes late."

"And then my dad and the twins came when they knew Kyle would be gone for a few hours, packed me up, and took me to D and D's parent's house. Apparently, I wasn't quite as good at covering up bruises as I thought I was. What nobody but Vic knew was that I was seven months pregnant. I wasn't showing much because of the stress."

I place my hand on my stomach and close my eyes. The first time he hit me, I was so worried that I'd miscarry. I was too afraid to leave and felt like I didn't have anywhere safe to go if I did.

Charlie goes eerily still next to me, and I can sense him struggling to keep a tight leash on his emotions. He balls one hand into a fist and places the other comfortingly on my leg. "I was terrified. I never wanted to be a mother, especially a young one, and I tried to be so careful to make sure it didn't happen. Vic was the only person who knew. She helped me sneak to all my doctor appointments."

Kyle didn't care if I wanted to use protection. He didn't care if I wanted to have sex or whether I was comfortable doing something or not. He got what he wanted when he wanted it. And if I tried to hold boundaries, he let his fists fly. There's nothing more degrading and demoralizing than being pressured, coerced, threatened, and manipulated into not just having sex but doing things with your body that you're not comfortable doing with someone who is supposed to love you and protect you.

"A few weeks after I left, Mildred and Kyle showed up demanding to see me. My oh-so-loving and caring mother saw me buying prenatal vitamins at the drugstore, and instead of checking on me, she called my abusive ex and spilled the beans. Only Tam and I were home when they showed up. She tried to stall and get them to leave, but Kyle got impatient, busted down the door, and forced his way in. Terrified, I had locked myself in a bedroom and called my dad, Tim, and the cops by this point, but the bedroom door was no match for a raging Kyle." My hands tremble, and my heart races as the sound of Kyle's boots stomping up the stairs and his rough voice screaming at me rings through my mind.

Charlie's hands are balled into fists in his lap, and I can feel rage radiating off him in waves. "If anyone ever lays a hand on you again, I will unleash my carefully contained violence without a second thought," he vows. Daniel responded much the same when he found out what Kyle had done.

"My dad was gone on a work trip. I don't even remember where anymore. Afterward, he blamed himself that I ended up in the hospital and had to have an emergency c-section. He felt like he had failed me for going on that trip. But he didn't know I was pregnant. And none of us realized just how unhinged Kyle had become."

Charlie flips a page in the photo album and sucks in a sharp hiss, the muscles in his leg going rigid under my hand. He takes a few deep, steadying breaths, sets his shoulders, and places his large, warm hand over my small, cold one. My eyes go out of focus, welling with tears, as the old, familiar terror floods through me. Charlie turns my head with a knuckle under my chin. "No one will ever hurt you again so long as we are together," he vows again. The tightness in my chest eases, and I continue.

"He pulled me out of the bedroom and down the stairs by my hair. Then accused me of cheating, convinced the baby was Darren's. He was so angry at me because I 'ran.' Furious that I dared to hide and bear another man's child. I pleaded with him. Told him I had always been faithful to him and that it didn't matter anyway because I wasn't going to keep the baby. That admission made him go berserk. He started smashing things and throwing furniture. Tam was pleading with him to leave, trying to stand between me and him to protect me while my mom just stood there watching, a smug, satisfied expression plastered on her face."

"Tam told him to leave before the cops arrived, which shredded his last bit of restraint. He shoved her out of the way and laid into me, as you can see," I say, nodding to the photos of a young, bruised, and battered Ronnie. How my mother stood by and watched someone beat her child, who was carrying her grandchild, I'll never understand.

"Did—" his voice breaks on the word. He pauses and clears his throat before trying again. "Did you lose the baby?" he asks, voice gentle but laced with steel.

I take a long, steadying breath and deliberately dance around the answer. "Put me in the hospital for a few days. Put him behind bars for a bit more than a few days, but not nearly long enough. I mourned for him, for the boy I knew growing up. For the boy who had been one of my best friends for so long, and for the brief glimpse I got of the man he could have been. I still can't figure out why he chose the path he did. He used to vow to us that he would never be like his father." For a long time, I blamed myself. His criticisms and his warped reality had burrowed so deep inside me that I genuinely believed his behavior and his actions were my fault. If I had just been able to be a better girlfriend, to be more supportive and less needy, if I had just bottled up more of myself and given him whatever he wanted whenever he demanded it, then he wouldn't have acted the way he did.

I gesture with my chin at the photo album, and Charlie quickly turns the page.

"Charlie?" I say. His head snaps up, kind eyes searching mine.

"Do you need a break, my love?" he inquires. I offer him a shy smile in response.

"I promise to finish. The soup was great, but I'm still famished."

"I'll order burgers from the pub."

"Let's get out of here. Some fresh air and a change of scenery is sorely needed," I say. He tidies up the living room while I change. I pop into the bathroom to grab my favorite pair of bright-ass pink, glittery flamingo earrings, studiously avoiding my reflection, knowing full well how terrible I look after one of my episodes.

When I emerge, Charlie stands by the door, hands tucked into the pockets of his black slacks. I pause on the threshold, studying his handsome, wary face, then pat his arm affectionately as I pass. He matches my slow pace as we descend the stairs. I bump his arm, grateful for his reassuring presence at my side.

The lights are still on in the office, spotlighting Kali and Kellan and the animated way they move their hands when they talk. It would be easy to slip out unnoticed, but I'm facing my issues tonight instead of running from them, so I ask Charlie to wait and make my way across the darkened gallery. I embrace each of them fiercely for long seconds before pulling our chairs into a circle and briefly explain everything. They wave away my apologies, but internally, I vow to quit being so consumed by my own issues and be a better friend to them.

As I head back to Charlie, Kali's teasing voice calls out, "We expect you back at work Monday morning. And I'm hiding your depressing paint colors, too." I roll my eyes and shake my head. Charlie ducks his head to hide his amusement.

Before Charlie and I escape, Kellan chimes in, voice ringing with laughter, "Bring back the rainbow, Ron. It's so depressing in here. I'm tired of dealing with my sister's moping brought on by your sudden love of monotone." She snorts, and we hear a loud thwack, followed by a round of cursing. I raise both hands, flip them off, and disappear into the frigid night with Charlie by my side.

Beg for Your Present

Charlie

I love hearing her laugh and I am so thankful for Kellan and Kali. They certainly have a knack for bringing levity to a heavy situation with their incessant teasing and wicked sense of humor. Conflicting emotions swirl violently through me as we amble down the twilight-lit pavement. I long to touch her, to reassure myself that she's okay, but I know she needs space right now. One minute, my heart soars, ecstatic to be reunited with her. The next, it plummets, chagrined by the obvious pain I have caused her.

My pulse quickens, and my vision darkens with rage as I reflect on the beginning of her story. If I ever come face to face with Kyle. . .. my free hand balls into a fist, and I let the thought fall away lest I allow it to take root and fester. And fucking Mildred. Never have I ever wanted to harm a little old lady, but thinking of the abuse she inflicted upon her three eldest daughters, essentially causing one of them to take her own life, and the residual effect it has had on my beloved Veronica makes me want to cause her unspeakable harm. Forcefully tamping down that train of thought, I also surreptitiously study Veronica out of the corner of my eye. Under all the pain, I sense a newfound peace blooming within her.

Compassion ignites in my chest, flowing out to my fierce, strong, yet fragile Veronica, silently encompassing her. She has endured too much hardship. Her tenacity and ability to remain kind and compassionate after the world has dealt her such a shitty hand humbles me. Joy, humiliation, rage, compassion, and humility eddy through me, converging into a singular storm of raw emotion, then separating once again into individual streams, pummeling me from all sides while I struggle to reign myself under control.

And through it all flows a thread of trepidation: will I lose her for good despite her quick forgiveness?

Veronica pulls her coat tighter around herself, burrowing deep into the fur-lined hood. I watch her shiver for a few steps before I tentatively wrap an arm around her to share my warmth. Her shoulders feel thin even through the layers separating us, but the sickly pallor of her skin is already fading. Light and life brighten in her eyes more and more with each passing minute. Thank fuck. If I had lost her. . ..

I contemplate apologizing again, throwing myself at her feet and begging for forgiveness. But I do not. We each made our own choices that brought us to this moment, and now, we must both take accountability for them. I crave her forgiveness to ease my burdened conscience, but managing my emotions is my responsibility, not hers, and vice versa. Moving forward, I have the power to make different choices and to show her with my actions how much I love her and value her. For now, I will trust that we can endure this turbulence together.

"Here we are, my love," I say, opening the door.

"Ronnie. Charlie." The regular, middle-aged male host greets us. "Will it be the bar tonight or the table?" he inquires.

Veronica's face lights up, delight softening the sharp angles of her skeletal face, and my heart squeezes in my chest again, both reveling in her joy and sorrowing in the pain I detect underneath.

"Our table is available?" Her tentative hope is a balm for my conflicted soul.

"Yes, dear, it is," he replies, eyes twinkling, and gestures down the aisle toward *our* table.

"Allow me," I offer, helping Veronica out of her coat and into her seat. I watch her intently as she stares wistfully at the incredible view of London.

"Charlie," she says, her voice barely audible above the clamor surrounding us: clinking tableware, shouts from the kitchen, and the din of overlapping conversations.

"Yes, my love?"

"Do you remember the first time we came here?"

"I could never forget that night."

"Me neither," she says, eyes lighting on mine, shining with such adoration my heart leaps into my throat.

"Veronica," I begin, deciding it is necessary to offer one final, earnest apology. "I am so deeply sorry for my actions and the pain I caused. I am sorry I was not there for you when you needed me. And I am sorry I did not come to my senses sooner." I take a deep breath and exhale while she keeps her eyes locked on mine. "If you still want to be with me, I cannot promise that I will never make another mistake, but I can promise that I will learn to temper my temper. I will be your staunchest supporter and your anchor. Even if I never hear your whole story, I trust you."

She inhales as if to speak, but I hold up my hand, needing to get it all out before she replies. "V, I love you. I know you may never be able to reciprocate the feeling, and I respect that. I desperately want you in my life. I promised not to ask for your past or future, but I will beg for your present. I will get down on my knees, right here, right now, and grovel at your feet if that is what it takes to get one more chance. And if you give me one, I will cherish every moment we have together," I finish, voice ragged. She considers me, head tilted, lips pursed.

"Charlie. I am just as much at fault for what happened and just as sorry. I already told you that I forgive you. Although I am tempted to make you beg, I rather like you on your knees and at my mercy," she says, voice low and sultry. "It's not necessary. I want you, Charlie." Eyes boring into mine with fierce passion, she reaches across the table and grasps my hand.

"We both made shitty choices. Maybe I should be the one on my knees, begging for forgiveness. How ignorant of me to think we could have a healthy relationship built on omission, blind trust, and half-assed commitment. Especially with a man whose past is riddled with women who only valued his reputation and the number of zeros in his bank account, and the truth is, Charlie, I do love you."

A multitude of emotions, joy, passion, determination, and the desire to possess her fully for the rest of my life, explode in my chest, and without a conscious decision, I rise, pulling her out of her chair into my arms. I cup her beloved face in my hands and kiss her, tenderly at first, until she makes a small moan of contentment into my mouth, and I lose all composure, deepening the kiss to devour her and claim her as my own for all the world to see.

We break apart reluctantly and settle back into our chairs, fingers entwined. The waiter brings our food—cheeseburgers, of course—and we eat in companionable silence, sharing knowing smiles and muffled giggles.

"So, tell me, my love, how many other men did you accost and assault whilst commando simply because one dared speak to you? Before I came along and wooed you, of course?" I inquire playfully.

Her shoulders shake, and she sets down her fork, folding her hands in front of her. "The *assault* only happened that one time, and he deserved it," she answers primly. "The accost, on the other hand . . . Every social interaction felt like an attack after everything happened. I did my best to ignore it most of the time."

"What changed? You did not ignore me."

"You were respectful and safe." I tilt my head. "I figured there was no way we'd ever see each other again, so. And also, I wanted to be normal again, to have a normal social life again, but it's so hard when a simple word or sound or smell can turn into a debilitating trigger."

Pain flashes in her chocolate eyes. I rub soothing circles on the back of her hand and remain quiet.

"The last time I almost," she tilts her head and lolls her tongue out of her mouth, then drags her thumb across her throat, "I badly wanted to end the pain, but I just couldn't do it. While standing on the precipice, staring down the side of a cliff, I decided that it was time to get out of limbo and learn to live again."

"From my perspective, you have built quite a life for yourself here." I give her fingers an encouraging squeeze.

"I have. It's been challenging, but being with you has made it easier. You have provided a safe space and become my steadfast anchor. Thank you," she says, reverentially cupping my face with one hand. I bring her other hand to my lips and kiss it tenderly.

"Always."

She looks into my eyes for a long moment, searching. I lay my soul bare to her, and hope it is enough. After a terrifying moment, her shoulders relax and her decadent mouth spreads into an easy smile. She orders dessert and refills and settles in to share more of her heartbreaking, yet remarkable story.

"The next part is relatively easy to tell," she says, raising her glass and clinking it to mine.

She settles comfortably into her dessert and her story. After Kyle went to prison, she stayed with Tim and Tam for a few months to regain her strength and make a plan for her future. She finished her nursing degree and secured a labor and delivery nursing position where she met Catherine and Sophie.

"I built a quiet, wonderful, fulfilling life for myself. Shall we?" She gestures towards the door and I help her into her coat.

A group of giggling young women pass by and stumble into the ladies room as we move toward the exit.

"Why is it," I muse playfully, "that women always use the loo in groups?"

She motions for me to lean in closer, then whispers, "I can't tell you. It's an industry secret and you don't possess the necessary. . .. equipment," she answers, flashing me a cheesy grin.

"Well, now, love. That is an easy fix," I say, leaning even closer, voice growing husky with desire. "I want to possess you, Veronica. All of you. Claim every inch of you with my mouth and my body. I want to fuck you until you are screaming my name and begging for mercy. Make love to you until you forget the pain and feel nothing but pleasure and love and joy."

A beautiful crimson flush rises up her chest and settles on her protruding cheekbones; a sensual, arrogant look radiates from her dilated eyes. Under the table, her fingernails rake sensuously up the inside of my thigh.

"What are you waiting for, Mr. Wright?"

The Half of It

A rare February (I almost shit myself when I found out that January had come and gone without my notice) sun filters through the wall-length windows in Charlie's bedroom, settling softly on my sleep-warmed skin and gently caressing me awake. A shiver runs down my spine when I remember Charlie's caresses from the previous night: hot and demanding, merciless, tender and thorough, gentle, possessive, ardent, and passionate. Being back in Charlie's embrace, felt like a homecoming.

The familiar sounds of Charlie in the kitchen and the smell of bacon frying lure me out of bed and bolster my resolve to finish my story and commit fully to a future with Charlie.

Well, get on with it then, V.

"Good morning, my love," I say as I plop onto a stool. "What are you making? It smells divine in here."

"A bit of this, a bit of that," he answers cryptically.

"Are you 'meal-prepping' again," I tease.

"Yes, I am. We are not going anywhere or doing anything for a long time," he replies, dragging out the 'o' in long. "I took some days off, and I hope you do not mind, but I also called Kal and Kel. They adore *their* Ronnie. They want you back in the office but understand. In fact, they gave me strict instructions to, and I quote, "Do whatever it takes to bring back the rainbow." And who am I to deny them? Only one night in, and it has already been such hard, grueling work," he says, sighing dramatically.

"Oh, you poor, poor baby. I didn't hear you complaining about it last night," I retort, head tilted, eyebrows raised.

"Couldn't hear much over you moaning and screaming and begging for mercy, now could we," he counters teasingly.

I pluck a warm, flaky pastry off a platter and chuck it at his face. He deftly swipes it out of the air, sticks the whole thing in his mouth, and winks at me, "Thanks, love. I'm famished."

We take our time eating breakfast, sticking to light-hearted topics and flirting. It feels good to be in Charlie's kitchen again.

God, I fucking missed this.

He grows serious when I share the sentiment with him.

"I did, too, my love."

I take a deep, steadying breath and square my shoulders. "Let's clean up and get this over with." I rise and step toward the kitchen, but Charlie gestures me away.

"Most everything is taken care of already. Go get settled on the sofa. I will be right along."

I follow his advice, and he joins me a few minutes later with two steaming cups of tea and my photo album tucked under an elbow. From the kitchen, we hear his phone vibrate, but he waves it off, raising his eyebrows at the black leather cover protecting the secret I am finally sharing after hoarding it for so long. I nod, and he flips through the pages that correspond with the part I told him last night. He stops when the photos change from me, Cat, and Soph with a handful of shots including Vicki and the twins, into a whole lot of me and Daniel, till he reaches the first photo where it's obvious that we are no longer in the friend zone.

I close my eyes and imagine Daniel's face, young and full of life. My fingers twitch with the desire to caress his beloved face. I exhale, release the image, and begin.

"He took me dancing," I say fondly, as Charlie studies a photo of me and Daniel at a bar. "We had a blast until some drunk idiot grabbed me around the waist and tried to force me onto the dance floor despite my loud protestations. Daniel beat the shit out of him. It took two dudes to pull him off the other guy. He was especially protective because of what Kyle did."

"I am glad you had someone; that you finally found someone to protect you, to defend you, to simply be there for you."

"Me too. It was so fucking hot, hmmm," I hum, closing my eyes and rubbing my throat. "Watching him unleash that masculine violence in my defense. Afterward, I didn't leave his side. By the end of the night, we couldn't keep our hands off each other. Not in an overtly sexual way, but in that sweet way, you know? Holding hands, bumping shoulders, finding every excuse to simply be near each other."

Charlie's nostrils flare, eyes narrowing. "I did not realize that was a turn-on for you. I assumed all women abhor violence. 'Hands to yourself' and 'use your words' and all that bloody nonsense," Charlie scoffs and glares over his shoulder at his vibrating phone.

"Women abhor mindless violence, uncontrolled violence. We respect and appreciate a man who knows when to unleash it and does so in a calculated manner. We are viscerally attracted to a man who unleashes his contained, calculated violence in our defense."

"Interesting," he purrs, and I quickly draw us back on track before we are entirely derailed by the thoughts I see swirling in his eyes.

"He kissed me for the first time that night when he dropped me off. On those steps right there, actually," I nod toward the photo of me and Daniel, his arms wrapped around me, standing in front of my cute little cottage.

"Man, I loved that house. It was my haven. The place where I matured and found peace. When Daniel and I got serious, we lived there for a few years. And those were all good memories, too."

Charlie's neutral facade slips, and he rubs his stubbled jaw.

"You two never fought, or argued, or went to bed even remotely annoyed with each other?"

I shake my head. "We had both been in shitty relationships where fighting was the norm. And I watched my parents fight all the time growing up while he watched his parents communicate in healthy ways. So, I guess we kinda had this unspoken pact to just figure out how to truly be on the same team. And it worked for us. We still had our disagreements, but we both refused to let them escalate."

"It was a challenge for me, learning how to communicate in healthy ways, but Daniel was a patient teacher. We couldn't bear being upset with each other. The first time we had a disagreement, and he raised his voice, I flinched and curled into myself. He dropped to his knees, apologized profusely, and never did it again. Daniel helped me learn how to trust people again."

Charlie contemplates my words while flipping through a few more pages of photos. "You look so happy with him. So bloody fucking happy I would be lying if I said it did not make me a smidge jealous."

Smidge is an understatement. Charlie is somewhat possessive. We both chuckle, and I pull my legs onto the couch, crossing them under one another.

"Are you gonna get that," I ask when his phone vibrates for the third time.

"No. What was it like besides that? Your relationship with him."

"It was calm. Safe. Sweet, tender, careful. Wonderful, so wonderful. He was kind and thoughtful, gentle, and funny. Consistent. I don't think he ever once broke a promise in all the years we were together, not even a small inconsequential one."

"He treated you well, then," he says as a statement, not a question.

"Yeah, he did. And I fucking loved him so much."

Another jarring vibration cuts through the silence, and Charlie huffs a sigh, dropping a kiss on the top of my head as he rises, smooth and graceful like a jungle cat. He answers with a gruff, "What is so bloody important, James, that you cannot wait until I return your call?"

Tuning out the one-sided conversation, my mind wanders to the part that comes next, and a dull ache blooms in my chest when I acknowledge the past I am about to face. What will Charlie think of me once he's heard the whole truth? Will I break apart so completely with the telling that I can never be put back together again? Or will I be cleansed and absolved, free of the burden of secrecy?

Charlie plops onto the sofa and scrubs a hand over his face. Alarm bells ring in my head. "What's wrong?"

"My mum. You know she has severe arthritis and a weak immune system. She suffers from chronic pain, and my dad worries every day that she will catch an illness that her body will not be able to fight off. She is in the hospital with pneumonia."

"Oh my God. Charlie. Your sweet mom. You need to go see her right away. I can come with you if you want. Or I can take care of things here. Whatever you need from me."

"V, she is okay. James said that she is responding well to the antibiotics and will be released tomorrow. I doubt Dad will let us come see her until she is healthy anyway, so we will wait on standby for now."

"Okay, okay. We can do that. You should call her or your dad at least."

"I will tomorrow. James said they are both exhausted and to wait until they get some rest," he replies, a frown creasing his eyebrows.

I hate seeing him upset like this, slouched into the cushions, eyes unfocused, and face void of its usual humor. "Charlie, love. What do you need right now? How can I help?"

"Play a few tunes for me, love," he replies, eyes pinched shut.

Eager to ease his worry, I bound up the dais and settle on the bench, plucking out as many upbeat songs as I know by heart. I watch him as I play; relief floods through me as his shoulders relax, dropping away from his ears, and the lines on his face disappear. After my third round through the small repertoire I have memorized, Charlie motions for me to join him on the sofa. Calmed myself by the music, I melt into his side and place my hand on his chest, watching it rise and fall with every breath. I am so damn thankful for each one of those breaths, and I beg to universe to give him millions and millions more, enough so that he outlasts me on this earth.

"Are you up for telling me more, V?" he asks into the silence. I sit up and contemplate him before answering.

"Are you up for it after the news you just got?"

"Yes, love, I am," he replies, sitting up and flipping to the next page in the photo album. His body goes rigid, the muscles in his jaw tensing. And, boom, there's the engagement photos.

Just wait till you see what surprise comes after the wedding.

He looks at me, poorly concealed hurt and betrayal shadowing his eyes as he flips through engagement and wedding photos. I don't need to elaborate; everything is plain to see right in front of him, but I make the mistake of risking a peek at the photo album right as he turns to one of my favorite photos. Try as I might to hold them back, silent tears stream down my face.

"Married," he mutters without looking at me. The word stabs into my chest, slashing through me like a knife, ripping me open, baring all that I've been hiding for so long. Silent sobs crash through me like an angry sea, obliterating the last of my barriers. Wave after wave of anguish, heartache, longing, desperation, anger, and self-loathing pummel my heart, shattering it to pieces once again.

Green eyes averted, Charlie strides to the window. Intense emotions radiate off him. For what feels like an eternity he glares at the majestic London skyline bathed in gold from the rare mid-afternoon sun, while I fall to pieces alone—again. In a clinical, detached way, I understand his intense reaction. Emotionally, however, it makes me angry and frustrated. Is he so surprised that I had a life before him? I've lived a decade longer than him. It should not come as a shock that I've had other lovers. But I get it. It's one thing to have other lovers; it's a completely different thing to have another great love.

I let my emotions run free, and frustration bubbles up and spills over. An anguished, angry sob escapes between my lips. Charlie's head whips around, and his face crumples, transforming from hurt and betrayal to chagrined and apologetic.

"Veronica," he says, impassioned. He takes two powerful strides across the room, scoops me into his arms, and cradles me in his lap. "Shh, shh. I am here; I am sorry. I am here, I promise."

Charlie

Bloody hell, Chuckie. Pull your head out of your arse, mate.

I have no right to be upset that she was married or that she had a life before me. And I should not be surprised. I have been assuming someone important to her died. Given how much it affected her, it would make sense that that person was her husband. Regardless, this is not about me, and I need to be strong for her like I promised.

That sound she made, the one that snapped me out of my self-indulgent trance, slashed through me, straight through my fucking heart. I almost do not want to hear the rest of her story. It kills me to see her suffer like this. No wonder she has been on the run for the past six years. And I have the feeling I do not even know the half of it.

I carefully cradle her head in my lap and run my fingers through her hair while the sobs wracking her body, curled into a fetal position under a pile of blankets, slowly calm then fade away altogether, and she falls into a deep sleep. I watch her, drinking her in her beauty, her strength, her tenacity.

I want to sit here all night, but a nervous energy courses through me, and I am afraid my incessant jitters will disturb her. I reluctantly slip my legs out from under her and pad quietly down the hall to release my torrent of emotions on a punching bag.

That Simple

Charlie

Trepidation slithers down my spine as Veronica sinks onto the sofa next to me. She looks refreshed after a good night's sleep, and her skin has regained its normal rosy, pink glow. I pull her in tight to my side and kiss her tenderly, nuzzling her neck when she pulls away. Giggling, she swats playfully at my face. Fuck I needed to see her smile, to see the light shining in her eyes.

I do not want to see the heartache in her eyes when she confirms my assumption that her husband died. I swear there is something else, too, not that losing a spouse is not a good cause for this much pain and sorrow. But, I feel as though I am missing a piece of the puzzle that is Veronica's past. I take a few deep breaths, bolstering my resolve to be strong for her.

I run a hand through my hair to settle my nerves before looking at her with raised eyebrows. She nods, and I open the photo album, turning back to their wedding photos. A stab of jealousy pulses through me, but I firmly push it away. She just looks so fucking happy, absolutely stunning, eyes shining with obvious affection for her new husband. I have never wanted to get married, but at this moment, it is hard not to wish it was me in a tux standing next to her. I push that thought away, too. I promised her I was happy to just be with her—no label needed—and I meant it.

I flip through a few more pages until she stops me, her small, soft hand on my forearm.

"I know it's probably irritating you to no end to not know what happened. I can see the wheels turning, Charlie. We're getting close, love, I promise. But as we get closer, it gets harder. It feels like telling you makes it more real than ever. When you know the whole truth, I can no longer run. I can no longer hide. And that scares the shit out of me. I'm not strong enough to keep shattering only to pick up the pieces and try to put them back together, knowing the whole time it's pointless because I'll just have to do it again and again and again."

I cup her cheek tenderly. "Veronica, you are the strongest person I know. But you do not always have to be strong, love. I will always be here, ready to help you put the pieces together when you come back from the past, okay? You do not have to go through this alone anymore. I am your anchor. You can let go and drift with the tides, love. I will reel you back in whenever you veer too far off course. Let me do that for you." She nods, giving me a sad yet grateful smile.

Her hand reaches out tentatively to lovingly stroke the photo of her and Daniel dancing at their wedding. It is the first time she has touched the photo album since I pulled it down from the shelf in her closet.

"It was the happiest day of my life. He was so good to me; he was just a wonderful human being in general. I think you would've liked him or respected him, at the very least. He was like you. He had a strong, unshakeable sense of what it means to be a man. Do you know what I mean? Like. . .. how do I explain it? Charlie, you are also just a wonderful human being. You're kind, honest, confident, mostly humble." We share a knowing look at that statement. "You easily earn other people's respect because you treat everyone with respect. Daniel was like that, too. But I know with you, as I knew with him, there's a closely contained violence in there," she pokes my chest, "and you wouldn't hesitate to release it to protect the people you love. I trusted Daniel to protect me, and I trust you as well."

A ball of pride gets stuck in my throat, choking me up. I am honored to have earned this woman's trust and respect. I feel validated to be seen as the kind of man she describes. Society is trying its damnedest to vilify masculine men, but it is our duty to protect our women, children, and others in need. A woman carries the world on her shoulders, bearing children, managing households, building careers, and caring for everyone too often at the expense of herself. As for us men, it is our sacred duty to protect our women from the cruelties of this world.

When I tell Veronica as much, she launches herself into my lap and clings to my neck.

"Every woman deserves to be loved by a man like you, a man like him. Every child deserves to be raised by a kind but dangerous father. To know they are safe and protected.

I love my dad so much, but he failed us in this. My mom was a monster. He should've done a better job to protect us from her. There are still times when I feel anger towards him, but mostly, I've forgiven him. He did the best he could, which is more than a lot of fathers out there, and I'm thankful for that."

"I would burn this world to the ground to protect you. I would do unspeakable harm to anyone who dares to lay a finger on you. If your mom was not an invalid in a care home, I would hunt her down and unleash my carefully contained violence. If Kyle ever gets out. . .. I will send him six feet under and go to prison, a satisfied smile on my face," I vow, a deadly calm settling in my chest.

She briefly studies my face, then kisses me, silently accepting my vow.

"Actually, he is out. Well, he got out. He only served four years for the assault. But then he got locked up again, or he was supposed to," she states, tone carefully neutral.

"What," I exclaim. "Why?"

"We're getting there," she replies.

My vision goes dark, and rage coils through me, curling my hands into fists. "He came after you again," I say darkly.

"I wish it were that simple."

"What do you mean, Veronica? That simple? A man attacking you is not fucking simple. Do not downplay your worth like that, V. Do not—"

"Charlie," she warns, grabbing my arm and yanking me back onto the couch with enough force to surprise me. I didn't even realize I was standing.

"I'm not downplaying my worth," she vehemently retorts. "Fuck Charlie, you don't understand. It would have been so much easier if he had just come after *me*. But that's not what happened. I wish every day that it was, though," she says, deflating. "Then maybe they would still be alive."

"Bloody fucking hell, Veronica! Seriously." I'm standing again.

Wait, they. They. . .. *they would still be* alive?

I sit back down and, impassioned, ask, "What do you mean *they* would still be *alive*? Who, Veronica? Who would still be alive?" I beg her to explain.

Her hands fly to her face, and silent sobs wrack her body. Wave after wave of grief pummels through her, threatening to drown her. I am on my knees, simultaneously comforting her and begging her to tell me to share her burden so I can help carry it.

"Please, love. Tell me. I am here. I will hold you together. Share your burden with me, love. Let me help you carry it. You are not alone in this anymore."

"They're not a *burden,* Charlie," she screams at me.

There is that 'they' a*gain.*

"I know that, love. That is not what I meant." I pull her into my lap and hold her. She pummels my chest with her fists while hurling profanities at the universe and all its unfair cruelties. When I feel her slacken against me, her rage spent, I settle us back on the couch and gently say, "Tell me about them, V."

In a small but determined voice, she demands, "Turn. The. Page."

I don't know what I was expecting, but it is not a sucker punch to the gut or the invisible hand ripping my heart out of my chest. I cannot even begin to imagine the depths of pain she must feel seeing this photo.

I stare dumbfounded at the photo of Veronica and Daniel. . . —and three beautiful brown-haired, brown-eyed girls who look exactly like their mother.

"Oh my God, Veronica," I whisper.

"They're dead," she shrieks. Then whispers, "My beloved husband and my beautiful daughters. Dead," and shatters in my arms.

Veronica

Tears and snot run rivulets down my face. My whole body shakes uncontrollably from the force of my heart shattering.

They're gone. They're gone, they're gone, they're gone. No. No no no no no! Please, God, no.

My girls. My beautiful, kind, sweet, witty, intelligent girls. Gone.

I can't breathe. I am drowning in pain. Drowning in grief. Drowning in despair.

My chest aches from trying to force air past the ball of rage lodged in my throat.

"Why?" I rage out loud. "Why?" I scream. "Why?" I beg.

Why them? Why all of them and not me?

"It should have been me," I lament.

I wish it had been me.

The sides of my fists ache from pounding out my rage on the flesh that anchors me, preventing me from being carried out to sea by the undertow of despair. My throat is raw, sandpaper grating against my anguish as I release it from my chest.

I miss them. God, I miss them so much. All of them. So. Fucking. Much.

My sister. My Dad. My husband. My precious daughters.

"How, Charlie? How? How is one person supposed to survive *this much loss?*" I plead, desperate for an answer of hope, words I can cling to like a life raft in this thrashing storm.

He gently grabs my arms, forcing me to stop pacing and look at him.

"Exactly the way you are," he answers, carefully enunciating each word. I stare at him blankly, unwilling to believe him.

"Allow me to elaborate. Exactly the way you are at *this* moment. You need to rage, to beat out your frustration on living flesh. You do it right here." He jabs a finger into his chest. "You need to scream. Lament your torments to the universe. Cuss out whoever dared to deal you such a shitty hand. You do it here." He gestures to the room around us.

"You need to cry? You do it here." He gestures to his shoulders. "And when you are done, I will wipe away your tears. You need to fall apart? You do it here." He gestures to his arms. "I will hold your pieces close and help you put them back together when you are ready. Whatever you need, I got you," he finishes, impassioned.

My eyes lock onto his, boring into him down to his soul, searching for the truth in his words. I find it engraved on his heart: his intense love for me and his promise to be my anchor.

I launch myself at him, crashing my lips against his, desperately needing to feel *alive*, to be brought back to the present fully, to strengthen and reinforce the tether between me and my anchor, to be reminded that my life without them is still beautiful, still worth living.

Charlie grips my legs hard, kissing me ferociously, and backs me into the wall. He grinds his erection against me, and a current of fierce need rages through me. He pulls back just far enough to look at me with those intense green eyes, and I release a sob.

"You need a reminder of what it feels like to be alive," he rasps, then grabs my small, cold hands, pinning them against the wall above us, one sizeable warm hand completely swallowing both of mine. "I will feed you big-ass juicy cheeseburgers. I will take you to the theatre. I will climb mountains and cross oceans with you. And," he says, lowering to whisper in my ear, "I will worship your body with my hands, my tongue, my cock" promises, grinding between my legs.

"I will fuck you in limos and glass-walled lifts. I will fuck you till you forget your pain, your name, your past, and your future. Make love to you till all you know is the feeling of me worshiping your body, the feeling of me buried deep inside you, and the pleasure, oh Veronica, the pleasure that life has to offer."

He drops his hand back to my leg and carries me across the room, snatching a blanket off the back of the sofa on his way past. I luxuriate in the feel of his hair between my fingers and his tongue in my mouth, his hard body pressed against mine. Without breaking contact, he slams the lid on the baby grand piano and tosses the blanket on it. I rip off my shirt and his, and then he sets me down long enough for us to both shed the rest of our clothes.

"On your hands and knees, love," he demands, gesturing towards the piano with an arrogant jerk of his chin. With exaggerated movements, I climb onto the blanket-draped lid and look at him over my shoulder. "Oh, I like this view," he says as his hand connects with my ass. I yelp in surprise, then arch my back for more. His hand connects with the other cheek, and my need drips down my legs.

Charlie slowly wipes my wetness up my legs one side at a time, then, with the same maddeningly slowness, slips two fingers inside me. I moan, dropping my head and arching my back, pushing my hips back into his hand.

"Look me in the eye when my fingers are inside you," he demands. I obey, and he thrusts his fingers while lazily circling my clit with his other hand. The sensation abruptly stops, and I whimper his name. His eyes flare, and a wicked smile spreads across his face as he moves closer to my exposed, sensitive flesh.

He grabs my ass firmly and licks me from clit all the way up the back, over and over, slow and even. I'm panting and whimpering, begging, so close to release, but he refuses to push me over the edge. When I'm trembling so hard I can barely hold myself up, he sucks my clit into his mouth and finally, finally, sends me into a powerful climax.

When I've come back down from the high, he pulls my legs off the piano, then nudges them apart with his knee. He enters me quickly and forcefully, setting a hard, fast rhythm. I look back at him over my shoulder, devouring the sight of him, head thrown back in ecstasy, fingers gripping my hips, muscles contracting as he pounds into me relentlessly until he finds his own release.

"Come on, love," Charlie coaxes after, as he deftly lifts me off the piano, where I lay slumped, completely and utterly exhausted. I snuggle into his slick, muscular chest and surrender control, allowing my mind to flow freely, trusting Charlie to prevent me from drowning in pain and despair.

"Here, love. Lie down here for a minute while I get the tub ready," he murmurs, setting me gently on a padded bench in his en suite. Thoughts of Daniel and our girls, my life before, and how much I miss them swirl through my brain, mingling with thoughts of Kali and Kellan and my studio, my budding love for Charlie, and how much I truly enjoy my new life here in London. A torrent of emotions interlaces with these thoughts, creating a maelstrom within me, but for once, I don't fight it. I flow with it, allowing myself to feel the emotions. I drift through the memories, trusting Charlie to reel me back in.

"Do you feel up to telling me the rest, love?" Charlie asks tentatively the next morning after we finish the remainder of his meal-prepped breakfasts. I'm sure it's driving him crazy, waiting to find out how it ends. But I need to know something first.

"How's your mom?"

"She is getting better. I talked with her this morning. My dad said that she is responding to the antibiotics well and that the doctors expect a full recovery."

I rest my hand against his stubbled cheek. "You must feel so relieved." He rubs his cheek against my hand. "I am, too. Your mom is the sweetest lady. Can we go see her when she's better?"

"I would like that very much." We snuggle on the sofa for a time, each lost in our own thoughts. My tea is long gone, and my legs are stiff from being tucked under me for so long when Charlie breaks the silence.

"Care to indulge my curiosity?"

I stretch out my legs as he flips through pages and pages of the girls' milestones. I cannot look at the photos without falling apart. Sometimes at night, instead of nightmares, I wake to phantom crying and tiny voices whispering, "Mommy." For a long time after I lost them, I would wake up feeling frantic and tear the house apart, looking for my girls. Or I would make lunch and holler for them to come eat until my voice was hoarse. And then my heart would break again and again with each repeated realization that they were gone.

It took months to break the habit of searching for Daniel in our shop when I couldn't find him in the house. My heart would race with worry every time the school bus drove past and didn't stop to drop off my girls. My entire life was built on the foundation of my and Daniel's marriage and revolved around raising our girls.

"Daniel and I were a few weeks away from our tenth wedding anniversary," I start, wishing desperately that we had been allowed to experience that milestone.

Charlie looks from me to the photo and back, calculating. "You were only married for ten years?" I nod, and he points to one of my daughters, who's clearly older than ten. I wait for him to figure it out. His eyes snap to mine the moment he does. "You never answered when I asked about Kyle's baby."

"No, I didn't. I almost lost her. She was in the NICU for two months. During that time, I debated whether to keep her or put her up for adoption. But, when I was finally able to bring her home and everyone—my dad and Vicki, Daniel, Darren, Tim, and Tam—was so helpful and supportive, I knew I couldn't let her go. So, I finally named her Bella and plowed ahead as a single mom. I was determined to give her a good life and be the mother I had wanted growing up. I did, too," I say, smiling through my tears.

Charlie swipes a thumb across my cheeks to wipe them away. "I have no doubt that you were a wonderful mother. And your dad, was he smitten with his granddaughter?"

"Yes," I chuckle. "She had him wrapped around her little finger from the moment he first saw her. They all doted on her. I was lucky to have the 'village' they say it takes to raise kids."

"And your mom?" he asks, voice carefully neutral.

"She never met Bella or her sisters. I tried, at first, to mend our relationship. I so badly wanted my mom to be there, helping me become a mother myself, even after everything she had done. But, deep down, I always knew she'd never change. I didn't cut her off immediately because I didn't want to lose my baby sister, Valerie, too. It didn't matter though. The less I spoke to Mildred, the less Val spoke to me until I decided it wasn't worth the abuse and heartache anymore."

"That must have been hard on you," Charlie says, eyes full of sympathy.

"It was, but also. ... it freed up all the mental energy I spent trying to be good enough for them to put toward raising my daughter and rebuilding my life." I pause to sip some water while Charlie flips back through the photos, considering them in light of this new information. If he questions why I omitted photos of Bella until after Daniel and I's wedding, he doesn't ask.

When I made this photo album, I subconsciously knew I might use it to tell my story in the unlikely event that I ever did. I always hated the judgment I received for being a young single mom. It's not like I was reckless. I had, had to take birth control in secret, and Kyle refused to use protection. He also wouldn't take no for an answer. So, I bore and raised a child who was conceived not out of love and consent but out of demand and manipulation. And I'd be damned if I let anyone see her and sully the life I built for her before they had the full context of the situation. My sweet, kind Bella.

I miss you so much, baby girl.

Fists balled in his lap, white knuckles stark against his black sweats; Charlie releases a long exhale. "Veronica, I look at these," he points at the photos, "and I see a strong, determined, tenacious young woman who took the shitty hand life dealt her and turned it into a winner."

"You're right, I did. And when I lost them, I was convinced I'd never have the will or strength to do it again. And then you found me."

"And then I found you," he parrots. "Your dad," he ventures gently, "passed. . ."

"A few months before the wedding. I was devastated. Tim walked me down the aisle, and I cried the whole way. When we stopped before the altar, he wiped my tears, kissed my forehead, and whispered in my ear, 'Feel the sun kiss your face, and the breeze flow through your hair, and know that he's here by your side.' He handed me off to his son, a beaming, ecstatic bride."

Daniel looked magnificent up there, the sun in his hair and joy shining from his eyes. I would give anything to go back and relive that day over again.

"And this photo," Charlie says, reeling me back to the present.

"Is our last family photo. It was taken a few weeks before the accident. Bella was carefree, officially an adult for just a few short days, and a brand-new high school graduate. She hadn't yet decided what she was going to do in the future. We were content to have her at home a little longer and in no hurry to see her go. Miss Avery had recently turned nine. Yes, I got pregnant right away. Yes, it was planned. Started planning the minute we got engaged."

Charlie chuckles, holding up his hands. "I was not going to say anything."

"Bullshit," I reply, chuckling as well. "I saw you calculating."

"Now, I call bullshit. You are the one with the glass face. But I. . .. have a poker face."

"But you forget, Lady Gaga, that I know your tells." I raise my eyebrows at him and continue before the grief has a chance to well up and drown me. "Avery was a social butterfly. She loved everyone, and everyone loved her. Her schedule was always packed full of activities: dance, theatre, chess club, hockey, and soccer. All the girls loved soccer." Daniel had played and shared his love of the game with our girls.

"Danielle, our youngest, had also recently had a birthday. She was eight and quite the spitfire.

"I can see that," Charlie says ruefully.

I chuckle and, holding back tears, ask, "Which photo are you looking at?"

"She's chasing after her sisters in a scary Halloween mask."

"That fucking creepy clown mask. Dani and her dad terrorized the rest of us with that stupid mask. It used to make me so mad. But, when the time came, I almost couldn't bring myself to get rid of it." I trail off, wishing she were still alive to torment her sisters.

"So," Charlie's voice gently pulls me back to the conversation. "Their birthdays were close together?"

"Yes. That's partly why I call November through May 'the bad months.'"

He raises his eyebrows. "Because of the reminders?" he asks softly.

I nod. "I can generally deal with the end of June, July, August, September, and the beginning of October. There are no big holidays or missed birthdays. But those other months. . .. Halloween hits, and then it's Thanksgiving, Christmas, and New Year's straight into the birthday season. My dad's, my sister Vera's, my hus—Daniel's, and all three of the girls'. And to top it off, they were killed in May, two weeks before Daniel and I's wedding anniversary."

Charlie threads his fingers through mine. "Every year, from Halloween till your anniversary in June, you are bombarded with reminders. Boom, boom, boom. One after another." I nod once, pleading with my eyes for Charlie to understand my utter devastation.

"My love," he says, releasing my hand and opening his arms. I fall into his chest, relishing his solid strength. "I cannot imagine how difficult it is to endure that year after year. Your strength and tenacity amaze me with each new chapter of your story. I will do whatever you need to help you through 'the bad months'. … help make them a little more bearable."

"Just be there, Charlie. Be my safe space. Hold me together while I fall apart. Be my anchor. That's what I need."

I feel him nod and place a kiss on the top of my head.

"Did you say they were killed?"

You don't miss a thing, do you, Charlie?

Last Night Together

After a long day in the shop with Daniel, I relaxed on the sofa while he and the girls gathered our favorite snacks, drinks, and some blankets for a movie night, joking and laughing the entire time. A content grin crept across my face, and gratitude settled warmly in my chest. I never dreamed my life could be this fucking amazing.

When I was pregnant with Avery, we built a bigger version of our beloved cottage to accommodate our growing family. Our career—Daniel and I owned a woodworking and epoxy business together—was thriving. We started it as a side hustle when Danielle was two. By the time we sent her off to kindergarten, we had both quit our jobs to keep up with the demands of our small business.

I fucking loved my life. It was all the positive adjectives, but it was far from perfect. I struggled to be a wife and mother. My mental health cycled through, often turbulent, highs and lows. I invested a lot of time, money, and other resources into healing. I desperately wanted to be the best version of myself for my family.

Despite my diligent self-improvement work, I still had moments where I got so overwhelmed that I just couldn't deal with life without completely disengaging and distancing myself from my family. Daniel was my saving grace in those moments.

A chorus of adoring voices calling, "Mommy," pulled me out of my thoughts as a pile of bodies settled around me. Sticky hands, heavy limbs, and my husband's loving caresses assaulted me from multiple angles, and I pushed back a wave of irritation. I knew I was tired and would miss those snuggles someday. If only I had known just how soon someday would come.

The girls squabbled over which movie we'd watch until Daniel settled the matter with his usual calm reason. He simply turned one on, and one by one, the girls quieted, their focus shifting to the TV, their squabbling quickly forgotten.

I didn't watch the movie. I watched my girls, memorizing their faces and freezing them in my mind so I could look back and remember them in each stage of life. I studied them more closely than usual that night. Maybe my subconscious knew what was coming. Regardless, I'm glad to have those clear, sharp, detailed memories, even though I rarely visit them.

Dani never lasted more than half a movie before she crashed. She curled up next to me, her brown curls spread across my lap. I ran my fingers through the silky strands and caressed her soft cheeks.

Bella untwined her long, toned limbs from mine and disappeared to her room with a carefree, "G'night," tossed over her shoulder. She rarely hung out with us anymore, but we did our best to cherish every moment she chose to spend with us. She became more independent every day, and I knew our days with her at home were numbered. If only that number hadn't been so small.

Avery quickly occupied the empty spot next to me, draping half her body over me. My first instinct was to push her away, but I pulled her into a hug and dropped a kiss on the top of her head instead. My fingers trailed designs up and down her arms, admiring her strength and fearless, determined attitude. There's no doubt she would have achieved a great many things in life had she had the chance.

Soon, she was sleeping, too, and a few silent tears slid down my face. Daniel caught my eye and tilted his head.

"They're happy tears, sweetheart," I answered his silent question.

"We've built an amazing life," he stated simply as he gracefully rose from his spot on the floor in front of us. He gently pried Avery off me and carried her to bed. I followed him up the stairs with a warm, limp Dani carefully cradled in my arms. I lingered longer than usual in each of the girls' rooms that night; even Bella indulged me with a hug and an, "I love you too, Mom."

As I shut her door behind me, Daniel caught me around the waist and pressed me into the wall with his hips. He reached behind me and pulled my hair free of its messy bun, burying his hands in it. "Hmm. Fuck, I love your hair," he whispered in my ear before his mouth claimed mine. I almost pushed him away. Almost told him, 'No, not tonight'. But the same *subconscious premonition that had permeated the evening settled in the back of my mind and said that I'd regret it.*

We made love that last night with more passion and fervor than we had in a long time. We connected deeply, our bodies tuned, and souls synced to each other so completely that each time one of us stirred during the night, the other was instantly aroused, and we made love a second, third, and fourth time during the night.

The vivid memory I possess of that night has been a balm to my scarred soul more than once since I lost them. If our last night together had gone any other way, I would have succumbed to despair long ago.

I woke the following day feeling content and grateful, but as they often did, my feelings flipped and soured with each demand, request, and responsibility placed on my shoulders until I snapped when I stubbed my toe while working in the shop with Daniel. I let out a string of cuss words and slammed the side of my fist into the wall, breathing heavily through my nose in an unsuccessful attempt to calm my surging emotions.

"Ron, honey. What's wrong, sweetheart?" Daniel caught me around the waist, spinning me to face him. I planted my hands on his chest and pushed him away more forcefully than necessary.

"Daniel, please stop. I love you. I love the girls. I love our life. But I need a fucking break, okay?"

"Okay," he answered, completely accepting of my need for space. He was always so patient and kind when I got overwhelmed. He knew how my less-than-ideal upbringing made it challenging for me to recognize what I needed, let alone when and how to ask for it. He gently and briefly touched my shoulder, his way of showing silent support, and then pulled his phone out of his pocket.

"Hey, Vic," he said after only one ring.

"Hey, Dan." I heard my sister's faint reply.

"Whatcha up to today?"

"That depends. . ."

"You and Ron should spend the day together. Go to lunch, shopping, get pedicures. Dinner and drinks. Whatever, ya know?"

"Ahhh," she acknowledged Daniel's unspoken plea for help. The three of us had been down that road multiple times before. "I'll swing by in an hour."

"Thank you, Vic," Daniel replied, relief evident in his voice. "Go get ready, sweetheart. I got things covered here," he told me, refraining from pulling me into his arms.

"Thank you, hun. I'm sorry. I have been trying to prevent myself from getting to this point. We've just been so busy lately, and the girls have been extra needy since your parents' last visit. And—"

"It's okay, Ron, I promise. I understand and see all the work you've been doing on yourself. Being a mom is hard, especially when you're re-parenting yourself and breaking generational cycles at the same time. There's nothing wrong with needing a break. Go. Have fun. I love you."

I almost almost *closed the distance between us and pulled him into my arms. God, how I wish I had, but I didn't. Instead, I replied, "I love you too, husband," and turned on my heel, practically sprinting into the house to get ready to go with Vicki. I didn't stop to see the girls on my way out either, taking for granted that they'd be there when I got home. But they weren't. I never got to hold them, kiss their soft cheeks, or tell them I love them again.*

Vicki and I had an incredible afternoon, thoroughly enjoying the unseasonably warm May afternoon. We ate lunch at our favorite hole-in-the-wall cafe. We got pedicures and bought a bunch of shit we didn't need, venting the whole time about our husbands, my kids, and life in general. Vicki was frustrated with her 'lackluster' first year of marriage, and I was overwhelmed by feeling like I had to be everything to everyone all the time.

As the hours ticked by and evening rolled in, we became frustrated with each other. My venting had quickly and smoothly morphed into gushing gratitude. I loved my girls and being their mom. "Yes," I had told Vic, "being a mother is hard. But it is also amazing and fun and fascinating. And the most fucking rewarding thing you'll ever do with your life." And I loved my husband so damn much. He was so patient and kind and would do anything to see me happy–as evidenced by his actions earlier that day.

Vic was annoyed by this change and confessed, rather vehemently, that she was seriously considering divorce. Knowing my sister didn't surprise me at all, and I would've supported her decision to do so. What I couldn't support, however, was going dancing with her for the sole purpose of being her wingman. She was hellbent on having a fling that night.

She begged and pleaded. She got downright manipulative and mean, but I didn't take it personally. I knew just how difficult it was to fight that urge myself, having been raised by the queen of mean and manipulative. Plus, we had a fair amount of alcohol running through our systems.

"Vic! For the fucking millionth time. I am not going to help you cheat on your husband!" *I practically screamed at her as I stood, scooting the chair back with an ear-splitting screech. People were staring, but I was a few cocktails past caring.*

"Ugh, Veronica," she sneered. "You're such a fucking killjoy." If we hadn't been in public, I would have punched her right in her stupid face. I put up with a lot of shit from my little sister, but I did not appreciate her using Mildred as a weapon.

She continued her rant, oblivious to the rage building inside me. "It's not the end of the world, Ronnie. He doesn't pay attention to me anyway. He cares more for his stupid fucking video games."

"Oh, Vic," I said, dropping back into my chair and grabbing her hands in mine. "I am so sorry that your marriage isn't what you expected. But this is not the way to get your husband's attention, okay? There's an excellent couples therapist that I used to refer patients to all the time. I'll give you her number. And we can still go dancing, just please, don't do something so drastic barely a year in."

She smiled a rueful smile, and the tension eased from my shoulders. The desire to go home to my husband and daughters became almost overwhelming, but I had always had a soft spot for my little sister. I planned on staying only for a dance, maybe two, just enough to placate her, but Vic called in reinforcements in the form of Sophie and Catherine, who wanted to grab dinner first. If only we had known how our last-minute change of plans would have life-altering, heart-breaking consequences.

"Seriously, Ron! Get off your phone already," Catherine chided playfully, slapping at my hand.

"Okay, okay. I haven't heard back from Daniel, and I'm starting to get worried. Bella's not answering either," I fired back, a knot of unease growing in my stomach.

"I'm sure everything is fine, but if it'll make you feel better, go call him," Sophie encouraged with a dismissive wave of her hand. I never got the chance.

"Oooo, somebody's in trouble," Sophie said in a singsong voice as I made to push away from the table. The sight of the cops twisted the knot of unease in my stomach.

"I've been a bad girl, officer," Vic chimed in, holding her wrists together in front of her. "Put me in cuffs and punish me." Their giggles grated on my already frazzled nerves. Despite my intuition, I told myself that everything was fine; Daniel and the girls were okay. There was no reason the police would be there to see me.

Except the hostess pointed at our table. As the police made their way toward us, I knew in my gut that something was very, very wrong. I froze in my seat, silently screaming at the universe, begging whoever was listening to prove me wrong.

"We're sorry to interrupt you, ladies," Officer One said, voice pinched and apologetic.

No. No. No, no, no.

His partner continued in that same sorrowful voice, "We need to speak with a. . ." he paused to check his notepad, "Veronica Gorski?" I didn't answer. I could see the bad news written all over their faces. Sophie and Catherine, seated to my left and right, each placed a hand on my arm and nodded at me.

"Will you step outside with us, ma'am?" Officer One asked gently. I stared blankly ahead, already numb. I didn't want to go with them. Didn't want to hear what they had to say.

My sister answered for me, "Yes. We'll all come." Someone threw money on the table, and someone else ushered me outside. I could barely walk, trembling so hard. The three of them had to hold me up.

"Ma'am," Officer Two started. "I am so, so sorry to tell you, but—"

"We're afraid," Officer One continued, "that there's been an accident. We need to take you in to identify the victims."

"Your husband and kids. . .. were in an accident. They didn't make it." Officer One's voice said from somewhere far, far away.

No. Not in this world. My husband and girls were alive and well in this world, waiting for me to come home.

I shook my head, vehemently denying their words.

"It was a drunk driver on 95. Hit them from behind. Pushed them off the road down into a ravine."

There was crying and questions. Arms wrapped around me, and comforts were offered. I registered none of it. Gone? All of them? My whole life is gone? Sophie, an ER nurse trained to deal with traumatic situations and the most level-headed of the three of them, grabbed my hand.

"Come on, V. I know you don't want to, but we have to go with them. We'll stay with you the whole time," she said through tears, and I snapped, ripping my hand from hers.

"No!" I screamed. "No! No, no, no, no." I crumpled to the pavement, tears streaming down my face. "They're not dead. They can't be dead, Soph. They're my whole life," I protested through sobs that shook my whole body.

Sophie, Catherine, and Victoria sat on the pavement, arms wrapped around me, holding me together until the officers kindly prodded us to our feet. I followed them like a robot, refusing to accept the truth that my beloved husband and precious daughters were dead.

Somehow, we ended up at the morgue. The coroner offered his condolences then we followed him down a cold hallway into a morbidly, humorously comfortable sitting room. He slid four photographs toward me, face down. While he explained the nature of their extensive injuries, I stared at the white rectangles, hoping beyond hope that they were wrong. Sophie whispered empty comforts in my ear and held my limp hand, but Cat and Vic stood behind me, a hand on each shoulder, their faces turned away.

"Alright, sweetie. I'm going to turn them over now," Sophie kindly murmured in my ear.

As she moved to flip the first photo, I screeched, "Wait! Which one is. . .. Which one is. . ." I choked on a sob, unable to say his name.

"Daniel," Sophie asked, and I rubbed my temples.

"I don't want to see the girls." The coroner pointed, and Sophie flipped. I screwed my eyes shut as tight as I could and shook my head.

"It's him. Daniel," Sophie choked.

I started violently shaking. "Please don't make me look. I don't want to remember him like that. Please," I begged, quickly becoming hysterical.

"It's not him, Soph. It can't be. You're wrong. You have to be wrong. My girls. Not my girls. I can't. How? What am I gonna do? I can't live without them. They can't be gone. All of them? No. No, no, no. Please, no. I can't do this."

Hands pulled me to my feet, leading me blindly out of the building. I refused to open my eyes until we got to Sophie and Turner's apartment, where I became hysterical again, begging them to take me home to see my family.

My sister grabbed me by both arms and gave me a gentle shake. "Ronnie. Look at me." Her eyes were bloodshot and swollen. "I'm so sorry, big sis, but they're gone. We're not going to take you home. You're gonna stay here tonight, okay?

"No, it's not okay, Victoria," I snapped back, voice dripping with venom. "This is your fault," I screamed in her face, ripping my arms out of her grip. "It's your fucking fault. If you hadn't insisted on cheating on your husband, then I would have been at home. Daniel and the girls—" my voice became cracked and jagged, tearing me to pieces on its way out "—wouldn't've been on the road. They'd still be alive!"

Strong arms wrapped around my heaving chest, hauling me off my feet and away from my dumbstruck sister. I beat at Turner's arms, screaming and kicking, begging and making threats until I felt a poke in my arm.

"I'm so sorry, sweetie," Sophie said, holding my hand while the drug pulled me into a blissfully numb oblivion.

No Real Justice

My chest is flayed open, my broken heart exposed, and my head throbs as memories recently released from their vault whip around violently inside my skull. Daniel proposing in a sea of wildflowers. New baby scent and soft skin so delicate you can trace the tiny blue veins just underneath the surface. Spring Concerts and soccer games and parent-teacher conferences. The smell of fresh-cut lumber and the calluses on my hands. The pride of building our own home. Daniel's beaming smile when we sold our very first epoxy river table and his quiet encouragement when I worried about quitting our 'real' jobs.

And the despair. The all-consuming despair that stripped life of its vibrant beauty and reduced me to an empty, translucent, broken being unable to interact with the irreversibly altered world around her.

The strong heartbeat thumping steadily against my cheek reels me back to the present, and Charlie's firm yet gentle embrace, wrapped around me, holds me together, just like he promised.

I pull away from his tear-stained shirt just enough to see his equally tear-stained face. He quickly swipes away his tears, then gently dries mine with the rough pads of his thumbs. He is still an enigma to me, with his luxury suits, plush corner office, and working man's hands. My favorite kind of hands, just like Daniel's.

A shiver runs down my spine as I luxuriate in the memories of both sets of hands, rough and reverent, and the way they both felt caressing my skin. I remember watching Daniel cradle our newborn daughters with such tenderness in one moment, then chop down an entire tree in the next. I've also watched Charlie's fingers delicately fly across a keyboard crunching numbers for a client, and although I haven't seen it, it's easy to imagine him working on his parent's farm, throwing hay bales and fixing a fence.

It's already easier to remember Daniel and my past with fondness while simultaneously anticipating my future with Charlie.

Charlie's thumbs continue to draw circles across my face while he stares deeply into my eyes. He drops his forehead against mine, and we rest for a minute, breathing the same air.

"V, my love," he says, breaking the silence. "Thank you for trusting me with your story. How do you feel now that it is out there?"

I pause to assess myself before answering. "I feel lighter. And, just as broken as the day it happened. But, for the first time since that day, I feel a thread of hope . . . and of peace. Like, now that I've let go of this heavy thing I've been carrying around and guarding for so long, I can release the heaviness. Shed the despair, sadness, anger, and rage that I've been holding onto so tightly for so long. I can let go of all of that and keep the rest: the joy, the love, the wonder. I feel peace flowing in and filling up the cracks in my heart, and I know that I can learn to miss what I have lost *and* anticipate what I'll gain. That both parts of me can co-exist peacefully."

"What a relief that must be . . . like shedding a stubborn outer shell. It protected you and kept you safe but also trapped your wings."

"It will take some time to learn to fly," I say to remind us both that I haven't been magically cured.

"I will be there every step of the way to catch you when you fall and to encourage you to try again."

I flash him a grateful smile, then rest my forehead against his chest. I memorize the unique rhythm of his heart, storing it away to use in those moments when I need an anchor and he's not physically present. I am under no illusion that it's all going to be smooth sailing from now on. But I do know that, from now on, I will face choppy waters with hope, and I trust that Charlie will be there to weather the storms by my side.

Eventually, we peel ourselves out of each other's arms and off the sofa, then walk hand-in-hand to Charlie's room down the hall. We take a shower, rinsing away the turmoil of emotions that have surrounded us since he rescued me off my closet floor.

It's cold and dark a few hours later, but we venture out anyway. I inhale huge lungfuls of the clean, crisp air, exhaling slowly to watch my breath gather in tiny clouds before me.

Charlie drives us to the pub, his warm hand cradling mine. We sit at the bar and chat with the bartenders. These simple interactions feel foreign without the usual undercurrent of despair and secrecy, but it's a good feeling, a relief.

I watch Charlie out of the corner of my eye while we eat our cheeseburgers. He fidgets frequently and inhales, setting his shoulders as if to speak, but exhales without saying anything a few times.

He doesn't miss a thing, does he, V?

After the bartender clears our plates, I turn and demand, "Alright then. Spit it out."

He regards me for a moment. "Did you at least get justice?" I stare at him blankly. "Did they catch the drunk driver," he clarifies.

I swallow hard and curl my hands into fists. "Yes. And that's where we get to Kyle." His eyes go wide, nostrils flaring. He slings an arm across the back of my barstool and rests a hand comfortingly on my shoulder.

"After the four short years he served for the assault, he settled with an old college teammate in Montana. He was told to stay out of Idaho. My attorney told us Kyle did well at first. He went to rehab and therapy and consistently attended AA meetings. Got a job. Rebuilt a decent life for himself."

"He should have spent his life in prison for what he did to you. Hopefully, his fellow inmates found out and gave him prison justice."

"They did. Let's just say the photo my attorney emailed me was darkly satisfying. What irritated me the most, though, was that he never asked about our baby. Not once during her life did he care until the very end. It was a relief, however, that he didn't, but it made us complacent. We didn't keep tabs on him, which is how we ended up delivering a dining room set to a customer in Montana who just so happened to be a friend of Kyle's. Last we knew, he was on the opposite side of the state."

I pause and take a long drink of water before continuing. "He was there when we showed up, visiting this friend. Bella was with us, and he did the math. Split before we ever even knew he was there. A few weeks later, our attorney called to inform us that Kyle had requested information about *his baby.*"

"Fucking prick," Charlie says darkly. "I can see where this is going." I purse my lips and nod.

"Yep," I reply, popping the 'p.' "I don't understand why, but he tried to get custody and visitation rights even though she was almost eighteen. She had known about him since she was little, knew what happened, and wanted absolutely nothing to do with him. I guess that set him off. He went on a bender and lost his job. In hindsight, I realize that we should have kept our personal and professional lives separate, but when the girls were little, it was easier having our shop at home. One Google search and he easily tracked us down."

Every damn day I wonder if they'd still be alive if Daniel and I would have had the foresight to keep our personal and professional lives separate. That we didn't contribute to the guilt that has been eating me from the inside out since the day they died.

"Fucking prick," Charlie repeats under his breath. "You said he is dead?" he asks, brows knit together. I nod. "So, what happened?"

"This is what I've been able to piece together. He stalked us for weeks. The day of the accident, he was so fucking drunk he thought it was me in the passenger seat. . . but it was Bella. My beautiful, witty, intelligent, strong-willed firstborn." My voice cracks, and I pause while Charlie rubs soothing circles on the small of my back.

"Come on, love. Let us go to the studio. You do not need an audience for this," he says, jerking his chin at the pub bustling around us.

The short walk steadies me, and I continue as soon as we settle on the sofa, hot tea in hand. "Daniel and the girls were on their way to the store to buy ingredients to make my favorite pick-me-up dessert. I found texts between Bella and her father discussing it and the recipe lying on the counter next to a bouquet of roses. They were brown and wilted by the time I was coherent enough to notice them. Kyle followed Daniel and our girls. He forced them off the highway and into the ravine."

Charlie carefully cradles me against his chest while I break apart. I squeeze my eyes shut so tightly that it hurts, but the visions pour in regardless. I can feel Daniel's anger and fear as he no doubt did everything in his power to save them. I can feel the girls' terror as they shot off the highway. I can hear their screams and see their broken bodies. Try as I might, I haven't been able to prevent myself from imagining their last moments. The images of what happened and what they must have felt repeat in my mind and heart. And the guilt consumes me.

"I should have gone home," I sob into Charlie's chest. "I should have been there. They never would have left the house if I hadn't decided to stay out later than planned."

"V, love. It was not your fault."

I shake my head, the raging currents of guilt and despair threatening to pull me under and drown me. "I was selfish, so selfish. There were so many other things I could have done to get that break. At the very least, I should have recognized it for the gift it was and hugged them each before I left, telling them I loved them. But no. I ran out, like always."

"Stop, Veronica. Stop berating yourself. *You* did *nothing* wrong. None of this was your fault. The only person to blame here is Kyle. He is the one who made and executed the decision that ended their lives. Not you. Even if you had stayed home that day, who is to say it would have changed the outcome? Stop drowning in what-ifs, love. Quit shouldering the guilt that belongs on no one's shoulders besides Kyle's." I grasp onto his words, a life raft in a raging sea, and hold on for dear life.

It's not your fault, V. It's not your fault.

"I just don't get it, Charlie. What happened? Where did it all go wrong? We were friends, *best friends*. The five of us. How does a person go from best friend to lover to abuser to, to. . . murderer?"

Charlie doesn't answer. No answer can offer me any sort of relief or comfort anyway. Instead, he silently holds space for me and my pain, firmly resting his hand on my thigh and giving it a tiny squeeze.

"Yes, he gave me Bella, and I am still so thankful to have gotten the time with her that I did. But I am also so fucking lucky that I was able to have more kids. The beating and emergency c-section caused debilitating issues."

"That's why you had a hysterectomy?"

"Yeah, and why the scars are still so noticeable after all this time. I had to have the younger two via c-section as well. My body and my give-a-shits were so beaten down when Bella was in the NICU that the incision got infected and didn't heal well, so the doctor who delivered Avery and Dani made those incisions above the original scar. I have used many products and done consistent scar tissue massage to reduce them and the stretch marks as much as I have. The hysterectomy also fucked with my hormones and caused major depression, with some anxiety, mood swings, brain fog, and chronic pain sprinkled in. Daniel was so patient and helpful as I recovered. In his kind but firm manner, he, in a way, forced me to get better. Without pressuring me, he made my mental health our number one priority, and I credit him fully with my smooth recovery after the surgery."

"Silver linings," he muses, giving me a rueful half-smile.

"Yeah," I agree, curling one side of my mouth in return. "Daniel was so good to me. Ya know what pisses me off most about the whole situation, besides the obvious, is that I don't even get the satisfaction of knowing he's rotting away in prison. When he sobered up and realized what he had done, he took the easy way out, the bastard."

"Suicide?"

"Yeah."

"Fucking prick."

"Yeah. I think that's the part that fuels the rage. I have suffered so much because of him, and I don't even get justice. I wish I'd had the chance to speak to him just one time. To rage and scream at him, to make him look me in the eye and take responsibility for his actions. To get some closure. When his attorney told me he couldn't handle the guilt of killing his child, I lost it. I mean, how dare he. He didn't know her. Didn't help raise her. He had no right, no fucking right to be upset."

"No, he did not," Charlie replies darkly.

"He wrote a letter, and there was no mention of the others, Daniel, Avery, or Danielle. No remorse for the childhood friend he murdered or the family he destroyed. No apology to his former best friend-turned-lover, the woman who bore his child and gave her a damn good life without a single ounce of his help. None."

"Oh, Veronica, my love."

"Even then, after everything, there was still a part of me that hoped he cared enough for me to be sorry for what he'd done," I whisper. A sob, filled with all the rage and disappointment that I carry because of Kyle's actions, escapes my chest on a forceful exhale. Charlie's body goes rigid next to me, but his hand on my thigh is gentle and reassuring.

"If I could, I would resurrect him. Make him kneel at your feet and apologize. Beg for forgiveness. Then throw him in a cell to face every torment he caused you over and over again for an eternity," Charlie declares, voice hard and flat.

I give him a grateful smile. "If only you could," I reply. "If I had gotten that closure, that outlet, to unleash all my pent-up emotions onto the person responsible for this mess, I might have been better able to deal. I might not have run if I hadn't had all the rage and anger boiling inside. Might have been able to move on without the distance, or avoidance, or omission. But we'll never know. And now," I say, gazing boldly into his intense green eyes.

"And now," he prompts after a long moment of silence.

"And now I am grateful that my path, however sorrowful, brought me here to London. . . —to you."

"I am, too," he replies, that brilliant smile I love so much spreading across his face. "I will never try to take the place of who you lost. I know it is impossible and would be bloody disrespectful. Instead, I will dedicate the rest of my life to you. I will do everything in my power to ensure your future is filled with peace, joy, and love. I will be your safe space and your anchor. That is if you will accept my vow for the future. If not, then the same stands for each moment of the present that you want me."

"Charlie," I breathe, then lean forward to press my lips softly against his. "I want you in every moment of my present *and* future."

Whatever You Need

Three months later, Charlie and I are both back to work full-time. I attend two therapy sessions and one life coaching session per week and strictly adhere to my routines. Vicki and I are slowly mending our relationship, and I've even spoken to Valerie a few times. She's still reluctant to see us without Mildred involved, but at least she's open to the idea this time.

I've had days when I couldn't function, but with Charlie, Kali and Kellan, and Catherine and Sophie's help, they've been fewer than in the past. I refuse to rely solely on others to get through the 'bad months,' so I've been diligent in helping myself. Letting go of the secrecy and facing my demons was the best thing I've done for myself since Daniel and the girls passed. I still miss them and will always miss them, but I am learning how to manage the pain and sorrow surrounding their deaths. The guilt, shame, rage, and betrayal that have plagued me since I lost them are still there, but they no longer consume me.

My phone vibrates on the small table behind me. I finish pouring purple resin into a line of earring molds, quickly tossing my gloves into the trash when I'm done. Enjoying the bright sunlight shining through the windows, I snatch my phone off the table as it vibrates a second time. A wide smile spreads across my covered face, and I hurry to the bathroom, where it's safe to remove the respirator.

"Hey, love," I answer, my face falling when Charlie speaks.

"It's my mum. She fell and broke her hip. Can you meet me at my flat?"

"I'll get there as fast as I can. I love you."

I crash into the office, startling Kali, and tell her why I must leave in such a rush. She calls me an Uber while I sprint upstairs to change and grab my purse. Kali and Kellan are waiting for me by the door when I sprint back down. I hug each twin swiftly and promise to keep them updated as I walk out the door and jump into the Uber. It's mid-afternoon, thank fuck, so I make it to Charlie's in less than twenty minutes.

He's not there when I step off the lift. I pull my phone out to call him but decide it's best not to distract him while he's driving. His office is on the other side of the city, and he likely had to dole out responsibilities to his employees before he could leave. I hurry through the flat, thinking I'll clean while I wait for him, but Charlie keeps this place immaculate. Unable to sit still, I pace until I hear the ding of the lift.

When the door opens, I pull Charlie into my arms. "Is your mom okay?"

"She is in surgery now, but James said it was a clean break and the doctor is optimistic that she will heal well and retain full use of her leg."

"Oh, thank fuck," I say, cupping his stubbled cheeks in my hands. "There's still plenty of daylight. Let's get on the road. Or, I can stay and take care of things here. Whatever you need."

He rubs circles on my lower back. "Veronica, love. James said he and Dad have everything handled right now. They asked if I would come in a few days to relieve them. And yes, I want you to come. I would very much appreciate you being there."

He pulls me into him, dropping his forehead onto my shoulder. I loop my arms around his waist and hold him tightly. "Whatever you need, love."

For the next thirty minutes, he moves through the flat, bouncing restlessly from room to room, packing half a suitcase and stuffing random items into his black leather messenger bag. He makes multiple calls to James and George Sr. to solidify their plans for Anne's Recovery. I try to help and be supportive, but I can tell he needs an outlet, something to occupy his hands and his brain because every fiber of his being is screaming at him to go take care of his mom.

"Charlie, love," I say, grabbing him by the biceps as he makes another aimless pass through the sitting room. "Take a deep breath. Anne is going to be okay. She's got your dad and James, Cynthia and the kids, and I know George Sr. made sure that she has the best doctors and nurses treating her. Go take out your restless energy on the punching bag. I'm going to run home and take care of a few things there. I'll be back in a few hours. Call me before then, and I'll come back right away."

Tension radiates off him in powerful waves, and he has trouble focusing his eyes on me. He kisses me deeply for a long minute before striding down the hallway, his long legs carrying him out of sight before the lift doors slide open. As the Uber maneuvers deftly through streets clogged from the dinner rush hour, I send out a volley of texts and call Cynthia. She sounds exhausted but reassures me that Anne is being well taken care of and that they have everything handled for now. We confirm the plans Charlie made with James and their father, and I promise to provide whatever help she needs from here and once we're there.

Legs bouncing and fingers drumming a staccato rhythm on the seat, I watch the city pass slowly by my window, fighting the urge to demand the Uber, a kind older gentleman with an easy smile, to drive faster. When he finally pulls up to the studio, I give him a large tip and barge into the gallery. There are a handful of customers littered throughout the space who, thankfully, don't seem to notice my frantic run to the office. I hug each of the twins, updating them about Charlie's mom and thanking them profusely for taking care of the studio and being genuinely good people.

Forcing myself to walk calmly, I head upstairs. I am packed and ready to go within twenty minutes. After another twenty minutes of pacing a line into the frayed grey carpet in the living room, I bounce down the stairs and slip into the workroom, losing myself in creating for an hour. Tension melts off me as I move a paintbrush across the canvas in large, bright arches. As I dab splotches of white around the edge of the canvas and top off the whole piece with a ton of glitter, I think about Charlie and his mom, hoping that she pulls through this setback so they can have more time together. I know precisely how devastated he and the rest of his family will be when Anne passes, and I beg the universe to wait as long as possible to take her from us.

I don't want to lose another person so soon after I finally came to terms with everyone else I've already lost. Even more than that, I can't bear to watch Charlie go through that pain.

Please give him more time with her.

I take the wet painting off its easel and carefully sidle into the office. With a private smirk for Kali and much ceremony, I turn the small canvas to face her and her brother. Kellan throws his head back in laughter, and Kali pulls an easel out of a corner, smiling broadly.

"Well played, Ron. Well played," she admits, patting me on the shoulder. I wink at her.

"That is . . . one bright-ass rainbow. I think it could use more glitter, though," Kellan jokes.

"I'll add more before you take it home and hang it above your mantel," I tease and place it on the easel. Kali doubles over into a fit of hysterics. I'm surprised Kellan hasn't noticed yet; he's such a detail-oriented man. I press my lips into a thin line but fail to suppress the giggles. Kellan looks between his sister and me a few times before Kali points to one end of the rainbow where a tiny, Kellan-shaped leprechaun perches on the edge of a pot of gold, legs crossed, elbow on his knee, and chin propped in his hand—Kellan's signature pose and the way he's sitting at this very moment.

Laughter rumbles in his chest, and he rolls his eyes dramatically before looking down at himself and saying, "Well, fuck. You got me there."

I exit the office, waving and grinning, and rush upstairs to take a quick shower. I should've changed into work clothes or at least put on my big apron because now I'm covered in paint and my hair has glitter in it.

Back at Charlie's, freshly washed and mind refreshed, I find him in a similar state, hair still damp, shoulders relaxed, and eyes clear. I walk straight to where he lounges on the sofa and straddle him, looping my arms around his neck.

"Feel better," I ask, pulling back to see his face.

"Yes, I am. Thank you. She is out of surgery. The doctor said it went well, and I even got to talk to her for a minute. She sounded tired but determined. I felt better after hearing her voice."

We kiss and cuddle on the sofa, sipping tea and watching the sunset paint the sky in soft pinks and purples. Charlie's chest is warm against my cheek, and I am content to sit here listening to his strong heartbeat. My watch buzzes on my wrist twice, and I sigh, pushing myself into a sitting position.

"Let's get out of here. Go have some fun?"

"That is a bloody brilliant idea, V."

While he changes, I text Kali to round up the troops, the troops being her, Kellan, and Theo, and meet us at a cocktail bar near Buckingham Palace. We opt for an Uber and grab some Five Guys on our way to the bar, buying the young female Uber driver dinner as well. She blushes profusely and stammers a thank you when Charlie hands her a fat cash tip and croons, "Thanks for the ride, love." I press my lips into a thin line to suppress my amusement but grab his ass and wink at her as we walk past her window. He chuckles, shaking his head, and I tuck my hand into the crook of his elbow. My goal for tonight is to see Charlie relaxed and smiling.

Our friends are tucked into a large corner booth strewn with half-eaten plates of hors d'oeuvres and empty bottles of wine. We didn't need an escort to the table, Kellan's booming laughter led us straight to them. Kali tosses a snide remark at her brother, and

Theo sits in the corner, smirking, eyes darting back and forth between the boisterous twins. They may be stoic and poised in a professional setting but also have a wild side. Theo is the perfect match for Kali. He can dish it just as well as her. I raise my eyebrows at Charlie and slide into the booth next to Kali. Charlie moves to sit next to Kellan, who stops him with a hand on his chest.

"Sit by your woman, mate. The rest of us don't want to watch you two make eyes at each other all night. At least if you're sitting next to her, you can feel her up under the table. Discreetly," he adds, looking pointedly between us. Charlie chuckles, and Kellan pats his chest a few times before looking at me. "Adonis is apt."

Laughing, I tease, "Green is so not a good color for you, Kel." Kali elbows me, then scoots closer to Theo, making room for Charlie to slip into the booth next to me. "What. Y'all two can't be jealous. After all the teasing and pushing and living vicariously through me. And me," I continue in mock exasperation, "providing you with so many juicy details."

"Excuse me," Charlie pipes in, pouring himself a glass of wine.

"Nothing, dear," I say, patting his arm. "So, Theo, how have *you* been?"

He tilts his hips in that arrogant, super attractive way guys do and drapes his arm behind Kali on the back of the booth. "Good," he shrugs a shoulder and continues, looking at Kali. "Can't complain."

I consider them for a moment before asking, "How good? I pried and pried, but she won't give me any details about you two." I trail off, holding my left hand up, my fingers in a circle, and I insert my other pointer finger into the circle. I click my tongue with the movement, and Charlie mutters, "Jesus, Veronica," into my ear, but he's laughing, and that is all that matters. Kali rolls her eyes, but I am sitting close enough to see her leg pressed against Theo's under the table. Kellan shakes his head and pours the rest of the wine into his glass.

"Why are you looking so smug over there, Mr. Bats-for-both-Teams? I saw you leave with that cute Spanish guy the last time we were here," I tease Kellan. Kali's mouth drops open, and he purses his lips. "How was he?" I ask sweetly.

"Okay, okay, ya randy," Charlie chimes in. "We all need—" he pauses, thoughtfully eyeing the empty bottles on the table, "well, I need a few more drinks if you are going to keep pestering everyone about their sex lives."

He scoots out of the booth, and I call after him, "I'll take a lemon drop martini, please." He halts, looking at me over his shoulder, eyebrows merged with his hairline. I nod and blow him a kiss, good-naturedly suffering a round of teasing aimed at me. Theo's telling a story about one of his and Kali's first dates, and we're all in a fit of hysterics when Charlie returns. A gorgeous blonde waitress follows, bearing a tray of martinis. Her eyes linger on Kellan, which isn't surprising because he looks incredible in grey slacks and a black silk shirt with undone top buttons, exposing his smooth, umber chest. I ask her when her shift ends and invite her to join us when she replies, "In about an hour."

Kali leans into me nonchalantly and whispers, "Smooth. Very smooth."

To which I reply, "I'd hate for him to be the fifth wheel all night. Plus, she's fucking hot. Someone should hit that if it can't be you or me."

"Ronnie."

"I'm kidding. But, you saw it too. She was giving him the 'fuck me' eyes so . . ." I shrug my shoulder and take a sip of my martini.

After everyone has their drink in hand, we toast to friendship and settle into a much-needed heartfelt conversation, discussing work and family, future goals and aspirations, and current projects, interspersed with a lot of light-hearted teasing and joking. The waitress, Amelia, joined us, and we instantly fell in love with her. She is hilarious and intelligent and slides seamlessly into our dynamic. Kali fairly gushes over her.

Charlie and I make out like teenagers during the drive back to his flat. We touch and kiss the whole ride up the lift, shedding clothes as soon as the door opens into the sitting room. We make love until the grey light of dawn lulls us to sleep, content and twined together.

The next few weeks are chaotic and jam-packed. We help Anne check out of the hospital and get settled into a guest room at James and Cynthia's. We bounce between their house and the farm, helping George Sr. prepare for an extended absence as he's staying in town with Anne during her recovery. Charlie hires three guys to run the farm, so he and James can get back to work and manage the firm in George Sr.'s absence. And I sent James and Cynthia to a hotel for the last week we were in Manchester, insisting that they take some time to themselves. We spend the next eight weekends in Manchester, helping on the farm, ferrying Anne to appointments, and babysitting Charlie's niece and nephew.

After Anne fully recovers, we return to a routine at home in London. *Wright &* *Sons* is in the middle of expanding, demanding grueling hours from Charlie. I continue aggressive therapy and life coaching sessions and focus on work-life balance. I prefer to work when Charlie works but find out the hard way that it is no longer sustainable for me to work that many hours. One day lost, spiraling into despair and depression, is one too many when I've been given a second chance to build a beautiful life for myself.

And that you have, V. And that you have.

To the Future

Three years later . . .

"Tell me again," I say to Charlie as I descend the stairs in my studio for the last time. He's waiting at the bottom, leaning against the banister with his arms crossed over his chest, ankles crossed in front of him, fairly oozing casual confidence. His intense aura permeates the space and sends a shock of electricity down my spine. "Why we're moving in the dead of fucking winter?"

"My dear Veronica," he replies, deftly swiping the box out of my hands and placing it carefully in the pile by the door. Today, we're moving the last of my stuff to my new studio, which occupies the entire main floor of a *beautiful* new building a few blocks down from Charlie's flat. With the help of an up-and-coming local architect, Charlie and I designed the building. It is the new home of *Studio V* and four other artists, each occupying half of the second and third floors, with *Wright & Sons* new offices occupying the entire top floor.

"We *have* to do it now if you want to be ready for the grand opening." I huff an exasperated sigh in response. Moving is bittersweet, and a part of me procrastinates. This is the place where I found closure for my old life and laid the foundation for my future.

The first round of 'the bad months' after I told Charlie about my life with Daniel and our girls was an emotional rollercoaster. Charlie rode steadfastly by my side and never wavered in his devotion to me or our relationship. He anchored me to the present and held me together every single time I fell apart, just as he promised he would. In turn, I did a lot of work on myself to make the ride less turbulent.

After we got through May and what should have been my 16th wedding anniversary, I was determined to focus on the future. Charlie and I spoke at length about living together, and after months of deliberating, I moved into his flat permanently. Wright Place was the deciding factor as the one luxury I refused to give up was having my living space and my studio located within a five-minute walk of each other. *Wright & Sons* provided a share of the financial backing for a highly anticipated new commercial construction firm. In return, they expertly expedited the erection and completion of Wright Place, their first major project.

In a few short months, *Studio V* and *Wright & Sons* will celebrate our new location with a grand re-opening and the grand opening of Wright Place and the four other art studios currently setting up shop there. Each artist is early in their career, unique in their methods, and hand-picked by me to receive a generous grant to jump-start their career. In three years, they can choose to stay permanently or move on to the next chapter of their career. Kali and Kellan will manage the building along with the five of us artists. With their business expertise and Charlie's financial wisdom, I have no doubt we'll succeed.

"I know, I know. But I hate it when you're *Wright*."

A mischievous smile spreads slowly across his face as he saunters toward me, wraps me in his arms, and kisses me passionately, sending a thrum of desire through me.

"Now, now, you two," Kellan chastises as he and Kali emerge from the office.

"You have our blessing to enjoy one last tryst before we lock up for the last time. But please, let's wait until *after lunch*, shall we?" Kali finishes playfully. A rap on the window rescues us from further teasing.

We slowly eat our way through multiple containers of food from all our favorite restaurants, savoring this last meal in the place that brought us all together. We reminisce and remember with fondness the growth, both personal and professional, gained within these walls, and we even shed a few tears when it's time to say goodbye.

"It's silly, I know," I say, chuckling while wiping tears from my eyes. "We're literally going to be doing this exact same thing next week. But I am going to miss this place—it brought us all together."

"On that note," Kali declares with a delicate, perfectly manicured finger in the air.

"We toast," Kellan finishes, fishing a bottle of Dom Perignon out of the messenger bag by his feet.

"To closed doors and new beginnings," he says, raising his glass in the air.

"To beautiful art and even more beautiful people," Kali adds, lifting her arm next to Kellan's.

"To friends who are closer than family and the woman who is so deeply grateful for each of you," I declare, thrusting my arm in the air and rising.

Charlie also stands and regards each of us for a moment before speaking. "To cheeseburgers and Broadway. To bloody brilliant business partners turned best mates. To the past remembered fondly and the present lived fully," he proclaims warmly, then his eyes lock on mine. "To us . . . and the future anticipated joyously."

"Cheers," we exclaim in unison, clinking glasses and throwing back champagne.

I did it. I rose from the depths of despair and created this beautiful, wonderful life.

I hold out my hand to my future. "Let's go love. It's time."

A wave of déjà vu ripples through me as the water cascades over me, easing the tension from my shoulders. Charlie's strong fingers massaging shampoo into my hair help a little, too. His hands wander down to my waist, and he pulls me against him.

"Are you ready for this, my love," he whispers in my ear. I wiggle my ass against him.

"Yes," I reply breathlessly, arching against him. We make love passionately, yet quickly. We have an open house to get ready for.

Kali and Kellan suggested waiting for their cue to join, but Charlie and I insisted on being there early. We waltz into Wright Place foyer hand in hand, me in the same little black dress and stilettos I wore at my first open house, at Charlie's gentle insistence. Today, however, my hair flows freely down my back in soft curls, and I seek out the twins, not as a crutch or shield, but to shower them with admiration and congratulate them on their hard work.

Kali and Kellan lead us into the studio. Charlie falls in step beside me, slipping his hand into mine. I feel another presence on my other side, and I swear for a second that I can feel Daniel's hand in mine, as solid and warm as Charlie's. I send him a silent nod of thanks and love and squeeze Charlie's hand.

A squeal of delight flies from my lips when the twins part in front of us to reveal the group of people already gathered in the middle of my studio. Sophie and Turner chat with Charlie's brother. Catherine and John stand next to Darren and his wife. My former in-laws, Tam and Tim, look around the room with awed expressions on their faces. My beloved sister-in-law, Cynthia, sternly reminds all the kids to keep their hands to themselves and behave. Theo steals Kali's attention, slipping his hand into hers. Kellan greets Romeo and his husband, Evan, with warm affection. Charlie and I attended their wedding two years ago, and they have visited us in London twice since. Charlie's parents relax on lounge chairs while Victoria, her husband in tow, flits from group to group, nervous excitement keeping her in motion.

We weren't sure if Anne would still be with us for this event, and we are thankful that she's not only still with us but able to be here today. After we get this place running, we're going to take a leave of absence to spend with Charlie's parents. It's not ideal, but it's necessary. Her doctors urged everyone to get in as much time as possible as her end is nearer than we care to accept.

Our friend's and family's heads turn in our direction collectively at my gasp, and all chaos breaks loose. We're hugged and congratulated by our closest friends and family. Vic assures me that Valerie didn't dip out. Their flight got delayed, but she, her husband, and the kids are on their way. Charlie's hand never leaves mine through it all, and I feel Daniel's comforting presence at my side. Our loved ones stay long past the last guest has left, their love and support painting the evening in vibrant hues.

We congregate in a loose circle, eating delicious food, drinking champagne and sparkling water, telling stories of the past, and sharing our dreams for the future. I recline comfortably in Charlie's arms, reveling in the love and camaraderie permeating the space. And I know in that moment, that no matter what life throws at me, I can weather the storm and come out the other side re-born and re-made stronger because I have the support and love of close family, good friends, and two remarkable men.

The End

About the Author

M. S. Gorza is a passionate wordsmith and romance author who loves to sweep readers off their feet with sizzling stories that bring their deepest fantasies alive. As a voracious reader from a young age, she always loves devouring a good book. As the author of her debut romance novel, *V,* she aims to entertain and inspire romance fans with electrifying tales that will give you a few laughs, make you cry, and always end with a feel-good happily ever after.

M. S. Gorza currently resides in Wyoming with her supportive husband and their 4 wonderful children. When she's not running her kids around the state for various activities, you can find her reading, dreaming up her next story idea, or indulging her passion for crafts. For more information, visit www.msgorza.com.